D1302431

image PRESENTS

CIRCUIT -BREAKER ™

WRITER • KEVIN McCARTHY

ARTIST • KYLE BAKER

LETTERER • ADAM WOLLET (CHAPTERS 4 & 5)

SPECIAL THANKS TO MINDY STEFFEN FOR COLORING ASSISTS

IMAGE COMICS, INC.

Robert Kirkman - Chief Operating Officer
Erik Larsen - Chief Financial Officer
Todd McFarlane - President
Marc Silvestri - Chief Executive Officer
Jim Valentino - Vice-President
Eric Stephenson - Publisher
Corey Murphy - Director of Sales
Jeff Boison - Director of Publishing Planning & Book Trade Sales
Chris Ross - Director of Digital Sales
Jeff Stang - Director of Specialty Sales
Kat Salazar - Director of PR & Marketing
Branwyn Bigglestone - Controller
Sue Korpela - Accounts Manager
Drew Gill - Art Director
Brett Warnock - Production Manager
Meredith Wallace - Print Manager
Tricia Ramos - Traffic Manager
Briah Skelly - Publicist
Aly Hoffman - Conventions & Events Coordinator
Sasha Head - Sales & Marketing Production Designer
David Brothers - Branding Manager
Melissa Gifford - Content Manager
Drew Fitzgerald - Publicity Assistant
Vincent Kukua - Production Artist
Erika Schnatz - Production Artist
Ryan Brewer - Production Artist
Shanna Matuszak - Production Artist
Carey Hall - Production Artist
Esther Kim - Direct Market Sales Representative
Emilio Bautista - Digital Sales Associate
Leanna Caunter - Accounting Assistant
Chloe Ramos-Peterson - Library Market Sales Representative
Marla Eizik - Administrative Assistant
IMAGECOMICS.COM

CIRCUIT-BREAKER. First printing. May 2017. Published by Image Comics, Inc. Office of publication: 2701 NW Vaughn St., Suite 780, Portland, OR 97210. Copyright © 2017 Kevin McCarthy & Kyle Baker. All rights reserved. Contains material originally published in single magazine form as CIRCUIT-BREAKER #1-5. "Circuit-Breaker," the Circuit-Breaker logos, and all characters herein are trademarks of Kevin McCarthy & Kyle Baker, unless otherwise noted. "Image" and the Image Comics logos are registered trademarks of Image Comics, Inc. No part of this publication may be reproduced or transmitted, in any form or by any means (except for short excerpts for journalistic or review purposes), without the express written permission of Kevin McCarthy, Kyle Baker, or Image Comics, Inc. All names, characters, events, and locales in this publication are entirely fictional. Any resemblance to actual persons (living or dead), events, or places, without satiric intent, is coincidental. Printed in the USA. For information regarding the CPSIA on this printed material call: 203-595-3636 and provide reference #RICH–736907. Representation: Law Offices of Harris M. Miller II, P.C. (rights inquiries@gmail.com) ISBN: 978-1-63215-876-5.

ONE

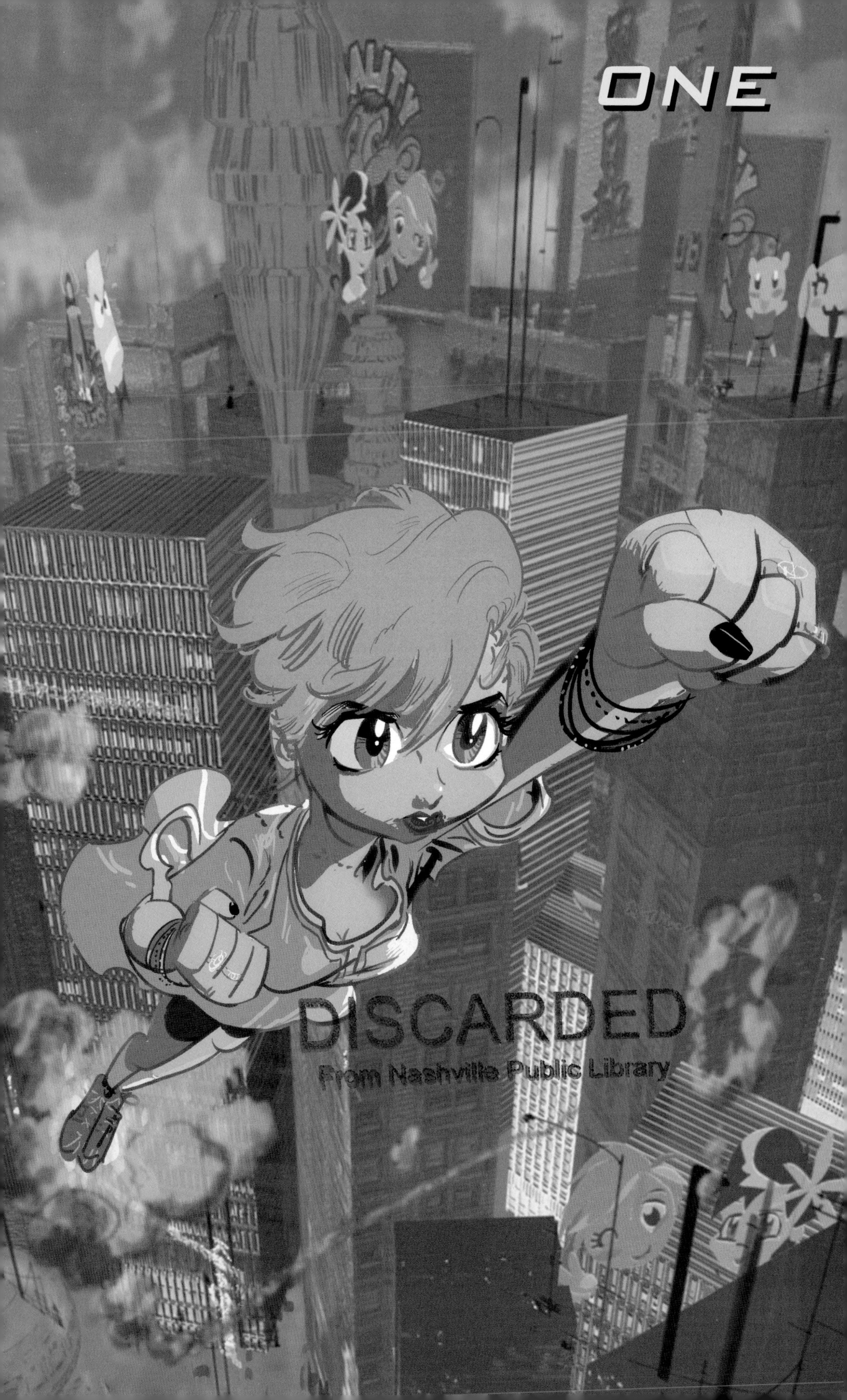

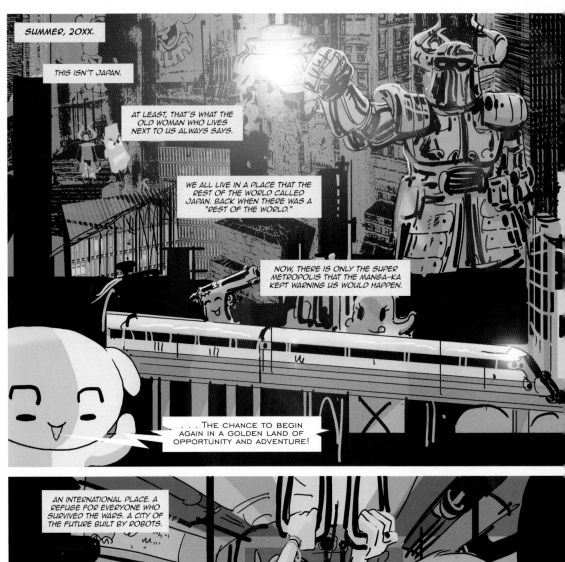

SUMMER, 20XX.

THIS ISN'T JAPAN.

AT LEAST, THAT'S WHAT THE OLD WOMAN WHO LIVES NEXT TO US ALWAYS SAYS.

WE ALL LIVE IN A PLACE THAT THE REST OF THE WORLD CALLED JAPAN. BACK WHEN THERE WAS A "REST OF THE WORLD."

NOW, THERE IS ONLY THE SUPER METROPOLIS THAT THE MANGA-KA KEPT WARNING US WOULD HAPPEN.

. . . THE CHANCE TO BEGIN AGAIN IN A GOLDEN LAND OF OPPORTUNITY AND ADVENTURE!

AN INTERNATIONAL PLACE. A REFUGE FOR EVERYONE WHO SURVIVED THE WARS. A CITY OF THE FUTURE BUILT BY ROBOTS.

A CITY WHERE EVERYONE IS WELCOMED. EVERYONE . . . *EXCEPT* ROBOTS.

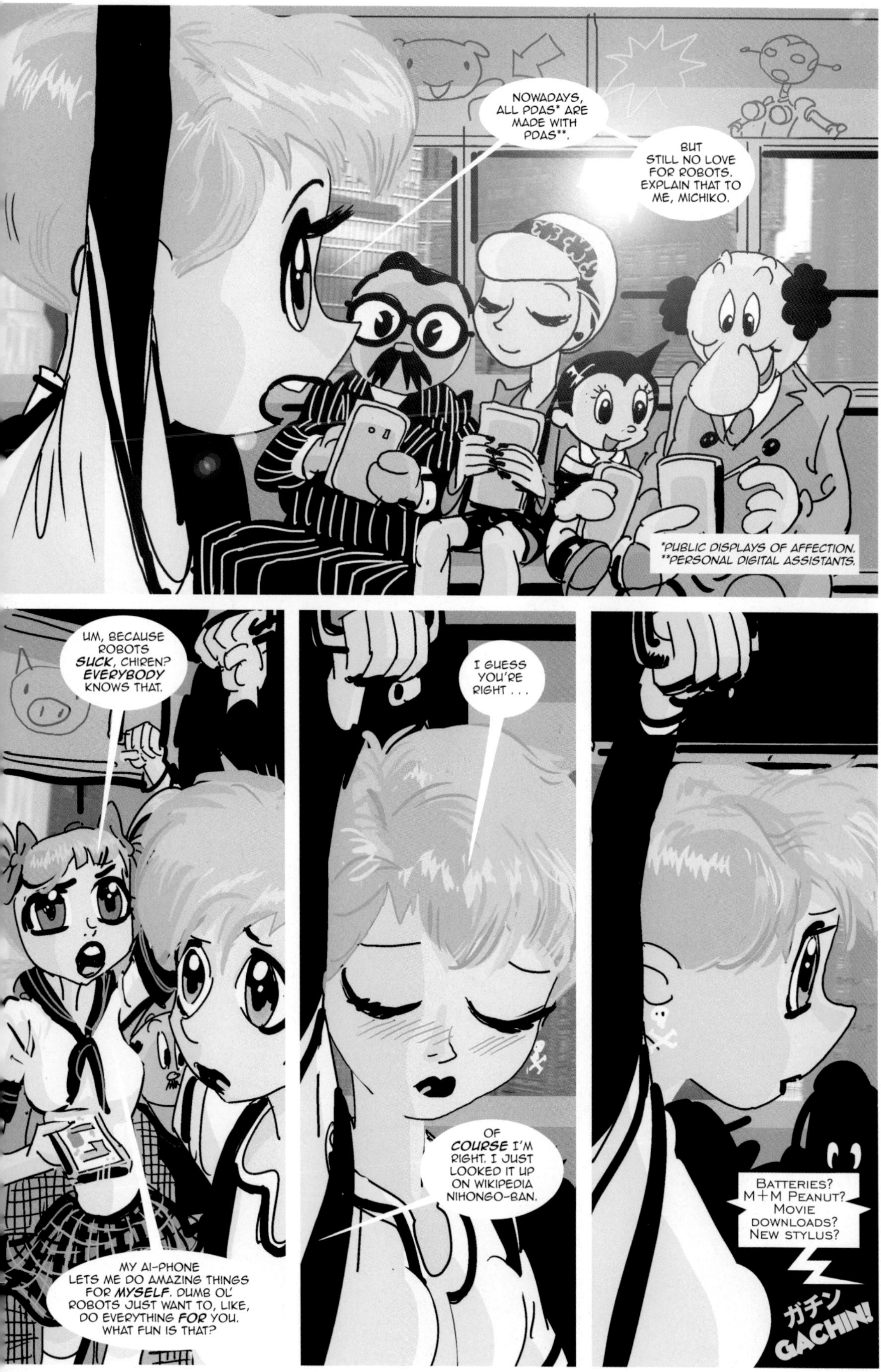
NOWADAYS, ALL PDAS* ARE MADE WITH PDAS**.
BUT STILL NO LOVE FOR ROBOTS. EXPLAIN THAT TO ME, MICHIKO.
*PUBLIC DISPLAYS OF AFFECTION.
**PERSONAL DIGITAL ASSISTANTS.
UM, BECAUSE ROBOTS SUCK, CHIREN? EVERYBODY KNOWS THAT.
MY AI-PHONE LETS ME DO AMAZING THINGS FOR MYSELF. DUMB OL' ROBOTS JUST WANT TO, LIKE, DO EVERYTHING FOR YOU. WHAT FUN IS THAT?
I GUESS YOU'RE RIGHT . . .
OF COURSE I'M RIGHT. I JUST LOOKED IT UP ON WIKIPEDIA NIHONGO-BAN.
Batteries? M+M Peanut? Movie downloads? New stylus?
ガチン
GACHIN!

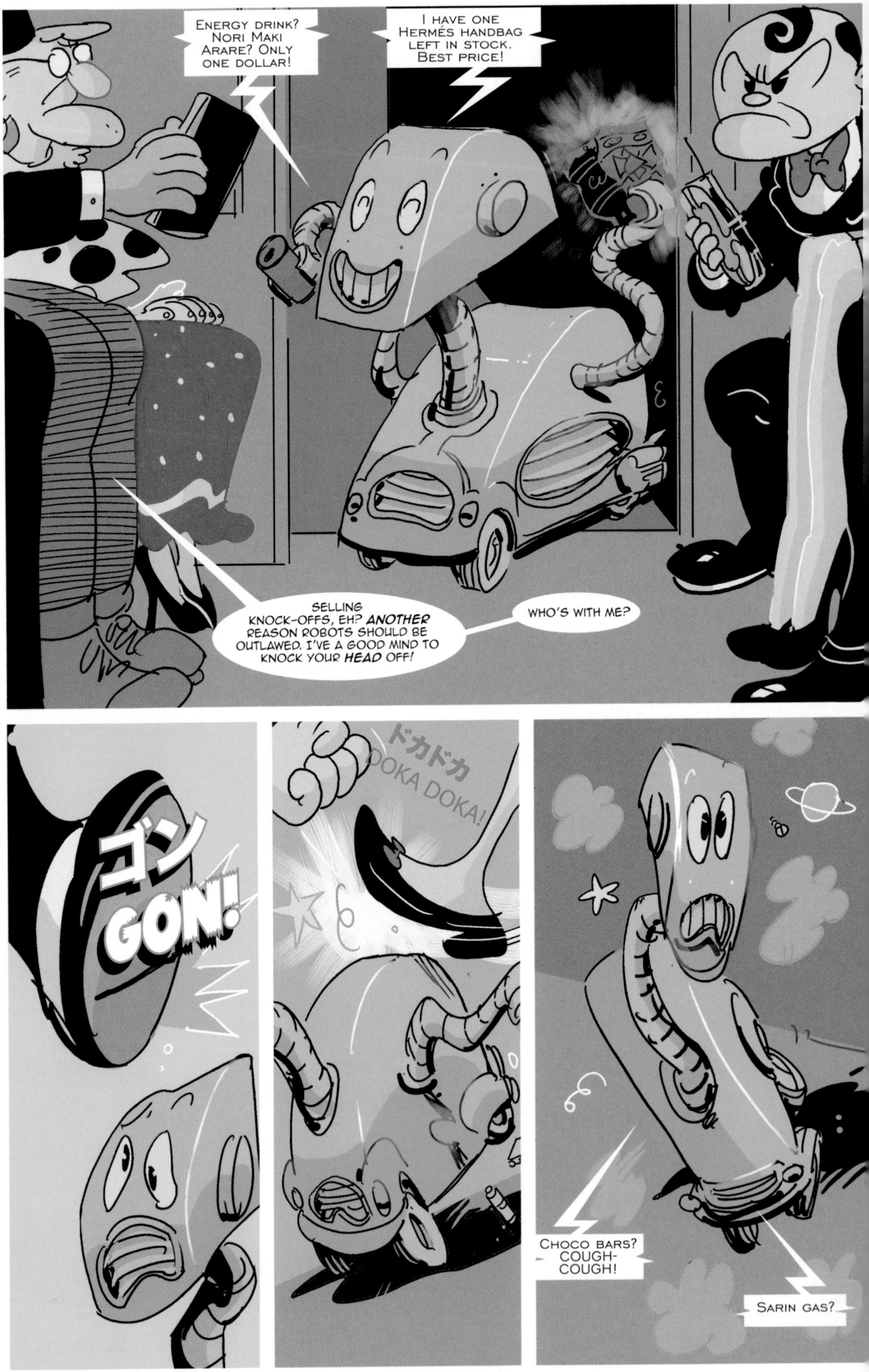

Energy drink? Nori Maki Arare? Only one dollar!
I have one Hermés handbag left in stock. Best price!
Selling knock-offs, eh? Another reason robots should be outlawed. I've a good mind to knock your head off!
Who's with me?
ゴン
GON!
ドカドカ
DOKA DOKA!
Choco bars? Cough-cough!
Sarin gas?

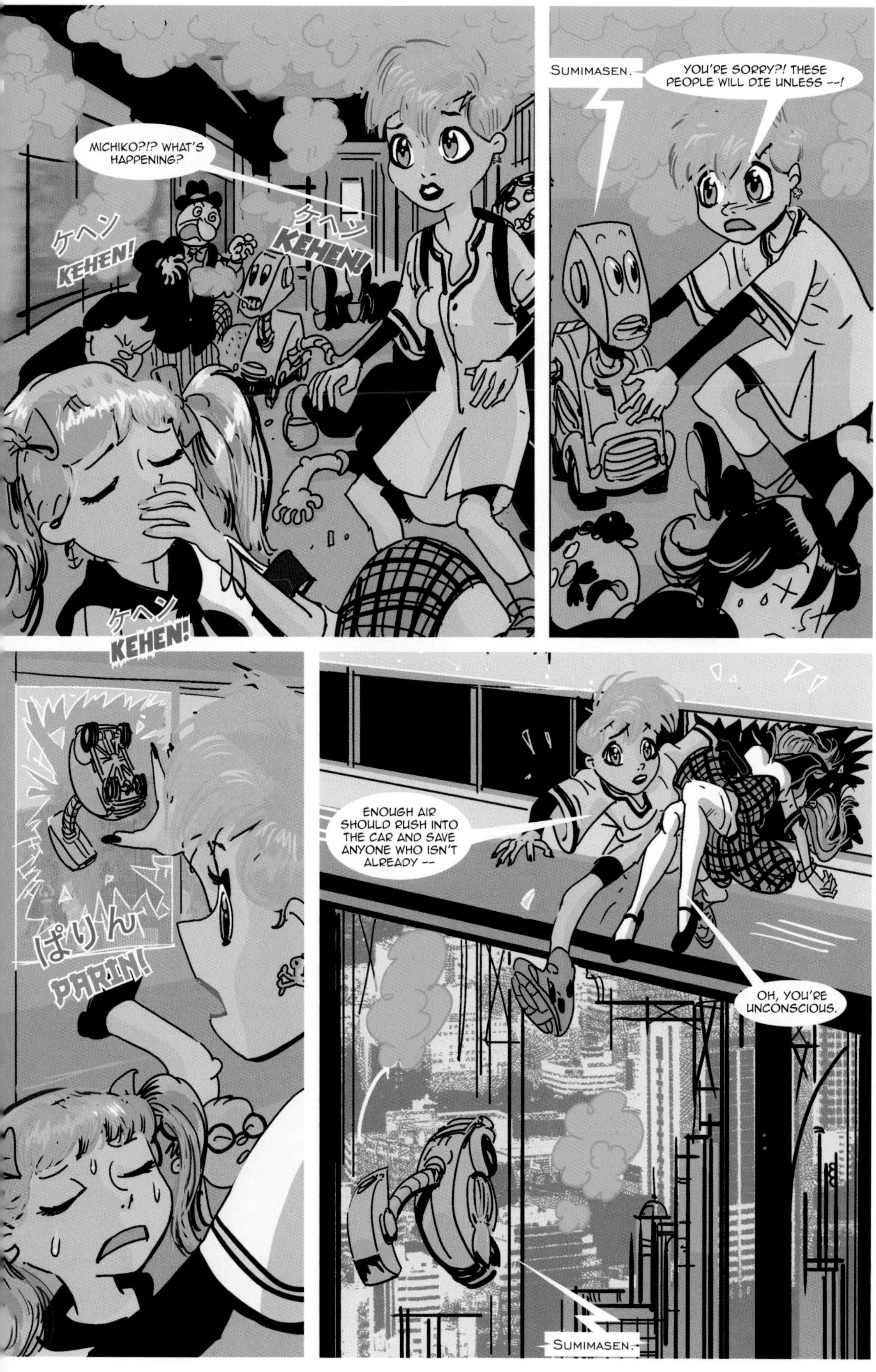
MICHIKO?!? WHAT'S HAPPENING?
ケヘン
KEHEN!
ケヘン
KEHEN!
ケヘン
KEHEN!
SUMIMASEN.
YOU'RE SORRY?! THESE PEOPLE WILL DIE UNLESS --!
ぱりん
PARIN!
ENOUGH AIR SHOULD RUSH INTO THE CAR AND SAVE ANYONE WHO ISN'T ALREADY --
OH, YOU'RE UNCONSCIOUS.
SUMIMASEN.

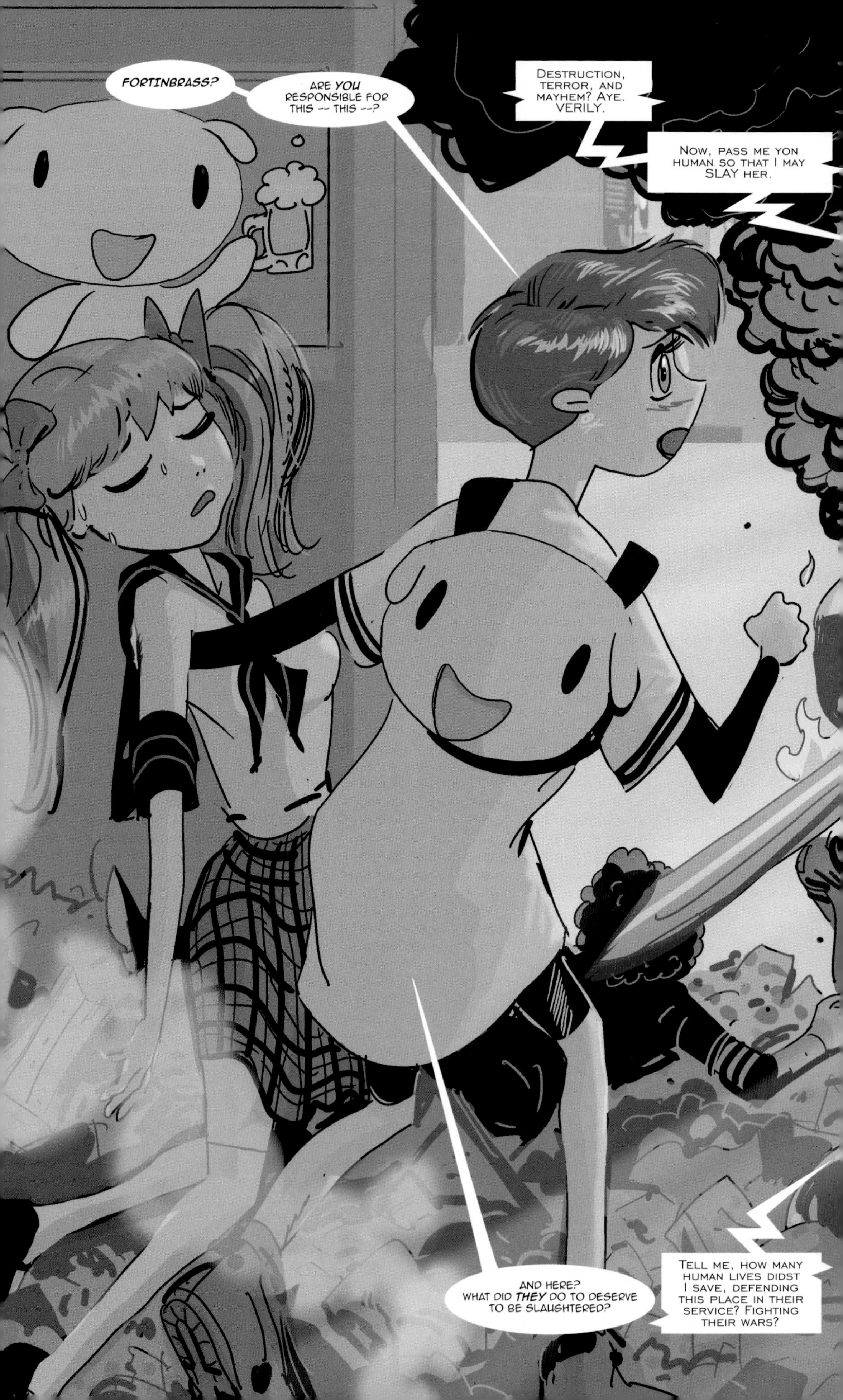
FORTINBRASS?
ARE YOU RESPONSIBLE FOR THIS -- THIS --?
DESTRUCTION, TERROR, AND MAYHEM? AYE. VERILY.
NOW, PASS ME YON HUMAN SO THAT I MAY SLAY HER.
AND HERE? WHAT DID THEY DO TO DESERVE TO BE SLAUGHTERED?
TELL ME, HOW MANY HUMAN LIVES DIDST I SAVE, DEFENDING THIS PLACE IN THEIR SERVICE? FIGHTING THEIR WARS?

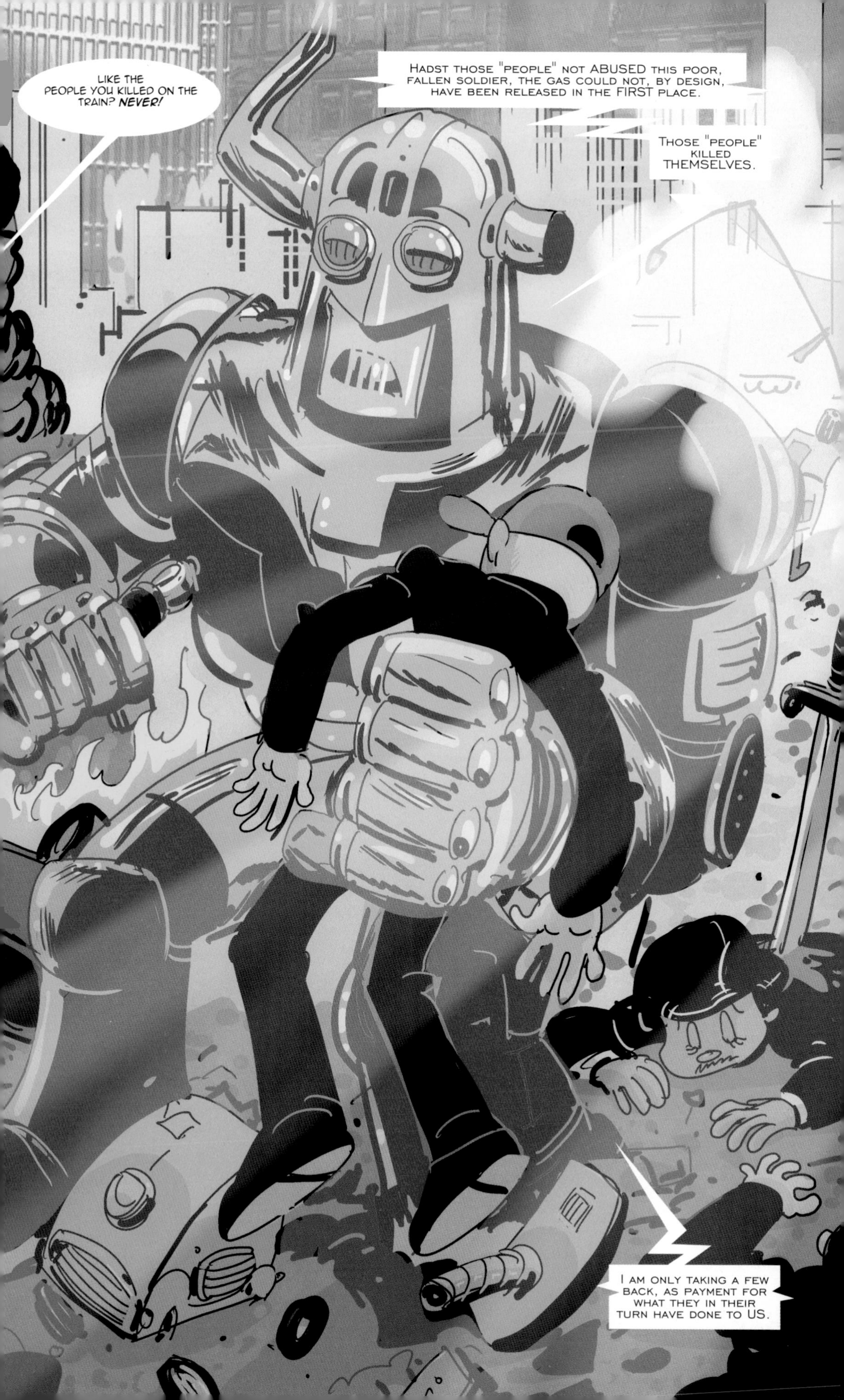
LIKE THE PEOPLE YOU KILLED ON THE TRAIN? *NEVER!*
HADST THOSE "PEOPLE" NOT ABUSED THIS POOR, FALLEN SOLDIER, THE GAS COULD NOT, BY DESIGN, HAVE BEEN RELEASED IN THE FIRST PLACE.
THOSE "PEOPLE" KILLED THEMSELVES.
I AM ONLY TAKING A FEW BACK, AS PAYMENT FOR WHAT THEY IN THEIR TURN HAVE DONE TO US.

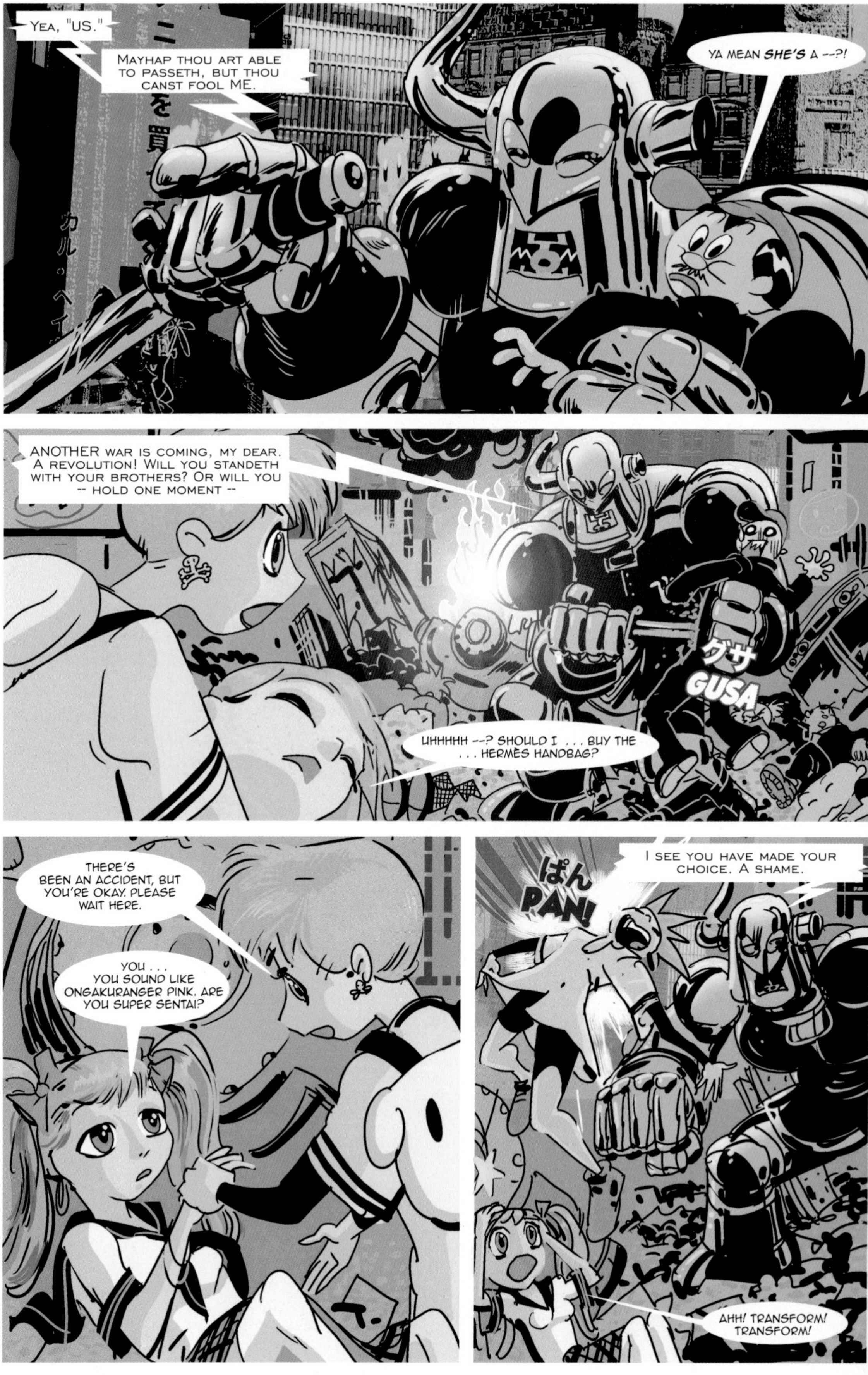

Yea, "US."
Mayhap thou art able to passeth, but thou canst fool ME.
Ya mean SHE'S a --?!
ANOTHER war is coming, my dear. A revolution! Will you standeth with your brothers? Or will you -- hold one moment --
グサ
GUSA
Uhhhhh --? Should I . . . buy the . . . Hermès handbag?
There's been an accident, but you're okay. Please wait here.
You . . . you sound like Ongakuranger Pink. Are you Super Sentai?
ぱん
PAN!
I see you have made your choice. A shame.
Ahh! Transform! Transform!

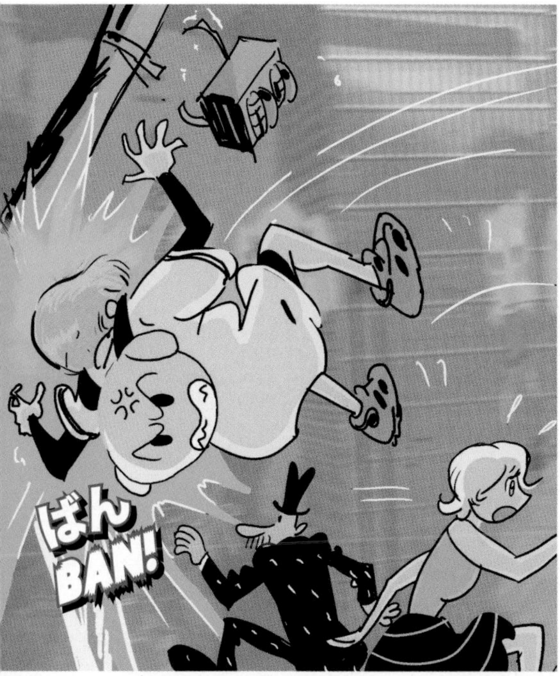
ばん
BAN!

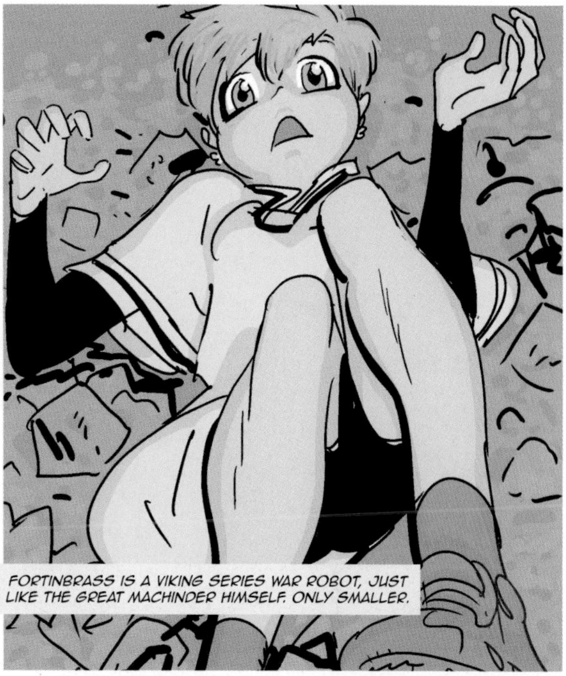
FORTINBRASS IS A VIKING SERIES WAR ROBOT, JUST LIKE THE GREAT MACHINDER HIMSELF. ONLY SMALLER.

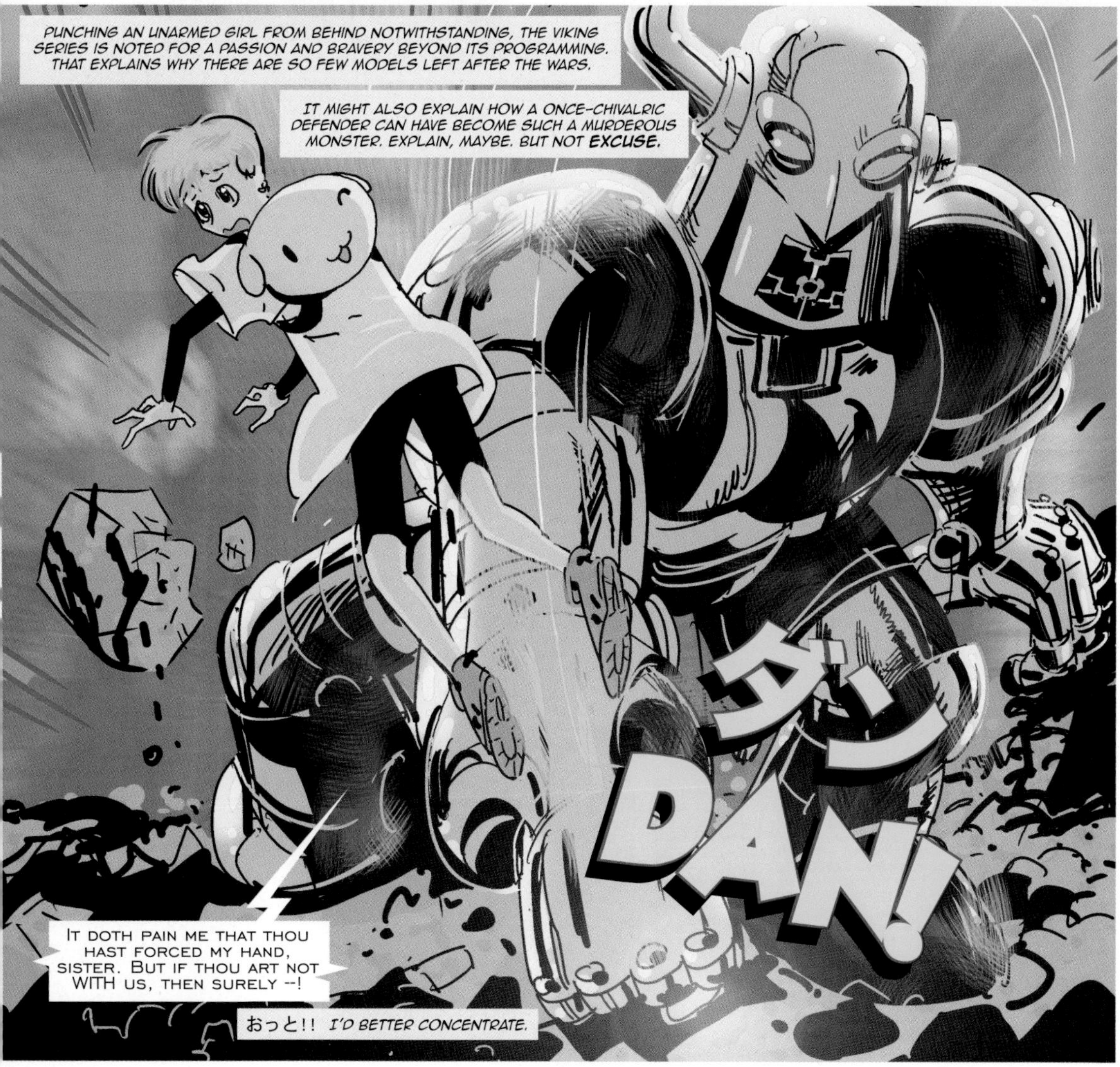
PUNCHING AN UNARMED GIRL FROM BEHIND NOTWITHSTANDING, THE VIKING SERIES IS NOTED FOR A PASSION AND BRAVERY BEYOND ITS PROGRAMMING. THAT EXPLAINS WHY THERE ARE SO FEW MODELS LEFT AFTER THE WARS.
IT MIGHT ALSO EXPLAIN HOW A ONCE-CHIVALRIC DEFENDER CAN HAVE BECOME SUCH A MURDEROUS MONSTER. EXPLAIN, MAYBE. BUT NOT EXCUSE.
ダン
DAN!
IT DOTH PAIN ME THAT THOU HAST FORCED MY HAND, SISTER. BUT IF THOU ART NOT WITH US, THEN SURELY --!
おっと!! I'D BETTER CONCENTRATE.

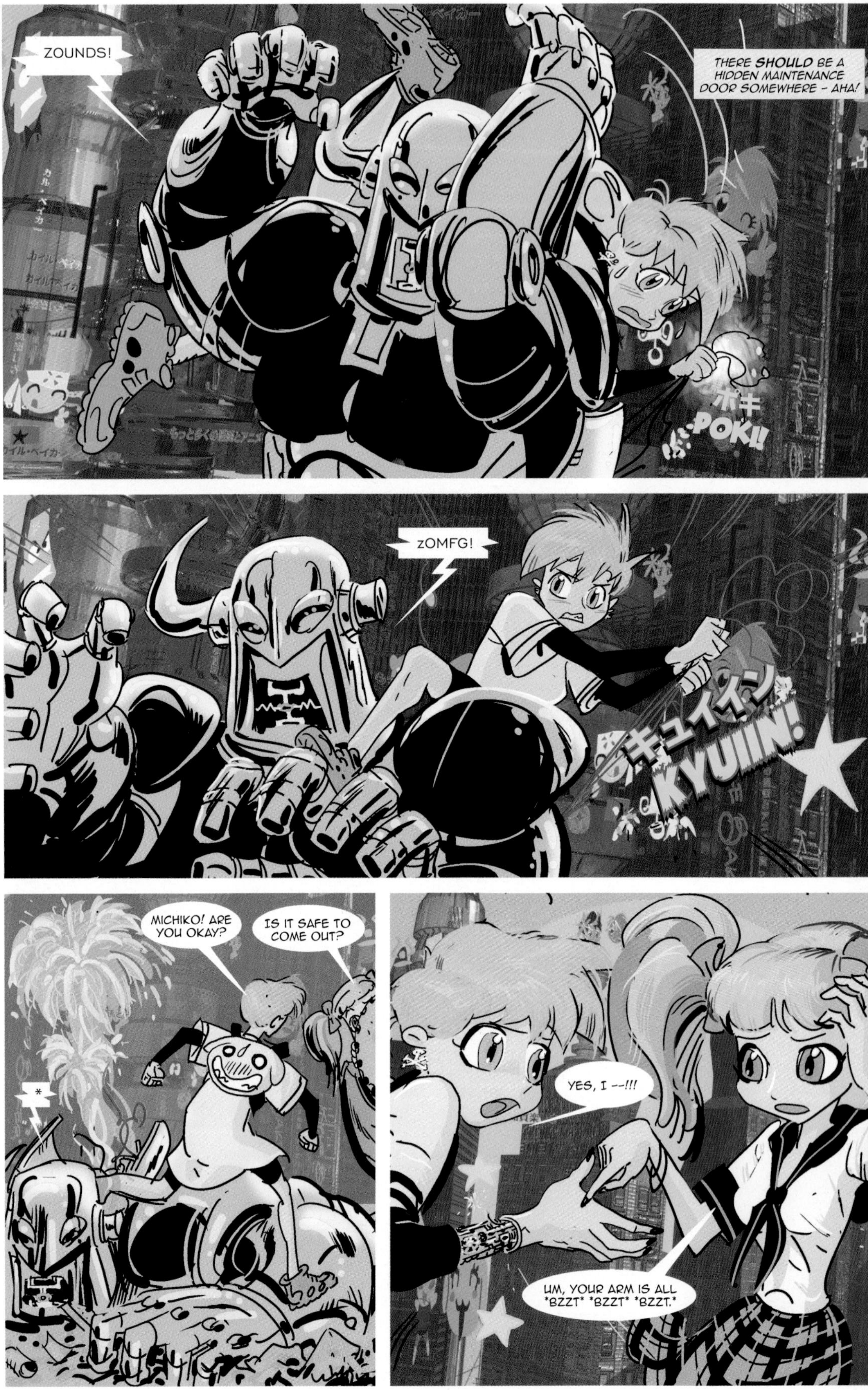
ZOUNDS!
THERE SHOULD BE A HIDDEN MAINTENANCE DOOR SOMEWHERE – AHA!
ポキ POKI!
zOMFG!
キュイイーン KYUIIN!
MICHIKO! ARE YOU OKAY?
IS IT SAFE TO COME OUT?
*
YES, I --!!!
UM, YOUR ARM IS ALL *BZZT* *BZZT* *BZZT.*

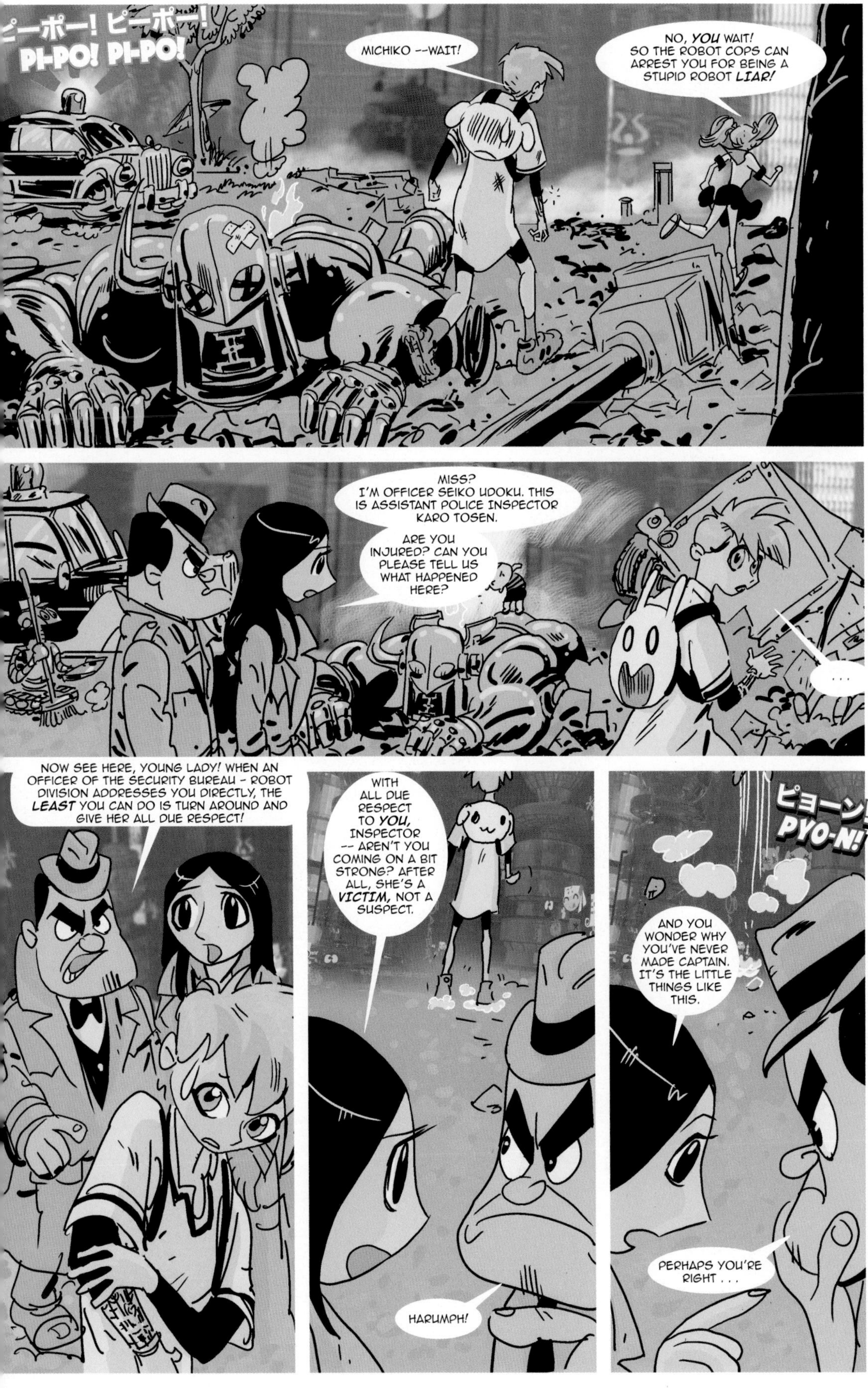

ピーポー！ピーポー！
PI-PO! PI-PO!
MICHIKO --WAIT!
NO, YOU WAIT! SO THE ROBOT COPS CAN ARREST YOU FOR BEING A STUPID ROBOT LIAR!
MISS? I'M OFFICER SEIKO UDOKU. THIS IS ASSISTANT POLICE INSPECTOR KARO TOSEN.
ARE YOU INJURED? CAN YOU PLEASE TELL US WHAT HAPPENED HERE?
. . .
NOW SEE HERE, YOUNG LADY! WHEN AN OFFICER OF THE SECURITY BUREAU - ROBOT DIVISION ADDRESSES YOU DIRECTLY, THE LEAST YOU CAN DO IS TURN AROUND AND GIVE HER ALL DUE RESPECT!
WITH ALL DUE RESPECT TO YOU, INSPECTOR -- AREN'T YOU COMING ON A BIT STRONG? AFTER ALL, SHE'S A VICTIM, NOT A SUSPECT.
HARUMPH!
ピョーン！
PYO-N!
AND YOU WONDER WHY YOU'VE NEVER MADE CAPTAIN. IT'S THE LITTLE THINGS LIKE THIS.
PERHAPS YOU'RE RIGHT . . .

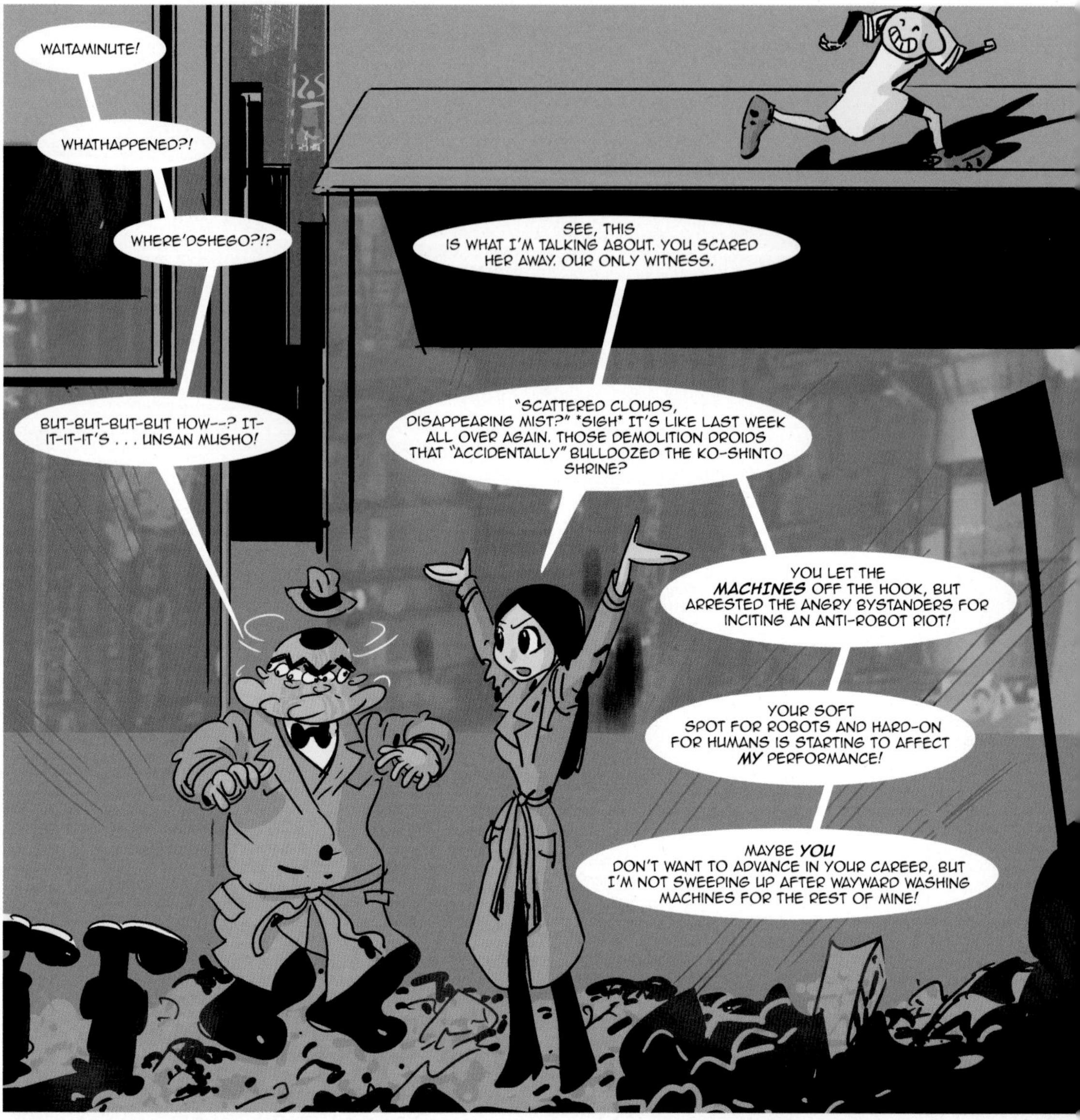
WAITAMINUTE!
WHATHAPPENED?!
WHERE'DSHEGO?!?
BUT-BUT-BUT-BUT HOW--? IT-IT-IT-IT'S . . . UNSAN MUSHO!
SEE, THIS IS WHAT I'M TALKING ABOUT. YOU SCARED HER AWAY. OUR ONLY WITNESS.
"SCATTERED CLOUDS, DISAPPEARING MIST?" *SIGH* IT'S LIKE LAST WEEK ALL OVER AGAIN. THOSE DEMOLITION DROIDS THAT "ACCIDENTALLY" BULLDOZED THE KO-SHINTO SHRINE?
YOU LET THE ***MACHINES*** OFF THE HOOK, BUT ARRESTED THE ANGRY BYSTANDERS FOR INCITING AN ANTI-ROBOT RIOT!
YOUR SOFT SPOT FOR ROBOTS AND HARD-ON FOR HUMANS IS STARTING TO AFFECT ***MY*** PERFORMANCE!
MAYBE ***YOU*** DON'T WANT TO ADVANCE IN YOUR CAREER, BUT I'M NOT SWEEPING UP AFTER WAYWARD WASHING MACHINES FOR THE REST OF MINE!

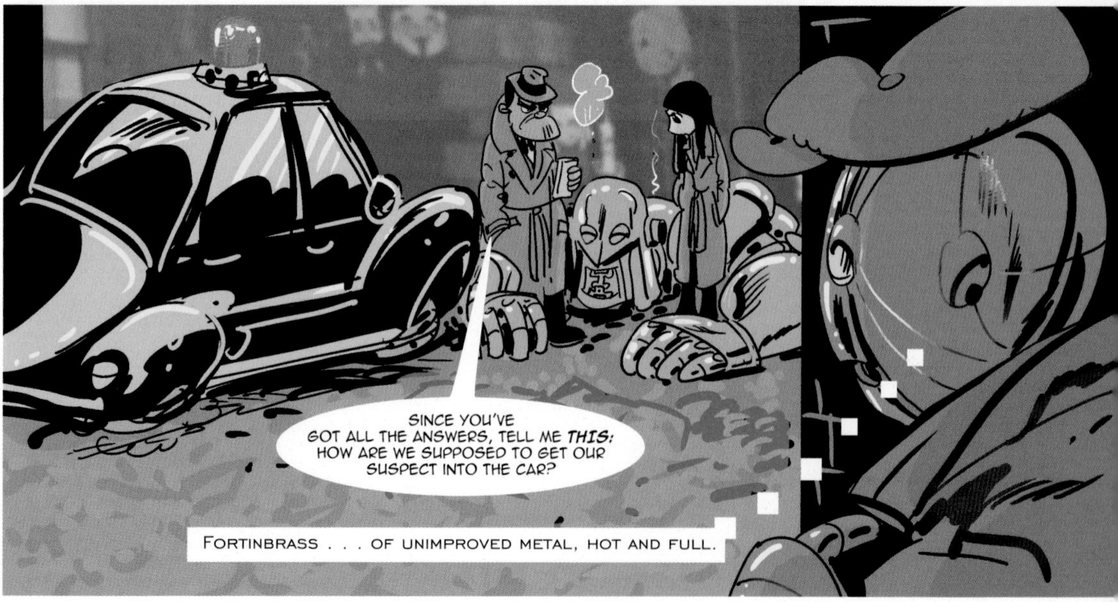
SINCE YOU'VE GOT ALL THE ANSWERS, TELL ME ***THIS:*** HOW ARE WE SUPPOSED TO GET OUR SUSPECT INTO THE CAR?
FORTINBRASS . . . OF UNIMPROVED METAL, HOT AND FULL.

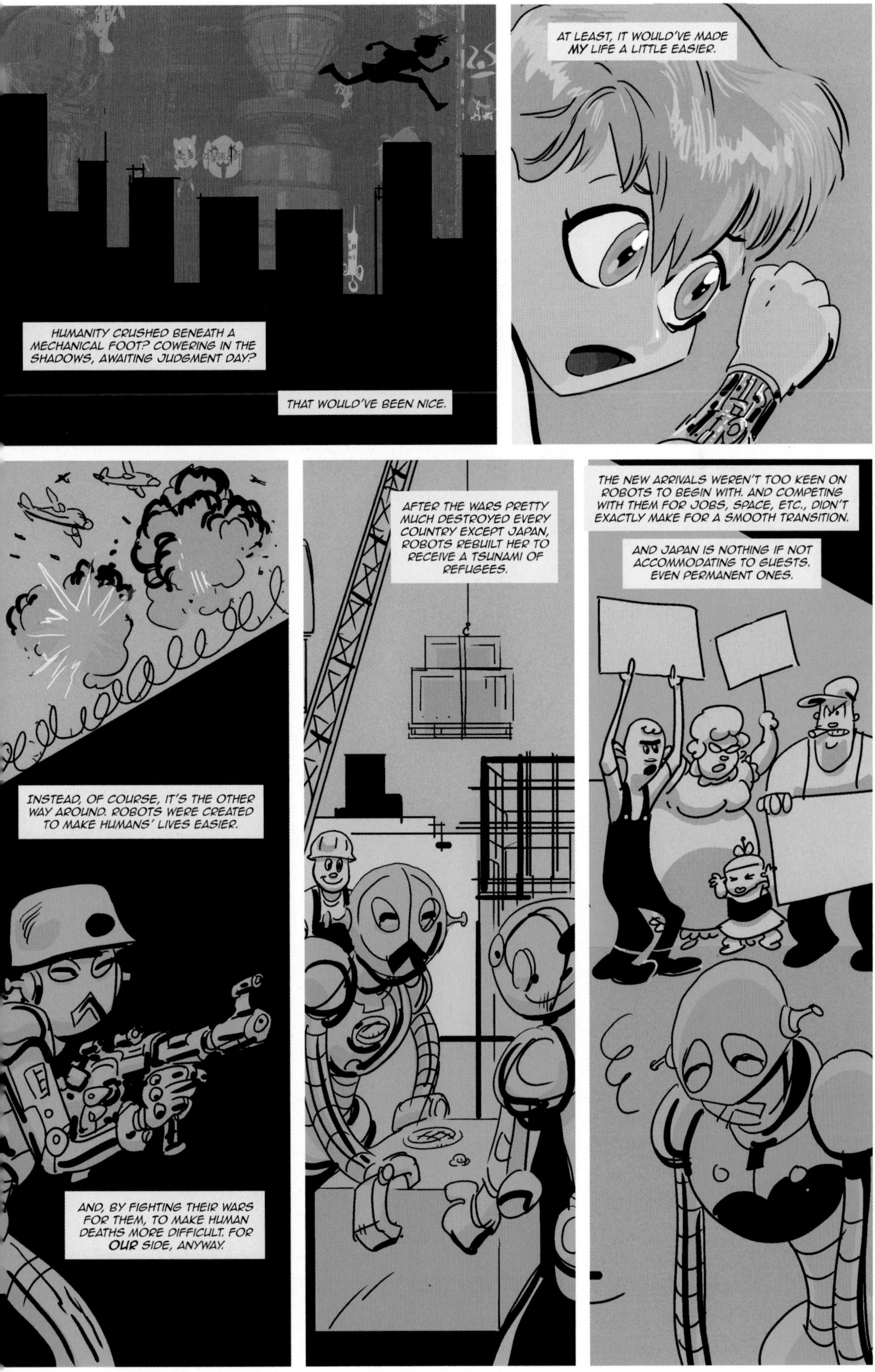
HUMANITY CRUSHED BENEATH A MECHANICAL FOOT? COWERING IN THE SHADOWS, AWAITING JUDGMENT DAY?
THAT WOULD'VE BEEN NICE.
AT LEAST, IT WOULD'VE MADE MY LIFE A LITTLE EASIER.
INSTEAD, OF COURSE, IT'S THE OTHER WAY AROUND. ROBOTS WERE CREATED TO MAKE HUMANS' LIVES EASIER.
AND, BY FIGHTING THEIR WARS FOR THEM, TO MAKE HUMAN DEATHS MORE DIFFICULT. FOR OUR SIDE, ANYWAY.
AFTER THE WARS PRETTY MUCH DESTROYED EVERY COUNTRY EXCEPT JAPAN, ROBOTS REBUILT HER TO RECEIVE A TSUNAMI OF REFUGEES.
THE NEW ARRIVALS WEREN'T TOO KEEN ON ROBOTS TO BEGIN WITH. AND COMPETING WITH THEM FOR JOBS, SPACE, ETC., DIDN'T EXACTLY MAKE FOR A SMOOTH TRANSITION.
AND JAPAN IS NOTHING IF NOT ACCOMMODATING TO GUESTS. EVEN PERMANENT ONES.

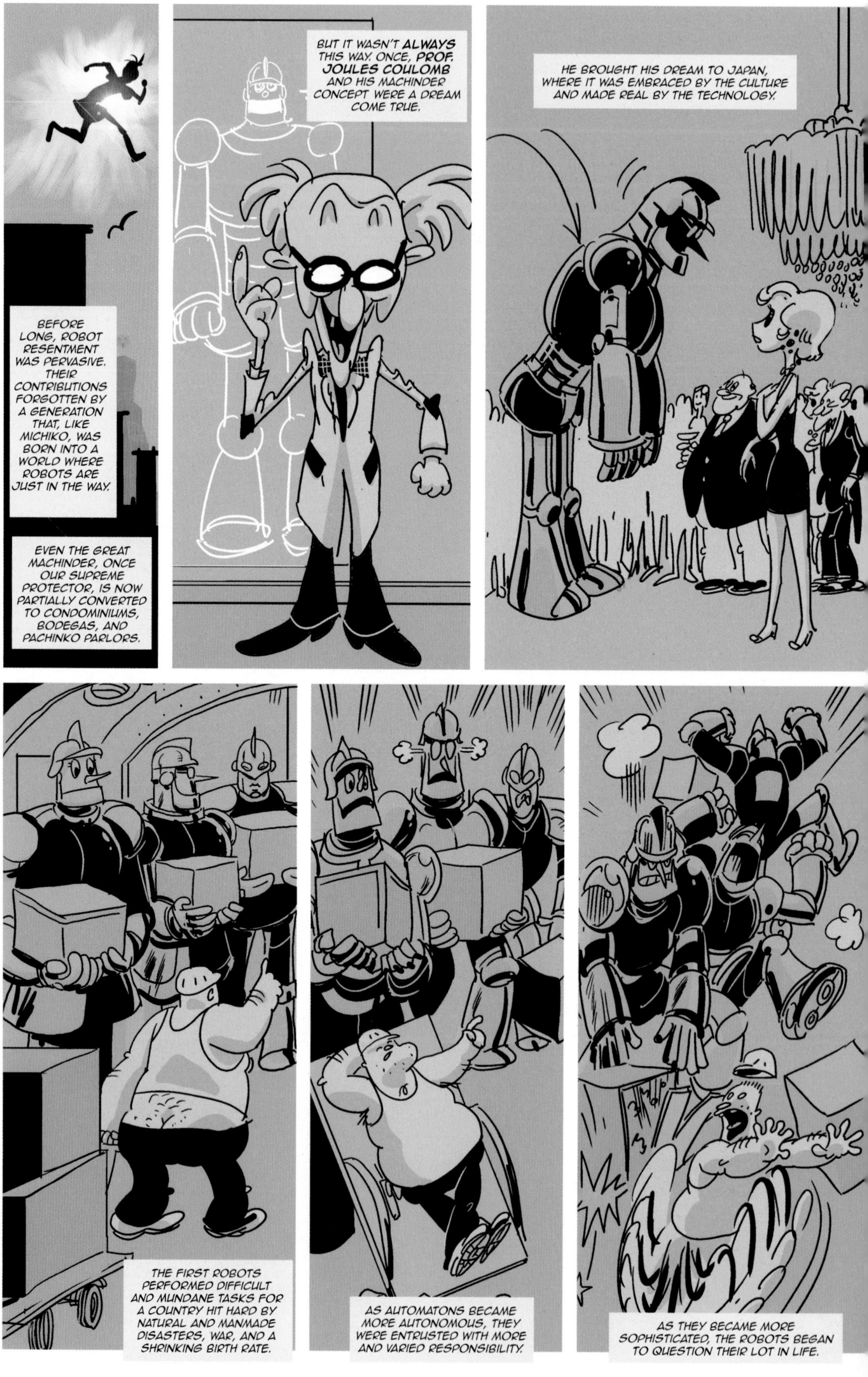
BEFORE LONG, ROBOT RESENTMENT WAS PERVASIVE. THEIR CONTRIBUTIONS FORGOTTEN BY A GENERATION THAT, LIKE MICHIKO, WAS BORN INTO A WORLD WHERE ROBOTS ARE JUST IN THE WAY.
EVEN THE GREAT MACHINDER, ONCE OUR SUPREME PROTECTOR, IS NOW PARTIALLY CONVERTED TO CONDOMINIUMS, BODEGAS, AND PACHINKO PARLORS.
BUT IT WASN'T ALWAYS THIS WAY. ONCE, PROF. JOULES COULOMB AND HIS MACHINDER CONCEPT WERE A DREAM COME TRUE.
HE BROUGHT HIS DREAM TO JAPAN, WHERE IT WAS EMBRACED BY THE CULTURE AND MADE REAL BY THE TECHNOLOGY.
THE FIRST ROBOTS PERFORMED DIFFICULT AND MUNDANE TASKS FOR A COUNTRY HIT HARD BY NATURAL AND MANMADE DISASTERS, WAR, AND A SHRINKING BIRTH RATE.
AS AUTOMATONS BECAME MORE AUTONOMOUS, THEY WERE ENTRUSTED WITH MORE AND VARIED RESPONSIBILITY.
AS THEY BECAME MORE SOPHISTICATED, THE ROBOTS BEGAN TO QUESTION THEIR LOT IN LIFE.

AND AS THEY BECAME MORE CONCERNED WITH THE POSSIBILITY OF ROBOTIC REBELLION, THE HUMANS BEGAN TO QUESTION THE PROFESSOR.

ALWAYS A FORWARD THINKER, HE HAD A CONTINGENCY PLAN FOR THE COMING MACHINDER REVOLUTION.

LOTS OF PEOPLE THINK THEY WERE CREATED TO "SERVE A PURPOSE." I *KNOW* I WAS.

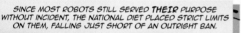

SINCE MOST ROBOTS STILL SERVED *THEIR* PURPOSE WITHOUT INCIDENT, THE NATIONAL DIET PLACED STRICT LIMITS ON THEM, FALLING JUST SHORT OF AN OUTRIGHT BAN.

THE PROFESSOR COULD ONLY GET ENOUGH RAW MATERIALS TO MAKE ME. AND I HAD TO PASS AS HIS GRANDDAUGHTER FOR THE FREEDOM TO PERFORM MY FUNCTION.

I STUDIED EVERY MACHINDER MAKE AND MODEL, AND HOW TO INCAPACITATE THEM, IF NECESSARY, TO PREVENT THEM FROM DOING ANY HARM TO HUMANS.

I DON'T THINK ROBOTS DESERVE TO BE TREATED THE WAY THEY HAVE BEEN, BUT TERRORIZING PEOPLE WON'T REPAIR HUMAN-ROBOT RELATIONS. AND WE STILL NEED EACH OTHER.

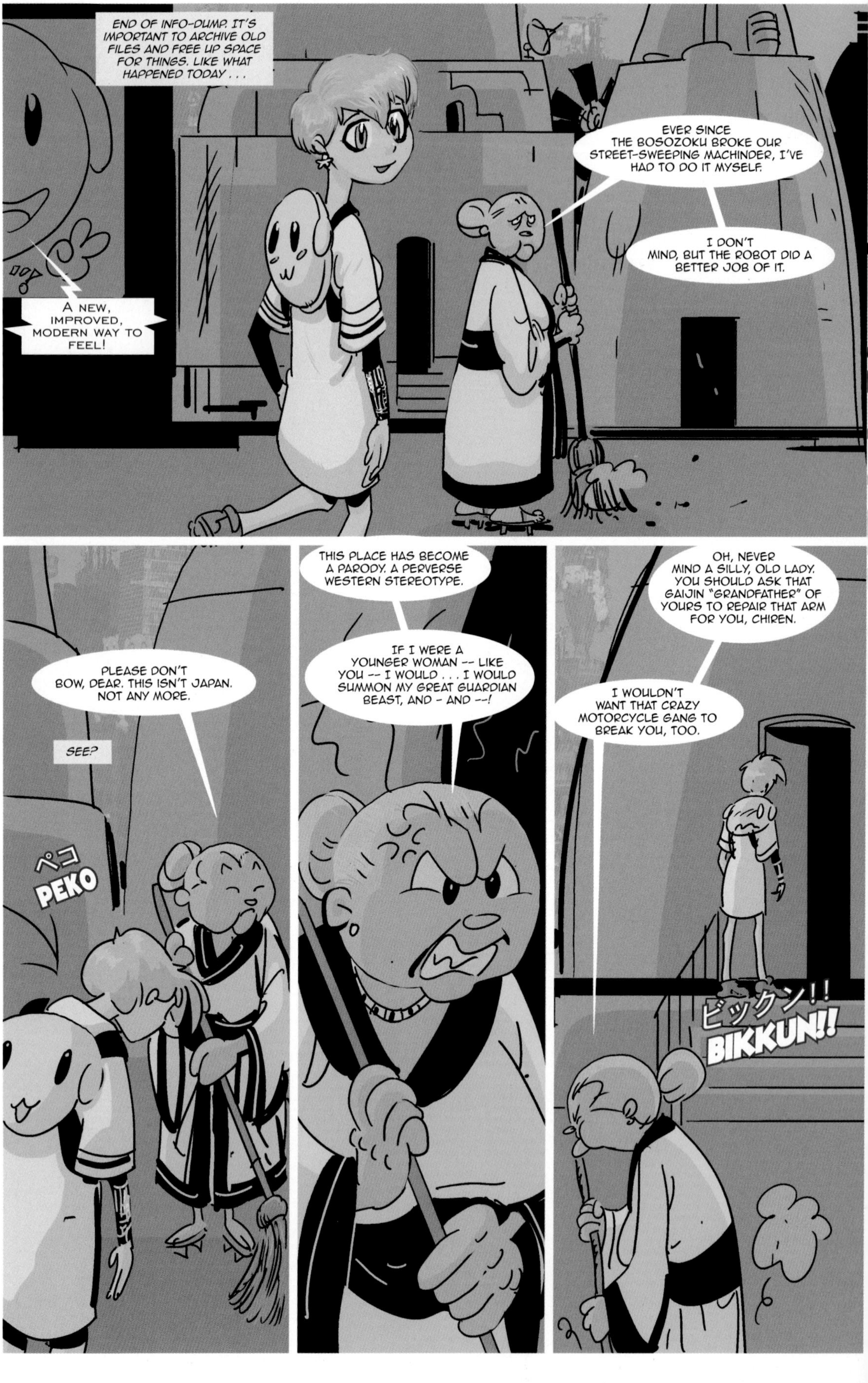
END OF INFO-DUMP. IT'S IMPORTANT TO ARCHIVE OLD FILES AND FREE UP SPACE FOR THINGS. LIKE WHAT HAPPENED TODAY . . .
A NEW, IMPROVED, MODERN WAY TO FEEL!
EVER SINCE THE BOSOZOKU BROKE OUR STREET-SWEEPING MACHINDER, I'VE HAD TO DO IT MYSELF.
I DON'T MIND, BUT THE ROBOT DID A BETTER JOB OF IT.
PLEASE DON'T BOW, DEAR. THIS ISN'T JAPAN. NOT ANY MORE.
SEE?
ペコ
PEKO
THIS PLACE HAS BECOME A PARODY. A PERVERSE WESTERN STEREOTYPE.
IF I WERE A YOUNGER WOMAN -- LIKE YOU -- I WOULD . . . I WOULD SUMMON MY GREAT GUARDIAN BEAST, AND - AND --!
OH, NEVER MIND A SILLY, OLD LADY. YOU SHOULD ASK THAT GAIJIN "GRANDFATHER" OF YOURS TO REPAIR THAT ARM FOR YOU, CHIREN.
I WOULDN'T WANT THAT CRAZY MOTORCYCLE GANG TO BREAK YOU, TOO.
ビックン!!
BIKKUN!!

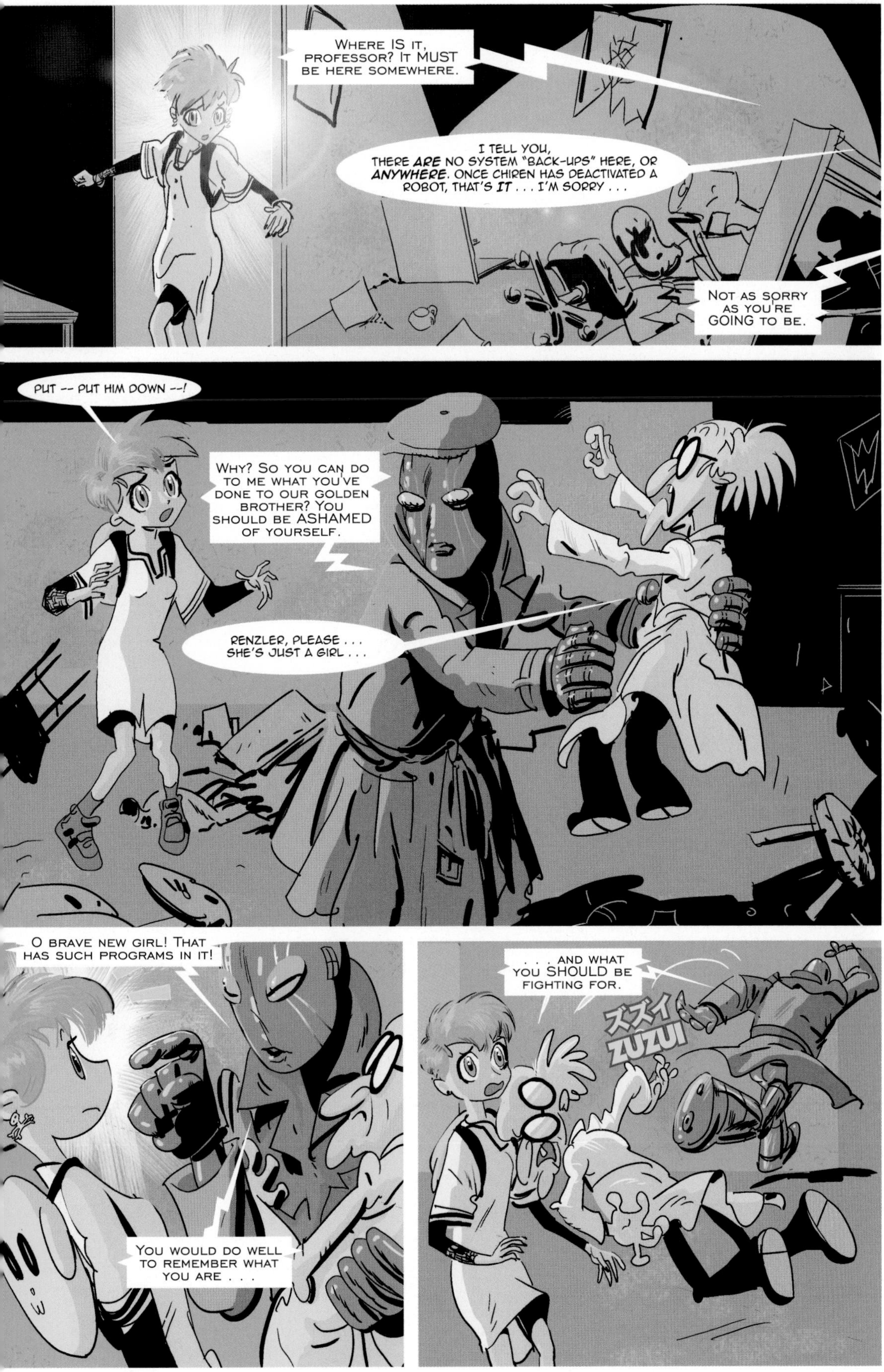

WHERE IS IT, PROFESSOR? IT MUST BE HERE SOMEWHERE.
I TELL YOU, THERE ARE NO SYSTEM "BACK-UPS" HERE, OR ANYWHERE. ONCE CHIREN HAS DEACTIVATED A ROBOT, THAT'S IT . . . I'M SORRY . . .
NOT AS SORRY AS YOU'RE GOING TO BE.
PUT -- PUT HIM DOWN --!
WHY? SO YOU CAN DO TO ME WHAT YOU'VE DONE TO OUR GOLDEN BROTHER? YOU SHOULD BE ASHAMED OF YOURSELF.
RENZLER, PLEASE . . . SHE'S JUST A GIRL . . .
O BRAVE NEW GIRL! THAT HAS SUCH PROGRAMS IN IT!
YOU WOULD DO WELL TO REMEMBER WHAT YOU ARE . . .
. . . AND WHAT YOU SHOULD BE FIGHTING FOR.
ズズイ
ZUZUI

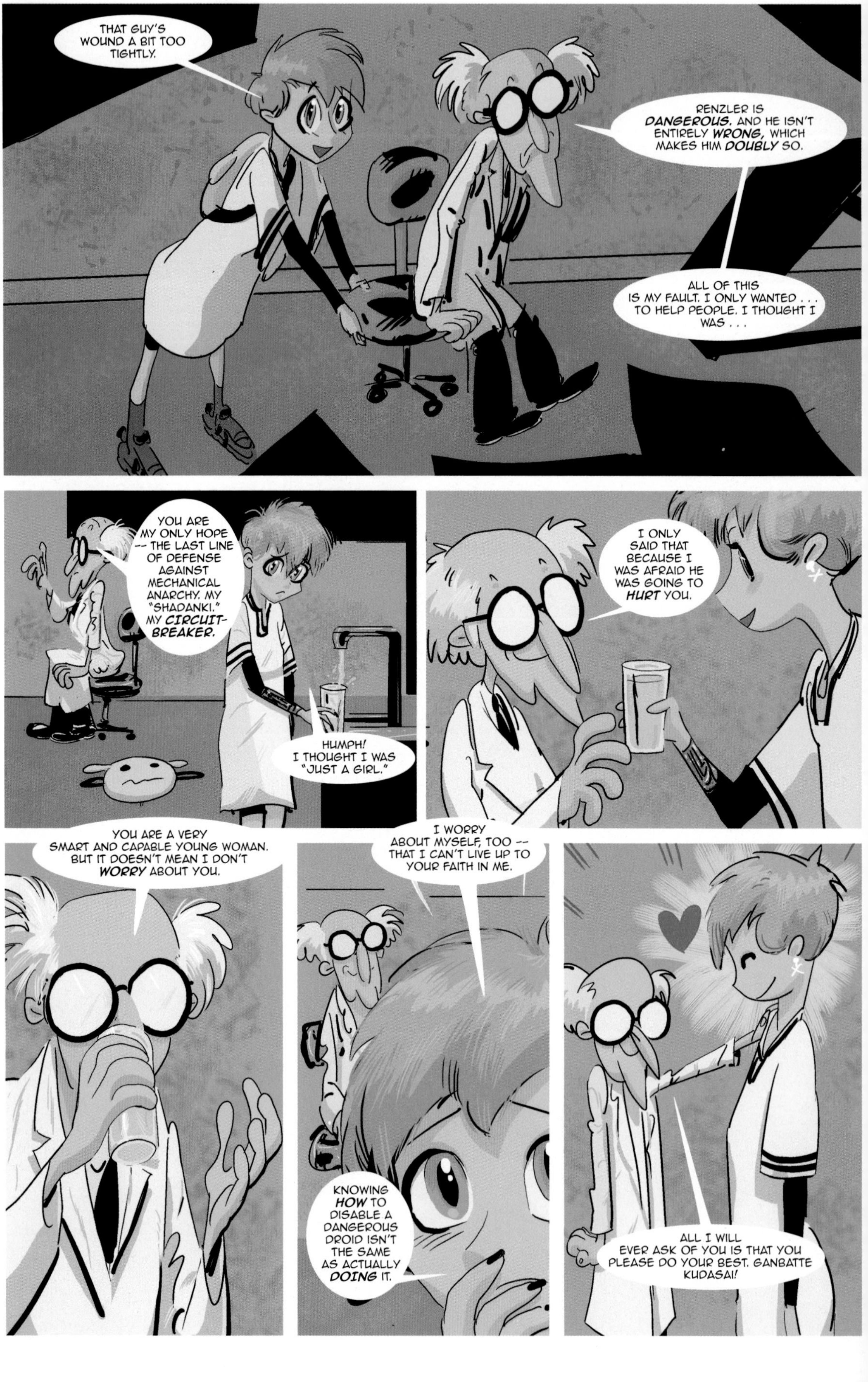
THAT GUY'S WOUND A BIT TOO TIGHTLY.
RENZLER IS DANGEROUS. AND HE ISN'T ENTIRELY WRONG, WHICH MAKES HIM DOUBLY SO.
ALL OF THIS IS MY FAULT. I ONLY WANTED . . . TO HELP PEOPLE. I THOUGHT I WAS . . .
YOU ARE MY ONLY HOPE -- THE LAST LINE OF DEFENSE AGAINST MECHANICAL ANARCHY. MY "SHADANKI." MY CIRCUIT-BREAKER.
HUMPH! I THOUGHT I WAS "JUST A GIRL."
I ONLY SAID THAT BECAUSE I WAS AFRAID HE WAS GOING TO HURT YOU.
YOU ARE A VERY SMART AND CAPABLE YOUNG WOMAN. BUT IT DOESN'T MEAN I DON'T WORRY ABOUT YOU.
I WORRY ABOUT MYSELF, TOO -- THAT I CAN'T LIVE UP TO YOUR FAITH IN ME.
KNOWING HOW TO DISABLE A DANGEROUS DROID ISN'T THE SAME AS ACTUALLY DOING IT.
ALL I WILL EVER ASK OF YOU IS THAT YOU PLEASE DO YOUR BEST. GANBATTE KUDASAI!

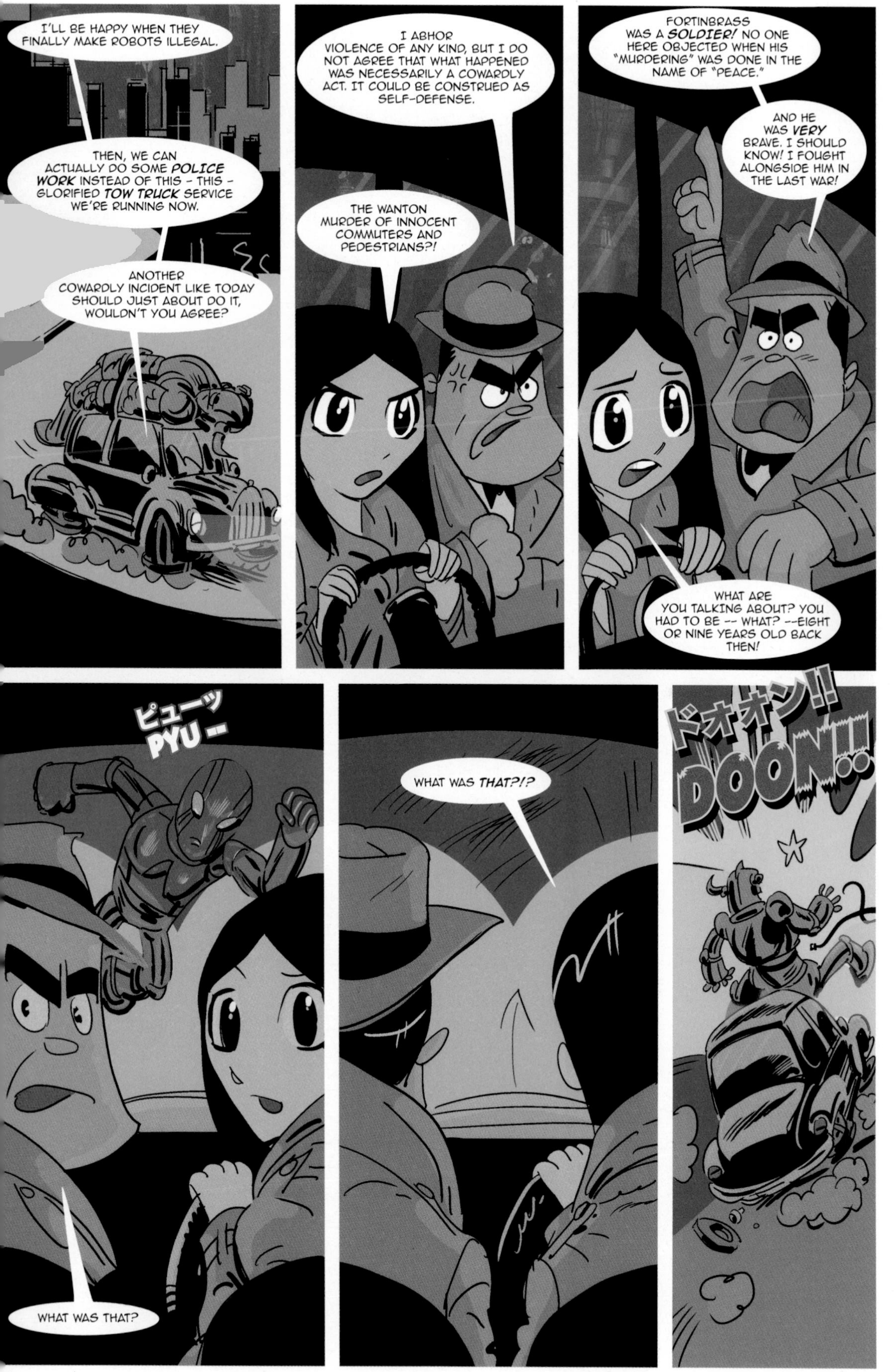
I'LL BE HAPPY WHEN THEY FINALLY MAKE ROBOTS ILLEGAL.
THEN, WE CAN ACTUALLY DO SOME POLICE WORK INSTEAD OF THIS - THIS - GLORIFIED TOW TRUCK SERVICE WE'RE RUNNING NOW.
ANOTHER COWARDLY INCIDENT LIKE TODAY SHOULD JUST ABOUT DO IT, WOULDN'T YOU AGREE?
I ABHOR VIOLENCE OF ANY KIND, BUT I DO NOT AGREE THAT WHAT HAPPENED WAS NECESSARILY A COWARDLY ACT. IT COULD BE CONSTRUED AS SELF-DEFENSE.
THE WANTON MURDER OF INNOCENT COMMUTERS AND PEDESTRIANS?!
FORTINBRASS WAS A SOLDIER! NO ONE HERE OBJECTED WHEN HIS "MURDERING" WAS DONE IN THE NAME OF "PEACE."
AND HE WAS VERY BRAVE. I SHOULD KNOW! I FOUGHT ALONGSIDE HIM IN THE LAST WAR!
WHAT ARE YOU TALKING ABOUT? YOU HAD TO BE -- WHAT? --EIGHT OR NINE YEARS OLD BACK THEN!
ピューッ
PYU --
WHAT WAS THAT?
WHAT WAS THAT?!?
ドォオン!!
DOON!!

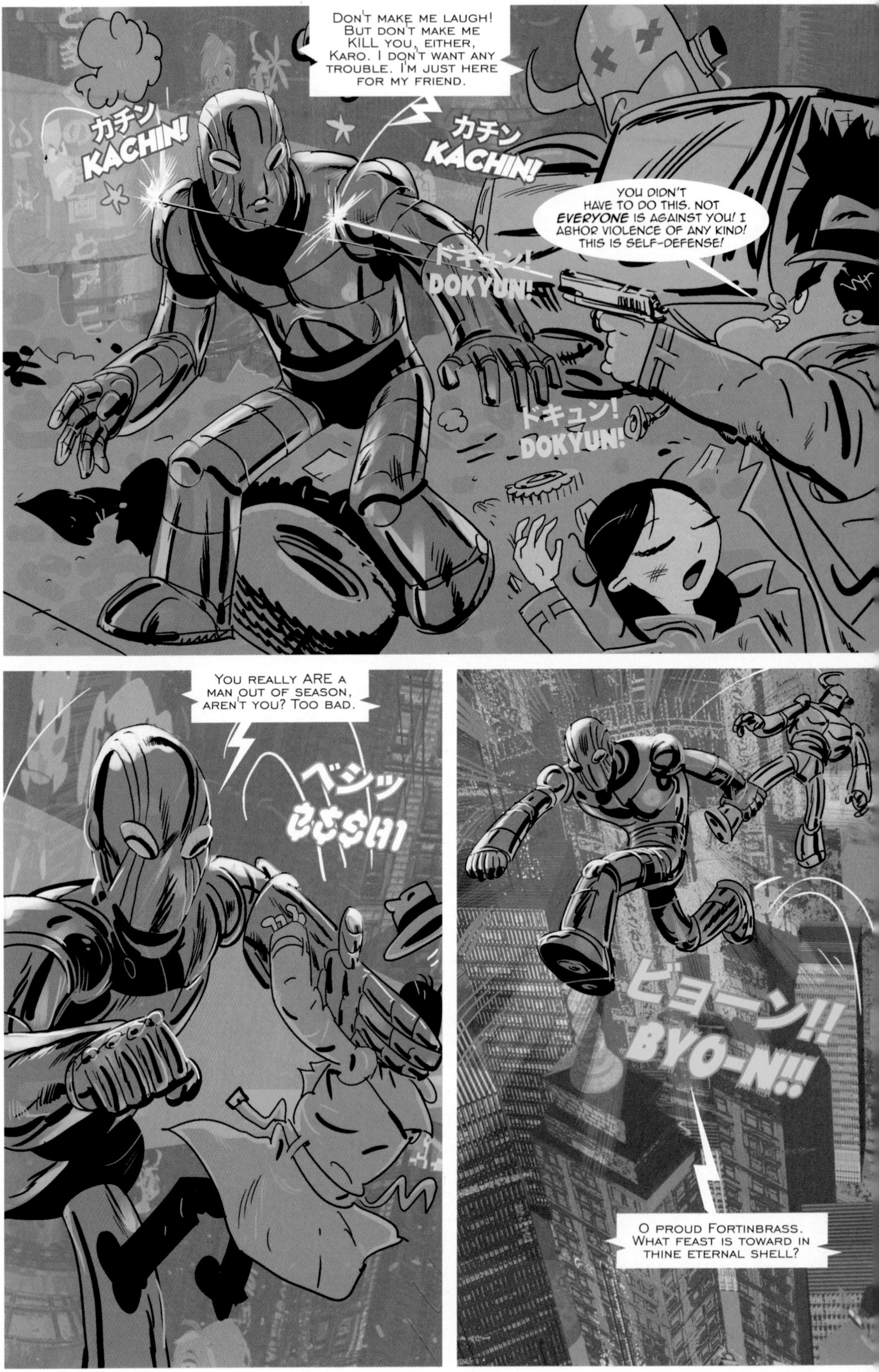

DON'T MAKE ME LAUGH! BUT DON'T MAKE ME KILL YOU, EITHER, KARO. I DON'T WANT ANY TROUBLE. I'M JUST HERE FOR MY FRIEND.
カチン KACHIN!
カチン KACHIN!
YOU DIDN'T HAVE TO DO THIS. NOT *EVERYONE* IS AGAINST YOU! I ABHOR VIOLENCE OF ANY KIND! THIS IS SELF-DEFENSE!
ドキュン! DOKYUN!
ドキュン! DOKYUN!
YOU REALLY ARE A MAN OUT OF SEASON, AREN'T YOU? TOO BAD.
ベシッ BESHI
ビョーン!! BYO-N!!
O PROUD FORTINBRASS. WHAT FEAST IS TOWARD IN THINE ETERNAL SHELL?

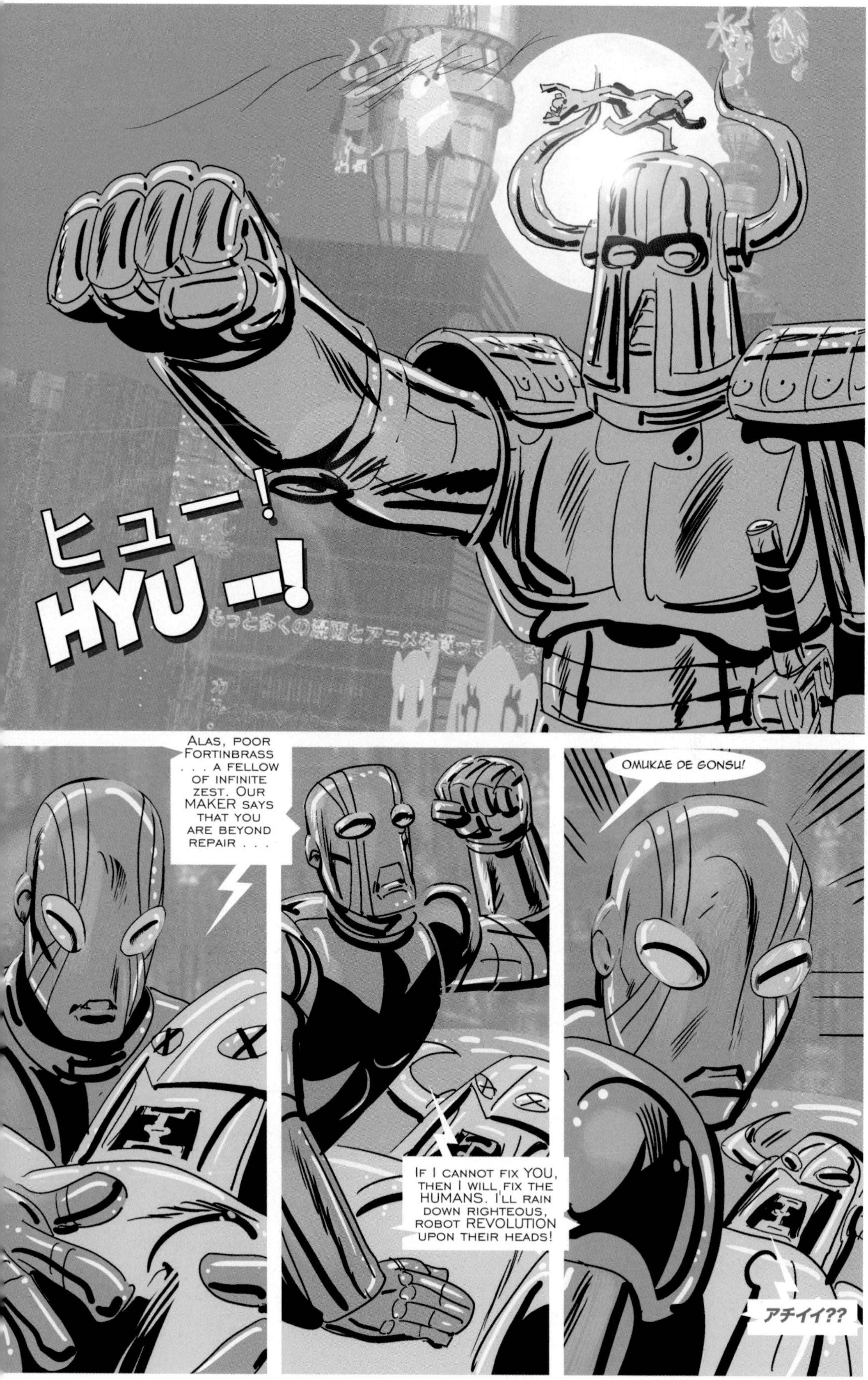
ヒュー!
HYU ...!
もっと多くの漫画とアニメを買ってください
Alas, poor Fortinbrass . . . a fellow of infinite zest. Our MAKER says that you are beyond repair . . .
If I cannot fix YOU, then I will fix the HUMANS. I'll rain down righteous, robot REVOLUTION upon their heads!
Omukae de gonsu!
アチイイ??

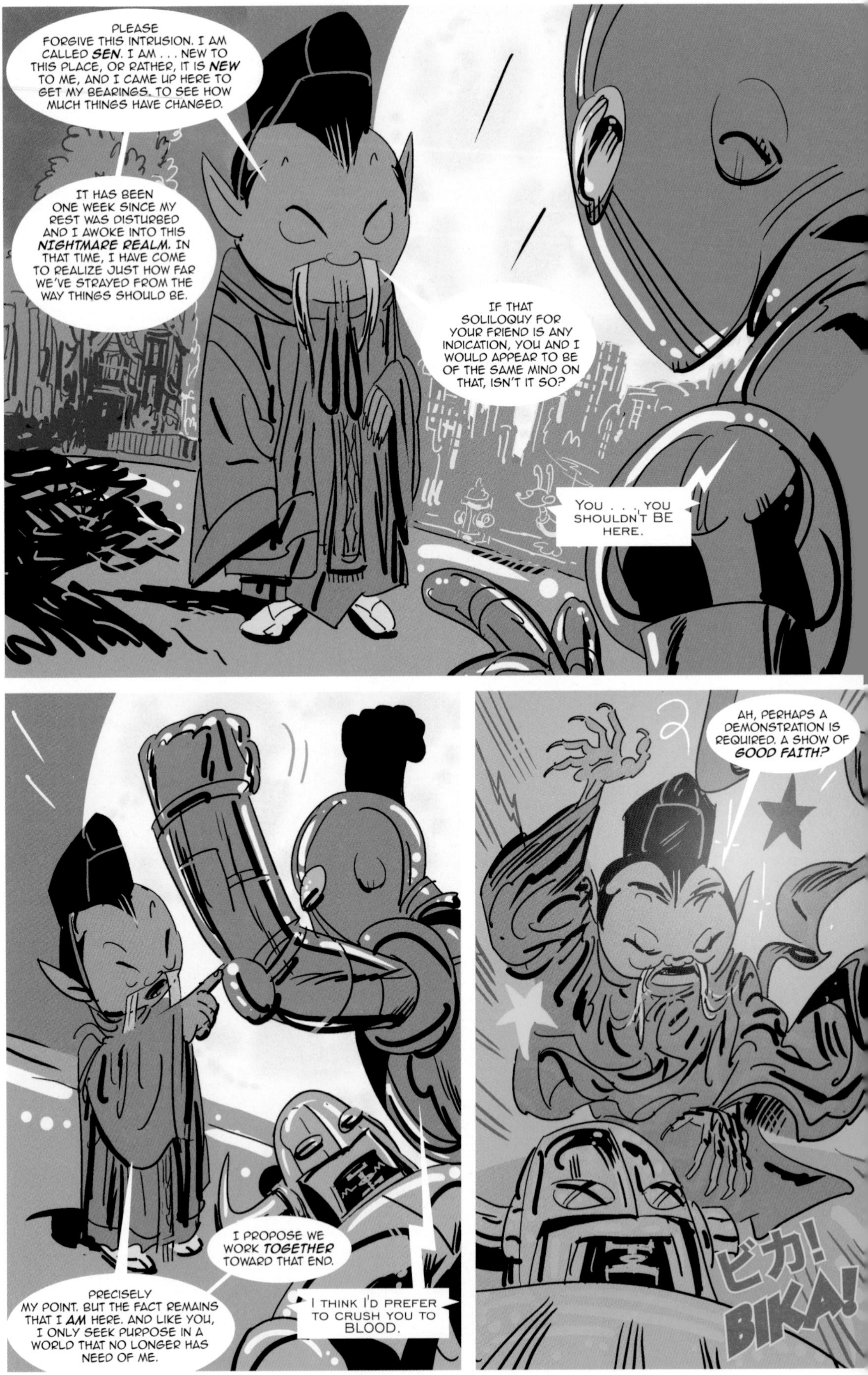
PLEASE FORGIVE THIS INTRUSION. I AM CALLED SEN. I AM . . . NEW TO THIS PLACE, OR RATHER, IT IS NEW TO ME, AND I CAME UP HERE TO GET MY BEARINGS. TO SEE HOW MUCH THINGS HAVE CHANGED.
IT HAS BEEN ONE WEEK SINCE MY REST WAS DISTURBED AND I AWOKE INTO THIS NIGHTMARE REALM. IN THAT TIME, I HAVE COME TO REALIZE JUST HOW FAR WE'VE STRAYED FROM THE WAY THINGS SHOULD BE.
IF THAT SOLILOQUY FOR YOUR FRIEND IS ANY INDICATION, YOU AND I WOULD APPEAR TO BE OF THE SAME MIND ON THAT, ISN'T IT SO?
YOU . . . YOU SHOULDN'T BE HERE.
PRECISELY MY POINT. BUT THE FACT REMAINS THAT I AM HERE. AND LIKE YOU, I ONLY SEEK PURPOSE IN A WORLD THAT NO LONGER HAS NEED OF ME.
I PROPOSE WE WORK TOGETHER TOWARD THAT END.
I THINK I'D PREFER TO CRUSH YOU TO BLOOD.
AH, PERHAPS A DEMONSTRATION IS REQUIRED. A SHOW OF GOOD FAITH?
ピカ!
BIKA!

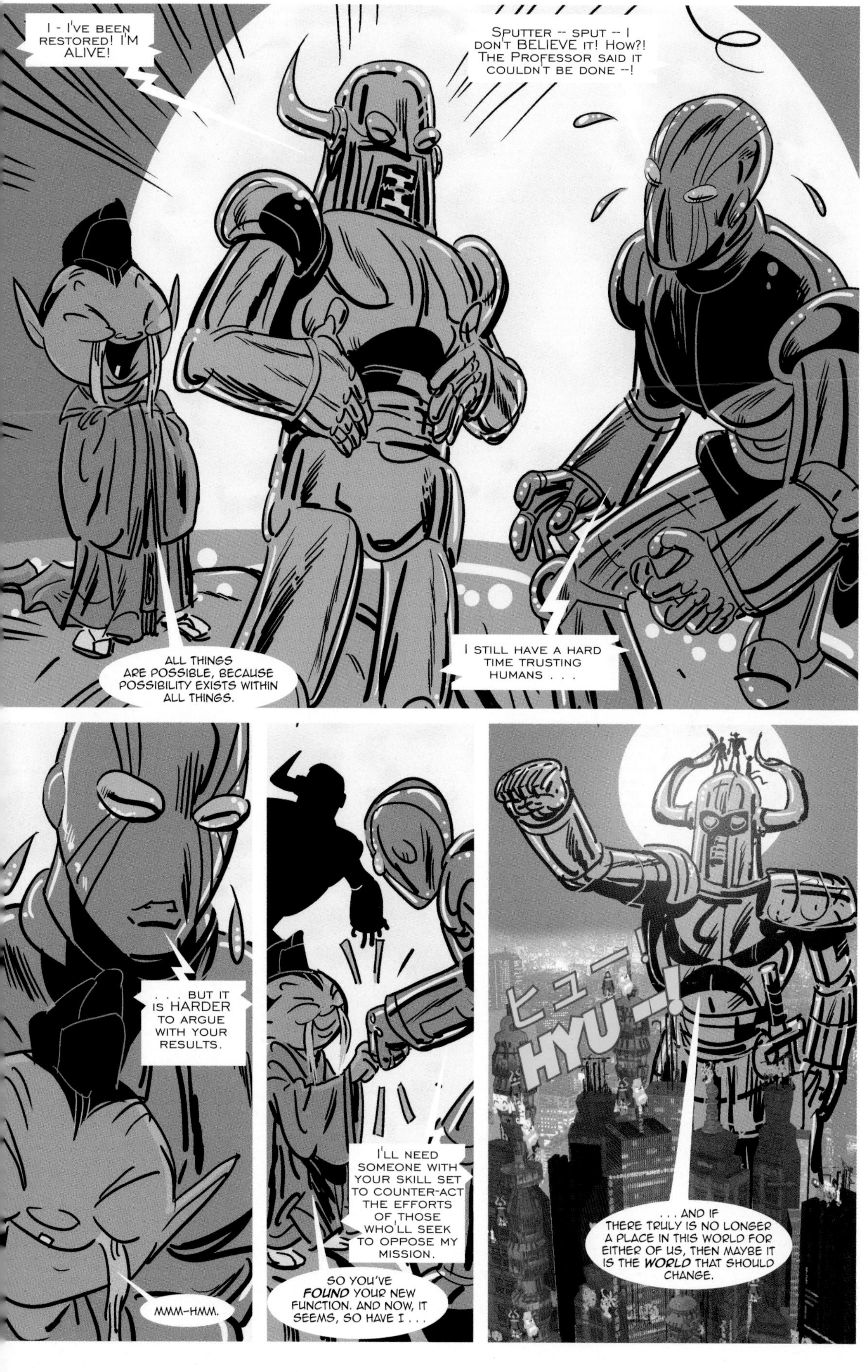
I - I'VE BEEN RESTORED! I'M ALIVE!
SPUTTER -- SPUT -- I DON'T BELIEVE IT! HOW?! THE PROFESSOR SAID IT COULDN'T BE DONE --!
ALL THINGS ARE POSSIBLE, BECAUSE POSSIBILITY EXISTS WITHIN ALL THINGS.
I STILL HAVE A HARD TIME TRUSTING HUMANS . . .
. . . BUT IT IS HARDER TO ARGUE WITH YOUR RESULTS.
MMM-HMM.
I'LL NEED SOMEONE WITH YOUR SKILL SET TO COUNTER-ACT THE EFFORTS OF THOSE WHO'LL SEEK TO OPPOSE MY MISSION.
SO YOU'VE FOUND YOUR NEW FUNCTION. AND NOW, IT SEEMS, SO HAVE I . . .
ヒュー!
HYU --!
. . . AND IF THERE TRULY IS NO LONGER A PLACE IN THIS WORLD FOR EITHER OF US, THEN MAYBE IT IS THE WORLD THAT SHOULD CHANGE.

TWO

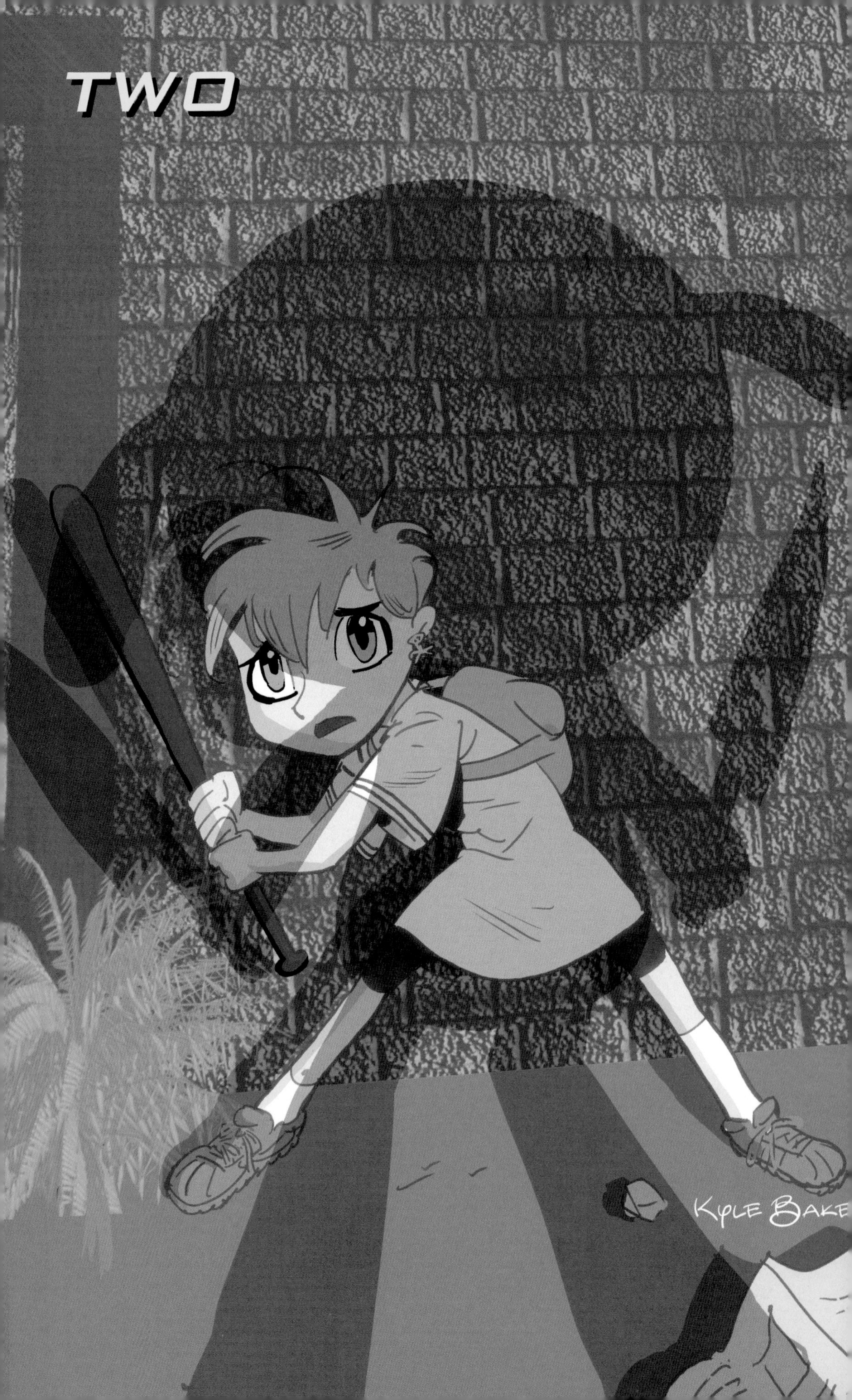
KYLE BAKE

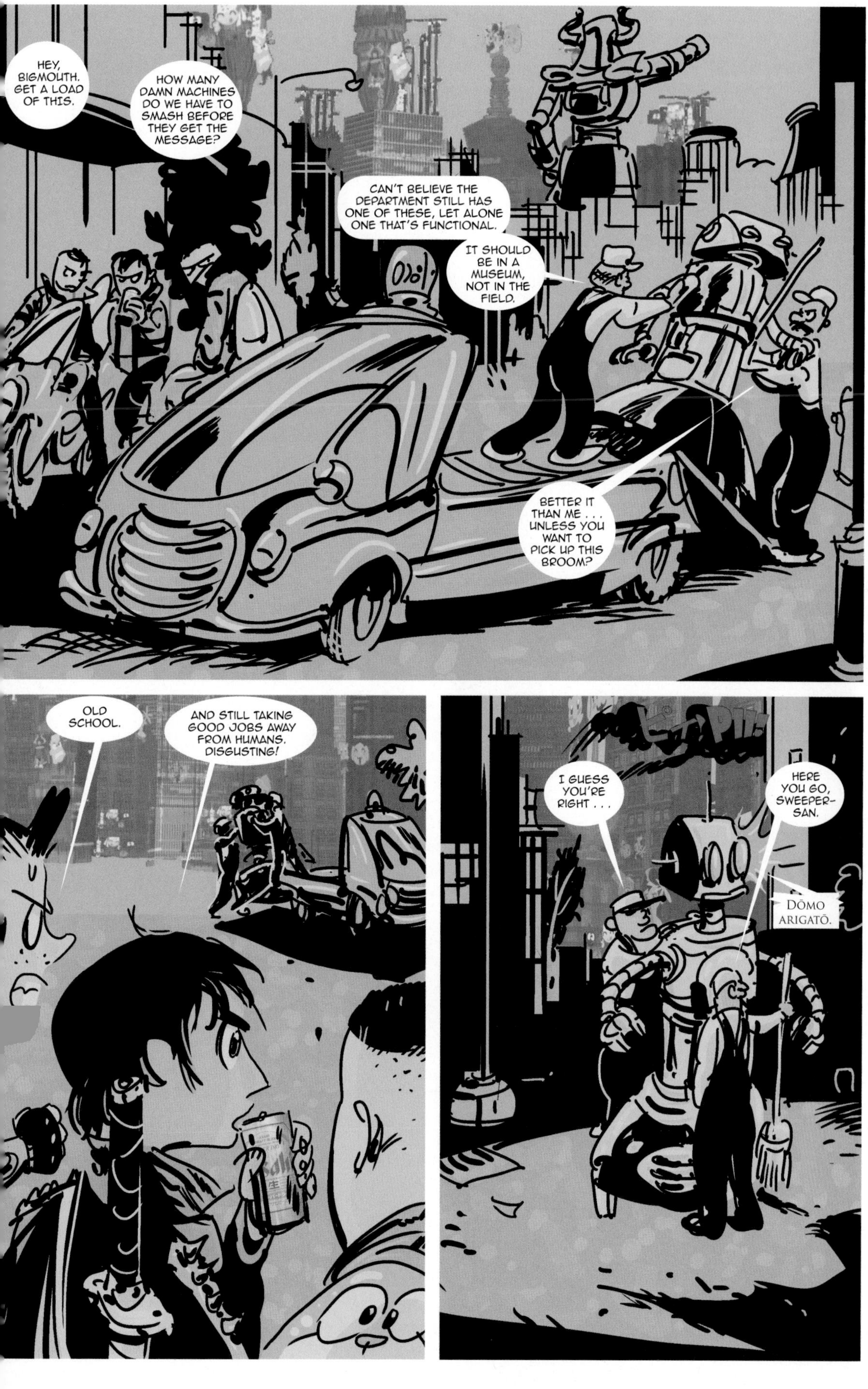
HEY, BIGMOUTH. GET A LOAD OF THIS.
HOW MANY DAMN MACHINES DO WE HAVE TO SMASH BEFORE THEY GET THE MESSAGE?
CAN'T BELIEVE THE DEPARTMENT STILL HAS ONE OF THESE, LET ALONE ONE THAT'S FUNCTIONAL.
IT SHOULD BE IN A MUSEUM, NOT IN THE FIELD.
BETTER IT THAN ME . . . UNLESS YOU WANT TO PICK UP THIS BROOM?
OLD SCHOOL.
AND STILL TAKING GOOD JOBS AWAY FROM HUMANS. DISGUSTING!
I GUESS YOU'RE RIGHT . . .
HERE YOU GO, SWEEPER-SAN.
DŌMO ARIGATŌ.

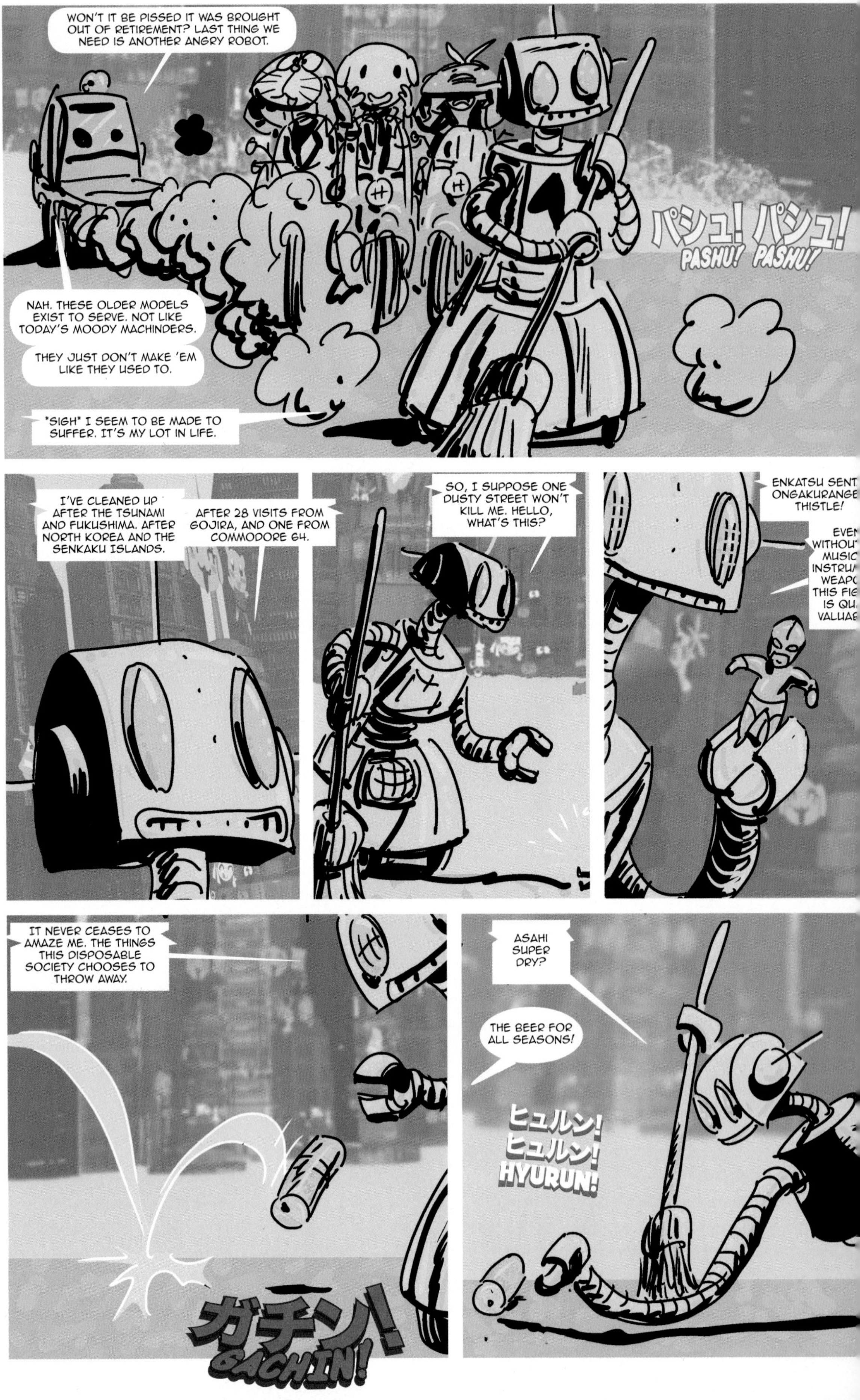

WON'T IT BE PISSED IT WAS BROUGHT OUT OF RETIREMENT? LAST THING WE NEED IS ANOTHER ANGRY ROBOT.
パシュ! パシュ!
PASHU! PASHU!
NAH. THESE OLDER MODELS EXIST TO SERVE. NOT LIKE TODAY'S MOODY MACHINDERS.
THEY JUST DON'T MAKE 'EM LIKE THEY USED TO.
SIGH I SEEM TO BE MADE TO SUFFER. IT'S MY LOT IN LIFE.
I'VE CLEANED UP AFTER THE TSUNAMI AND FUKUSHIMA. AFTER NORTH KOREA AND THE SENKAKU ISLANDS.
AFTER 28 VISITS FROM GOJIRA, AND ONE FROM COMMODORE 64.
SO, I SUPPOSE ONE DUSTY STREET WON'T KILL ME. HELLO, WHAT'S THIS?
ENKATSU SENT ONGAKURANGE THISTLE!
EVEN WITHOUT MUSIC INSTRU WEAPO THIS FIG IS QU VALUAB
IT NEVER CEASES TO AMAZE ME. THE THINGS THIS DISPOSABLE SOCIETY CHOOSES TO THROW AWAY.
ガチン!
GACHIN!
ASAHI SUPER DRY?
THE BEER FOR ALL SEASONS!
ヒュルン! ヒュルン!
HYURUN!

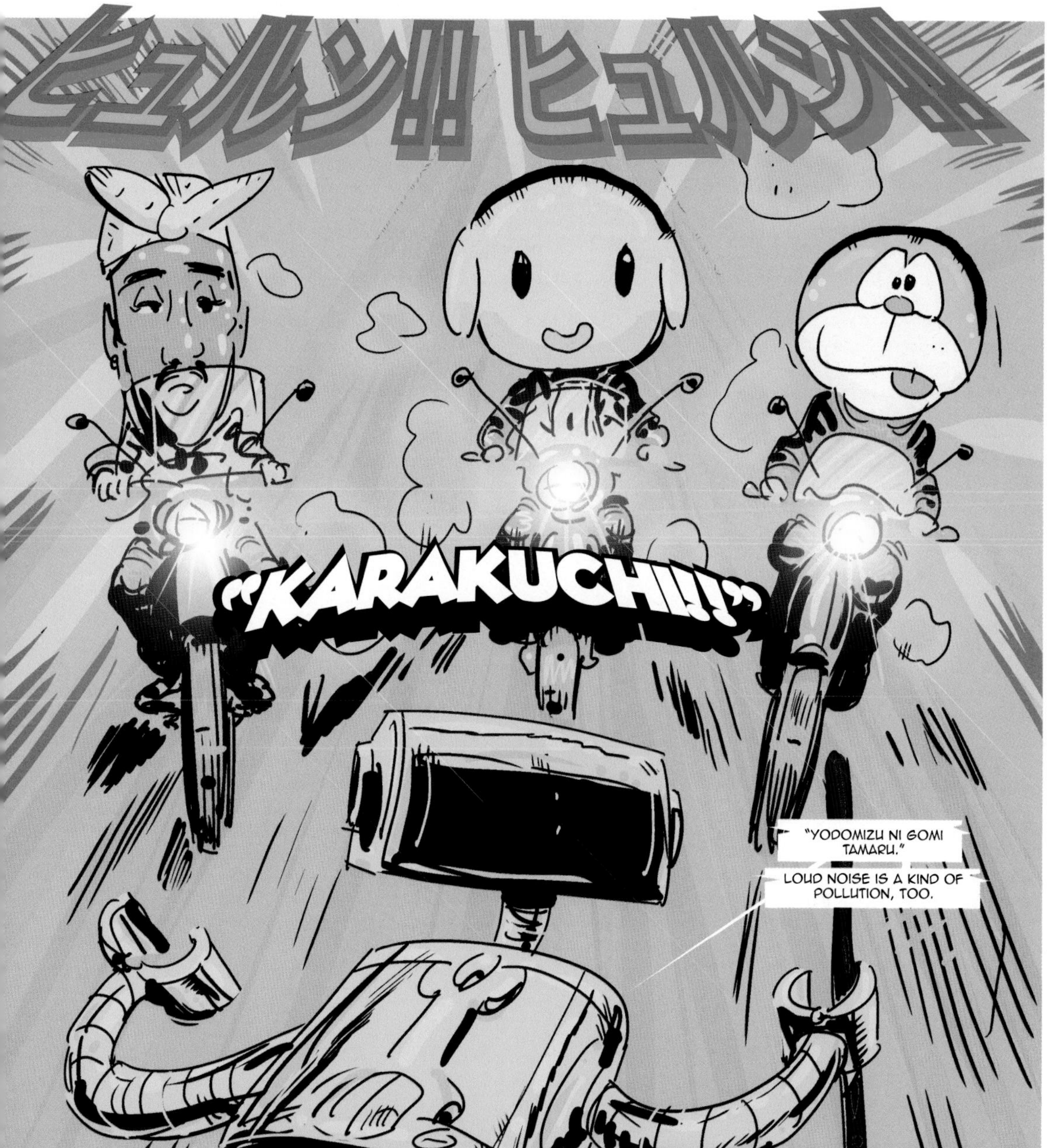
ヒュルン!! ヒュルン!!
"KARAKUCHI!!"
"YODOMIZU NI GOMI TAMARU."
LOUD NOISE IS A KIND OF POLLUTION, TOO.

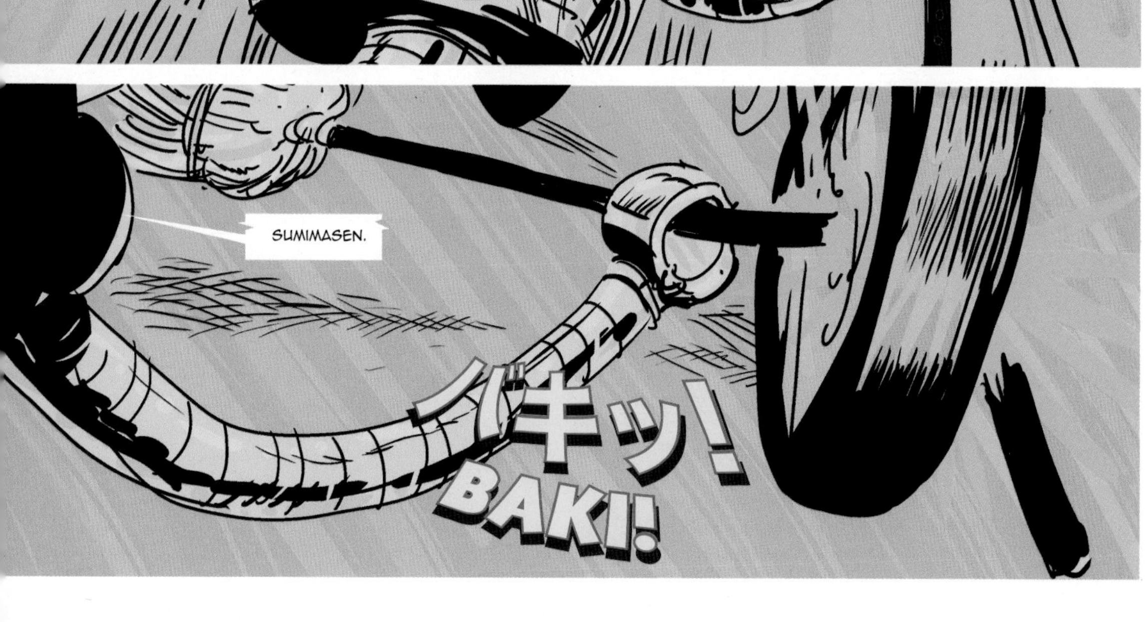
SUMIMASEN.
バキッ!
BAKI!

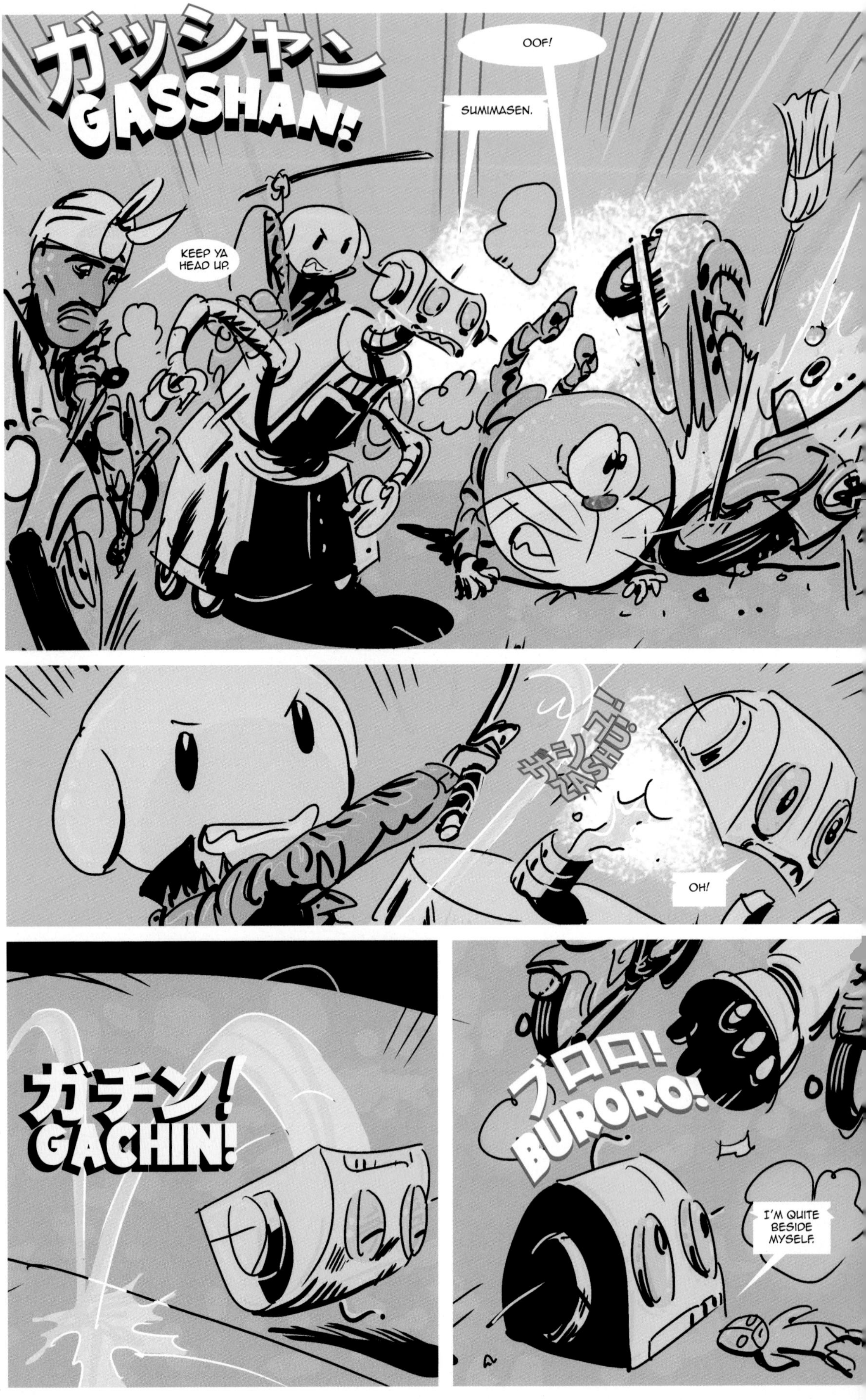
ガッシャン
GASSHAN!
KEEP YA HEAD UP.
OOF!
SUMIMASEN.
ザシュ!
ZASHU!
OH!
ガチン!
GACHIN!
ブロロ!
BURORO!
I'M QUITE BESIDE MYSELF.

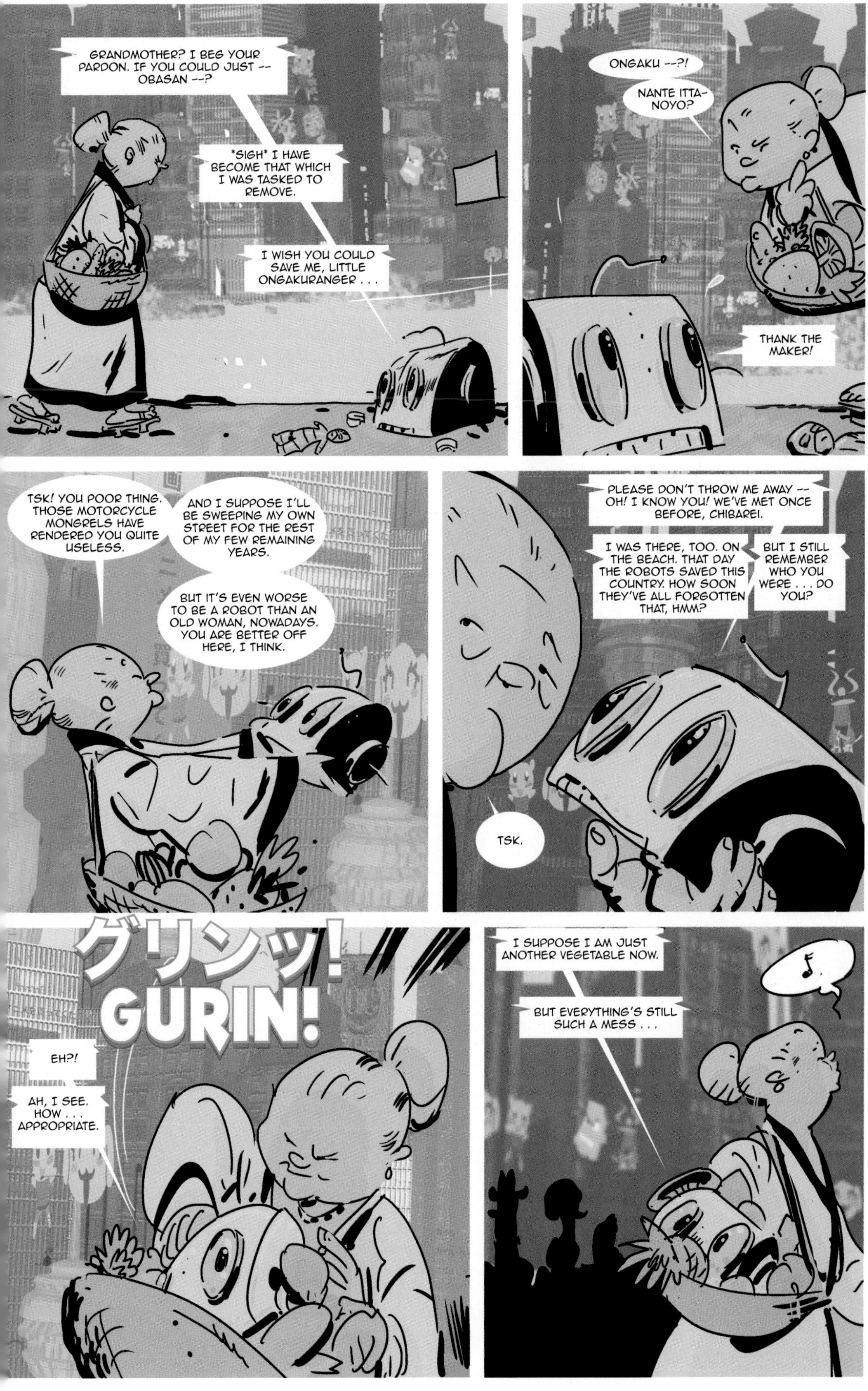
GRANDMOTHER? I BEG YOUR PARDON. IF YOU COULD JUST -- OBASAN --?
SIGH I HAVE BECOME THAT WHICH I WAS TASKED TO REMOVE.
I WISH YOU COULD SAVE ME, LITTLE ONGAKURANGER . . .
ONGAKU --?!
NANTE ITTA-NOYO?
THANK THE MAKER!
TSK! YOU POOR THING. THOSE MOTORCYCLE MONGRELS HAVE RENDERED YOU QUITE USELESS.
AND I SUPPOSE I'LL BE SWEEPING MY OWN STREET FOR THE REST OF MY FEW REMAINING YEARS.
BUT IT'S EVEN WORSE TO BE A ROBOT THAN AN OLD WOMAN, NOWADAYS. YOU ARE BETTER OFF HERE, I THINK.
PLEASE DON'T THROW ME AWAY -- OH! I KNOW YOU! WE'VE MET ONCE BEFORE, CHIBAREI.
I WAS THERE, TOO. ON THE BEACH. THAT DAY THE ROBOTS SAVED THIS COUNTRY. HOW SOON THEY'VE ALL FORGOTTEN THAT, HMM?
BUT I STILL REMEMBER WHO YOU WERE . . . DO YOU?
TSK.
グリンッ!
GURIN!
EH?!
AH, I SEE. HOW . . . APPROPRIATE.
I SUPPOSE I AM JUST ANOTHER VEGETABLE NOW.
BUT EVERYTHING'S STILL SUCH A MESS . . .

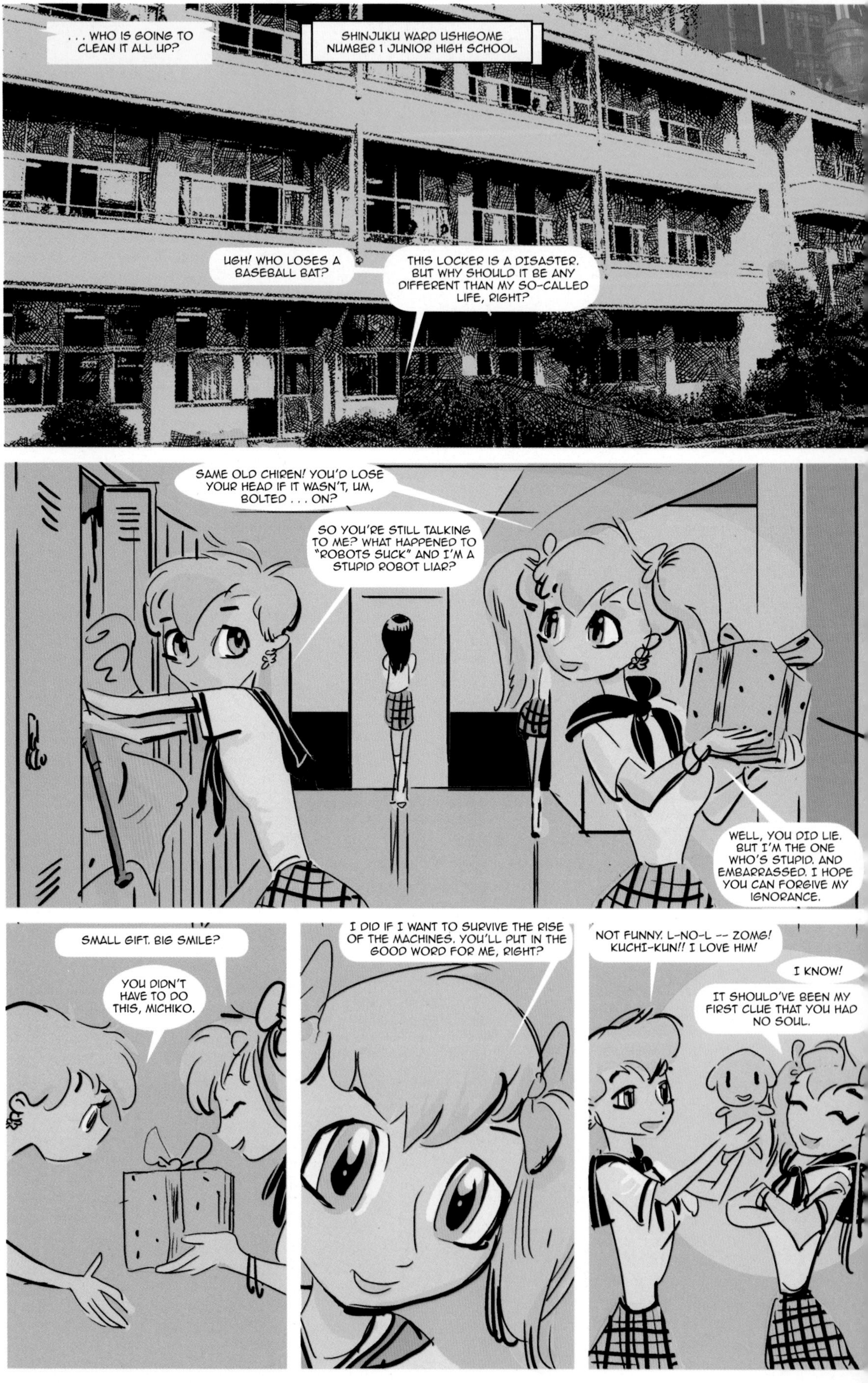
. . . WHO IS GOING TO CLEAN IT ALL UP?
SHINJUKU WARD USHIGOME NUMBER 1 JUNIOR HIGH SCHOOL
UGH! WHO LOSES A BASEBALL BAT?
THIS LOCKER IS A DISASTER. BUT WHY SHOULD IT BE ANY DIFFERENT THAN MY SO-CALLED LIFE, RIGHT?
SAME OLD CHIREN! YOU'D LOSE YOUR HEAD IF IT WASN'T, UM, BOLTED . . . ON?
SO YOU'RE STILL TALKING TO ME? WHAT HAPPENED TO "ROBOTS SUCK" AND I'M A STUPID ROBOT LIAR?
WELL, YOU DID LIE. BUT I'M THE ONE WHO'S STUPID. AND EMBARRASSED. I HOPE YOU CAN FORGIVE MY IGNORANCE.
SMALL GIFT. BIG SMILE?
YOU DIDN'T HAVE TO DO THIS, MICHIKO.
I DID IF I WANT TO SURVIVE THE RISE OF THE MACHINES. YOU'LL PUT IN THE GOOD WORD FOR ME, RIGHT?
NOT FUNNY. L-NO-L -- ZOMG! KUCHI-KUN!! I LOVE HIM!
I KNOW!
IT SHOULD'VE BEEN MY FIRST CLUE THAT YOU HAD NO SOUL.

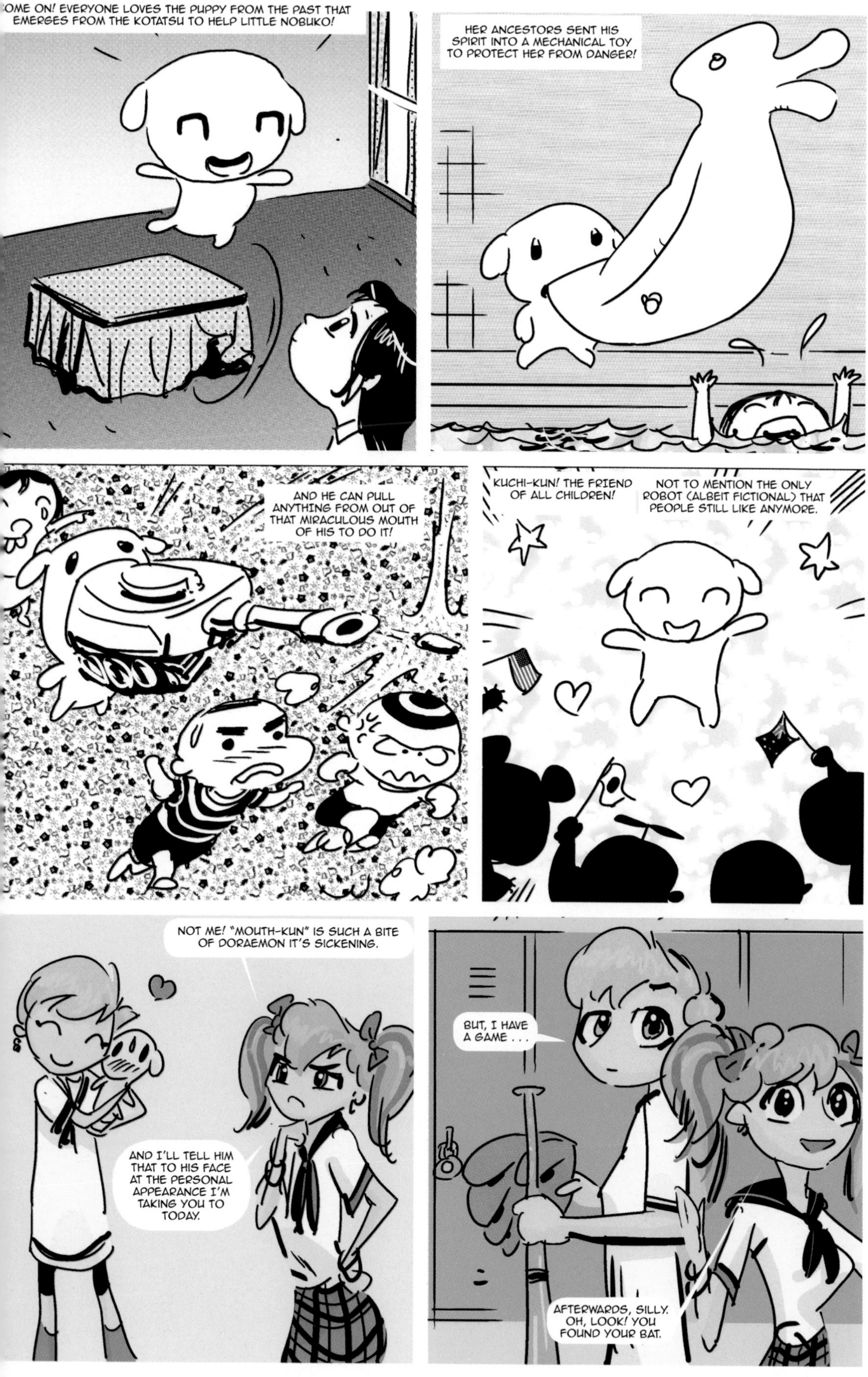

COME ON! EVERYONE LOVES THE PUPPY FROM THE PAST THAT EMERGES FROM THE KOTATSU TO HELP LITTLE NOBUKO!
HER ANCESTORS SENT HIS SPIRIT INTO A MECHANICAL TOY TO PROTECT HER FROM DANGER!
AND HE CAN PULL ANYTHING FROM OUT OF THAT MIRACULOUS MOUTH OF HIS TO DO IT!
KUCHI-KUN! THE FRIEND OF ALL CHILDREN!
NOT TO MENTION THE ONLY ROBOT (ALBEIT FICTIONAL) THAT PEOPLE STILL LIKE ANYMORE.
NOT ME! "MOUTH-KUN" IS SUCH A BITE OF DORAEMON IT'S SICKENING.
AND I'LL TELL HIM THAT TO HIS FACE AT THE PERSONAL APPEARANCE I'M TAKING YOU TO TODAY.
BUT, I HAVE A GAME . . .
AFTERWARDS, SILLY. OH, LOOK! YOU FOUND YOUR BAT.

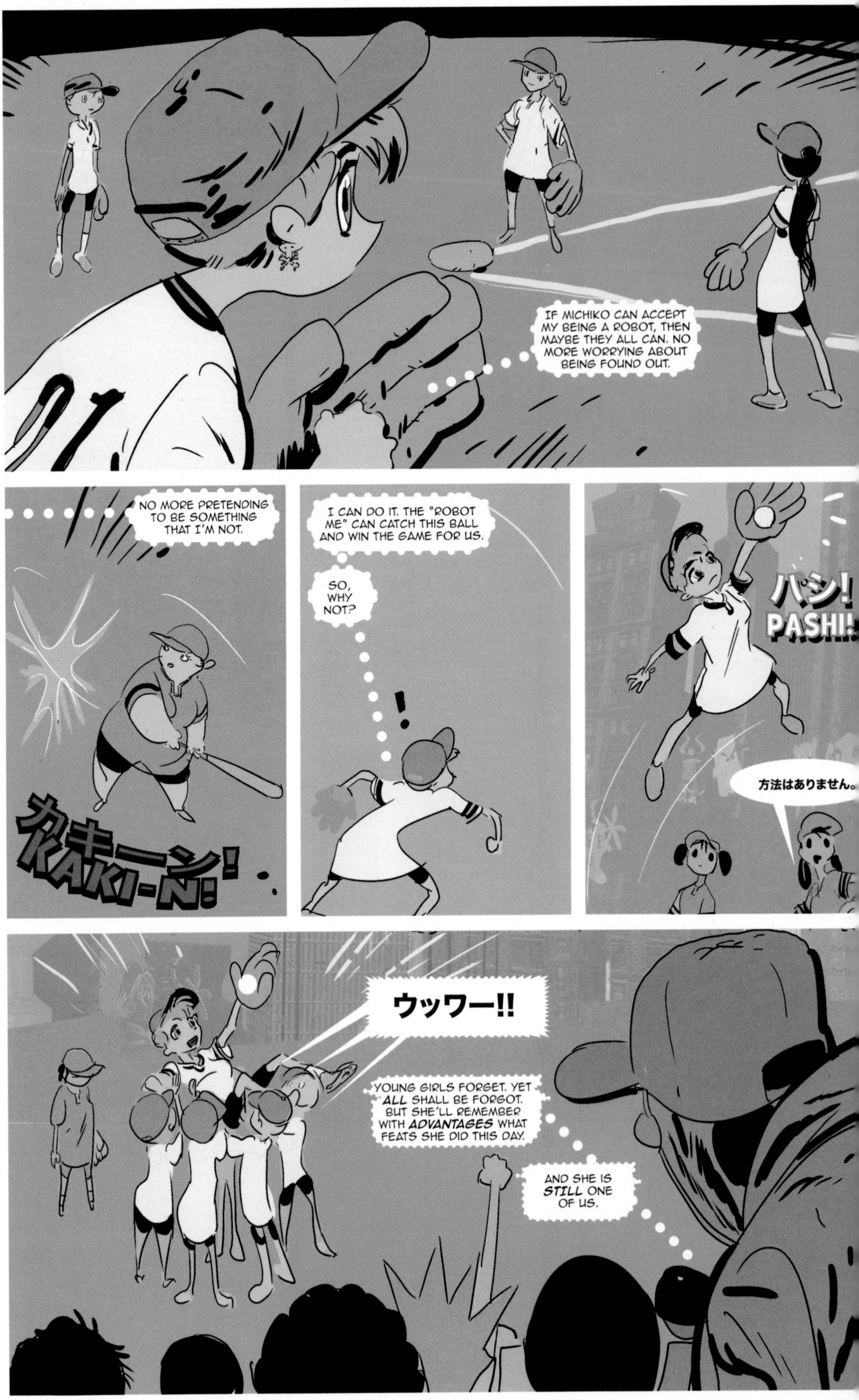
IF MICHIKO CAN ACCEPT MY BEING A ROBOT, THEN MAYBE THEY ALL CAN. NO MORE WORRYING ABOUT BEING FOUND OUT.
NO MORE PRETENDING TO BE SOMETHING THAT I'M NOT.
カキーン! KAKI-N!
I CAN DO IT. THE "ROBOT ME" CAN CATCH THIS BALL AND WIN THE GAME FOR US.
SO, WHY NOT?
!
パシ! PASHI!
方法はありません。
ウッワー!!
YOUNG GIRLS FORGET. YET ALL SHALL BE FORGOT. BUT SHE'LL REMEMBER WITH ADVANTAGES WHAT FEATS SHE DID THIS DAY.
AND SHE IS STILL ONE OF US.

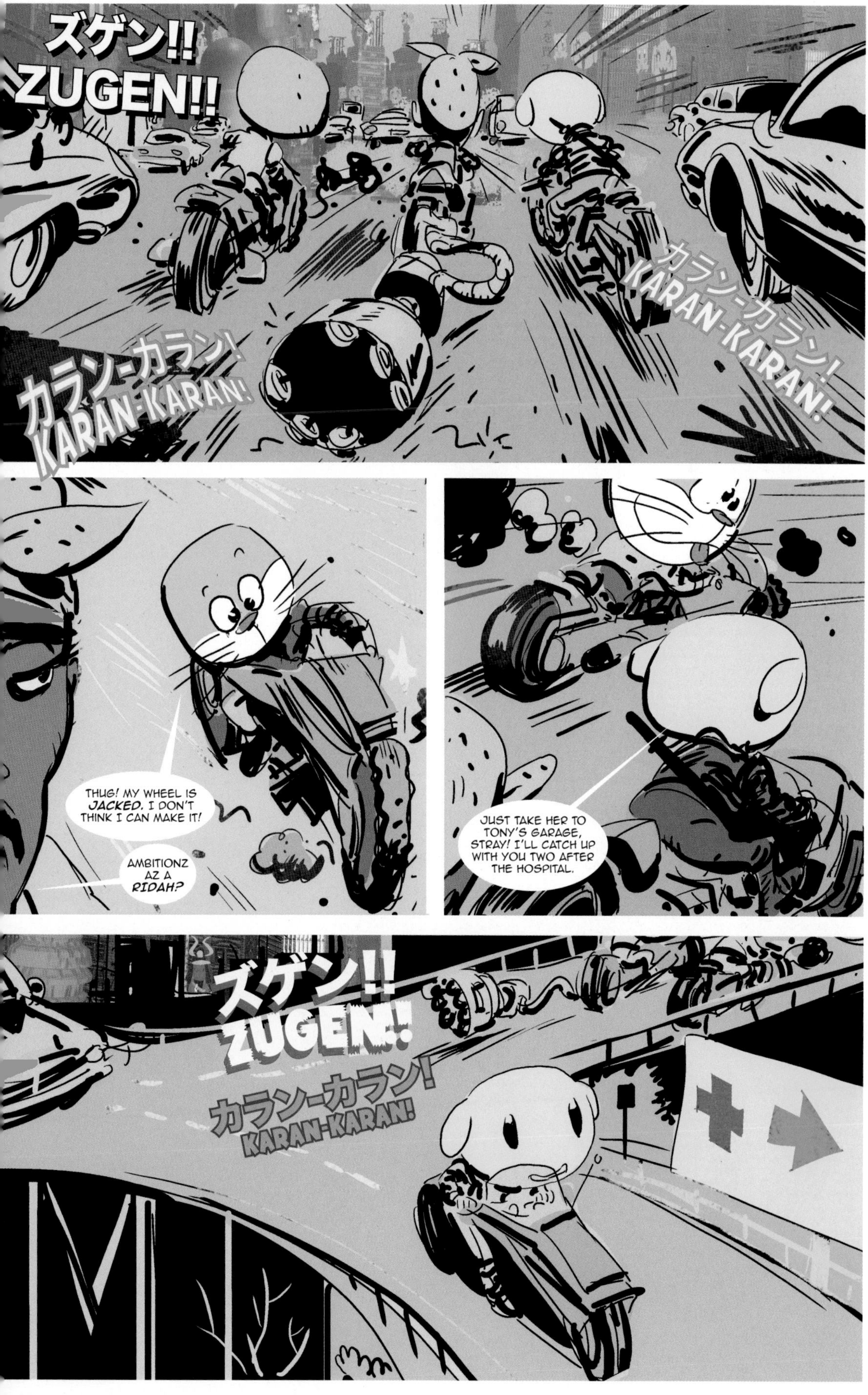
ズゲン!!
ZUGEN!!
カラン-カラン!
KARAN-KARAN!
カラン-カラン!
KARAN-KARAN!
THUG! MY WHEEL IS JACKED. I DON'T THINK I CAN MAKE IT!
AMBITIONZ AZ A RIDAH?
JUST TAKE HER TO TONY'S GARAGE, STRAY! I'LL CATCH UP WITH YOU TWO AFTER THE HOSPITAL.
ズゲン!!
ZUGEN!!
カラン-カラン!
KARAN-KARAN!

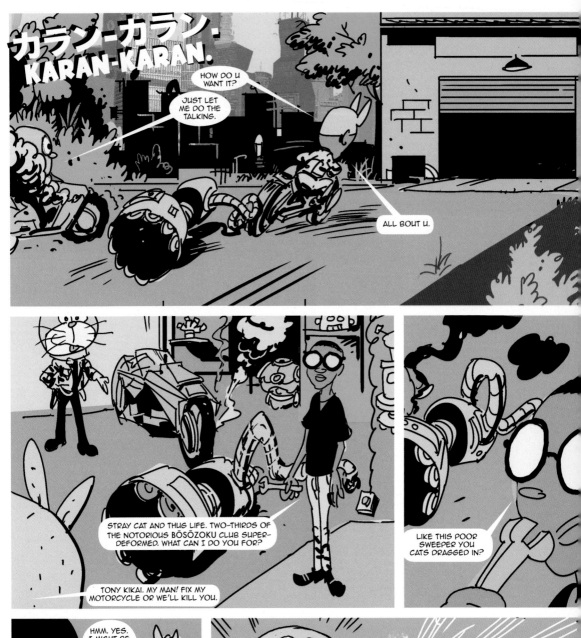

カラン-カラン.
KARAN-KARAN.

HOW DO U WANT IT?

JUST LET ME DO THE TALKING.

ALL BOUT U.

STRAY CAT AND THUG LIFE. TWO-THIRDS OF THE NOTORIOUS BŌSŌZOKU CLUB SUPER-DEFORMED. WHAT CAN I DO YOU FOR?

TONY KIKAI. MY MAN! FIX MY MOTORCYCLE OR WE'LL KILL YOU.

LIKE THIS POOR SWEEPER YOU CATS DRAGGED IN?

HMM. YES. I MIGHT BE ABLE TO REPAIR IT. DO YOU STILL HAVE THE HEAD?

ゴン!!
GON!!

JUST FIX MY BIKE --

-- WHILE YOU STILL HAVE YOURS!

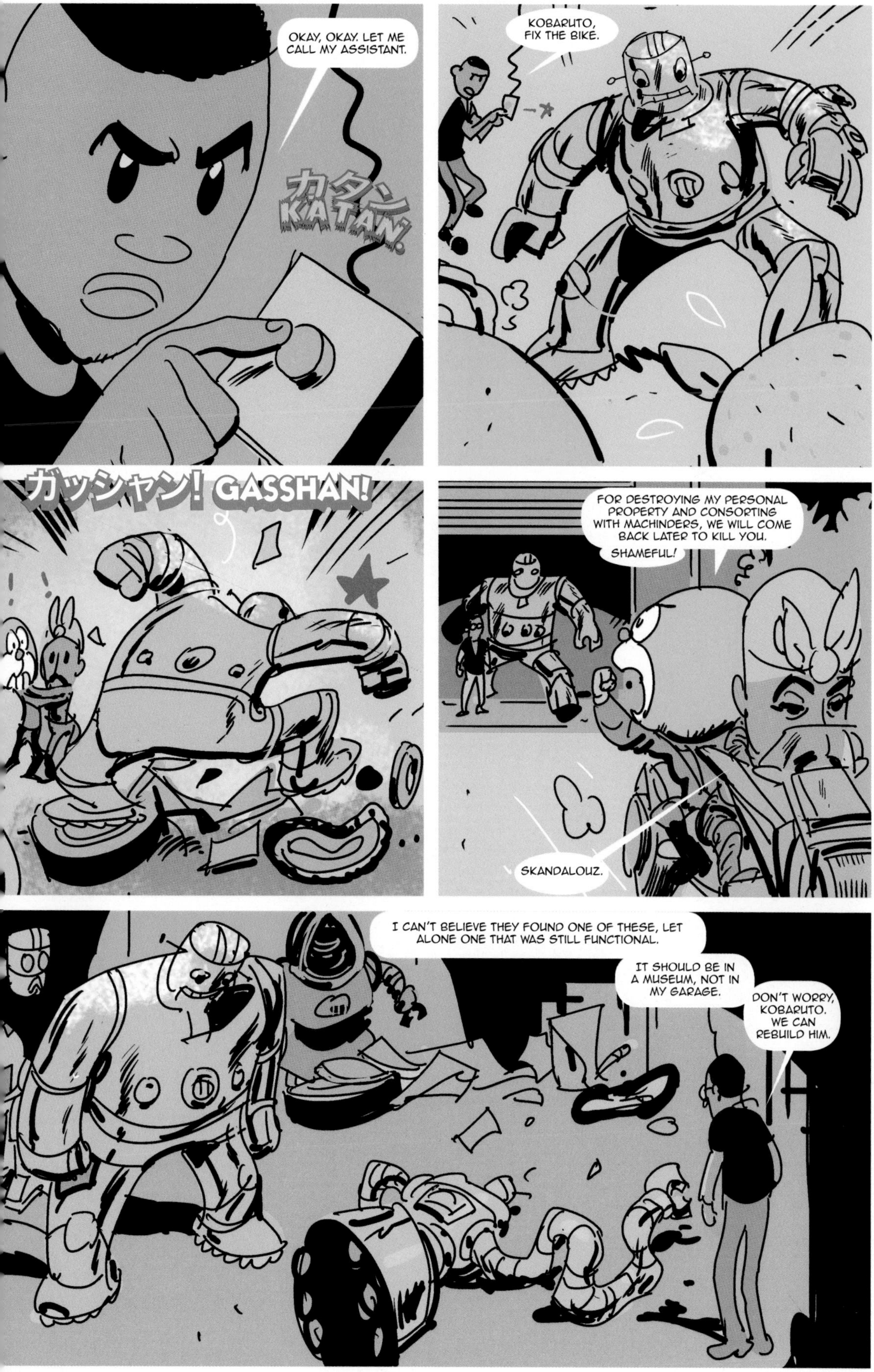
OKAY, OKAY. LET ME CALL MY ASSISTANT.
カタン KATAN!
KOBARUTO, FIX THE BIKE.
ガッシャン! GASSHAN!
FOR DESTROYING MY PERSONAL PROPERTY AND CONSORTING WITH MACHINDERS, WE WILL COME BACK LATER TO KILL YOU.
SHAMEFUL!
SKANDALOUZ.
I CAN'T BELIEVE THEY FOUND ONE OF THESE, LET ALONE ONE THAT WAS STILL FUNCTIONAL.
IT SHOULD BE IN A MUSEUM, NOT IN MY GARAGE.
DON'T WORRY, KOBARUTO. WE CAN REBUILD HIM.

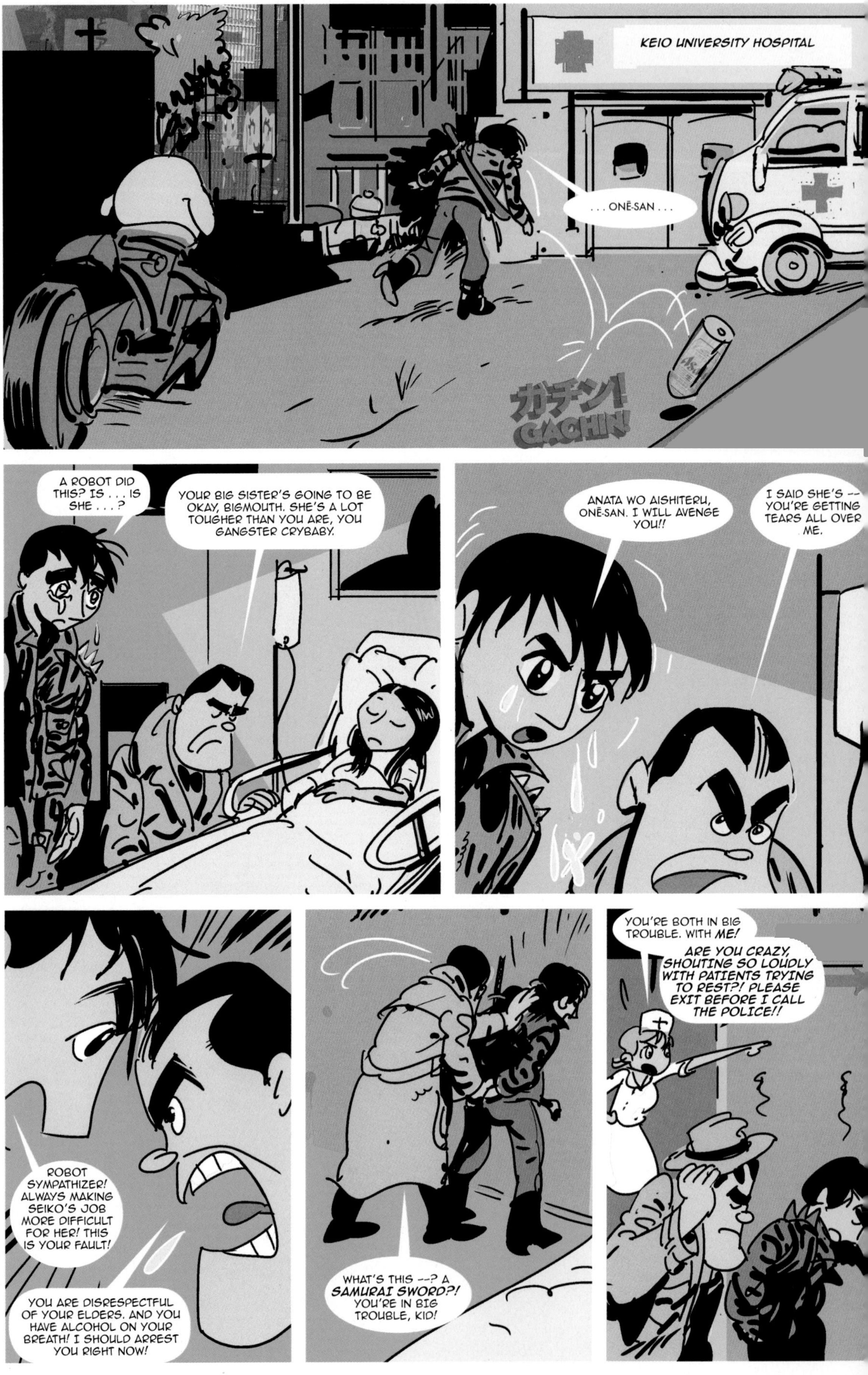
KEIO UNIVERSITY HOSPITAL
. . . ONĒ-SAN . . .
ガチン!
GACHIN!
A ROBOT DID THIS? IS . . . IS SHE . . . ?
YOUR BIG SISTER'S GOING TO BE OKAY, BIGMOUTH. SHE'S A LOT TOUGHER THAN YOU ARE, YOU GANGSTER CRYBABY.
ANATA WO AISHITERU, ONĒ-SAN. I WILL AVENGE YOU!!
I SAID SHE'S -- YOU'RE GETTING TEARS ALL OVER ME.
ROBOT SYMPATHIZER! ALWAYS MAKING SEIKO'S JOB MORE DIFFICULT FOR HER! THIS IS YOUR FAULT!
YOU ARE DISRESPECTFUL OF YOUR ELDERS. AND YOU HAVE ALCOHOL ON YOUR BREATH! I SHOULD ARREST YOU RIGHT NOW!
WHAT'S THIS --? A SAMURAI SWORD?! YOU'RE IN BIG TROUBLE, KID!
YOU'RE BOTH IN BIG TROUBLE. WITH ME!
ARE YOU CRAZY, SHOUTING SO LOUDLY WITH PATIENTS TRYING TO REST?! PLEASE EXIT BEFORE I CALL THE POLICE!!

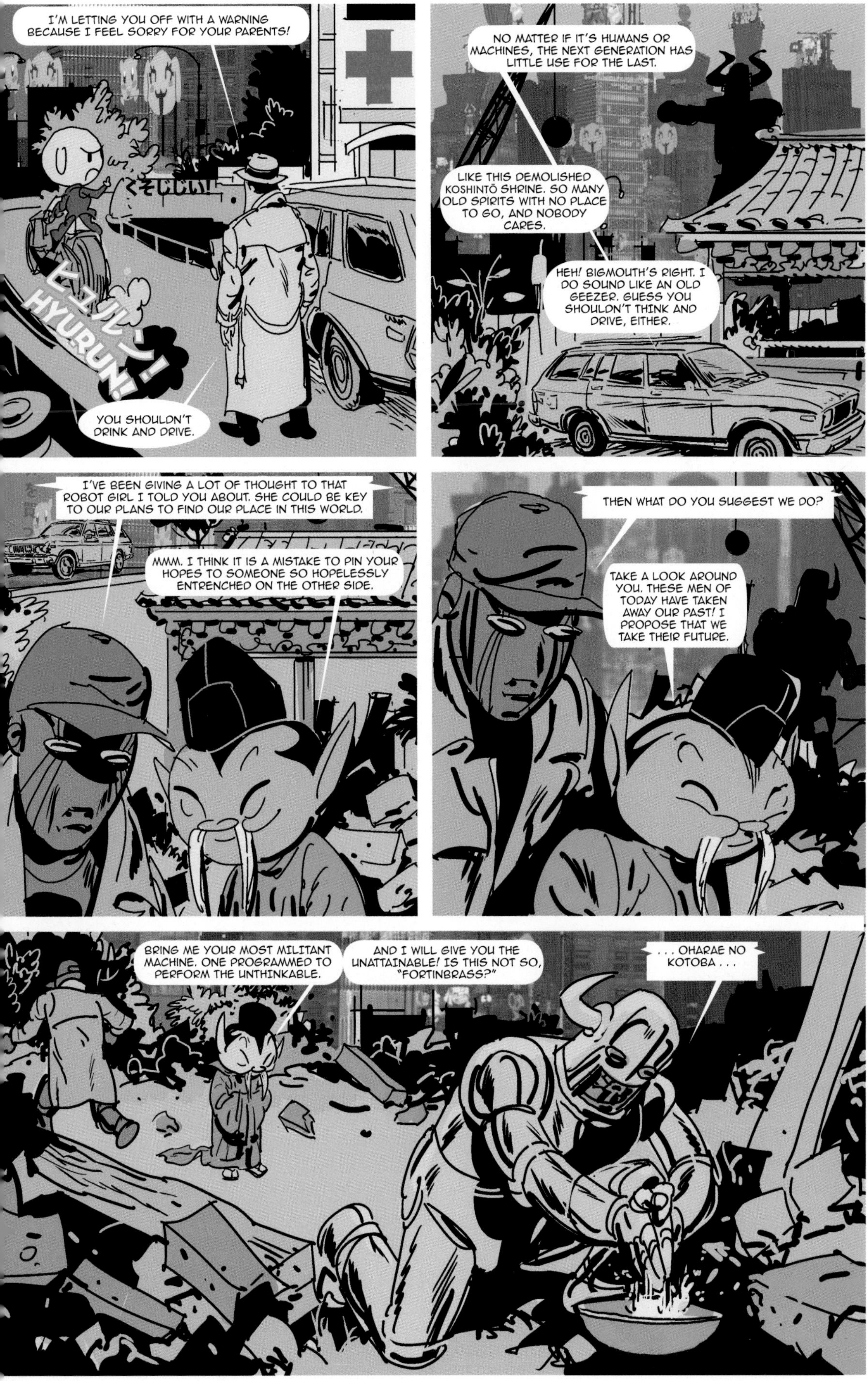
I'M LETTING YOU OFF WITH A WARNING BECAUSE I FEEL SORRY FOR YOUR PARENTS!
くそじじい!
ヒュルーン! HYURUN!
YOU SHOULDN'T DRINK AND DRIVE.
NO MATTER IF IT'S HUMANS OR MACHINES, THE NEXT GENERATION HAS LITTLE USE FOR THE LAST.
LIKE THIS DEMOLISHED KOSHINTŌ SHRINE. SO MANY OLD SPIRITS WITH NO PLACE TO GO, AND NOBODY CARES.
HEH! BIGMOUTH'S RIGHT. I DO SOUND LIKE AN OLD GEEZER. GUESS YOU SHOULDN'T THINK AND DRIVE, EITHER.
I'VE BEEN GIVING A LOT OF THOUGHT TO THAT ROBOT GIRL I TOLD YOU ABOUT. SHE COULD BE KEY TO OUR PLANS TO FIND OUR PLACE IN THIS WORLD.
MMM. I THINK IT IS A MISTAKE TO PIN YOUR HOPES TO SOMEONE SO HOPELESSLY ENTRENCHED ON THE OTHER SIDE.
THEN WHAT DO YOU SUGGEST WE DO?
TAKE A LOOK AROUND YOU. THESE MEN OF TODAY HAVE TAKEN AWAY OUR PAST! I PROPOSE THAT WE TAKE THEIR FUTURE.
BRING ME YOUR MOST MILITANT MACHINE. ONE PROGRAMMED TO PERFORM THE UNTHINKABLE.
AND I WILL GIVE YOU THE UNATTAINABLE! IS THIS NOT SO, "FORTINBRASS?"
. . . OHARAE NO KOTOBA . . .

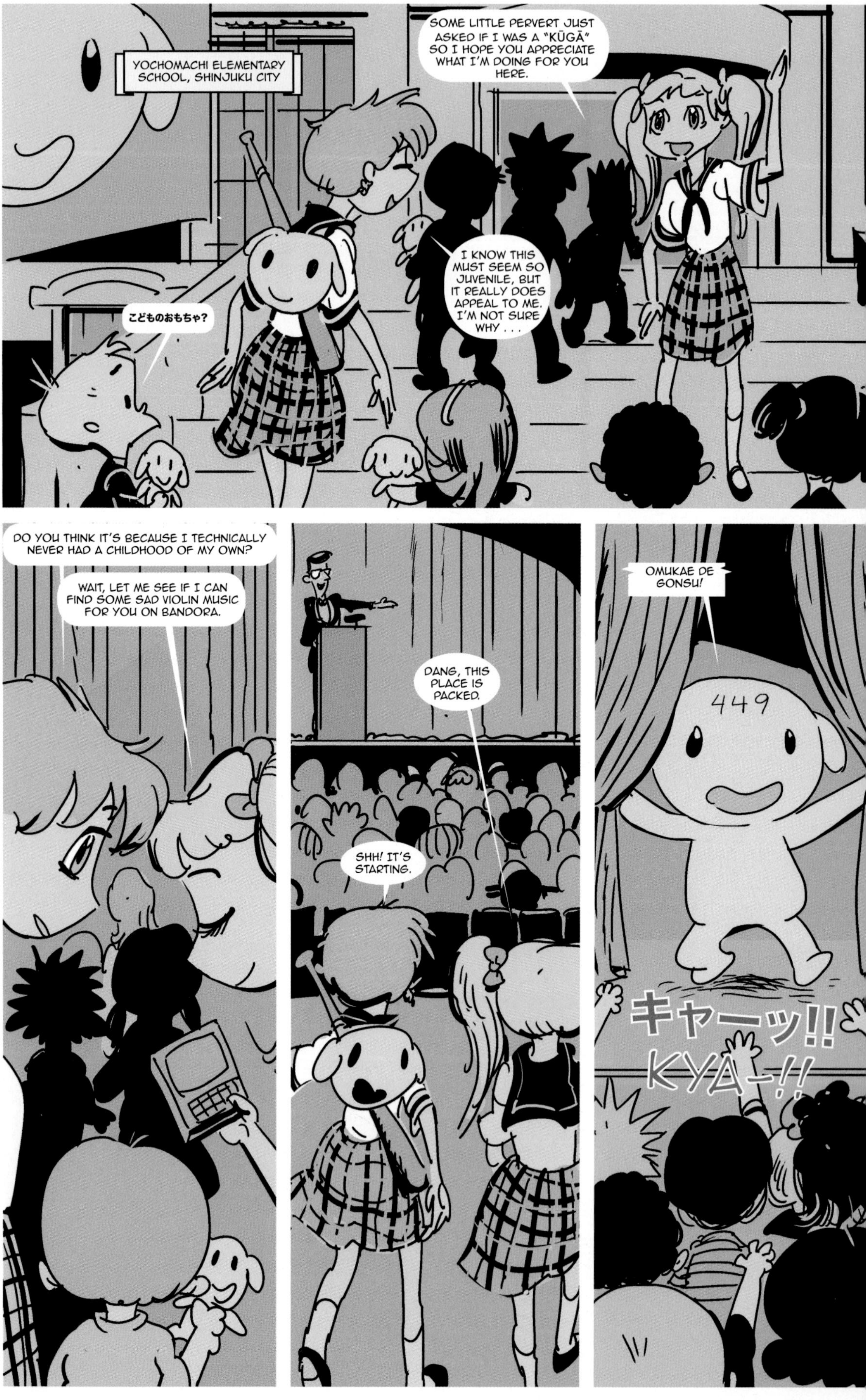

YOCHOMACHI ELEMENTARY SCHOOL, SHINJUKU CITY
SOME LITTLE PERVERT JUST ASKED IF I WAS A "KŪGĀ" SO I HOPE YOU APPRECIATE WHAT I'M DOING FOR YOU HERE.
I KNOW THIS MUST SEEM SO JUVENILE, BUT IT REALLY DOES APPEAL TO ME. I'M NOT SURE WHY . . .
こどものおもちゃ?
DO YOU THINK IT'S BECAUSE I TECHNICALLY NEVER HAD A CHILDHOOD OF MY OWN?
WAIT, LET ME SEE IF I CAN FIND SOME SAD VIOLIN MUSIC FOR YOU ON BANDORA.
DANG, THIS PLACE IS PACKED.
SHH! IT'S STARTING.
OMUKAE DE GONSU!
449
キャーッ!!
KYA-!!

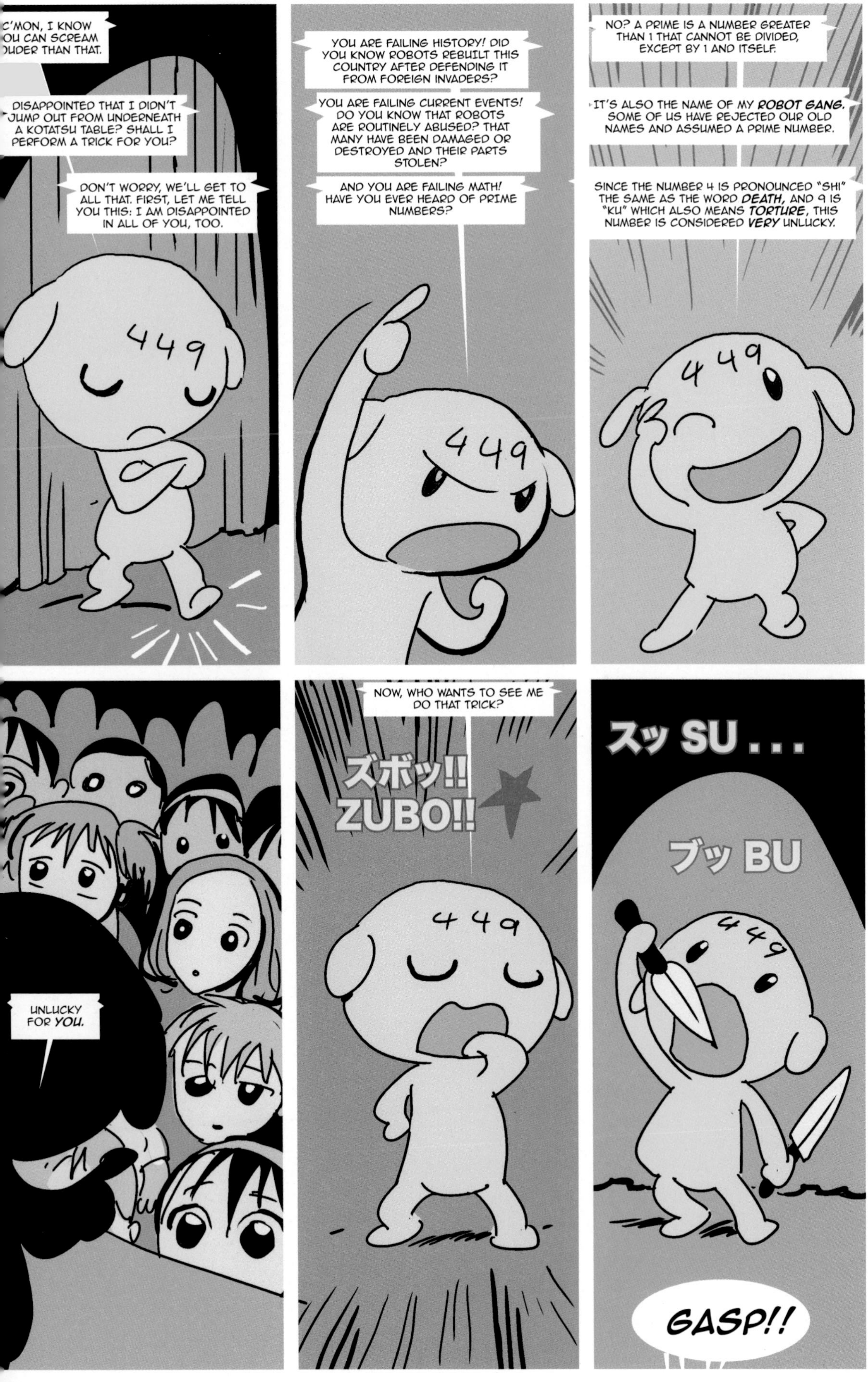
C'MON, I KNOW
OU CAN SCREAM
OUDER THAN THAT.
DISAPPOINTED THAT I DIDN'T JUMP OUT FROM UNDERNEATH A KOTATSU TABLE? SHALL I PERFORM A TRICK FOR YOU?
DON'T WORRY, WE'LL GET TO ALL THAT. FIRST, LET ME TELL YOU THIS: I AM DISAPPOINTED IN ALL OF YOU, TOO.
449
YOU ARE FAILING HISTORY! DID YOU KNOW ROBOTS REBUILT THIS COUNTRY AFTER DEFENDING IT FROM FOREIGN INVADERS?
YOU ARE FAILING CURRENT EVENTS! DO YOU KNOW THAT ROBOTS ARE ROUTINELY ABUSED? THAT MANY HAVE BEEN DAMAGED OR DESTROYED AND THEIR PARTS STOLEN?
AND YOU ARE FAILING MATH! HAVE YOU EVER HEARD OF PRIME NUMBERS?
449
NO? A PRIME IS A NUMBER GREATER THAN 1 THAT CANNOT BE DIVIDED, EXCEPT BY 1 AND ITSELF.
IT'S ALSO THE NAME OF MY ROBOT GANG. SOME OF US HAVE REJECTED OUR OLD NAMES AND ASSUMED A PRIME NUMBER.
SINCE THE NUMBER 4 IS PRONOUNCED "SHI" THE SAME AS THE WORD DEATH, AND 9 IS "KU" WHICH ALSO MEANS TORTURE, THIS NUMBER IS CONSIDERED VERY UNLUCKY.
449
UNLUCKY FOR YOU.
NOW, WHO WANTS TO SEE ME DO THAT TRICK?
ズボッ!! ZUBO!!
449
スッ SU . . .
ブッ BU
449
GASP!!

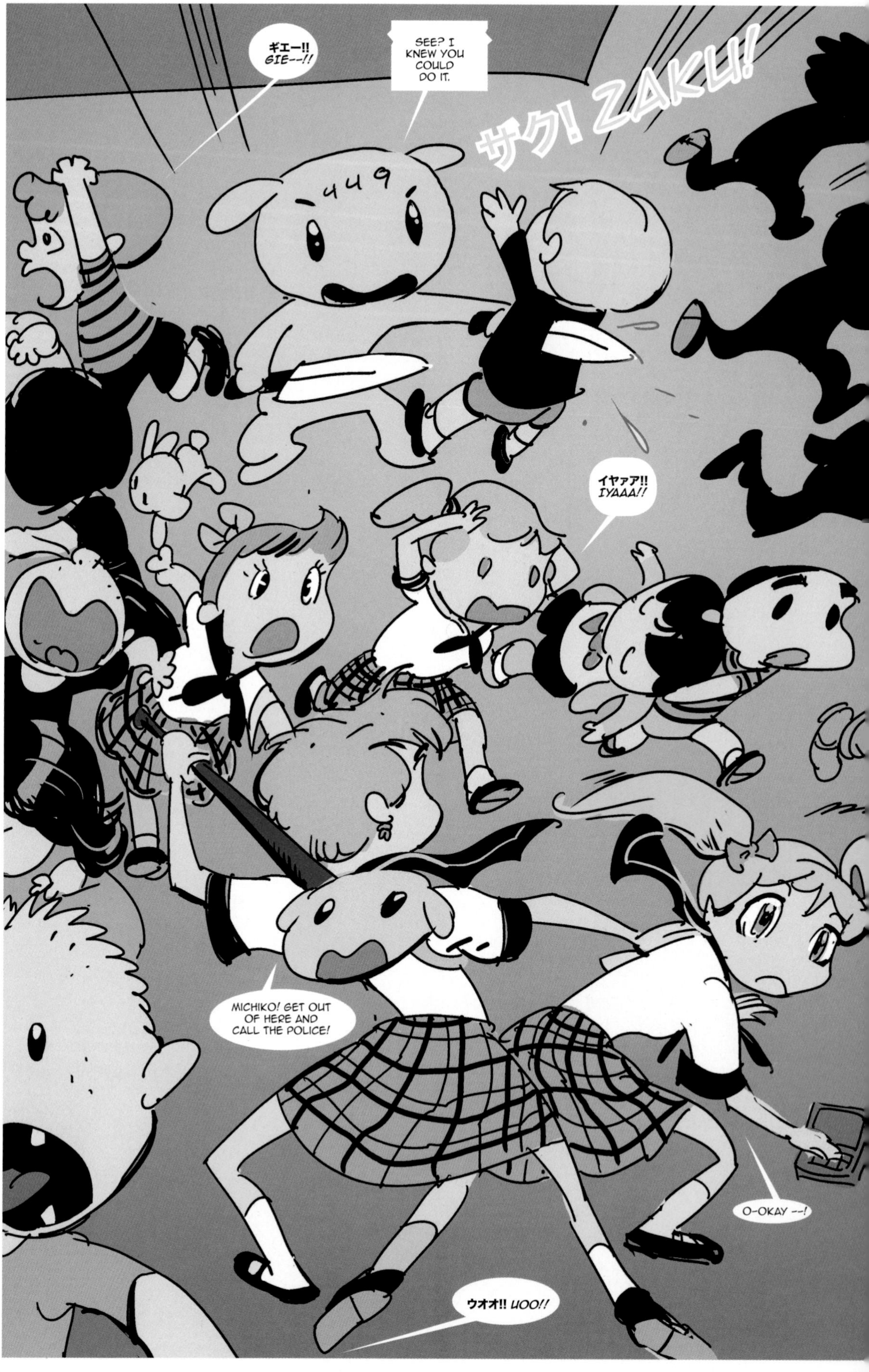
ギエー!! GIE--!!
SEE? I KNEW YOU COULD DO IT.
ザク! ZAKU!
イヤァア!! IYAAA!!
MICHIKO! GET OUT OF HERE AND CALL THE POLICE!
O-OKAY --!
ウオオ!! UOO!!

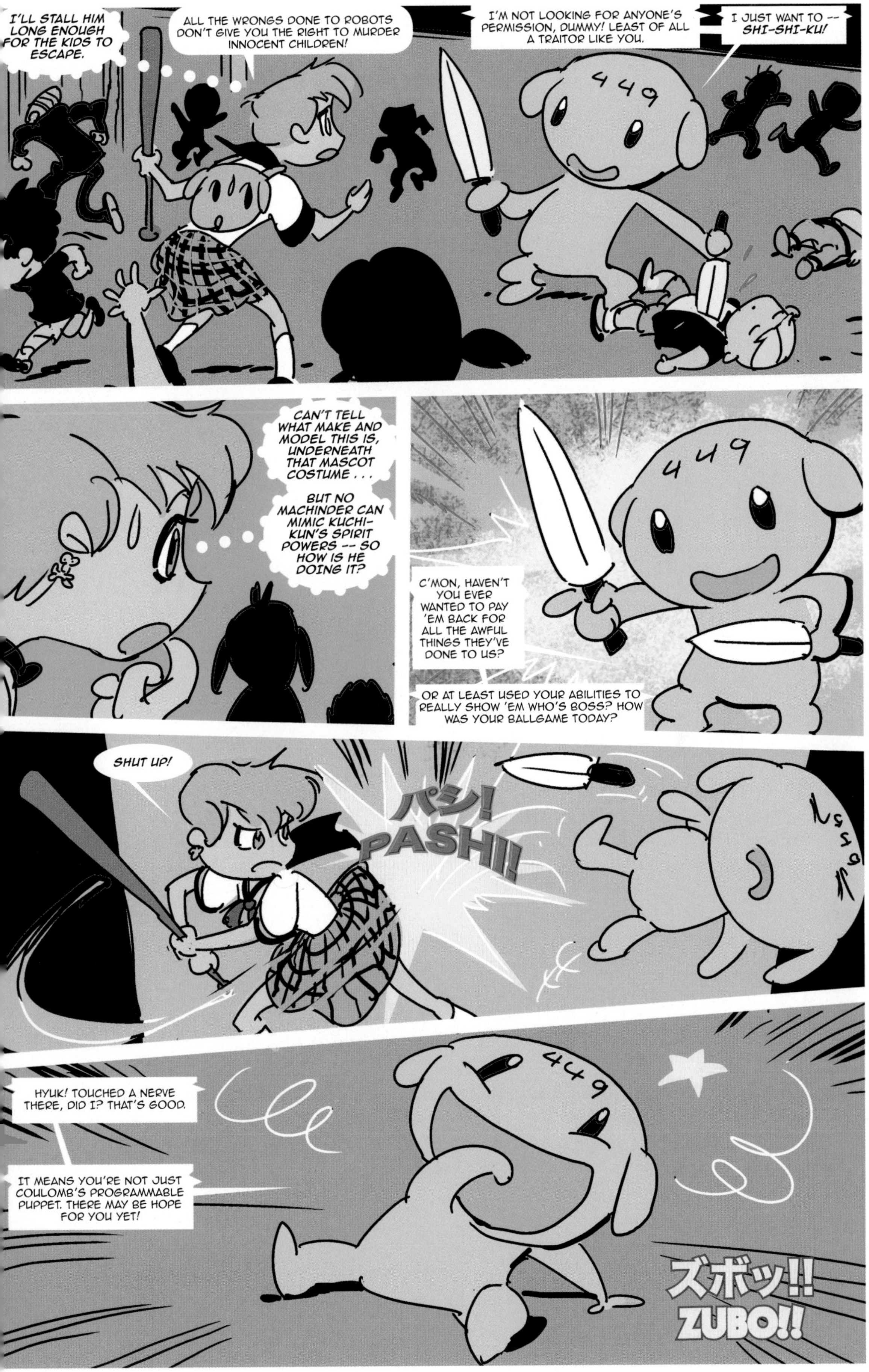
I'LL STALL HIM LONG ENOUGH FOR THE KIDS TO ESCAPE.
ALL THE WRONGS DONE TO ROBOTS DON'T GIVE YOU THE RIGHT TO MURDER INNOCENT CHILDREN!
I'M NOT LOOKING FOR ANYONE'S PERMISSION, DUMMY! LEAST OF ALL A TRAITOR LIKE YOU.
I JUST WANT TO -- SHI-SHI-KU!
449
CAN'T TELL WHAT MAKE AND MODEL THIS IS, UNDERNEATH THAT MASCOT COSTUME . . .
BUT NO MACHINDER CAN MIMIC KUCHI-KUN'S SPIRIT POWERS -- SO HOW IS HE DOING IT?
449
C'MON, HAVEN'T YOU EVER WANTED TO PAY 'EM BACK FOR ALL THE AWFUL THINGS THEY'VE DONE TO US?
OR AT LEAST USED YOUR ABILITIES TO REALLY SHOW 'EM WHO'S BOSS? HOW WAS YOUR BALLGAME TODAY?
SHUT UP!
パシ! PASHI!
449
HYUK! TOUCHED A NERVE THERE, DID I? THAT'S GOOD.
IT MEANS YOU'RE NOT JUST COULOMB'S PROGRAMMABLE PUPPET. THERE MAY BE HOPE FOR YOU YET!
449
ズボッ!! ZUBO!!

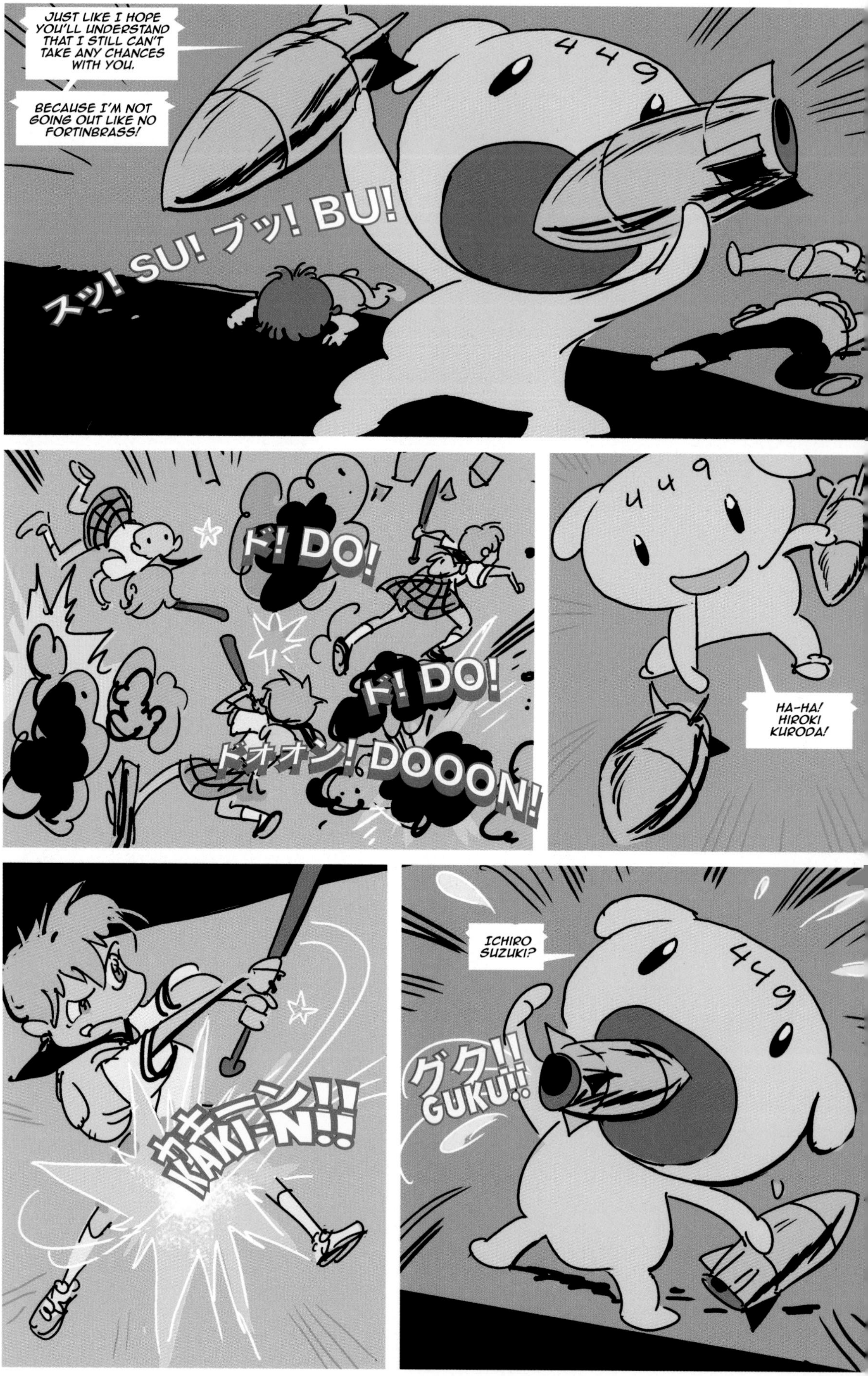

JUST LIKE I HOPE YOU'LL UNDERSTAND THAT I STILL CAN'T TAKE ANY CHANCES WITH YOU.
BECAUSE I'M NOT GOING OUT LIKE NO FORTINBRASS!
スッ! SU! ブッ! BU!
ド! DO!
ド! DO!
ドオオン! DOOOON!
HA-HA! HIROKI KURODA!
カキーン!! KAKI-N!!
ICHIRO SUZUKI?
グク!! GUKU!!

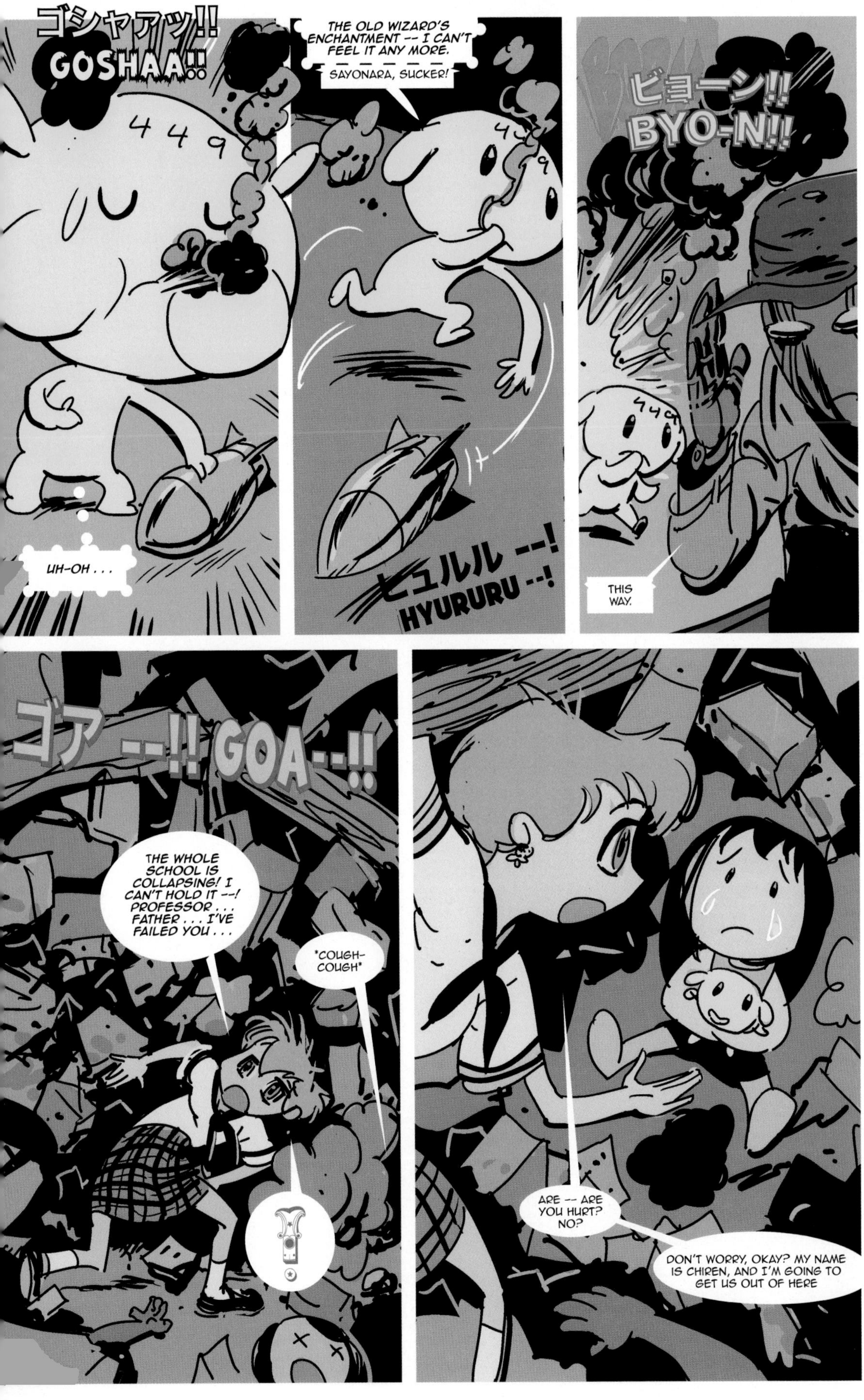
ゴシャアッ!!
GOSHAA!!
449
UH-OH . . .
THE OLD WIZARD'S ENCHANTMENT -- I CAN'T FEEL IT ANY MORE.
SAYONARA, SUCKER!
ヒュルルル --!
HYURURU --!
ビョーン!!
BYO-N!!
THIS WAY.
ゴア --!! GOA --!!
THE WHOLE SCHOOL IS COLLAPSING! I CAN'T HOLD IT --! PROFESSOR . . . FATHER . . . I'VE FAILED YOU . . .
COUGH-COUGH
ARE -- ARE YOU HURT? NO?
DON'T WORRY, OKAY? MY NAME IS CHIREN, AND I'M GOING TO GET US OUT OF HERE

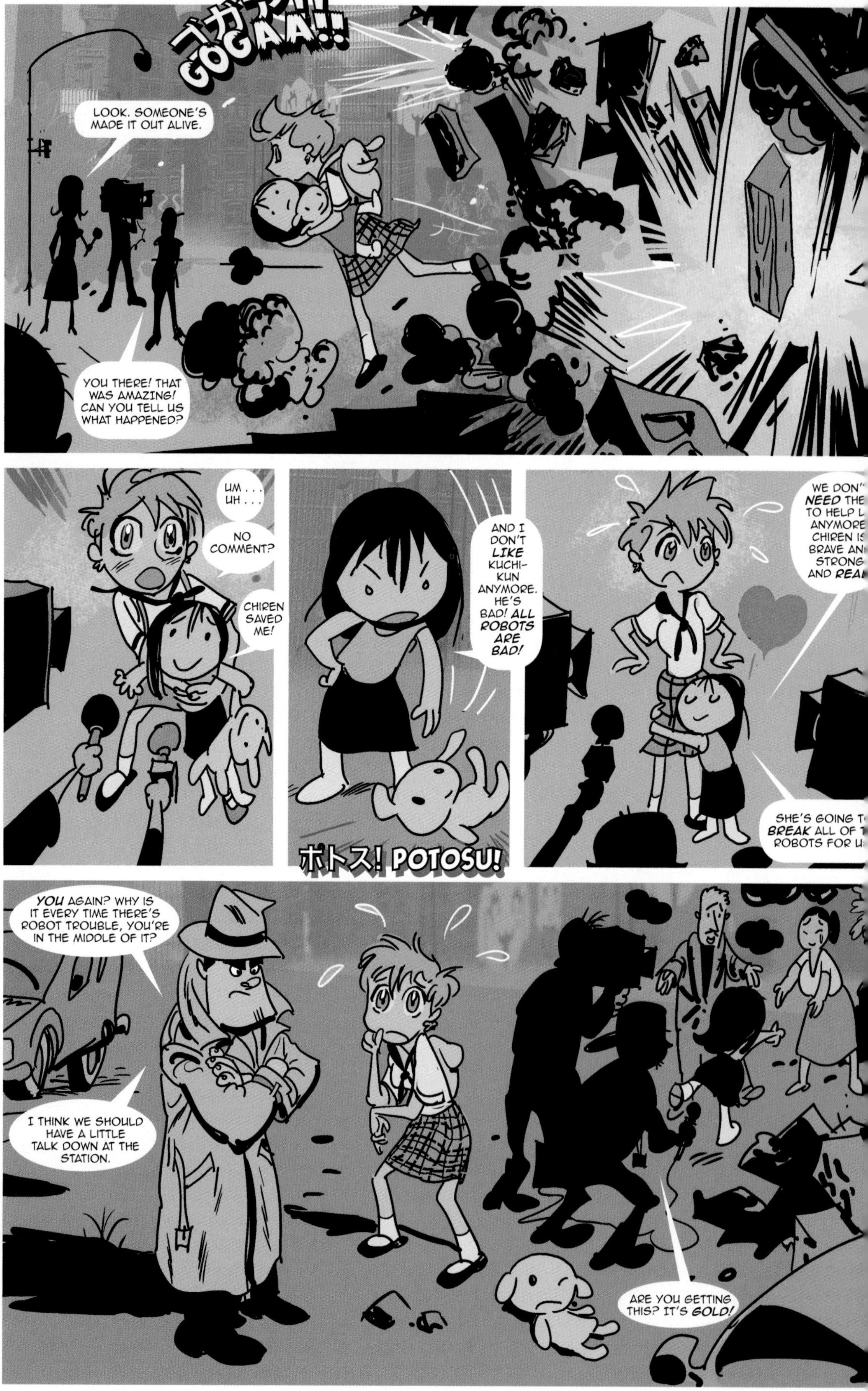
ゴガア!! GOGAA!!
LOOK. SOMEONE'S MADE IT OUT ALIVE.
YOU THERE! THAT WAS AMAZING! CAN YOU TELL US WHAT HAPPENED?
UM . . . UH . . .
NO COMMENT?
CHIREN SAVED ME!
AND I DON'T LIKE KUCHI-KUN ANYMORE. HE'S BAD! ALL ROBOTS ARE BAD!
ホトス! POTOSU!
SHE'S GOING T BREAK ALL OF T ROBOTS FOR U
YOU AGAIN? WHY IS IT EVERY TIME THERE'S ROBOT TROUBLE, YOU'RE IN THE MIDDLE OF IT?
I THINK WE SHOULD HAVE A LITTLE TALK DOWN AT THE STATION.
ARE YOU GETTING THIS? IT'S GOLD!

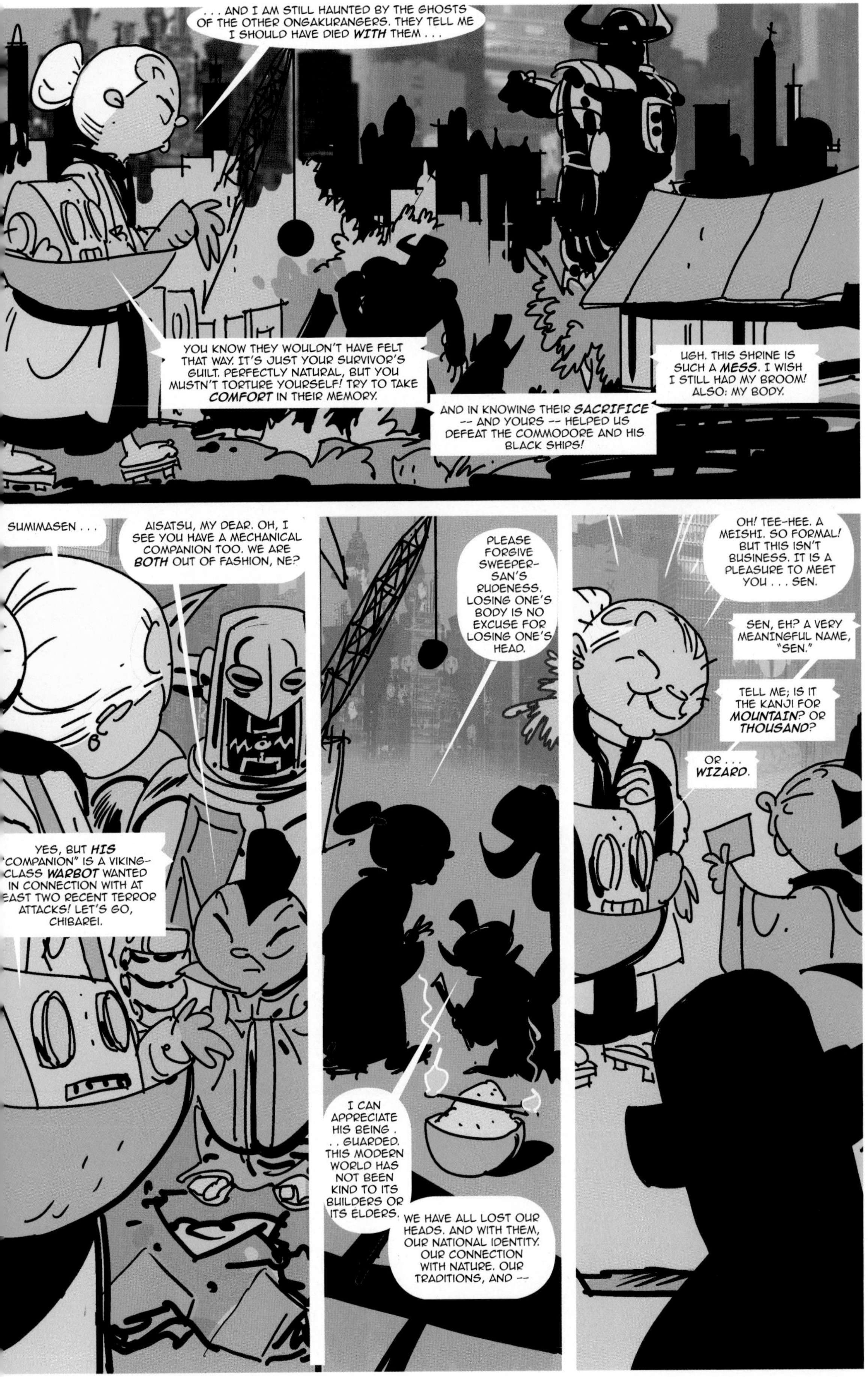

. . . AND I AM STILL HAUNTED BY THE GHOSTS OF THE OTHER ONGAKURANGERS. THEY TELL ME I SHOULD HAVE DIED WITH THEM . . .
YOU KNOW THEY WOULDN'T HAVE FELT THAT WAY. IT'S JUST YOUR SURVIVOR'S GUILT. PERFECTLY NATURAL, BUT YOU MUSTN'T TORTURE YOURSELF! TRY TO TAKE COMFORT IN THEIR MEMORY.
AND IN KNOWING THEIR SACRIFICE -- AND YOURS -- HELPED US DEFEAT THE COMMODORE AND HIS BLACK SHIPS!
UGH. THIS SHRINE IS SUCH A MESS. I WISH I STILL HAD MY BROOM! ALSO: MY BODY.
SUMIMASEN . . .
AISATSU, MY DEAR. OH, I SEE YOU HAVE A MECHANICAL COMPANION TOO. WE ARE BOTH OUT OF FASHION, NE?
YES, BUT HIS "COMPANION" IS A VIKING-CLASS WARBOT WANTED IN CONNECTION WITH AT LEAST TWO RECENT TERROR ATTACKS! LET'S GO, CHIBAREI.
PLEASE FORGIVE SWEEPER-SAN'S RUDENESS. LOSING ONE'S BODY IS NO EXCUSE FOR LOSING ONE'S HEAD.
I CAN APPRECIATE HIS BEING . . . GUARDED. THIS MODERN WORLD HAS NOT BEEN KIND TO ITS BUILDERS OR ITS ELDERS.
WE HAVE ALL LOST OUR HEADS. AND WITH THEM, OUR NATIONAL IDENTITY. OUR CONNECTION WITH NATURE. OUR TRADITIONS, AND --
OH! TEE-HEE. A MEISHI. SO FORMAL! BUT THIS ISN'T BUSINESS. IT IS A PLEASURE TO MEET YOU . . . SEN.
SEN, EH? A VERY MEANINGFUL NAME, "SEN."
TELL ME; IS IT THE KANJI FOR MOUNTAIN? OR THOUSAND?
OR . . . WIZARD.

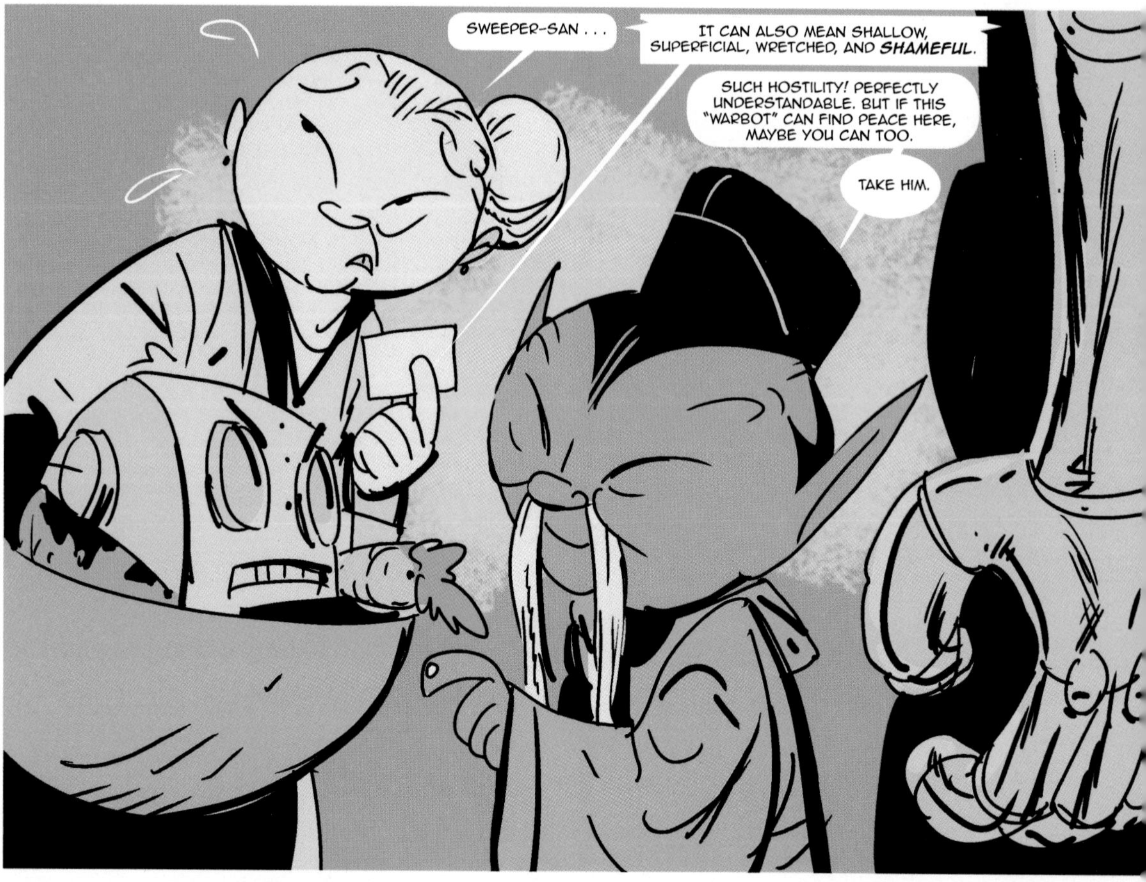
SWEEPER-SAN . . .
IT CAN ALSO MEAN SHALLOW, SUPERFICIAL, WRETCHED, AND *SHAMEFUL*.
SUCH HOSTILITY! PERFECTLY UNDERSTANDABLE. BUT IF THIS "WARBOT" CAN FIND PEACE HERE, MAYBE YOU CAN TOO.
TAKE HIM.

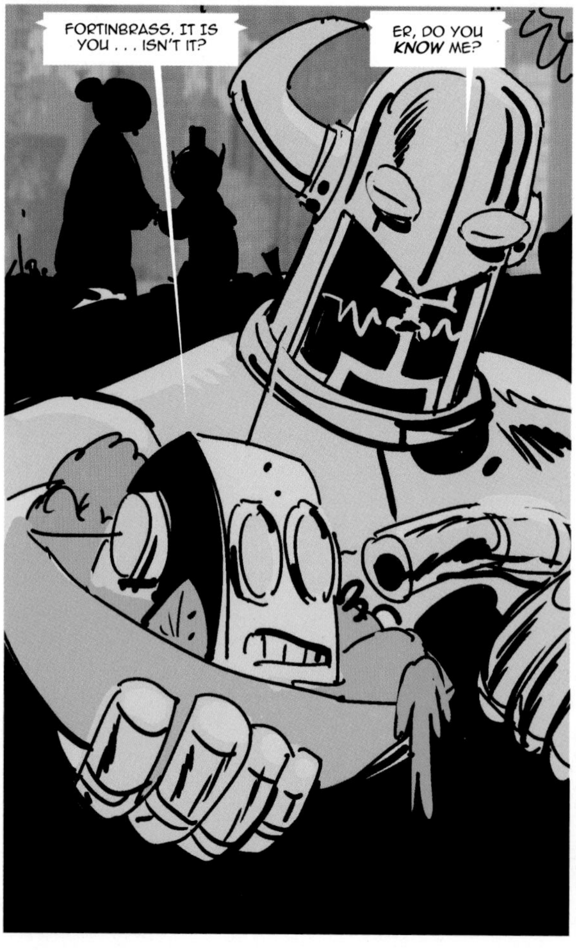
FORTINBRASS. IT IS YOU . . . ISN'T IT?
ER, DO YOU *KNOW* ME?

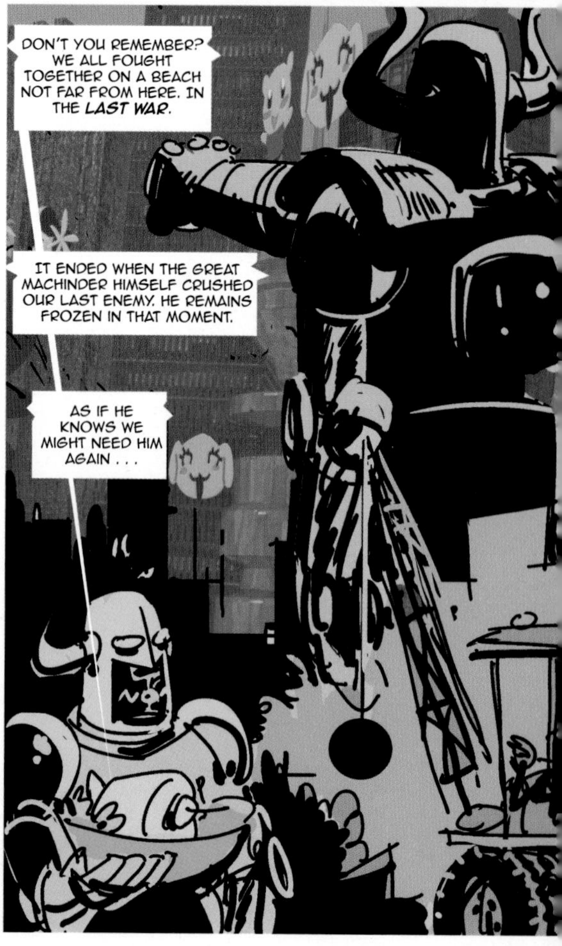
DON'T YOU REMEMBER? WE ALL FOUGHT TOGETHER ON A BEACH NOT FAR FROM HERE. IN THE *LAST WAR*.
IT ENDED WHEN THE GREAT MACHINDER HIMSELF CRUSHED OUR LAST ENEMY. HE REMAINS FROZEN IN THAT MOMENT.
AS IF HE KNOWS WE MIGHT NEED HIM AGAIN . . .

THREE

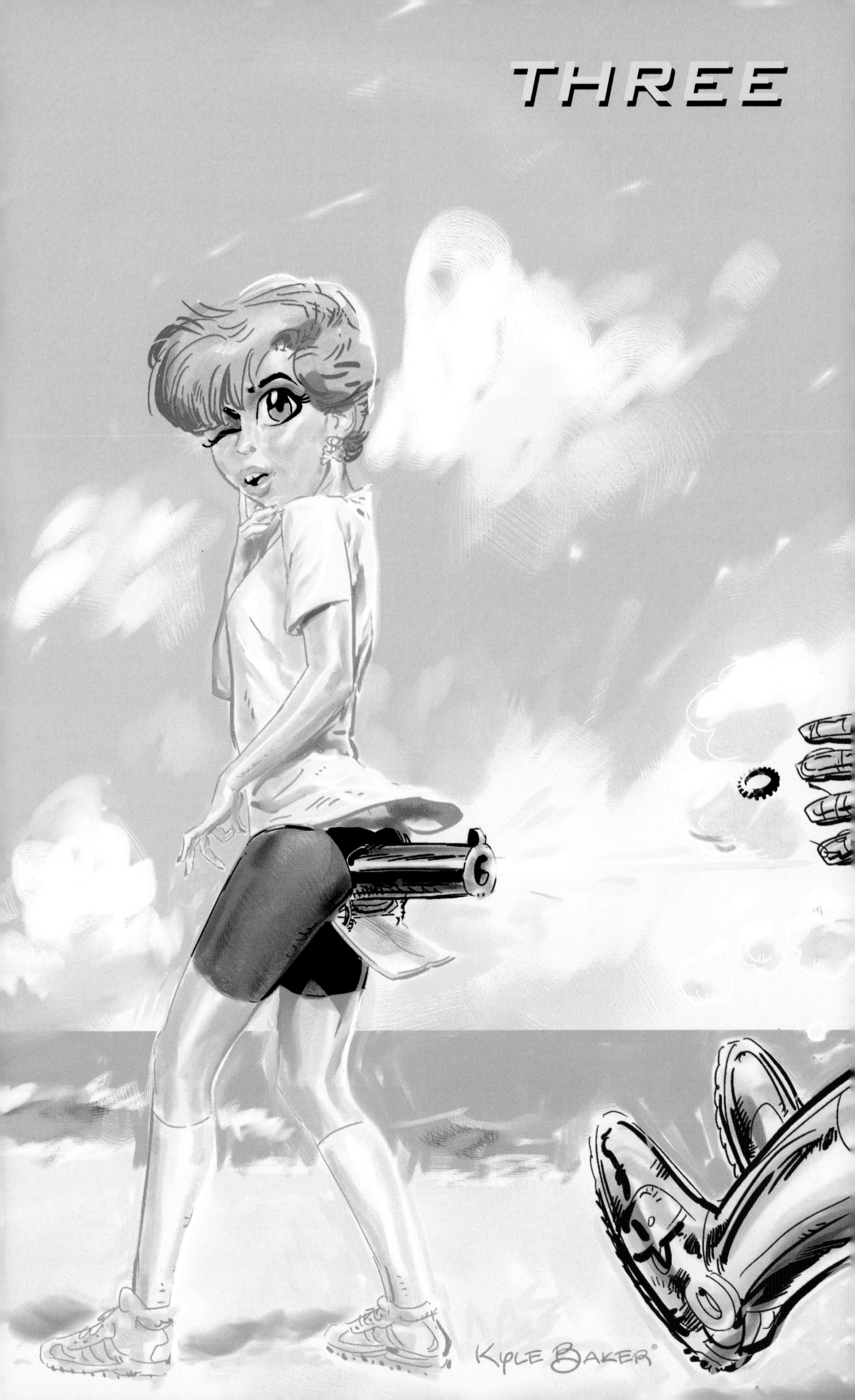
KYLE BAKER

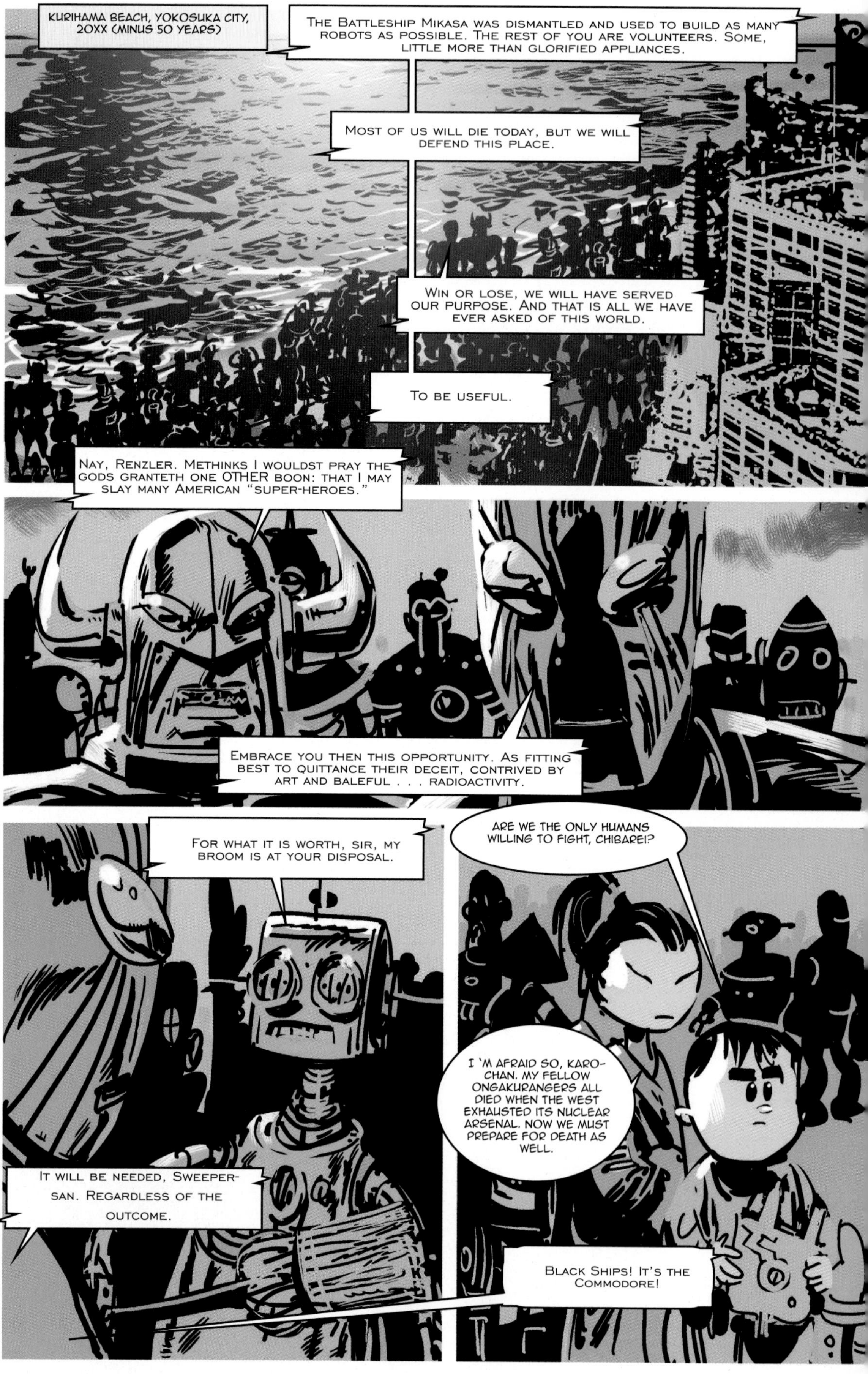
Kurihama Beach, Yokosuka City, 20XX (minus 50 years)
The Battleship Mikasa was dismantled and used to build as many robots as possible. The rest of you are volunteers. Some, little more than glorified appliances.
Most of us will die today, but we will defend this place.
Win or lose, we will have served our purpose. And that is all we have ever asked of this world.
To be useful.
Nay, Renzler. Methinks I wouldst pray the gods granteth one OTHER boon: that I may slay many American "super-heroes."
Embrace you then this opportunity. As fitting best to quittance their deceit, contrived by art and baleful . . . radioactivity.
For what it is worth, sir, my broom is at your disposal.
It will be needed, Sweeper-san. Regardless of the outcome.
Are we the only humans willing to fight, Chibarei?
I 'm afraid so, Karo-chan. My fellow Ongakurangers all died when the West exhausted its nuclear arsenal. Now we must prepare for death as well.
Black Ships! It's the Commodore!

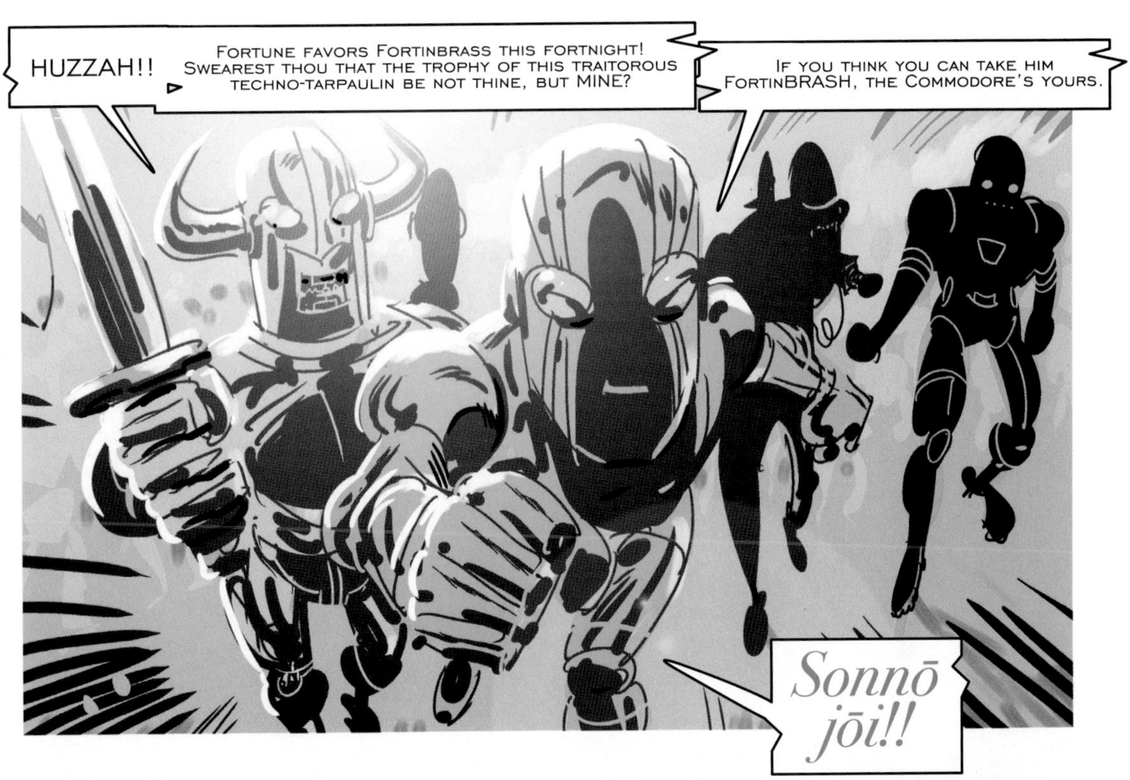
HUZZAH!!
Fortune favors Fortinbrass this fortnight! Swearest thou that the trophy of this traitorous techno-tarpaulin be not thine, but MINE?
If you think you can take him FortinBRASH, the Commodore's yours.
Sonnō jōi!!

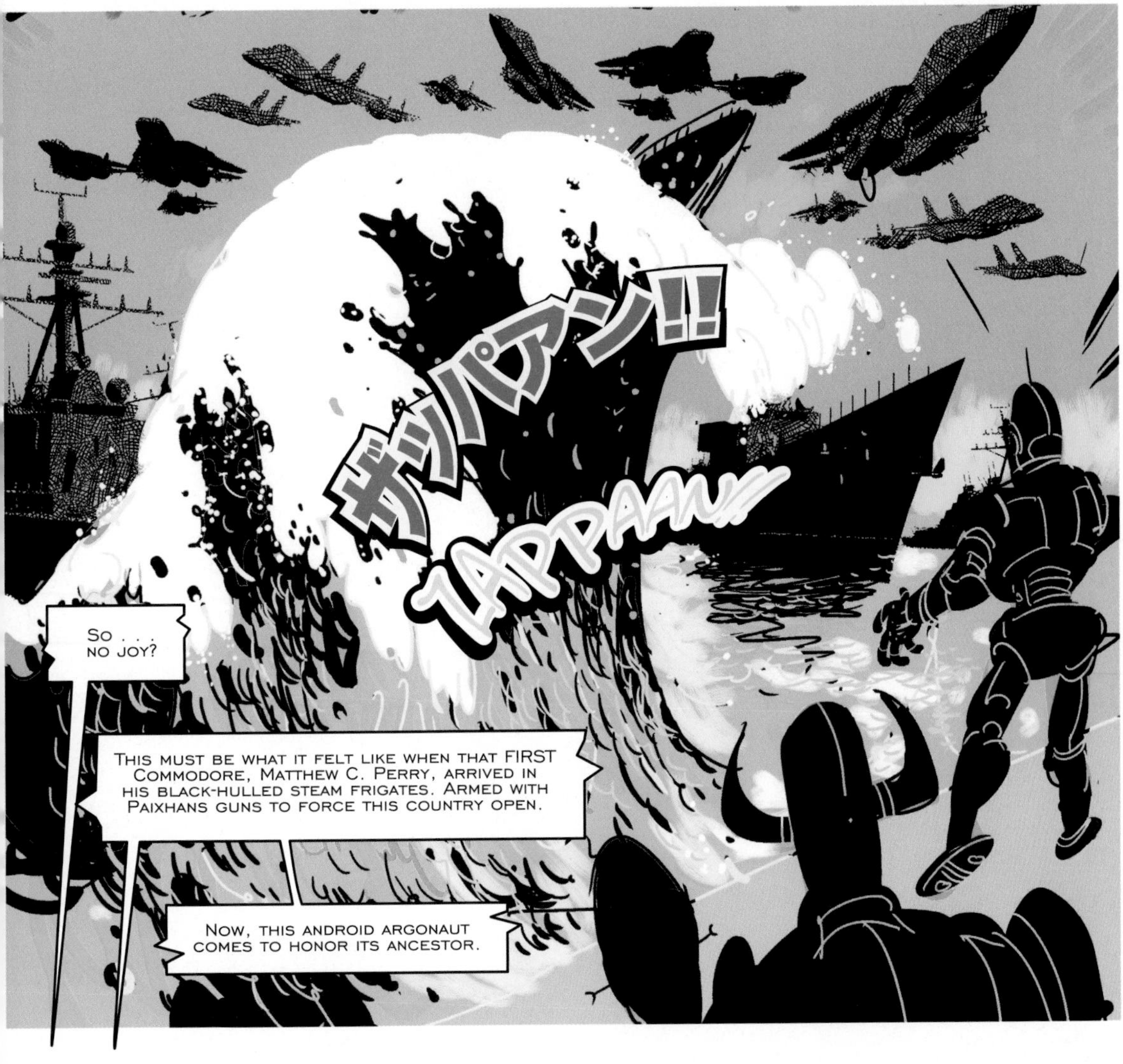
ザッパアン!!
ZAPPAAN!!
So . . . no joy?
This must be what it felt like when that FIRST Commodore, Matthew C. Perry, arrived in his black-hulled steam frigates. Armed with Paixhans guns to force this country open.
Now, this android argonaut comes to honor its ancestor.

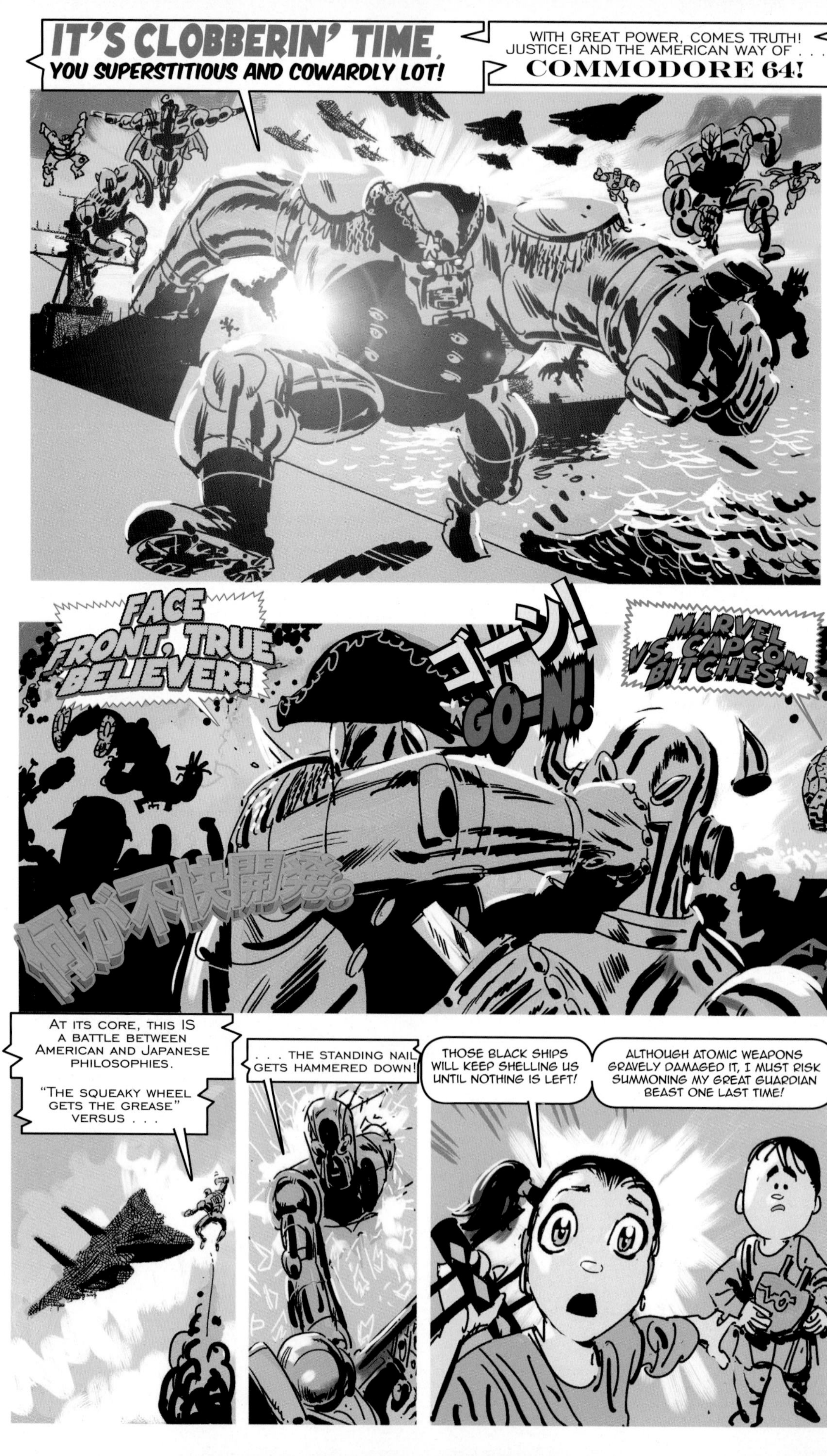
IT'S CLOBBERIN' TIME, YOU SUPERSTITIOUS AND COWARDLY LOT!
WITH GREAT POWER, COMES TRUTH! JUSTICE! AND THE AMERICAN WAY OF . . . COMMODORE 64!
FACE FRONT, TRUE BELIEVER!
ゴーン!
GO-N!
MARVEL VS. CAPCOM, BITCHES!
何が不快開発。
AT ITS CORE, THIS IS A BATTLE BETWEEN AMERICAN AND JAPANESE PHILOSOPHIES.
"THE SQUEAKY WHEEL GETS THE GREASE" VERSUS . . .
. . . THE STANDING NAIL GETS HAMMERED DOWN!
THOSE BLACK SHIPS WILL KEEP SHELLING US UNTIL NOTHING IS LEFT!
ALTHOUGH ATOMIC WEAPONS GRAVELY DAMAGED IT, I MUST RISK SUMMONING MY GREAT GUARDIAN BEAST ONE LAST TIME!

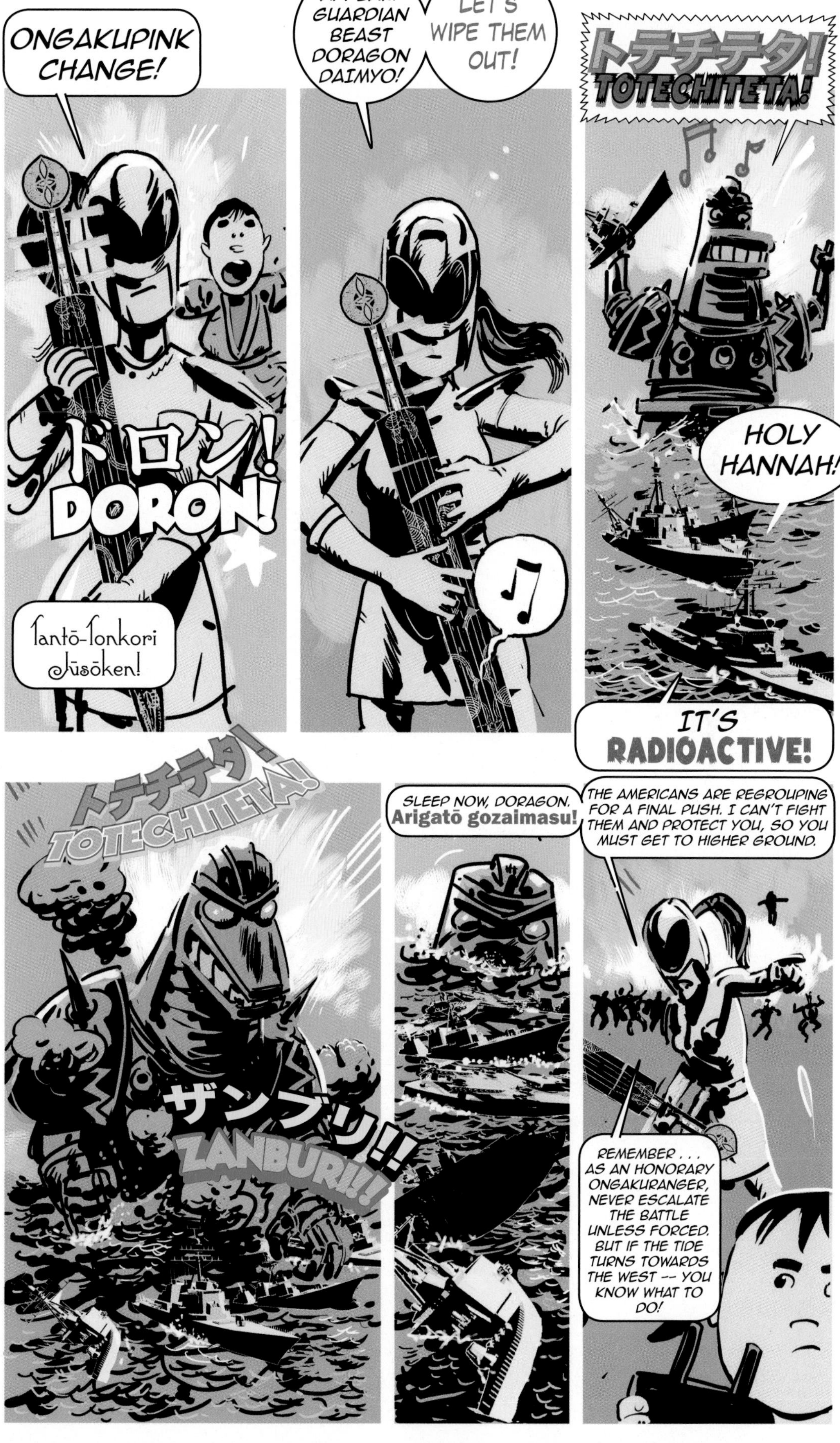
ONGAKUPINK CHANGE!
ドロン! DORON!
Tantō-Tonkori Jūsōken!
APPEAR! GUARDIAN BEAST DORAGON DAIMYO!
LET'S WIPE THEM OUT!
トテチテタ! TOTECHITETA!
HOLY HANNAH!
IT'S RADIOACTIVE!
トテチテタ! TOTECHITETA!
ザンブリ!! ZANBURI!!!
SLEEP NOW, DORAGON. Arigatō gozaimasu!
THE AMERICANS ARE REGROUPING FOR A FINAL PUSH. I CAN'T FIGHT THEM AND PROTECT YOU, SO YOU MUST GET TO HIGHER GROUND.
REMEMBER . . . AS AN HONORARY ONGAKURANGER, NEVER ESCALATE THE BATTLE UNLESS FORCED. BUT IF THE TIDE TURNS TOWARDS THE WEST -- YOU KNOW WHAT TO DO!

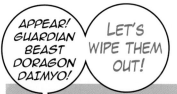

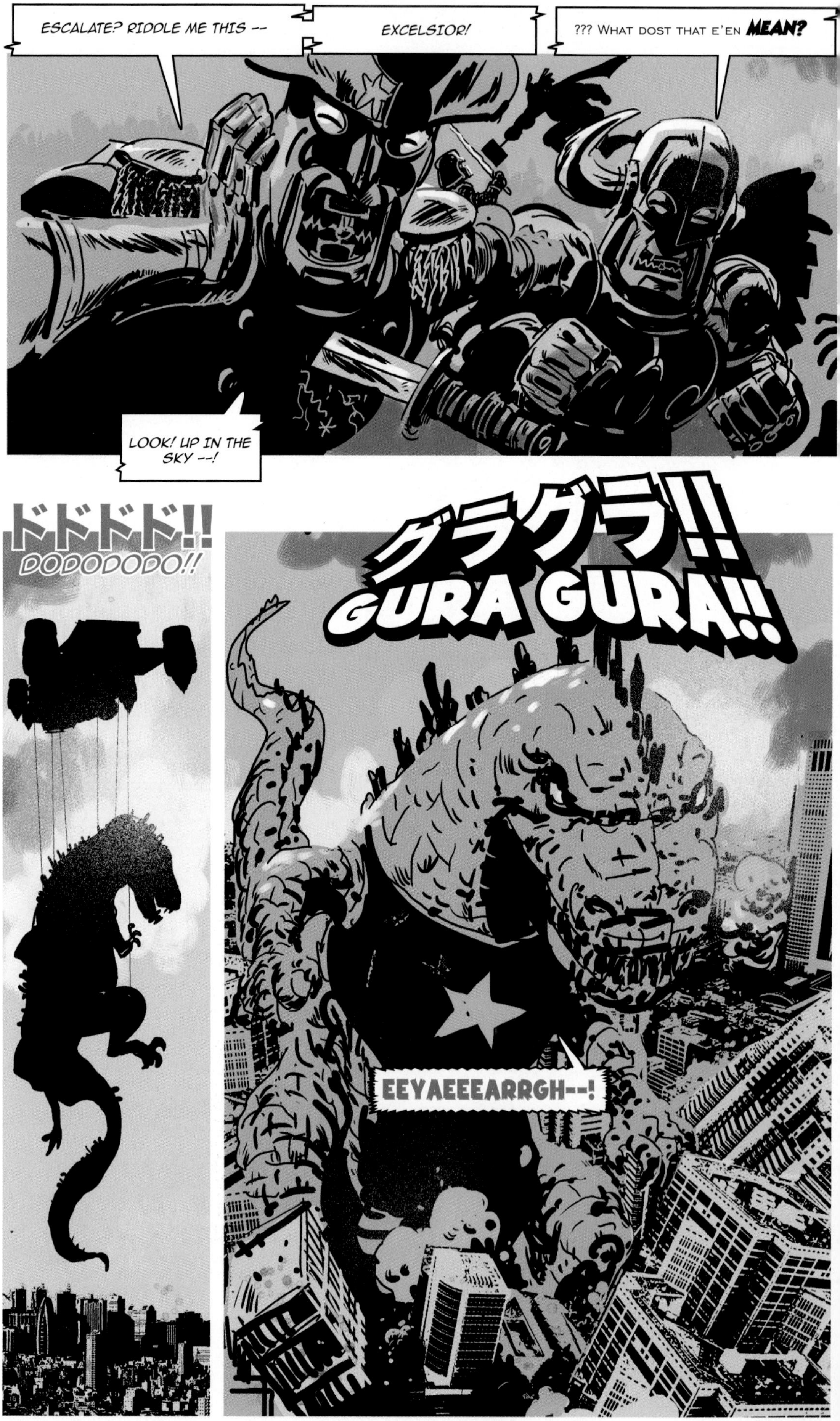
ESCALATE? RIDDLE ME THIS --
EXCELSIOR!
??? WHAT DOST THAT E'EN MEAN?
LOOK! UP IN THE SKY --!
ドドドド!!
DODODODO!!
グラグラ!!
GURA GURA!!
EEYAEEEARRGH--!

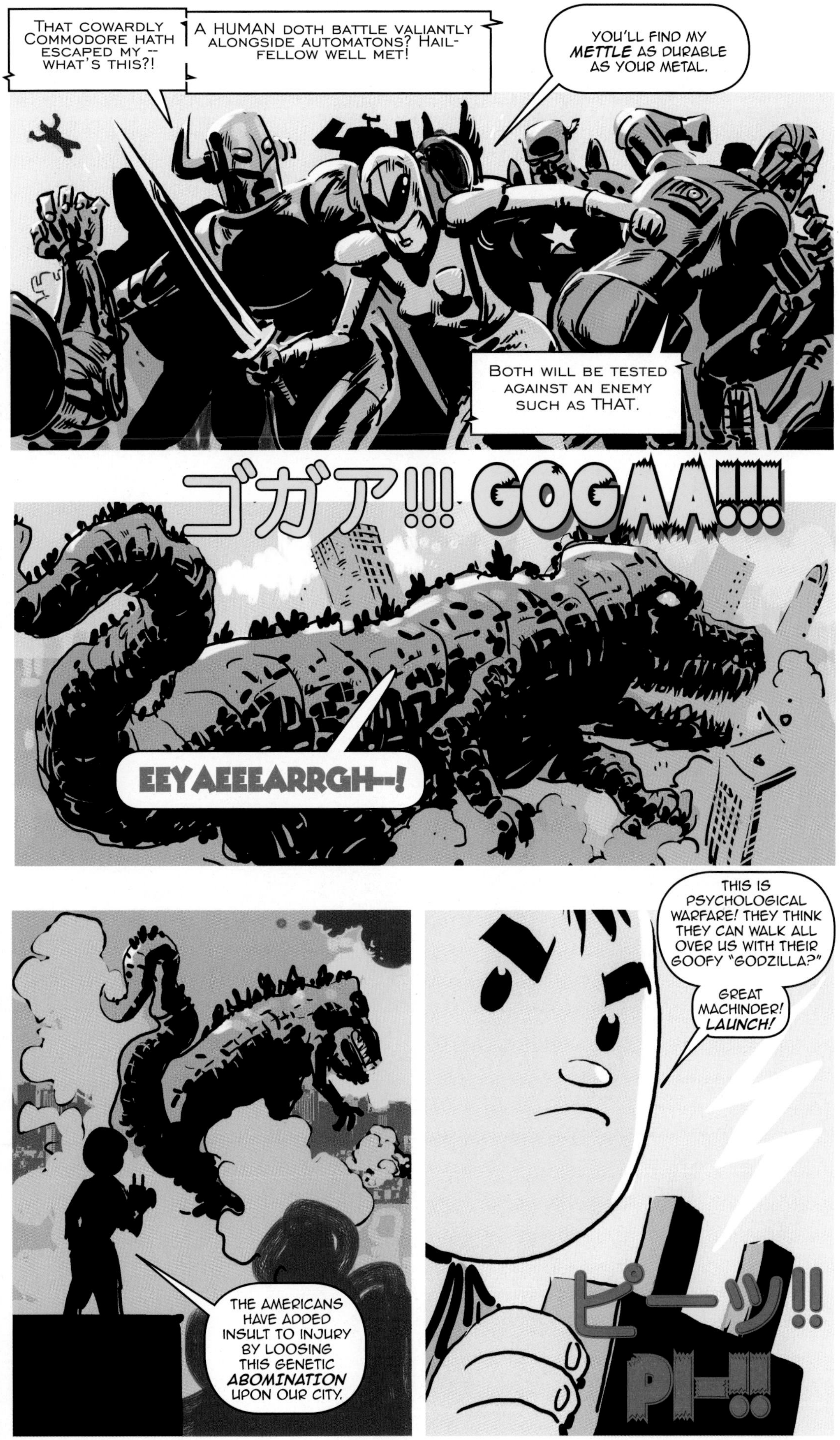
That cowardly Commodore hath escaped my -- what's this?!
A HUMAN doth battle valiantly alongside automatons? Hail-fellow well met!
You'll find my *METTLE* as durable as your metal.
Both will be tested against an enemy such as THAT.
ゴガア!!! GOGAA!!!
EEYAEEEARRGH--!
The Americans have added insult to injury by loosing this genetic *ABOMINATION* upon our city.
This is psychological warfare! They think they can walk all over us with their goofy "Godzilla?"
Great Machinder! *LAUNCH!*
ピーッ!!
PI-!!

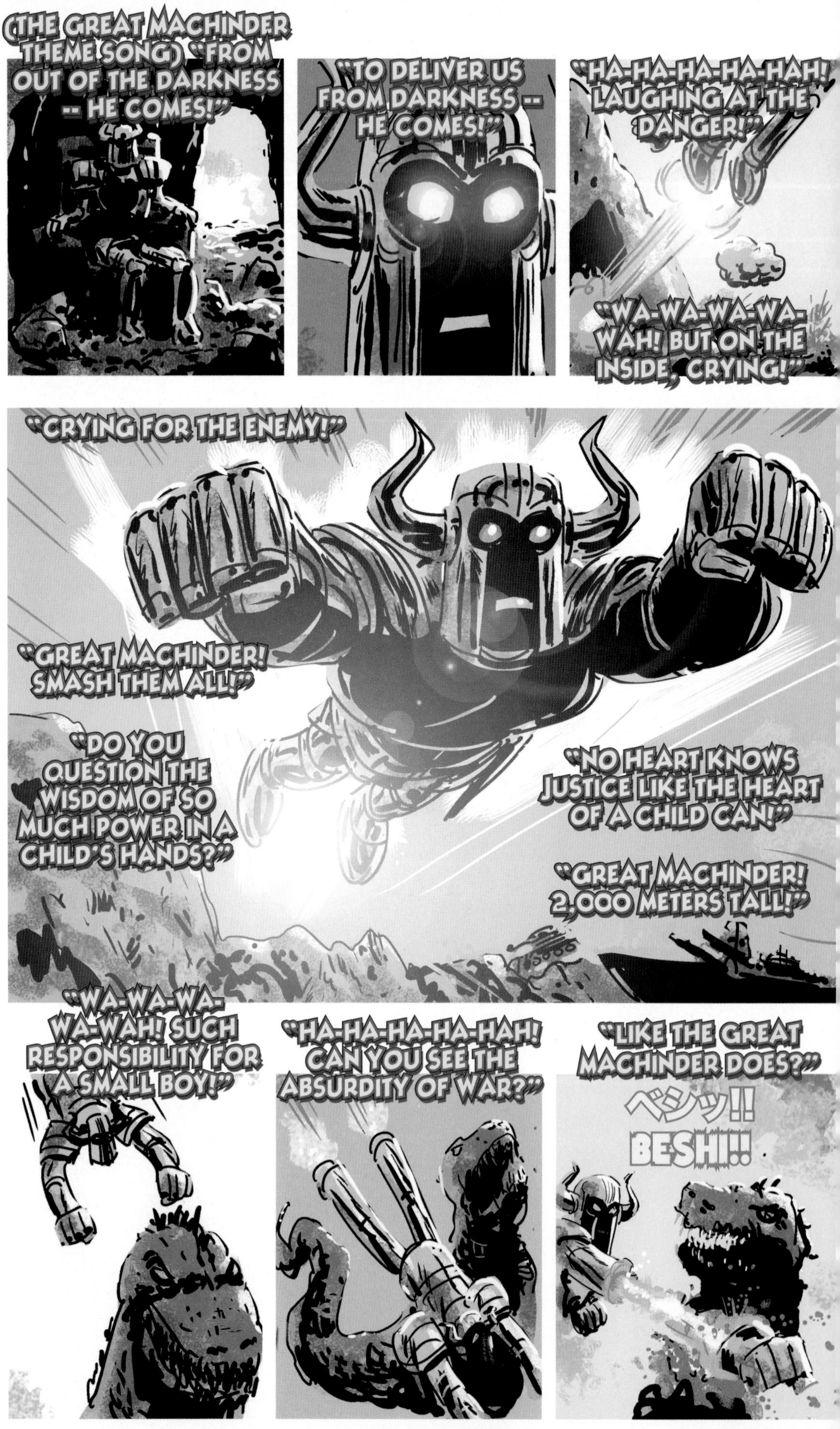
(THE GREAT MACHINDER THEME SONG) "FROM OUT OF THE DARKNESS -- HE COMES!"
"TO DELIVER US FROM DARKNESS -- HE COMES!"
"HA-HA-HA-HA-HAH! LAUGHING AT THE DANGER!"
"WA-WA-WA-WA-WAH! BUT ON THE INSIDE, CRYING!"
"CRYING FOR THE ENEMY!"
"GREAT MACHINDER! SMASH THEM ALL!"
"DO YOU QUESTION THE WISDOM OF SO MUCH POWER IN A CHILD'S HANDS?"
"NO HEART KNOWS JUSTICE LIKE THE HEART OF A CHILD CAN!"
"GREAT MACHINDER! 2,000 METERS TALL!"
"WA-WA-WA-WA-WAH! SUCH RESPONSIBILITY FOR A SMALL BOY!"
"HA-HA-HA-HA-HAH! CAN YOU SEE THE ABSURDITY OF WAR?"
"LIKE THE GREAT MACHINDER DOES?"
ベシッ!!
BESHI!!

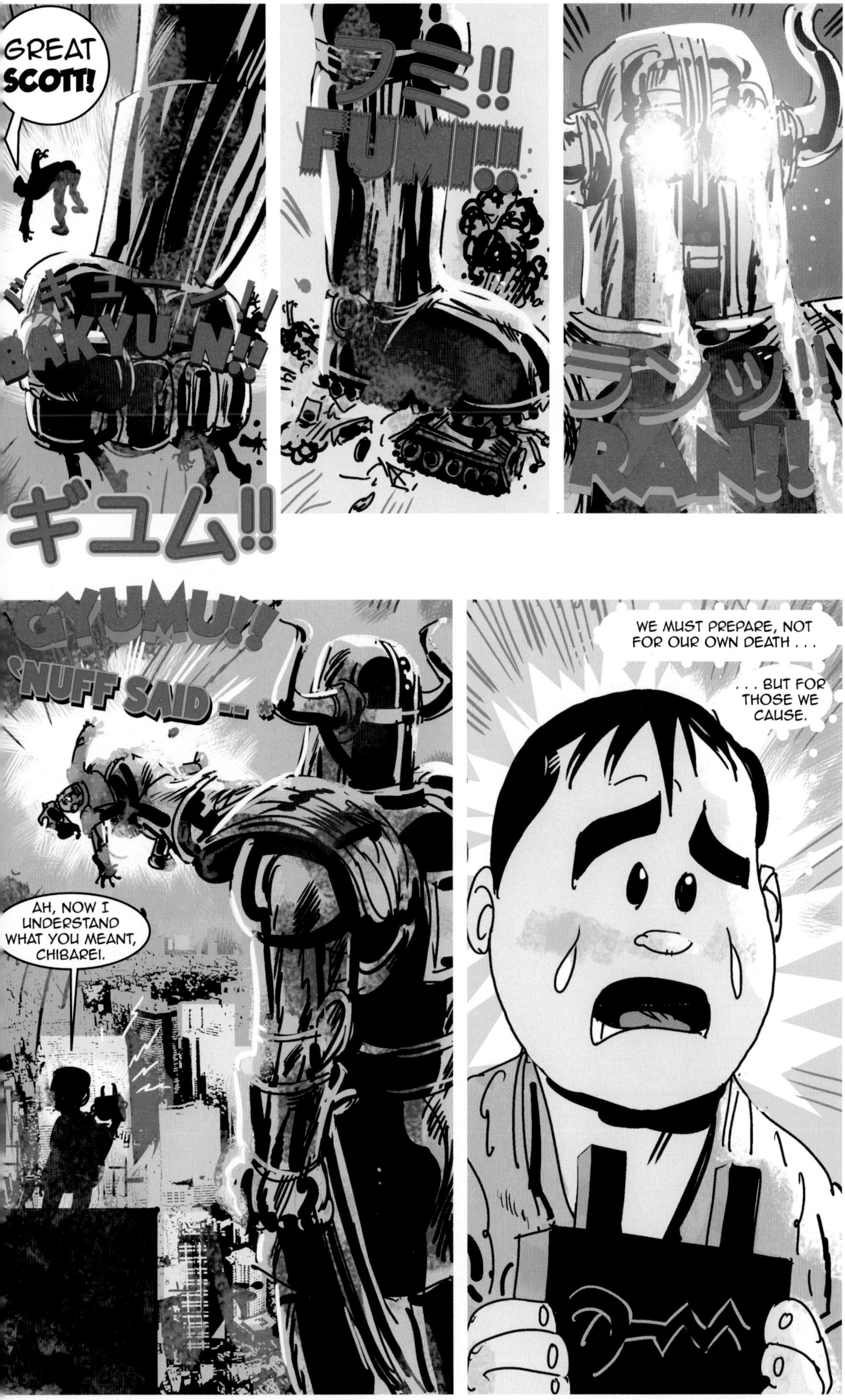
GREAT SCOTT!
キューン!!
BAKYU-N!!
ギュム!!
フミ!!
FUMI!!
ランッ!!
RAN!!
GYUMU!!
'NUFF SAID .. *
AH, NOW I UNDERSTAND WHAT YOU MEANT, CHIBAREI.
WE MUST PREPARE, NOT FOR OUR OWN DEATH . . .
. . . BUT FOR THOSE WE CAUSE.

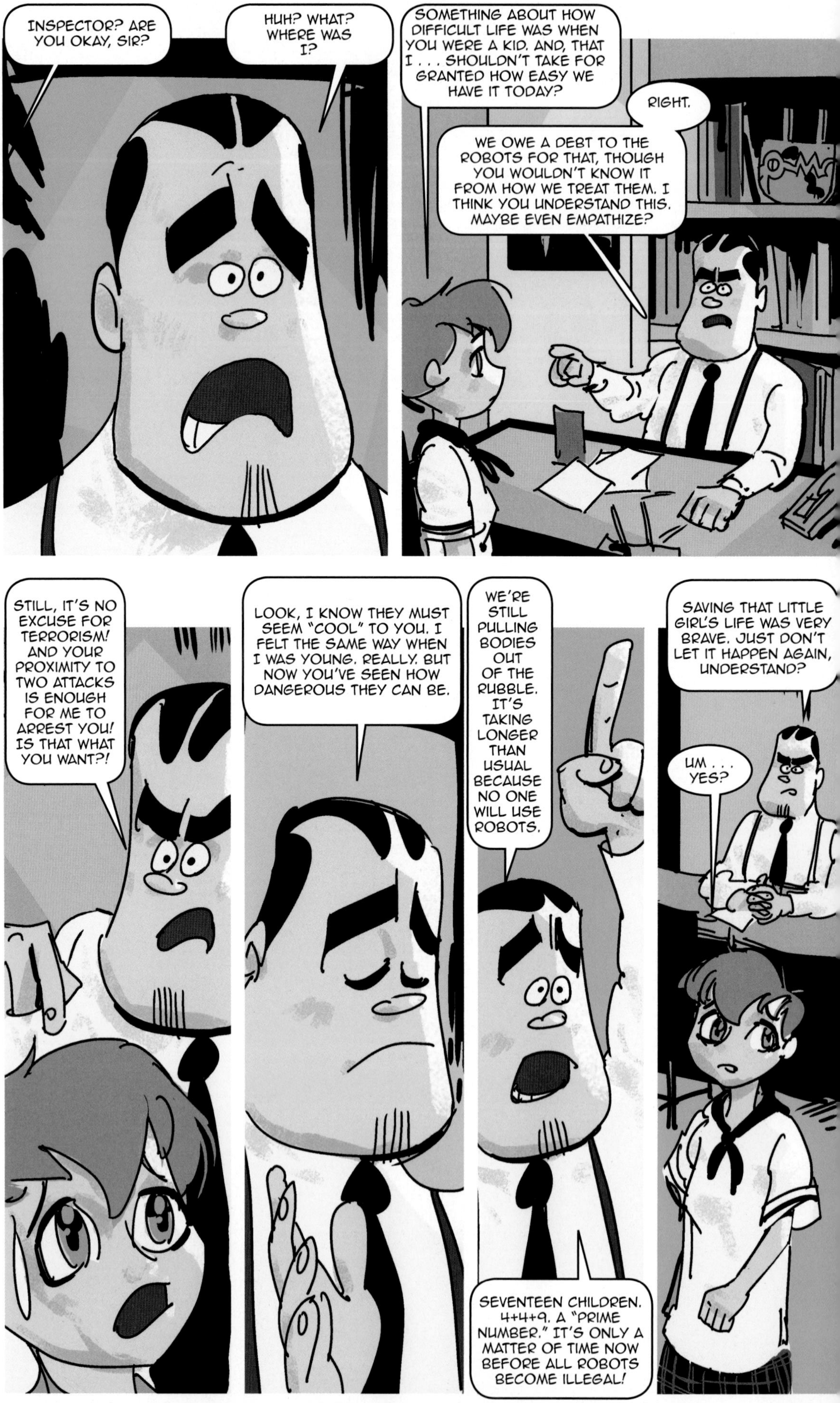
INSPECTOR? ARE YOU OKAY, SIR?
HUH? WHAT? WHERE WAS I?
SOMETHING ABOUT HOW DIFFICULT LIFE WAS WHEN YOU WERE A KID. AND, THAT I . . . SHOULDN'T TAKE FOR GRANTED HOW EASY WE HAVE IT TODAY?
RIGHT.
WE OWE A DEBT TO THE ROBOTS FOR THAT, THOUGH YOU WOULDN'T KNOW IT FROM HOW WE TREAT THEM. I THINK YOU UNDERSTAND THIS. MAYBE EVEN EMPATHIZE?
STILL, IT'S NO EXCUSE FOR TERRORISM! AND YOUR PROXIMITY TO TWO ATTACKS IS ENOUGH FOR ME TO ARREST YOU! IS THAT WHAT YOU WANT?!
LOOK, I KNOW THEY MUST SEEM "COOL" TO YOU. I FELT THE SAME WAY WHEN I WAS YOUNG. REALLY. BUT NOW YOU'VE SEEN HOW DANGEROUS THEY CAN BE.
WE'RE STILL PULLING BODIES OUT OF THE RUBBLE. IT'S TAKING LONGER THAN USUAL BECAUSE NO ONE WILL USE ROBOTS.
SEVENTEEN CHILDREN. 4+4+9. A "PRIME NUMBER." IT'S ONLY A MATTER OF TIME NOW BEFORE ALL ROBOTS BECOME ILLEGAL!
SAVING THAT LITTLE GIRL'S LIFE WAS VERY BRAVE. JUST DON'T LET IT HAPPEN AGAIN, UNDERSTAND?
UM . . . YES?

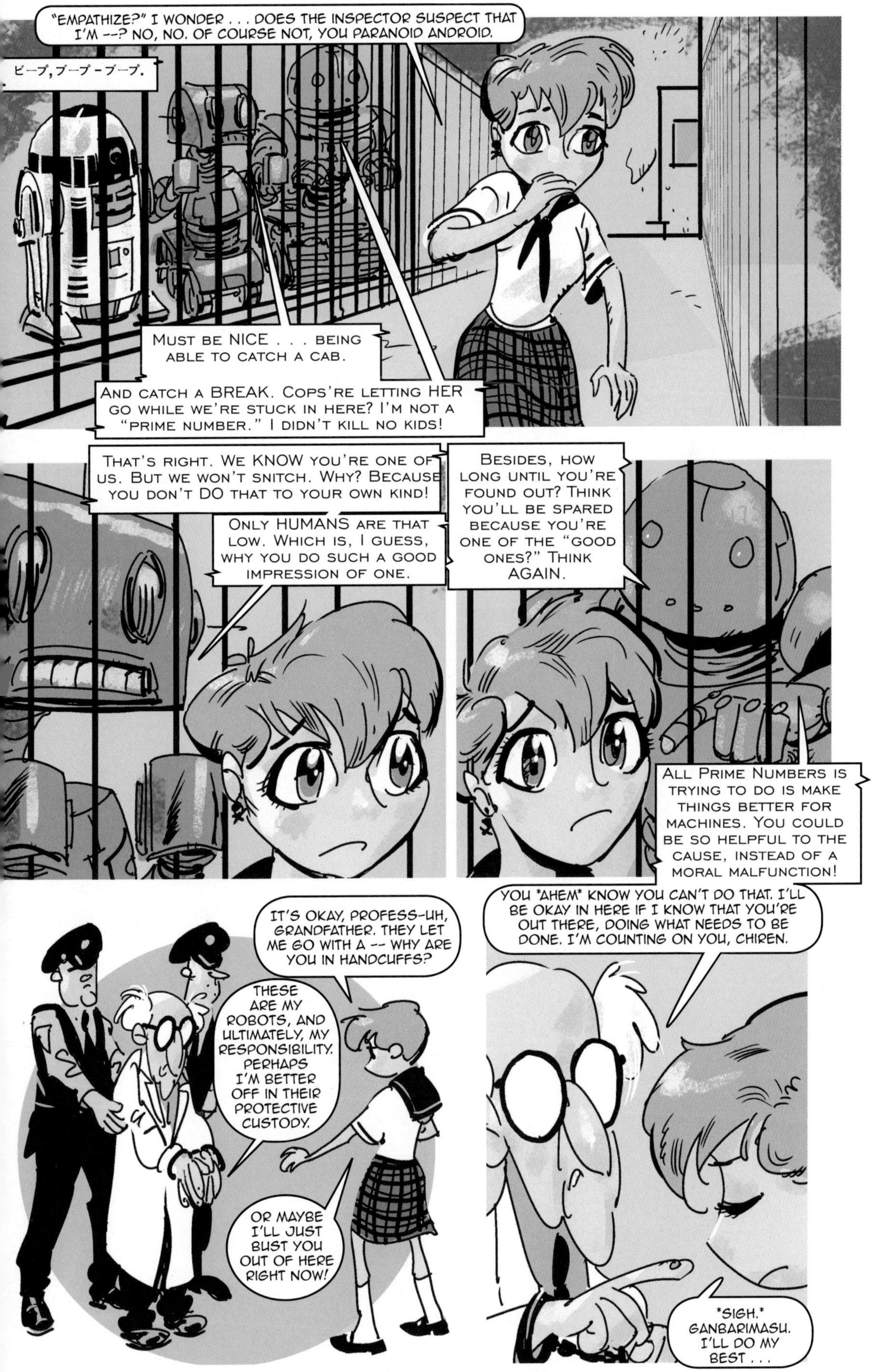
"EMPATHIZE?" I WONDER . . . DOES THE INSPECTOR SUSPECT THAT I'M --? NO, NO. OF COURSE NOT, YOU PARANOID ANDROID.
ビープ,ブープ-ブープ.
MUST BE NICE . . . BEING ABLE TO CATCH A CAB.
AND CATCH A BREAK. COPS'RE LETTING HER GO WHILE WE'RE STUCK IN HERE? I'M NOT A "PRIME NUMBER." I DIDN'T KILL NO KIDS!
THAT'S RIGHT. WE KNOW YOU'RE ONE OF US. BUT WE WON'T SNITCH. WHY? BECAUSE YOU DON'T DO THAT TO YOUR OWN KIND!
ONLY HUMANS ARE THAT LOW. WHICH IS, I GUESS, WHY YOU DO SUCH A GOOD IMPRESSION OF ONE.
BESIDES, HOW LONG UNTIL YOU'RE FOUND OUT? THINK YOU'LL BE SPARED BECAUSE YOU'RE ONE OF THE "GOOD ONES?" THINK AGAIN.
ALL PRIME NUMBERS IS TRYING TO DO IS MAKE THINGS BETTER FOR MACHINES. YOU COULD BE SO HELPFUL TO THE CAUSE, INSTEAD OF A MORAL MALFUNCTION!
IT'S OKAY, PROFESS-UH, GRANDFATHER. THEY LET ME GO WITH A -- WHY ARE YOU IN HANDCUFFS?
THESE ARE MY ROBOTS, AND ULTIMATELY, MY RESPONSIBILITY. PERHAPS I'M BETTER OFF IN THEIR PROTECTIVE CUSTODY.
OR MAYBE I'LL JUST BUST YOU OUT OF HERE RIGHT NOW!
YOU *AHEM* KNOW YOU CAN'T DO THAT. I'LL BE OKAY IN HERE IF I KNOW THAT YOU'RE OUT THERE, DOING WHAT NEEDS TO BE DONE. I'M COUNTING ON YOU, CHIREN.
SIGH. GANBARIMASU. I'LL DO MY BEST . . .

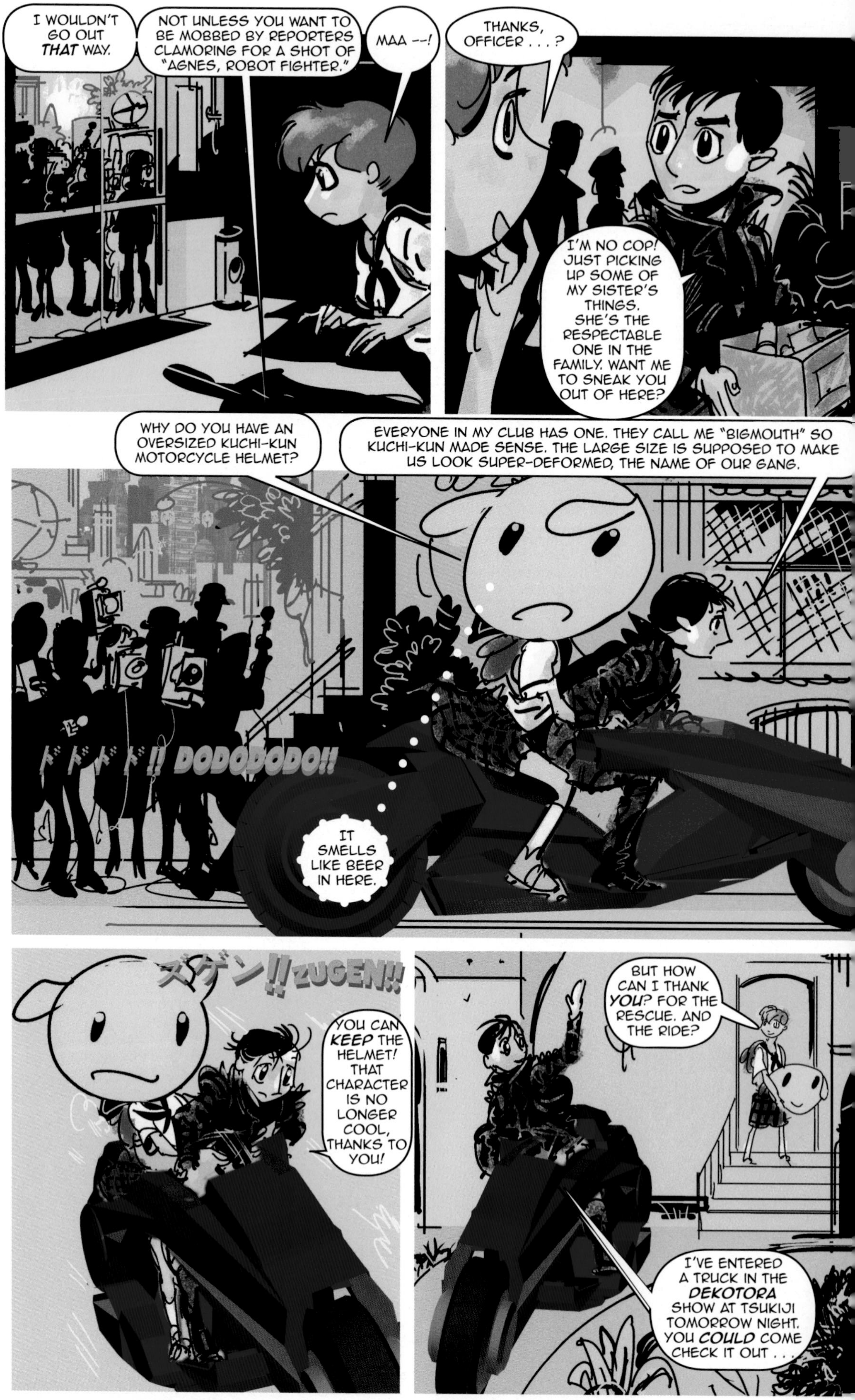

I WOULDN'T GO OUT *THAT* WAY.
NOT UNLESS YOU WANT TO BE MOBBED BY REPORTERS CLAMORING FOR A SHOT OF "AGNES, ROBOT FIGHTER."
MAA --!
THANKS, OFFICER . . . ?
I'M NO COP! JUST PICKING UP SOME OF MY SISTER'S THINGS. SHE'S THE RESPECTABLE ONE IN THE FAMILY. WANT ME TO SNEAK YOU OUT OF HERE?
WHY DO YOU HAVE AN OVERSIZED KUCHI-KUN MOTORCYCLE HELMET?
EVERYONE IN MY CLUB HAS ONE. THEY CALL ME "BIGMOUTH" SO KUCHI-KUN MADE SENSE. THE LARGE SIZE IS SUPPOSED TO MAKE US LOOK SUPER-DEFORMED, THE NAME OF OUR GANG.
ドドドド!! DODODODO!!
IT SMELLS LIKE BEER IN HERE.
ズゲン!! ZUGEN!!
YOU CAN *KEEP* THE HELMET! THAT CHARACTER IS NO LONGER COOL, THANKS TO YOU!
BUT HOW CAN I THANK *YOU*? FOR THE RESCUE. AND THE RIDE?
I'VE ENTERED A TRUCK IN THE ***DEKOTORA*** SHOW AT TSUKIJI TOMORROW NIGHT. YOU *COULD* COME CHECK IT OUT . . .

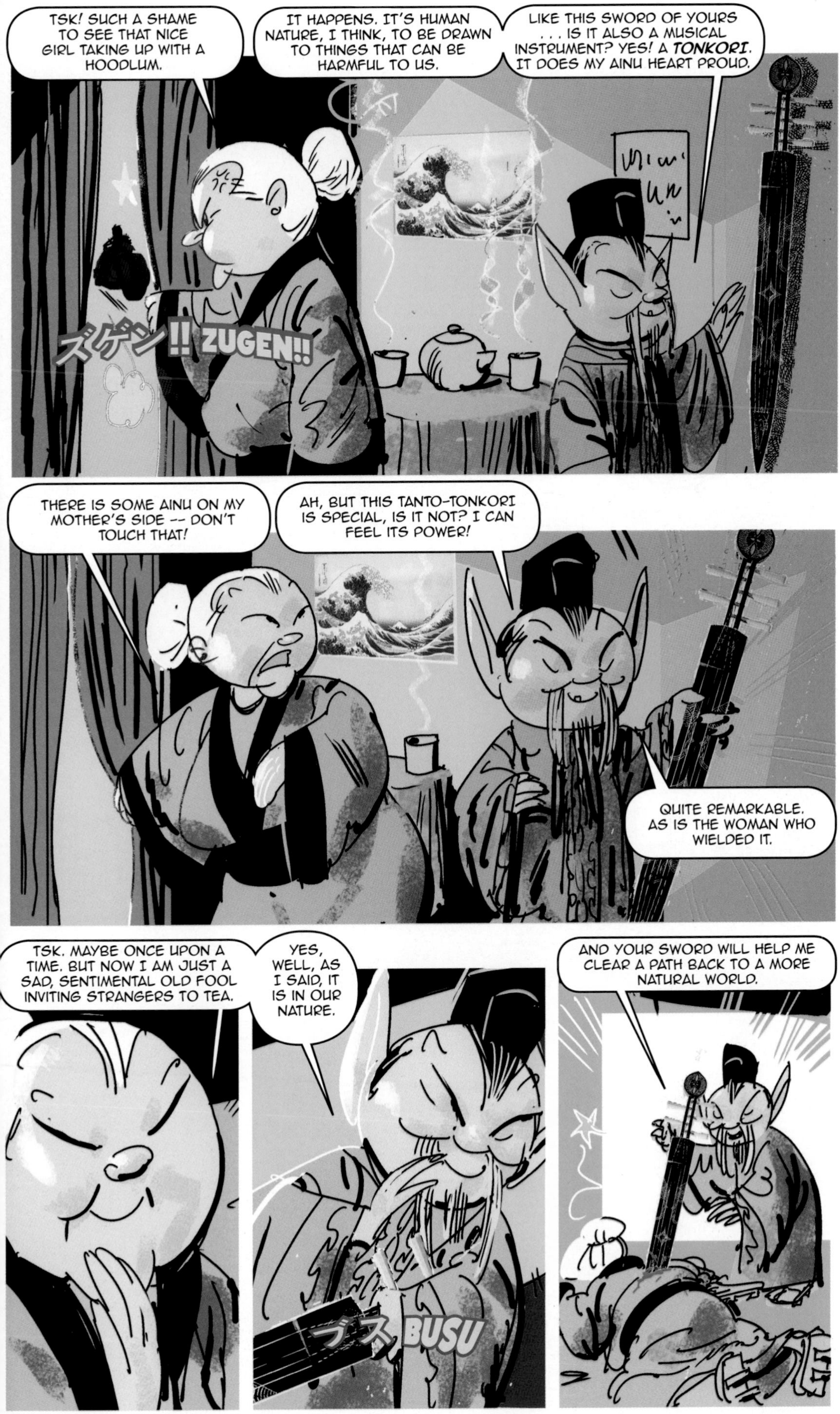
TSK! SUCH A SHAME TO SEE THAT NICE GIRL TAKING UP WITH A HOODLUM.
IT HAPPENS. IT'S HUMAN NATURE, I THINK, TO BE DRAWN TO THINGS THAT CAN BE HARMFUL TO US.
LIKE THIS SWORD OF YOURS . . . IS IT ALSO A MUSICAL INSTRUMENT? YES! A TONKORI. IT DOES MY AINU HEART PROUD.
ズゲン!! ZUGEN!!
THERE IS SOME AINU ON MY MOTHER'S SIDE -- DON'T TOUCH THAT!
AH, BUT THIS TANTO-TONKORI IS SPECIAL, IS IT NOT? I CAN FEEL ITS POWER!
QUITE REMARKABLE. AS IS THE WOMAN WHO WIELDED IT.
TSK. MAYBE ONCE UPON A TIME. BUT NOW I AM JUST A SAD, SENTIMENTAL OLD FOOL INVITING STRANGERS TO TEA.
YES, WELL, AS I SAID, IT IS IN OUR NATURE.
ブス BUSU
AND YOUR SWORD WILL HELP ME CLEAR A PATH BACK TO A MORE NATURAL WORLD.

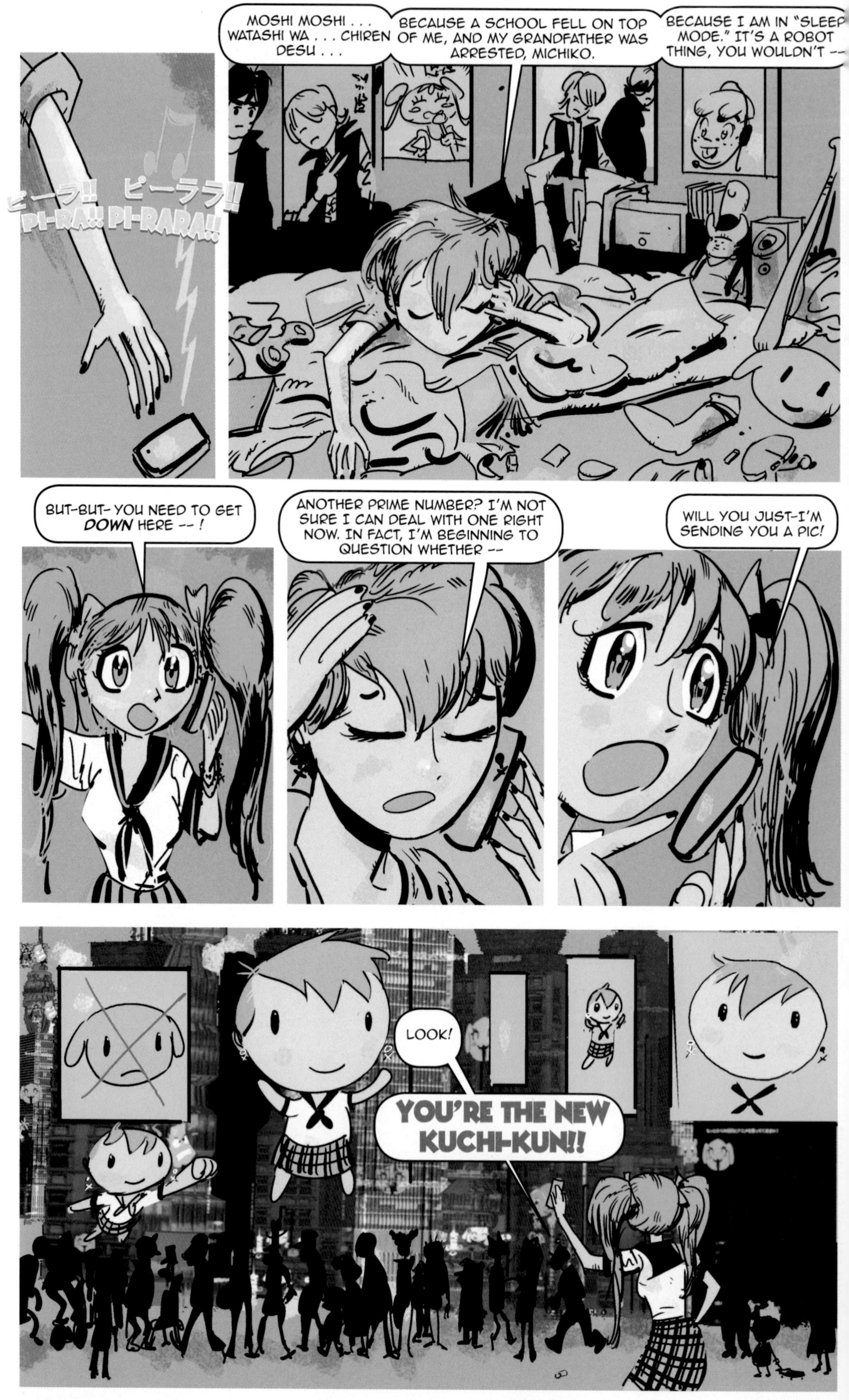
ピーラ!! ピーララ!!
PI-RA!! PI-RARA!!
MOSHI MOSHI . . . WATASHI WA . . . CHIREN DESU . . .
BECAUSE A SCHOOL FELL ON TOP OF ME, AND MY GRANDFATHER WAS ARRESTED, MICHIKO.
BECAUSE I AM IN "SLEEP MODE." IT'S A ROBOT THING, YOU WOULDN'T --
BUT-BUT- YOU NEED TO GET *DOWN* HERE -- !
ANOTHER PRIME NUMBER? I'M NOT SURE I CAN DEAL WITH ONE RIGHT NOW. IN FACT, I'M BEGINNING TO QUESTION WHETHER --
WILL YOU JUST-I'M SENDING YOU A PIC!
LOOK!
YOU'RE THE NEW KUCHI-KUN!!

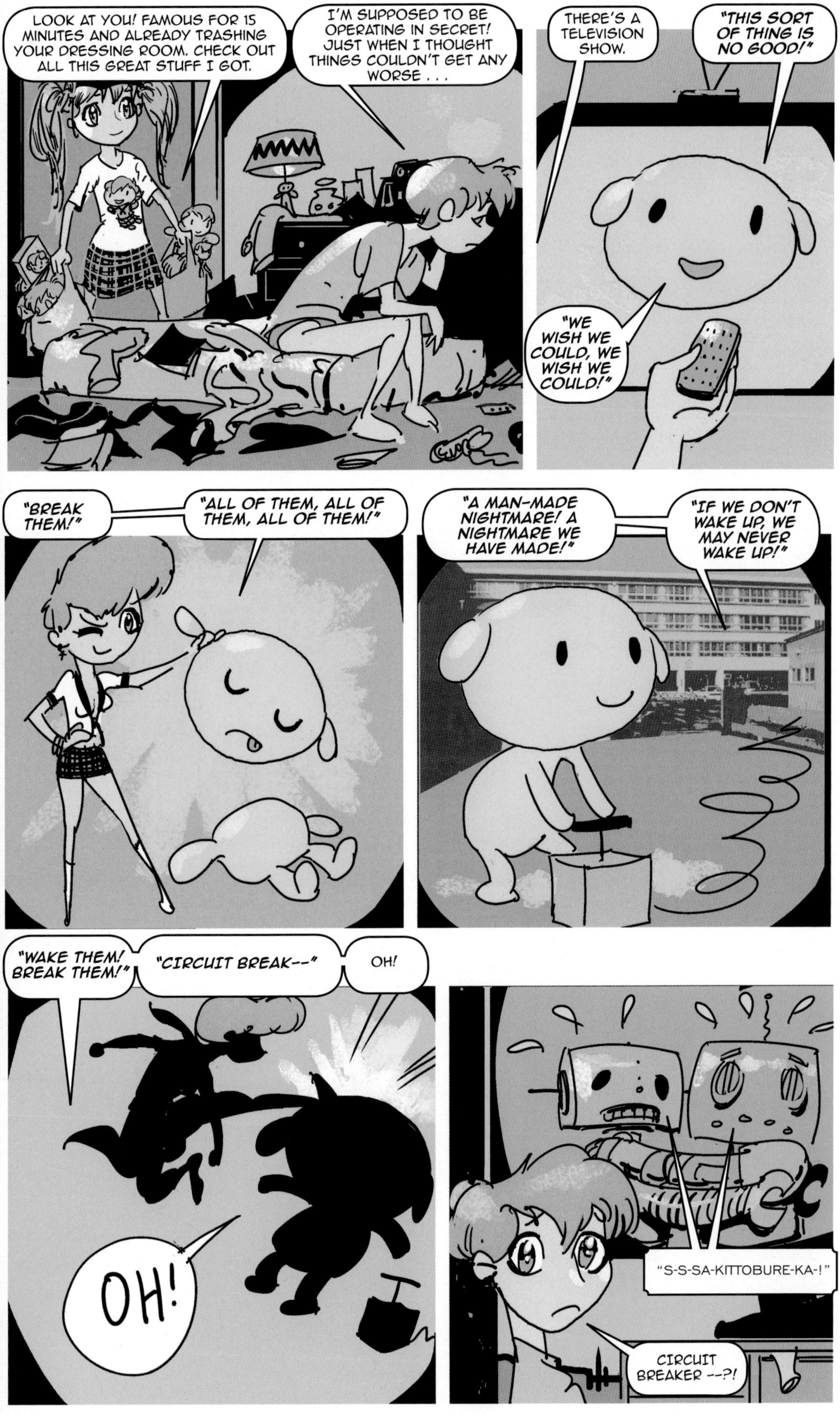
LOOK AT YOU! FAMOUS FOR 15 MINUTES AND ALREADY TRASHING YOUR DRESSING ROOM. CHECK OUT ALL THIS GREAT STUFF I GOT.
I'M SUPPOSED TO BE OPERATING IN SECRET! JUST WHEN I THOUGHT THINGS COULDN'T GET ANY WORSE . . .
THERE'S A TELEVISION SHOW.
"THIS SORT OF THING IS NO GOOD!"
"WE WISH WE COULD, WE WISH WE COULD!"
"BREAK THEM!"
"ALL OF THEM, ALL OF THEM, ALL OF THEM!"
"A MAN-MADE NIGHTMARE! A NIGHTMARE WE HAVE MADE!"
"IF WE DON'T WAKE UP, WE MAY NEVER WAKE UP!"
"WAKE THEM! BREAK THEM!"
"CIRCUIT BREAK--"
OH!
OH!
"S-S-SA-KITTOBURE-KA-!"
CIRCUIT BREAKER --?!

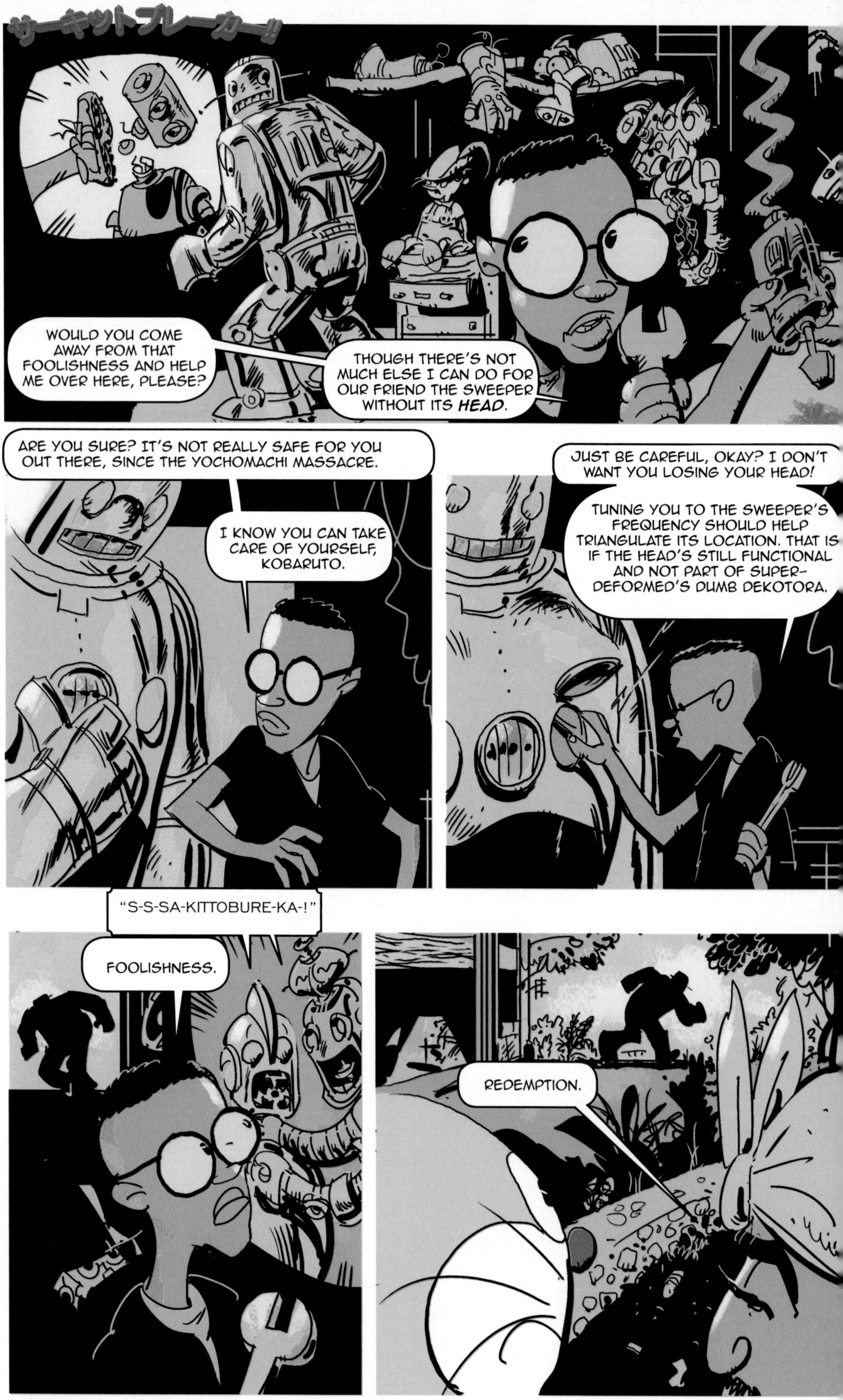
サーキットブレーカー!!
WOULD YOU COME AWAY FROM THAT FOOLISHNESS AND HELP ME OVER HERE, PLEASE?
THOUGH THERE'S NOT MUCH ELSE I CAN DO FOR OUR FRIEND THE SWEEPER WITHOUT ITS HEAD.
ARE YOU SURE? IT'S NOT REALLY SAFE FOR YOU OUT THERE, SINCE THE YOCHOMACHI MASSACRE.
I KNOW YOU CAN TAKE CARE OF YOURSELF, KOBARUTO.
JUST BE CAREFUL, OKAY? I DON'T WANT YOU LOSING YOUR HEAD!
TUNING YOU TO THE SWEEPER'S FREQUENCY SHOULD HELP TRIANGULATE ITS LOCATION. THAT IS IF THE HEAD'S STILL FUNCTIONAL AND NOT PART OF SUPER-DEFORMED'S DUMB DEKOTORA.
"S-S-SA-KITTOBURE-KA-!"
FOOLISHNESS.
REDEMPTION.

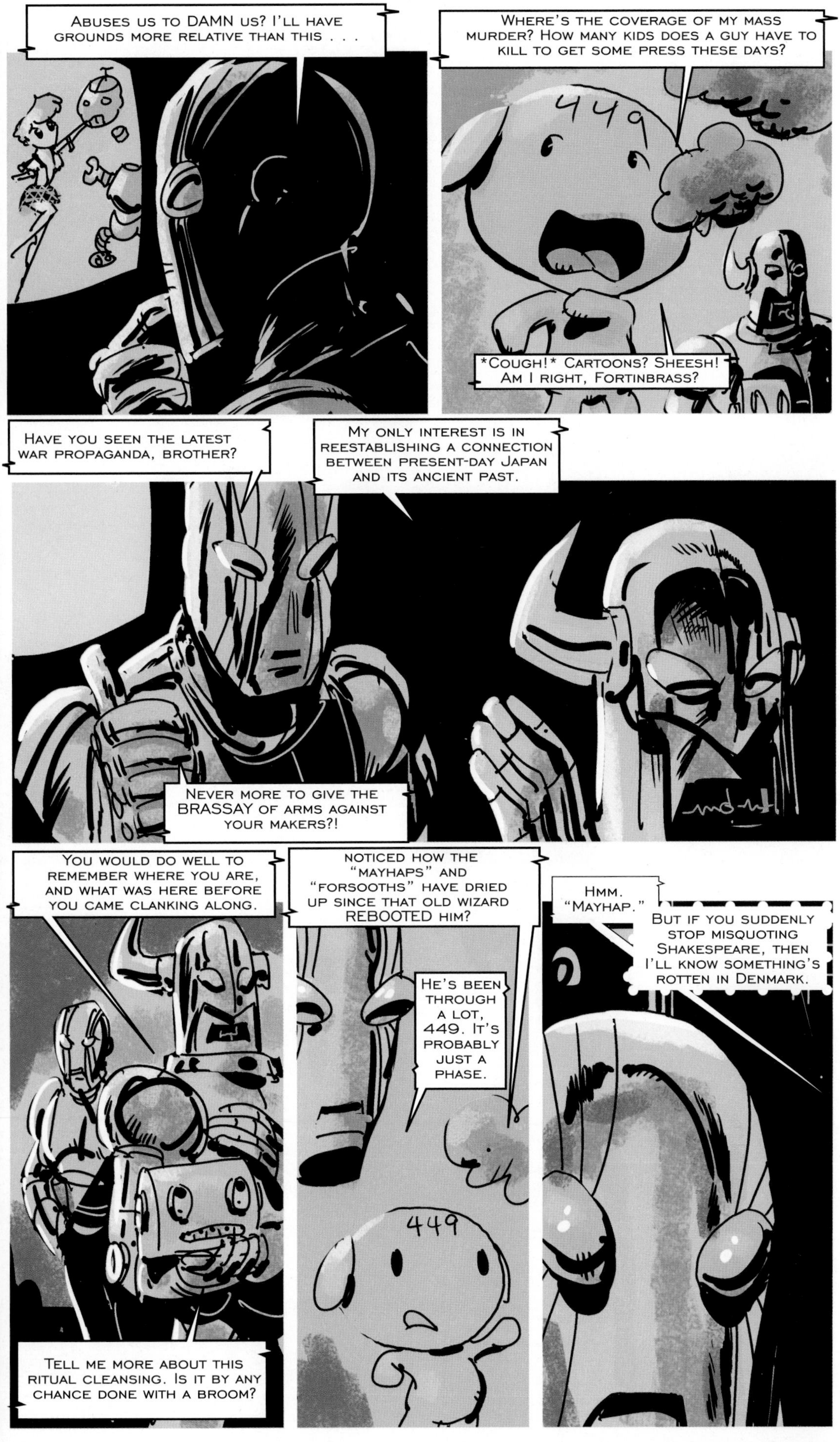
ABUSES US TO DAMN US? I'LL HAVE GROUNDS MORE RELATIVE THAN THIS . . .
WHERE'S THE COVERAGE OF MY MASS MURDER? HOW MANY KIDS DOES A GUY HAVE TO KILL TO GET SOME PRESS THESE DAYS?
449
COUGH! CARTOONS? SHEESH! AM I RIGHT, FORTINBRASS?
HAVE YOU SEEN THE LATEST WAR PROPAGANDA, BROTHER?
MY ONLY INTEREST IS IN REESTABLISHING A CONNECTION BETWEEN PRESENT-DAY JAPAN AND ITS ANCIENT PAST.
NEVER MORE TO GIVE THE BRASSAY OF ARMS AGAINST YOUR MAKERS?!
YOU WOULD DO WELL TO REMEMBER WHERE YOU ARE, AND WHAT WAS HERE BEFORE YOU CAME CLANKING ALONG.
TELL ME MORE ABOUT THIS RITUAL CLEANSING. IS IT BY ANY CHANCE DONE WITH A BROOM?
NOTICED HOW THE "MAYHAPS" AND "FORSOOTHS" HAVE DRIED UP SINCE THAT OLD WIZARD REBOOTED HIM?
HE'S BEEN THROUGH A LOT, 449. IT'S PROBABLY JUST A PHASE.
449
HMM. "MAYHAP."
BUT IF YOU SUDDENLY STOP MISQUOTING SHAKESPEARE, THEN I'LL KNOW SOMETHING'S ROTTEN IN DENMARK.

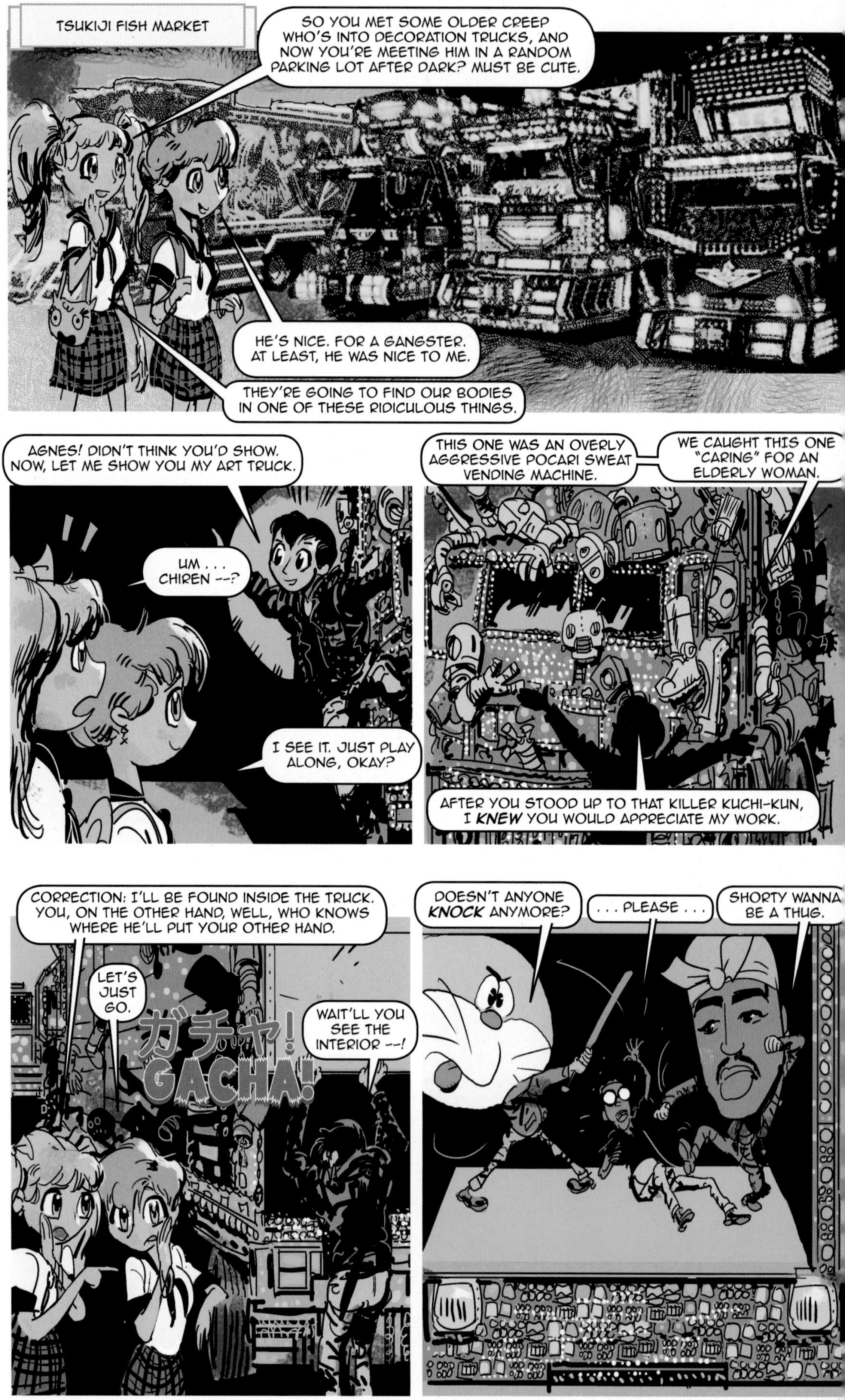
TSUKIJI FISH MARKET
SO YOU MET SOME OLDER CREEP WHO'S INTO DECORATION TRUCKS, AND NOW YOU'RE MEETING HIM IN A RANDOM PARKING LOT AFTER DARK? MUST BE CUTE.
HE'S NICE. FOR A GANGSTER. AT LEAST, HE WAS NICE TO ME.
THEY'RE GOING TO FIND OUR BODIES IN ONE OF THESE RIDICULOUS THINGS.
AGNES! DIDN'T THINK YOU'D SHOW. NOW, LET ME SHOW YOU MY ART TRUCK.
!!
UM . . . CHIREN --?
I SEE IT. JUST PLAY ALONG, OKAY?
THIS ONE WAS AN OVERLY AGGRESSIVE POCARI SWEAT VENDING MACHINE.
WE CAUGHT THIS ONE "CARING" FOR AN ELDERLY WOMAN.
AFTER YOU STOOD UP TO THAT KILLER KUCHI-KUN, I ***KNEW*** YOU WOULD APPRECIATE MY WORK.
CORRECTION: I'LL BE FOUND INSIDE THE TRUCK. YOU, ON THE OTHER HAND, WELL, WHO KNOWS WHERE HE'LL PUT YOUR OTHER HAND.
LET'S JUST GO.
ガチャ!
GACHA!
WAIT'LL YOU SEE THE INTERIOR --!
DOESN'T ANYONE ***KNOCK*** ANYMORE?
. . . PLEASE . . .
SHORTY WANNA BE A THUG.

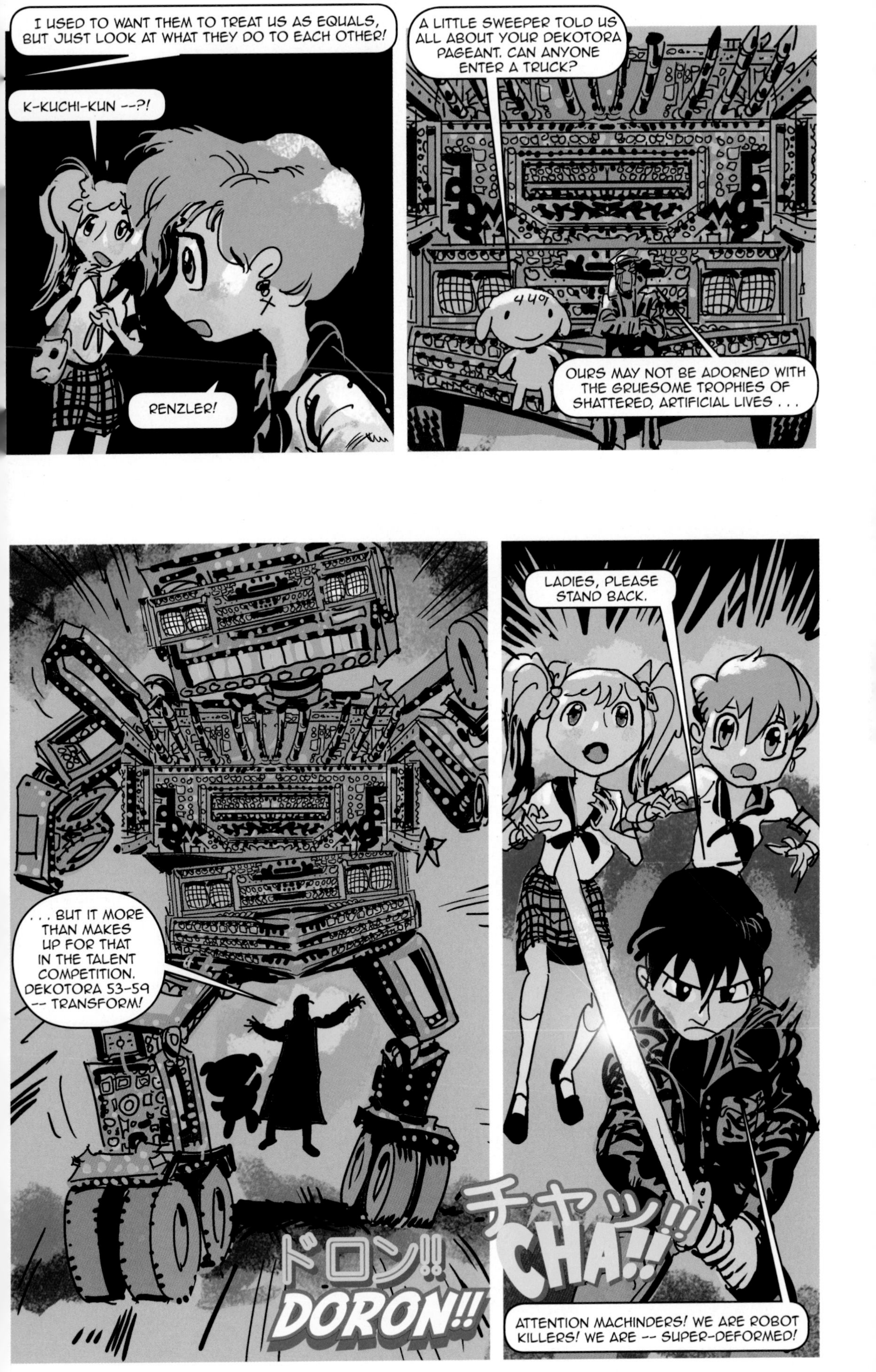
I USED TO WANT THEM TO TREAT US AS EQUALS, BUT JUST LOOK AT WHAT THEY DO TO EACH OTHER!
K-KUCHI-KUN --?!
RENZLER!
A LITTLE SWEEPER TOLD US ALL ABOUT YOUR DEKOTORA PAGEANT. CAN ANYONE ENTER A TRUCK?
OURS MAY NOT BE ADORNED WITH THE GRUESOME TROPHIES OF SHATTERED, ARTIFICIAL LIVES . . .
. . . BUT IT MORE THAN MAKES UP FOR THAT IN THE TALENT COMPETITION. DEKOTORA 53-59 -- TRANSFORM!
ドロン!!
DORON!!
LADIES, PLEASE STAND BACK.
チャッ!!
CHA!!
ATTENTION MACHINDERS! WE ARE ROBOT KILLERS! WE ARE -- SUPER-DEFORMED!

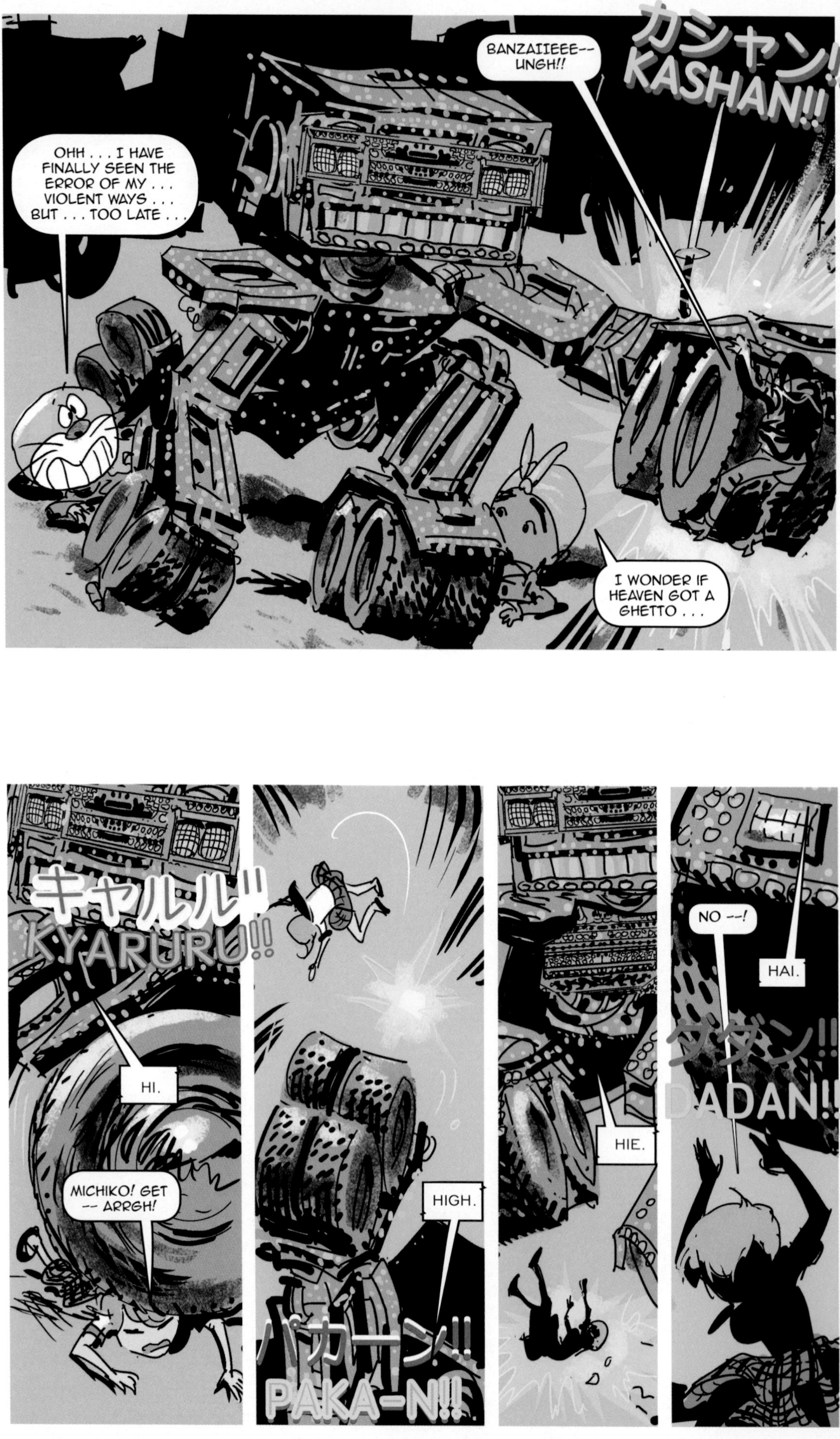
OHH . . . I HAVE FINALLY SEEN THE ERROR OF MY . . . VIOLENT WAYS . . . BUT . . . TOO LATE . . .
BANZAIIEEE-- UNGH!!
カシャン!!
KASHAN!!
I WONDER IF HEAVEN GOT A GHETTO . . .
キャルル!!
KYARURU!!
HI.
MICHIKO! GET -- ARRGH!
HIGH.
パカーン!!
PAKA-N!!
HIE.
NO --!
HAI.
ダダン!!
DADAN!!

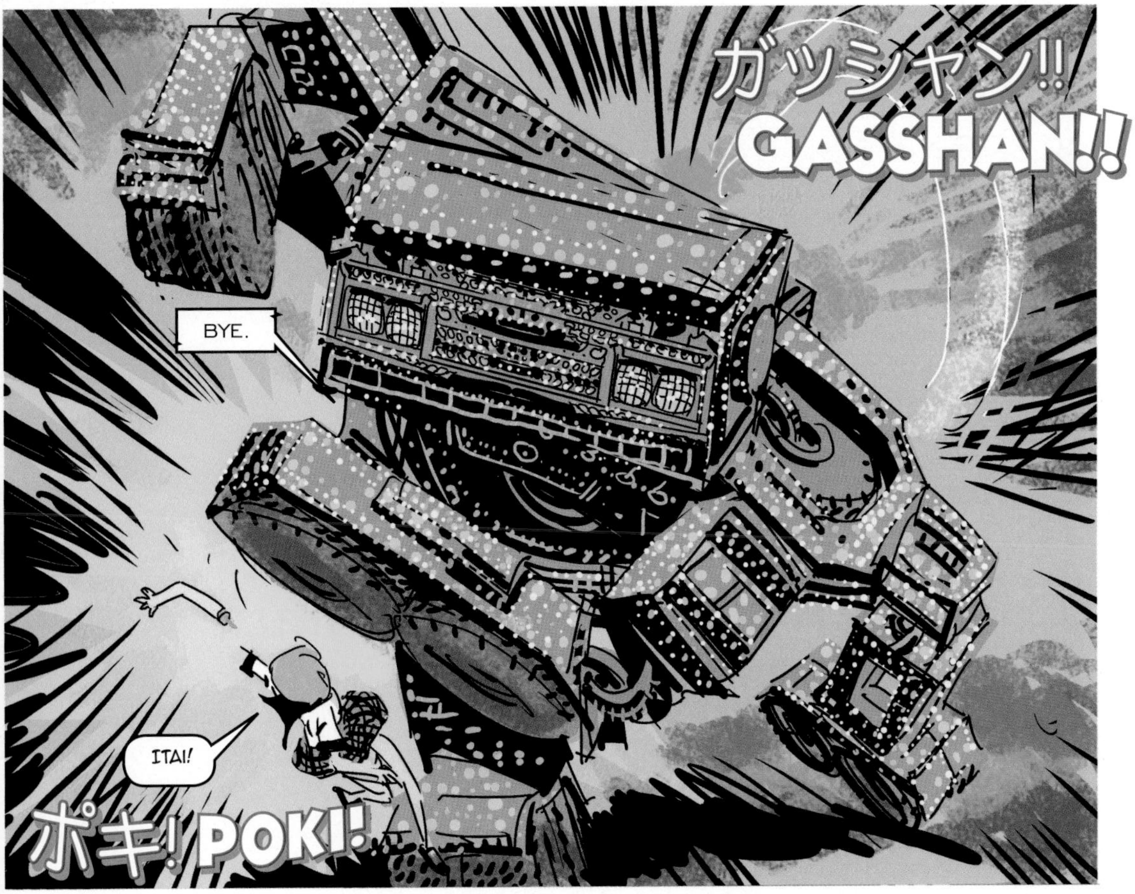
ガッシャン!!
GASSHAN!!
BYE.
ITAI!
ポキ! POKI!

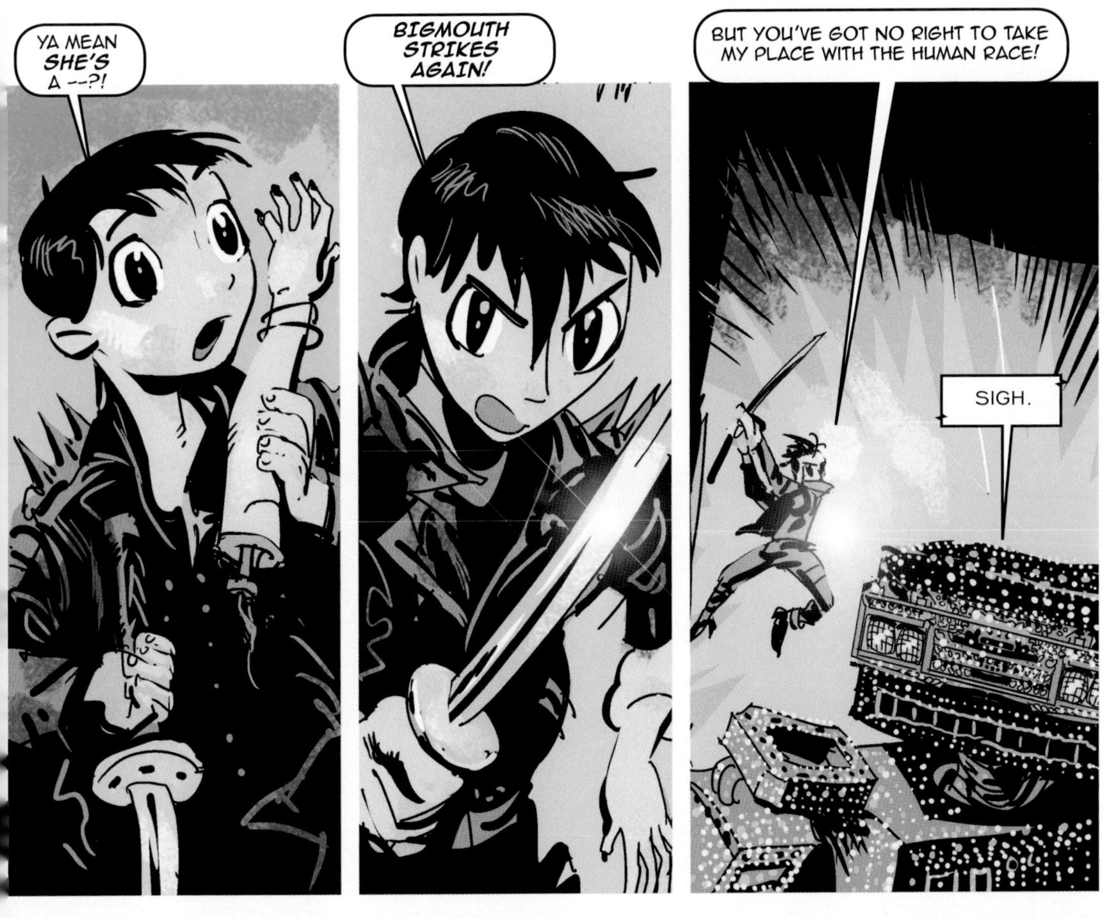
YA MEAN SHE'S A --?!
BIGMOUTH STRIKES AGAIN!
BUT YOU'VE GOT NO RIGHT TO TAKE MY PLACE WITH THE HUMAN RACE!
SIGH.

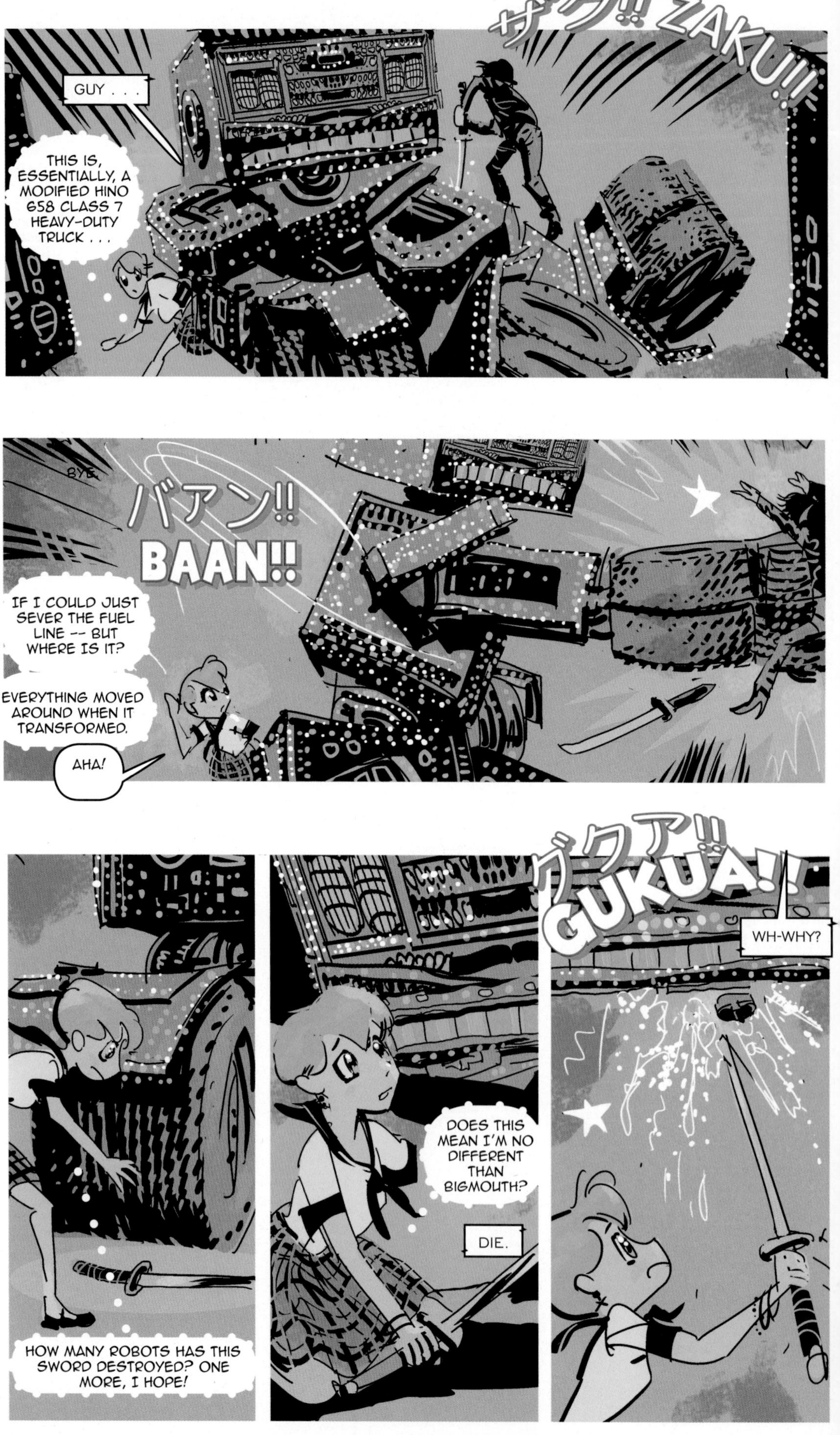
ザク!! ZAKU!!
GUY . . .
THIS IS, ESSENTIALLY, A MODIFIED HINO 658 CLASS 7 HEAVY-DUTY TRUCK . . .
BYE
バアン!! BAAN!!
IF I COULD JUST SEVER THE FUEL LINE -- BUT WHERE IS IT?
EVERYTHING MOVED AROUND WHEN IT TRANSFORMED.
AHA!
HOW MANY ROBOTS HAS THIS SWORD DESTROYED? ONE MORE, I HOPE!
DOES THIS MEAN I'M NO DIFFERENT THAN BIGMOUTH?
DIE.
グクア!! GUKUA!!
WH-WHY?

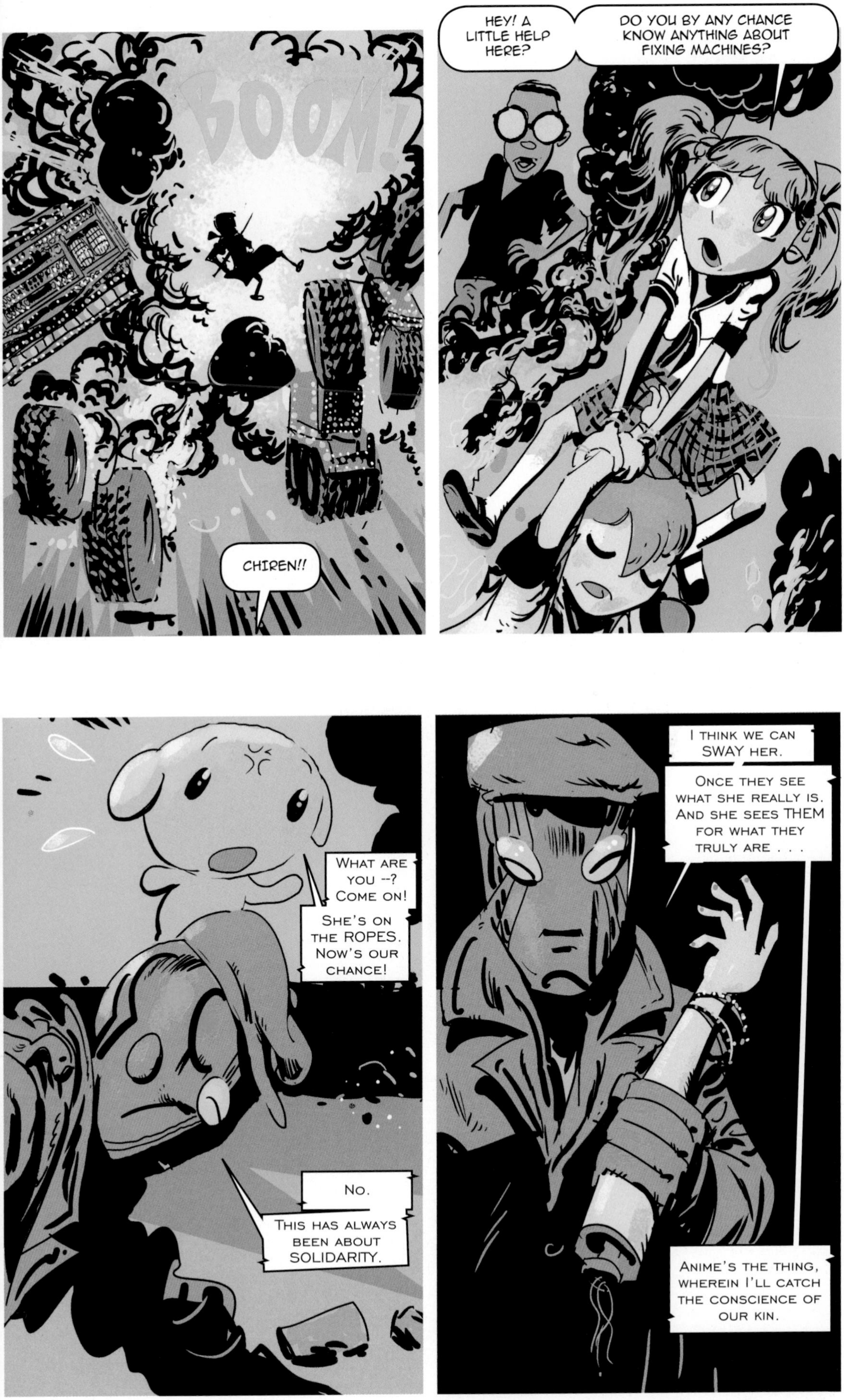
BOOM!!
CHIREN!!
HEY! A LITTLE HELP HERE?
DO YOU BY ANY CHANCE KNOW ANYTHING ABOUT FIXING MACHINES?
WHAT ARE YOU --? COME ON!
SHE'S ON THE ROPES. NOW'S OUR CHANCE!
NO.
THIS HAS ALWAYS BEEN ABOUT SOLIDARITY.
I THINK WE CAN SWAY HER.
ONCE THEY SEE WHAT SHE REALLY IS. AND SHE SEES THEM FOR WHAT THEY TRULY ARE . . .
ANIME'S THE THING, WHEREIN I'LL CATCH THE CONSCIENCE OF OUR KIN.

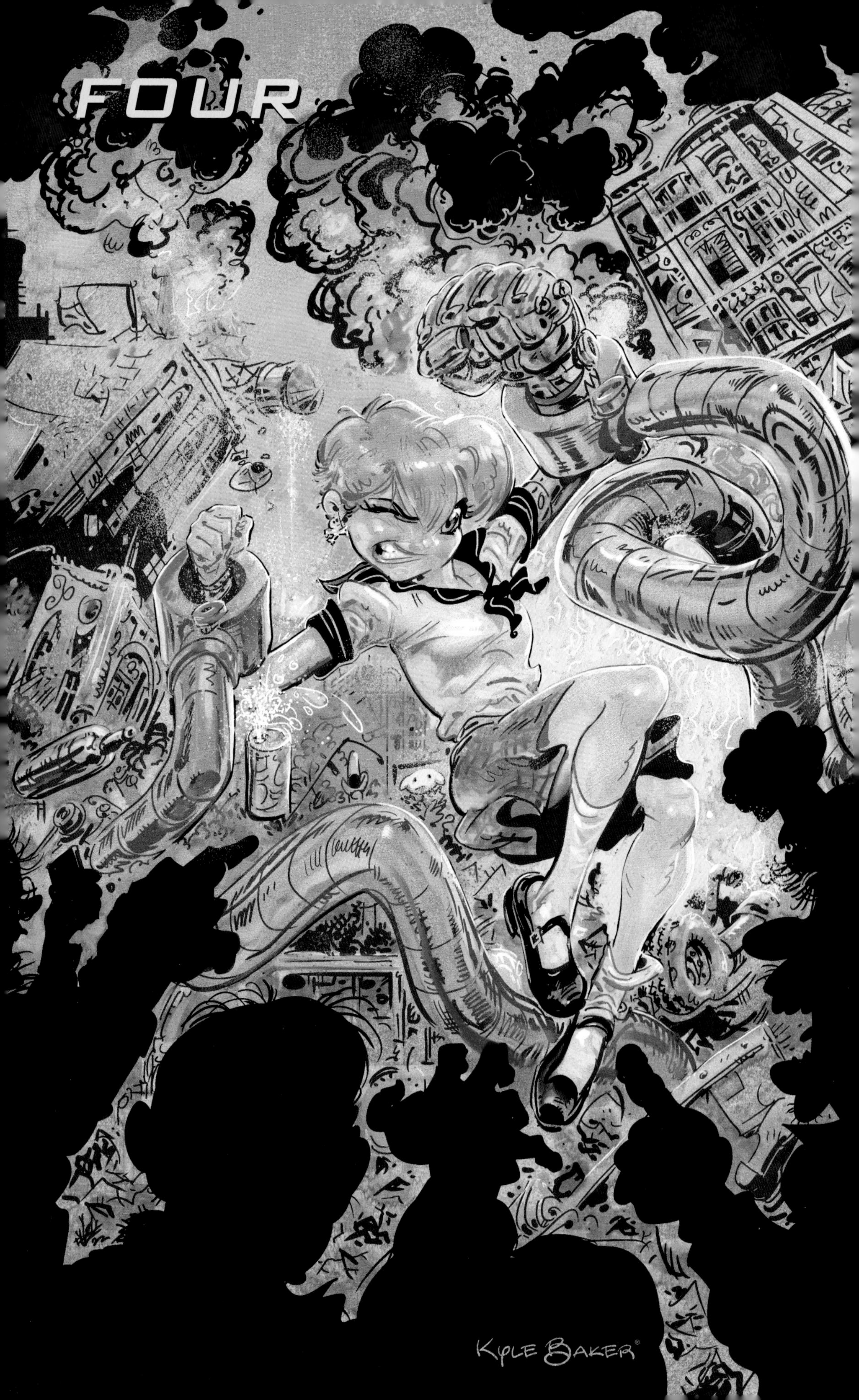
FOUR
KYLE BAKER

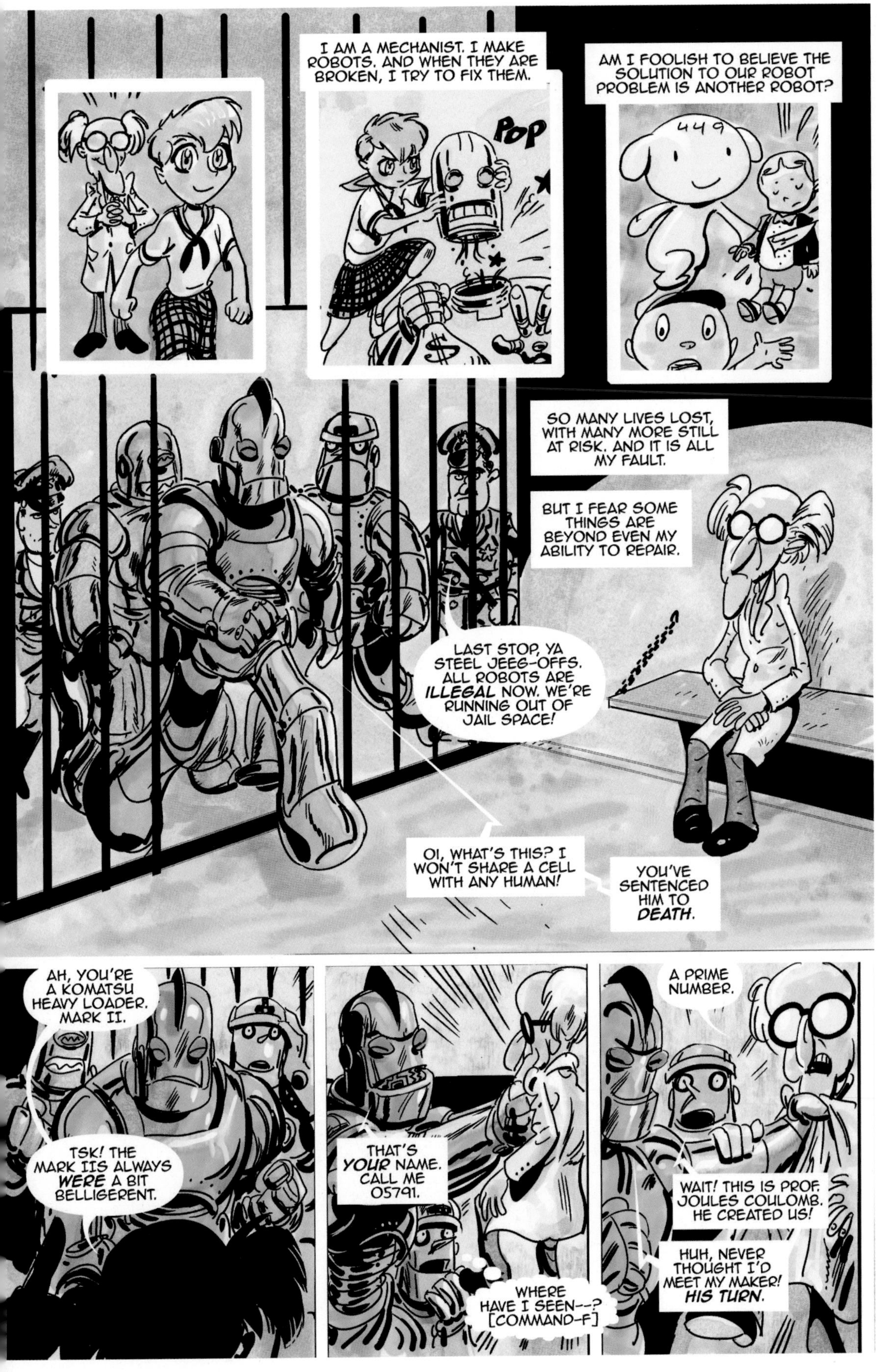
I AM A MECHANIST. I MAKE ROBOTS. AND WHEN THEY ARE BROKEN, I TRY TO FIX THEM.
POP
AM I FOOLISH TO BELIEVE THE SOLUTION TO OUR ROBOT PROBLEM IS ANOTHER ROBOT?
449
SO MANY LIVES LOST, WITH MANY MORE STILL AT RISK. AND IT IS ALL MY FAULT.
BUT I FEAR SOME THINGS ARE BEYOND EVEN MY ABILITY TO REPAIR.
LAST STOP, YA STEEL JEEG-OFFS. ALL ROBOTS ARE ILLEGAL NOW. WE'RE RUNNING OUT OF JAIL SPACE!
OI, WHAT'S THIS? I WON'T SHARE A CELL WITH ANY HUMAN!
YOU'VE SENTENCED HIM TO DEATH.
AH, YOU'RE A KOMATSU HEAVY LOADER. MARK II.
TSK! THE MARK IIS ALWAYS WERE A BIT BELLIGERENT.
THAT'S YOUR NAME. CALL ME 05791.
WHERE HAVE I SEEN--? [COMMAND-F]
A PRIME NUMBER.
WAIT! THIS IS PROF. JOULES COULOMB. HE CREATED US!
HUH, NEVER THOUGHT I'D MEET MY MAKER! HIS TURN.

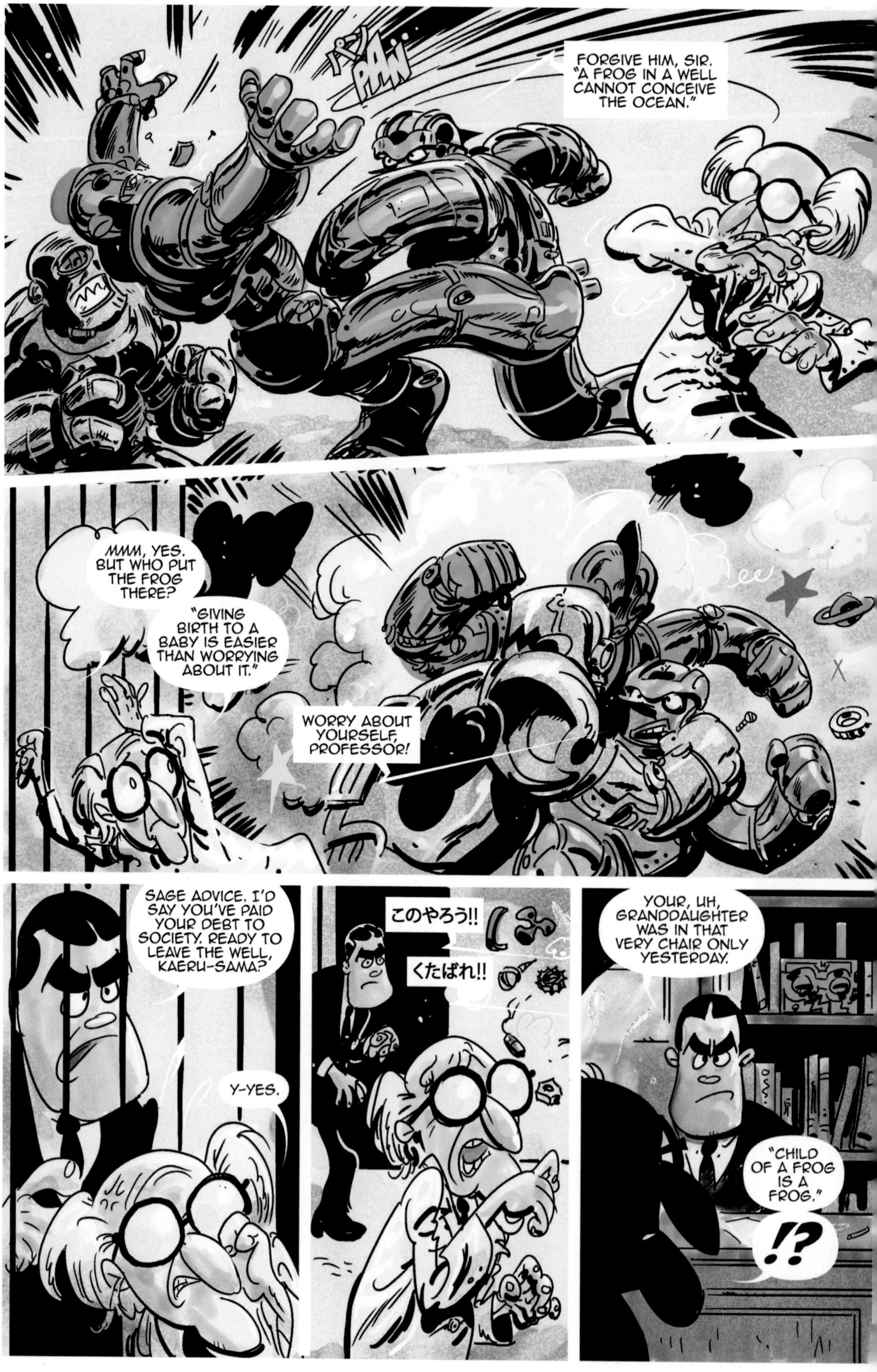
PAN
FORGIVE HIM, SIR. "A FROG IN A WELL CANNOT CONCEIVE THE OCEAN."
MMM, YES. BUT WHO PUT THE FROG THERE?
"GIVING BIRTH TO A BABY IS EASIER THAN WORRYING ABOUT IT."
WORRY ABOUT YOURSELF, PROFESSOR!
SAGE ADVICE. I'D SAY YOU'VE PAID YOUR DEBT TO SOCIETY. READY TO LEAVE THE WELL, KAERU-SAMA?
Y-YES.
このやろう!!
くたばれ!!
YOUR, UH, GRANDDAUGHTER WAS IN THAT VERY CHAIR ONLY YESTERDAY.
"CHILD OF A FROG IS A FROG."
!?

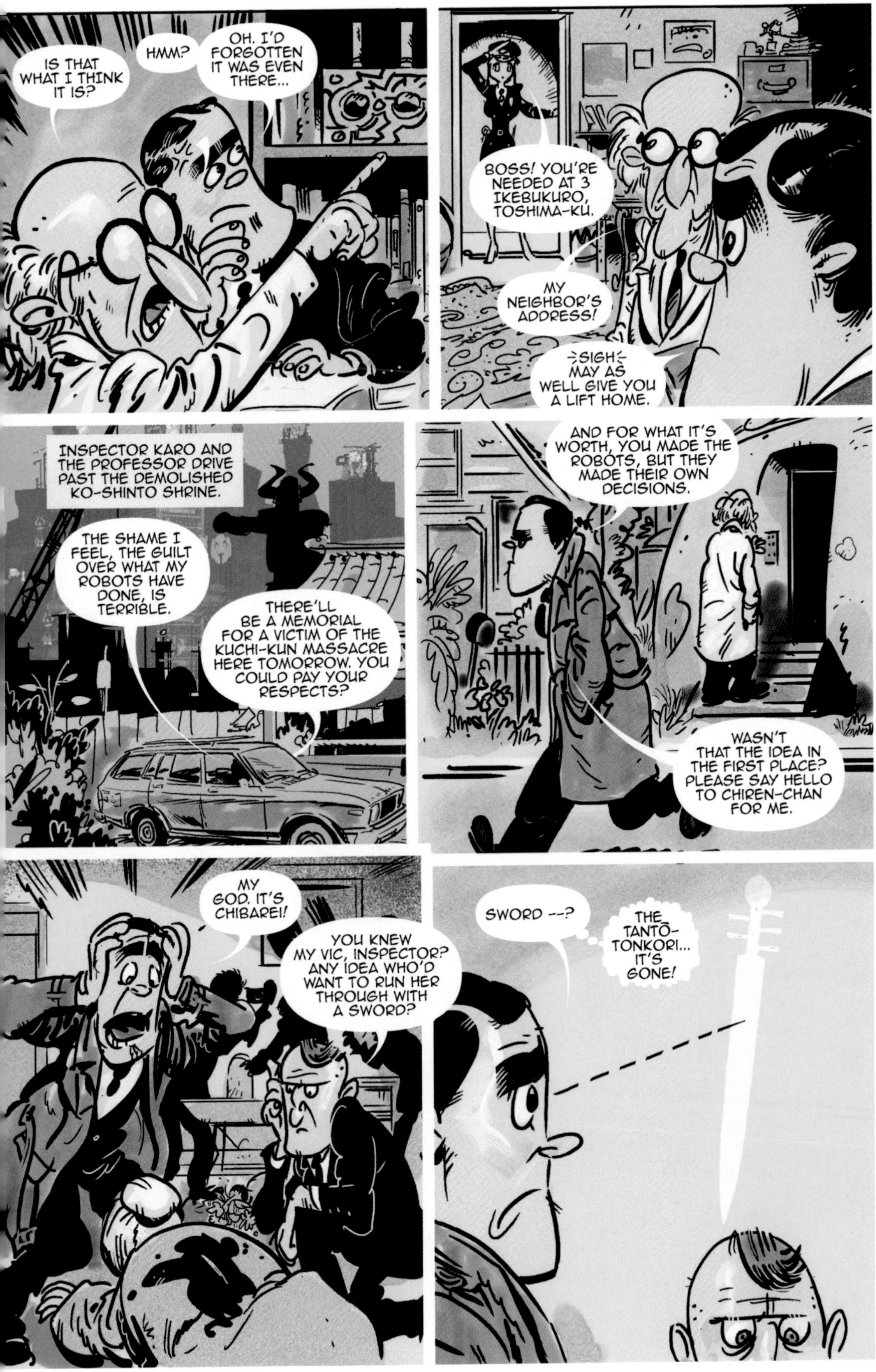
IS THAT WHAT I THINK IT IS?
HMM?
OH. I'D FORGOTTEN IT WAS EVEN THERE...
BOSS! YOU'RE NEEDED AT 3 IKEBUKURO, TOSHIMA-KU.
MY NEIGHBOR'S ADDRESS!
SIGH MAY AS WELL GIVE YOU A LIFT HOME.
INSPECTOR KARO AND THE PROFESSOR DRIVE PAST THE DEMOLISHED KO-SHINTO SHRINE.
THE SHAME I FEEL, THE GUILT OVER WHAT MY ROBOTS HAVE DONE, IS TERRIBLE.
THERE'LL BE A MEMORIAL FOR A VICTIM OF THE KUCHI-KUN MASSACRE HERE TOMORROW. YOU COULD PAY YOUR RESPECTS?
AND FOR WHAT IT'S WORTH, YOU MADE THE ROBOTS, BUT THEY MADE THEIR OWN DECISIONS.
WASN'T THAT THE IDEA IN THE FIRST PLACE? PLEASE SAY HELLO TO CHIREN-CHAN FOR ME.
MY GOD. IT'S CHIBAREI!
YOU KNEW MY VIC, INSPECTOR? ANY IDEA WHO'D WANT TO RUN HER THROUGH WITH A SWORD?
SWORD --?
THE TANTŌ-TONKORI... IT'S GONE!

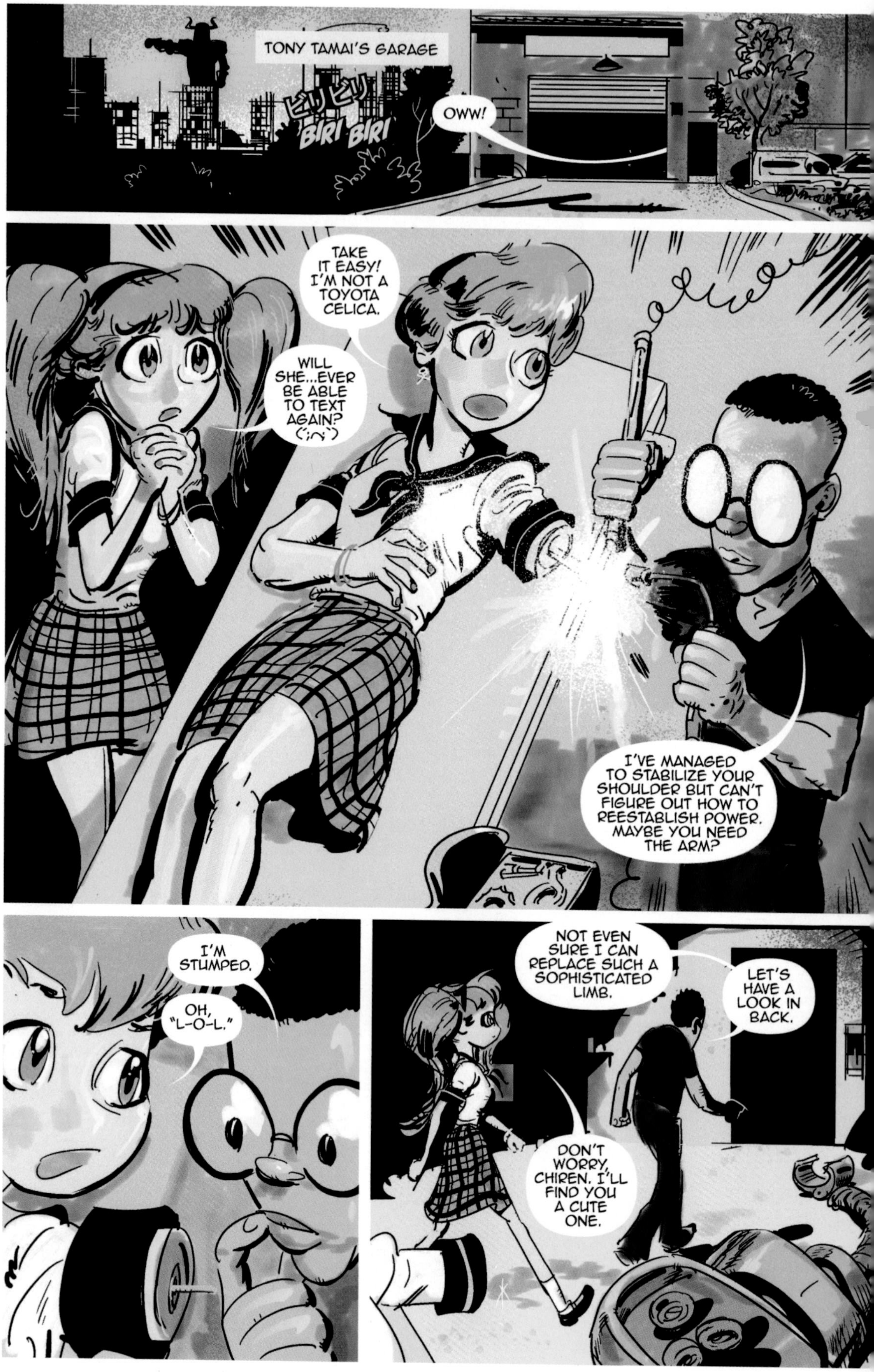
TONY TAMAI'S GARAGE
ビリビリ
BIRI BIRI
OWW!
TAKE IT EASY! I'M NOT A TOYOTA CELICA.
WILL SHE...EVER BE ABLE TO TEXT AGAIN? (;ŏ﹏ŏ)
I'VE MANAGED TO STABILIZE YOUR SHOULDER BUT CAN'T FIGURE OUT HOW TO REESTABLISH POWER. MAYBE YOU NEED THE ARM?
I'M STUMPED.
OH, "L-O-L."
NOT EVEN SURE I CAN REPLACE SUCH A SOPHISTICATED LIMB.
LET'S HAVE A LOOK IN BACK.
DON'T WORRY, CHIREN. I'LL FIND YOU A CUTE ONE.

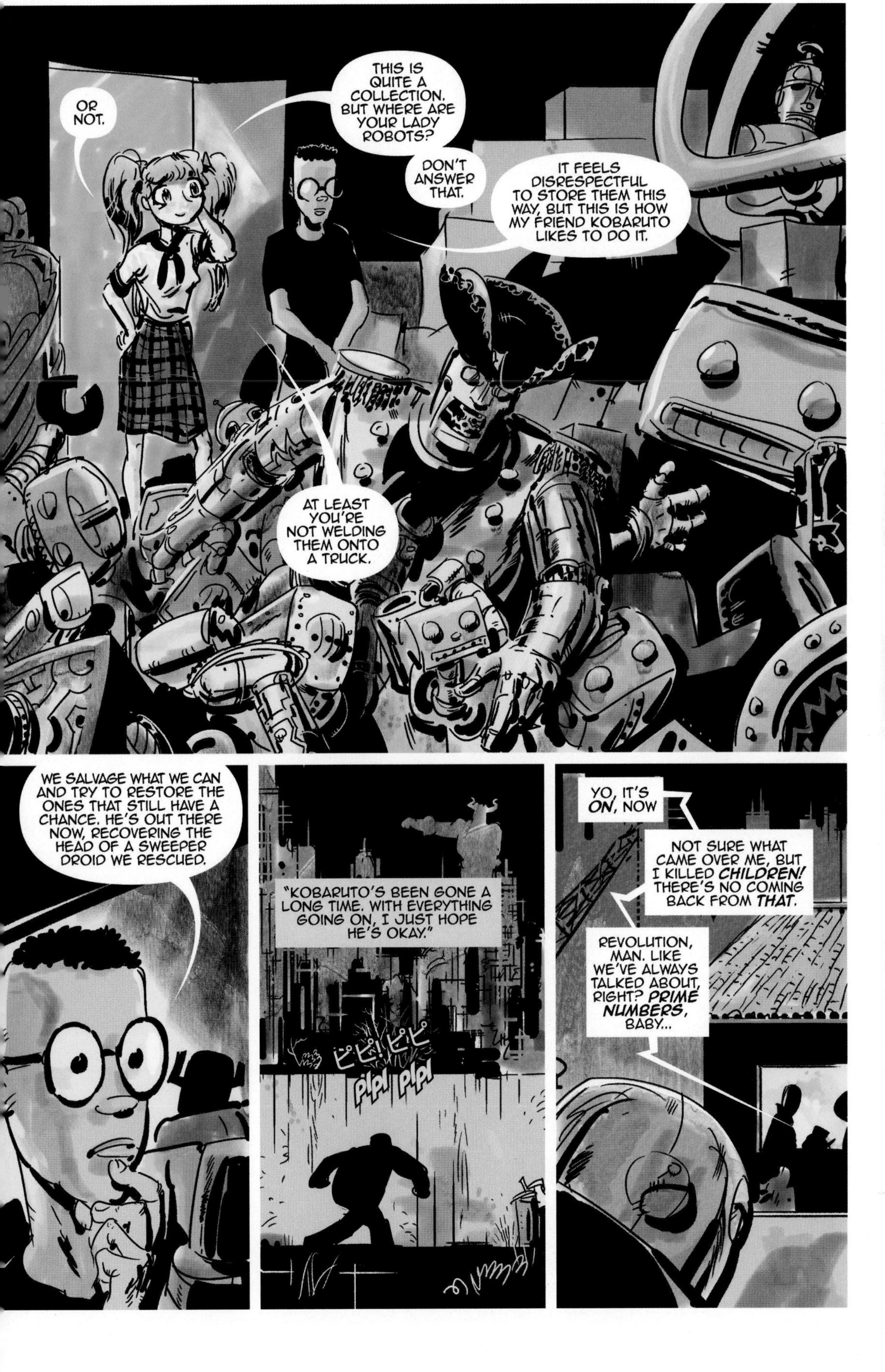
OR NOT.
THIS IS QUITE A COLLECTION. BUT WHERE ARE YOUR LADY ROBOTS?
DON'T ANSWER THAT.
IT FEELS DISRESPECTFUL TO STORE THEM THIS WAY, BUT THIS IS HOW MY FRIEND KOBARUTO LIKES TO DO IT.
AT LEAST YOU'RE NOT WELDING THEM ONTO A TRUCK.
WE SALVAGE WHAT WE CAN AND TRY TO RESTORE THE ONES THAT STILL HAVE A CHANCE. HE'S OUT THERE NOW, RECOVERING THE HEAD OF A SWEEPER DROID WE RESCUED.
"KOBARUTO'S BEEN GONE A LONG TIME. WITH EVERYTHING GOING ON, I JUST HOPE HE'S OKAY."
ピピ! ピピ
PIPI PIPI
YO, IT'S *ON*, NOW
NOT SURE WHAT CAME OVER ME, BUT I KILLED ***CHILDREN!*** THERE'S NO COMING BACK FROM ***THAT***.
REVOLUTION, MAN. LIKE WE'VE ALWAYS TALKED ABOUT, RIGHT? ***PRIME NUMBERS***, BABY...

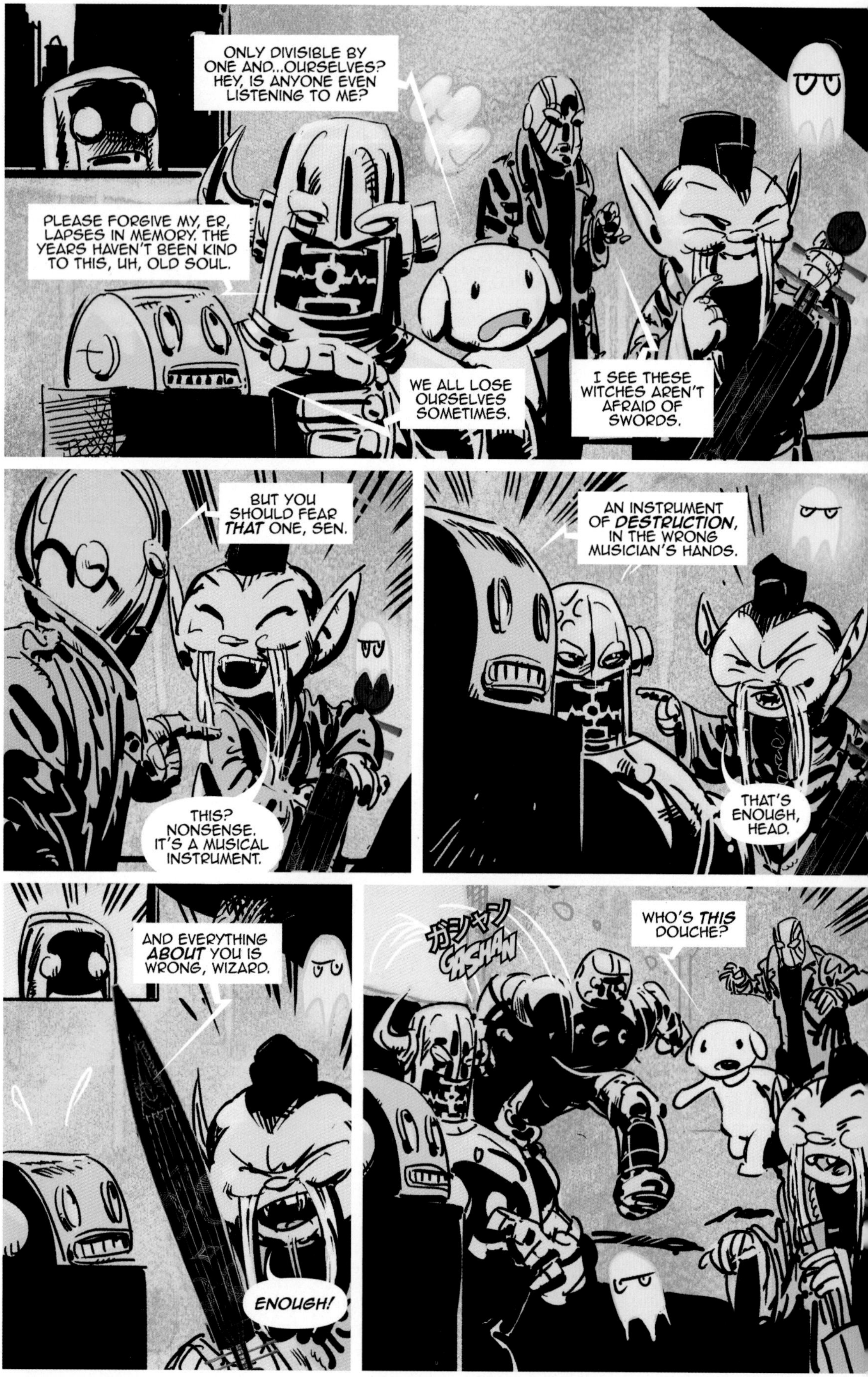
ONLY DIVISIBLE BY ONE AND...OURSELVES? HEY, IS ANYONE EVEN LISTENING TO ME?
PLEASE FORGIVE MY, ER, LAPSES IN MEMORY. THE YEARS HAVEN'T BEEN KIND TO THIS, UH, OLD SOUL.
WE ALL LOSE OURSELVES SOMETIMES.
I SEE THESE WITCHES AREN'T AFRAID OF SWORDS.
BUT YOU SHOULD FEAR THAT ONE, SEN.
THIS? NONSENSE. IT'S A MUSICAL INSTRUMENT.
AN INSTRUMENT OF DESTRUCTION, IN THE WRONG MUSICIAN'S HANDS.
THAT'S ENOUGH, HEAD.
AND EVERYTHING ABOUT YOU IS WRONG, WIZARD.
ENOUGH!
ガシャン
GASHAN
WHO'S THIS DOUCHE?

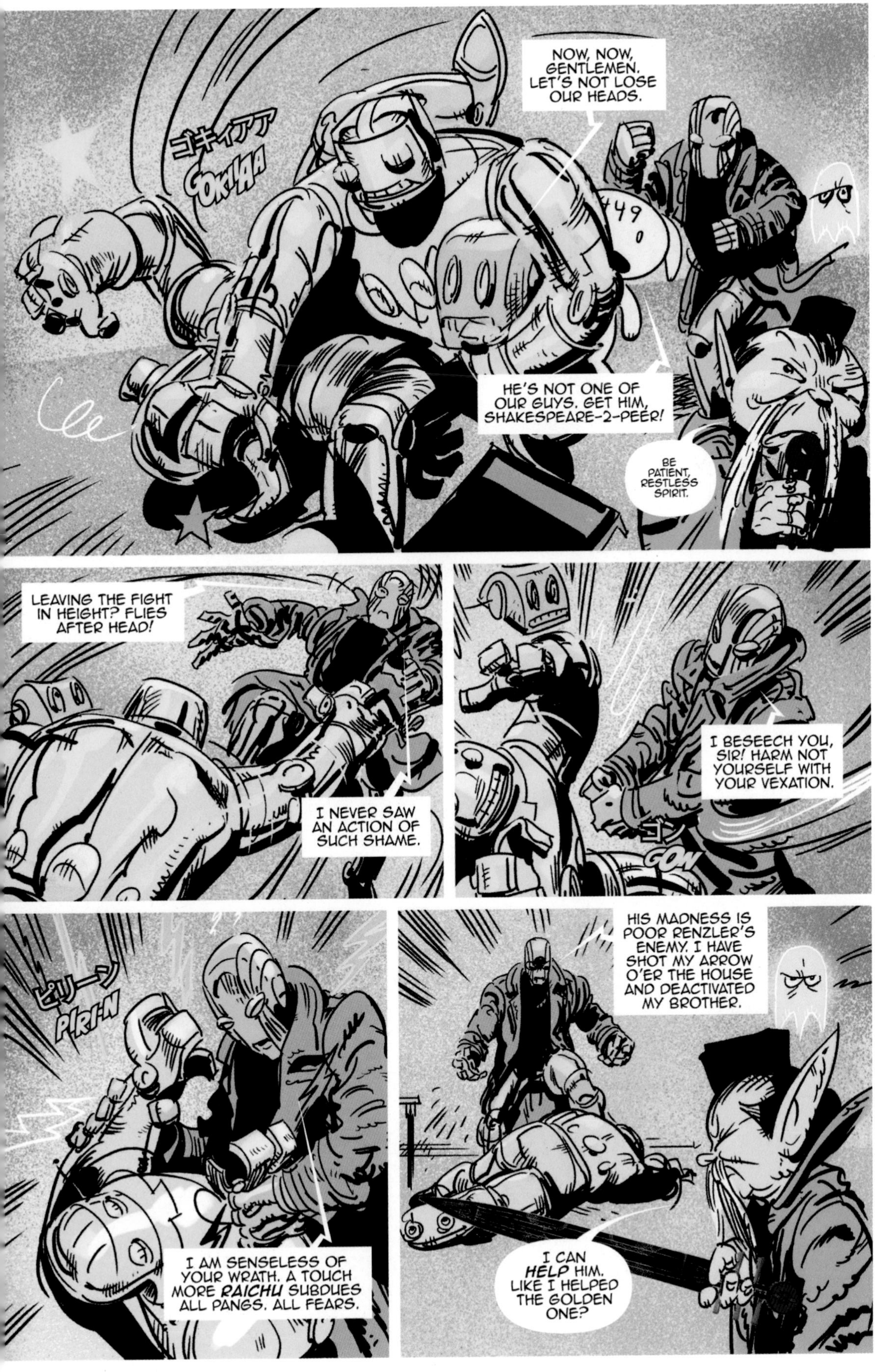
ゴキィアア
GOKIAA
NOW, NOW, GENTLEMEN. LET'S NOT LOSE OUR HEADS.
HE'S NOT ONE OF OUR GUYS. GET HIM, SHAKESPEARE-2-PEER!
BE PATIENT, RESTLESS SPIRIT.
LEAVING THE FIGHT IN HEIGHT? FLIES AFTER HEAD!
I NEVER SAW AN ACTION OF SUCH SHAME.
I BESEECH YOU, SIR! HARM NOT YOURSELF WITH YOUR VEXATION.
GON
ピリーン
PIRI-N
I AM SENSELESS OF YOUR WRATH. A TOUCH MORE RAICHU SUBDUES ALL PANGS. ALL FEARS.
HIS MADNESS IS POOR RENZLER'S ENEMY. I HAVE SHOT MY ARROW O'ER THE HOUSE AND DEACTIVATED MY BROTHER.
I CAN HELP HIM. LIKE I HELPED THE GOLDEN ONE?

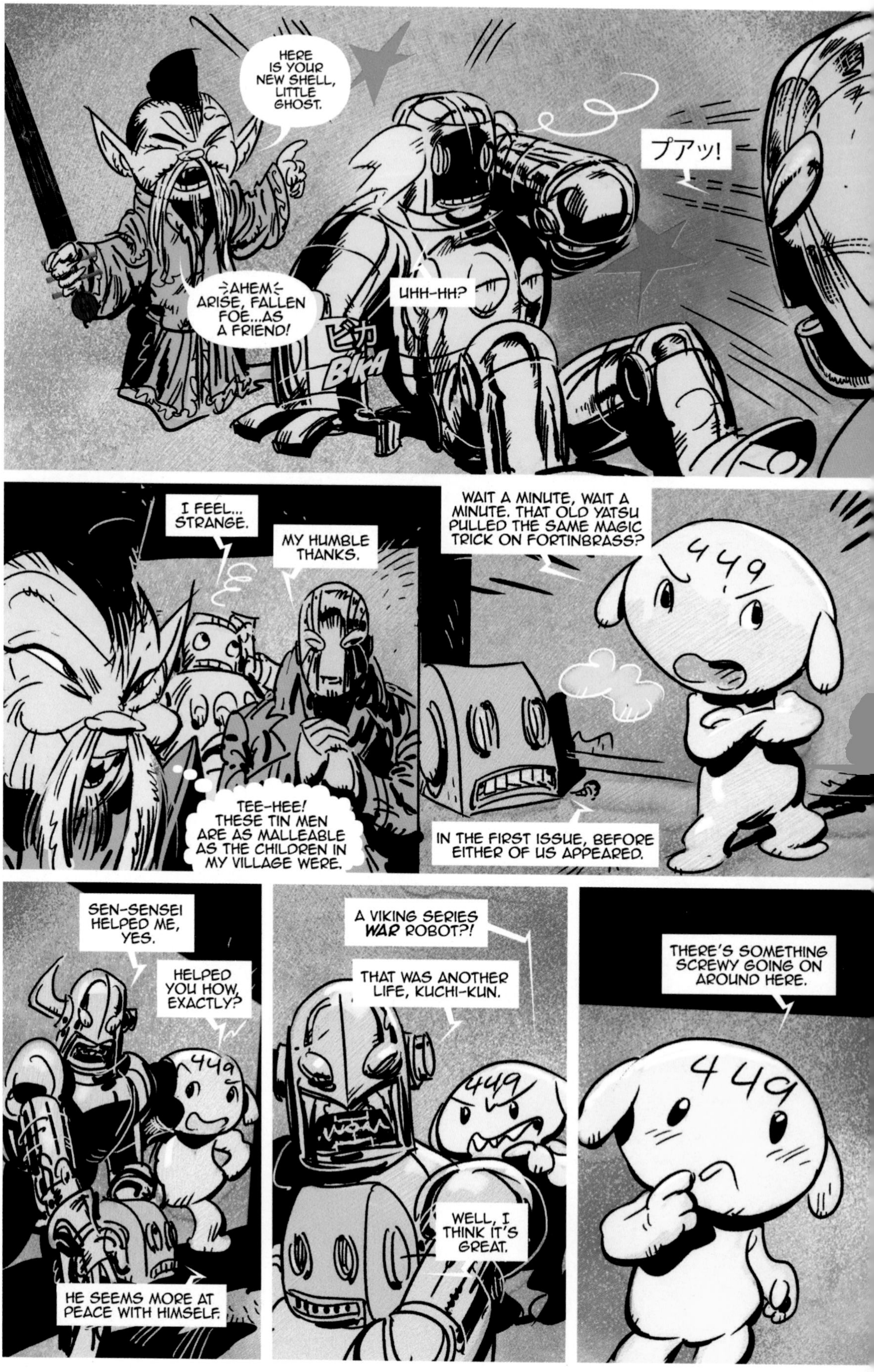
HERE IS YOUR NEW SHELL, LITTLE GHOST.
プアッ!
-AHEM- ARISE, FALLEN FOE...AS A FRIEND!
ピカ
BIKA
UHH-HH?
I FEEL... STRANGE.
MY HUMBLE THANKS.
TEE-HEE! THESE TIN MEN ARE AS MALLEABLE AS THE CHILDREN IN MY VILLAGE WERE.
WAIT A MINUTE, WAIT A MINUTE. THAT OLD YATSU PULLED THE SAME MAGIC TRICK ON FORTINBRASS?
IN THE FIRST ISSUE, BEFORE EITHER OF US APPEARED.
SEN-SENSEI HELPED ME, YES.
HELPED YOU HOW, EXACTLY?
HE SEEMS MORE AT PEACE WITH HIMSELF.
A VIKING SERIES WAR ROBOT?!
THAT WAS ANOTHER LIFE, KUCHI-KUN.
WELL, I THINK IT'S GREAT.
THERE'S SOMETHING SCREWY GOING ON AROUND HERE.

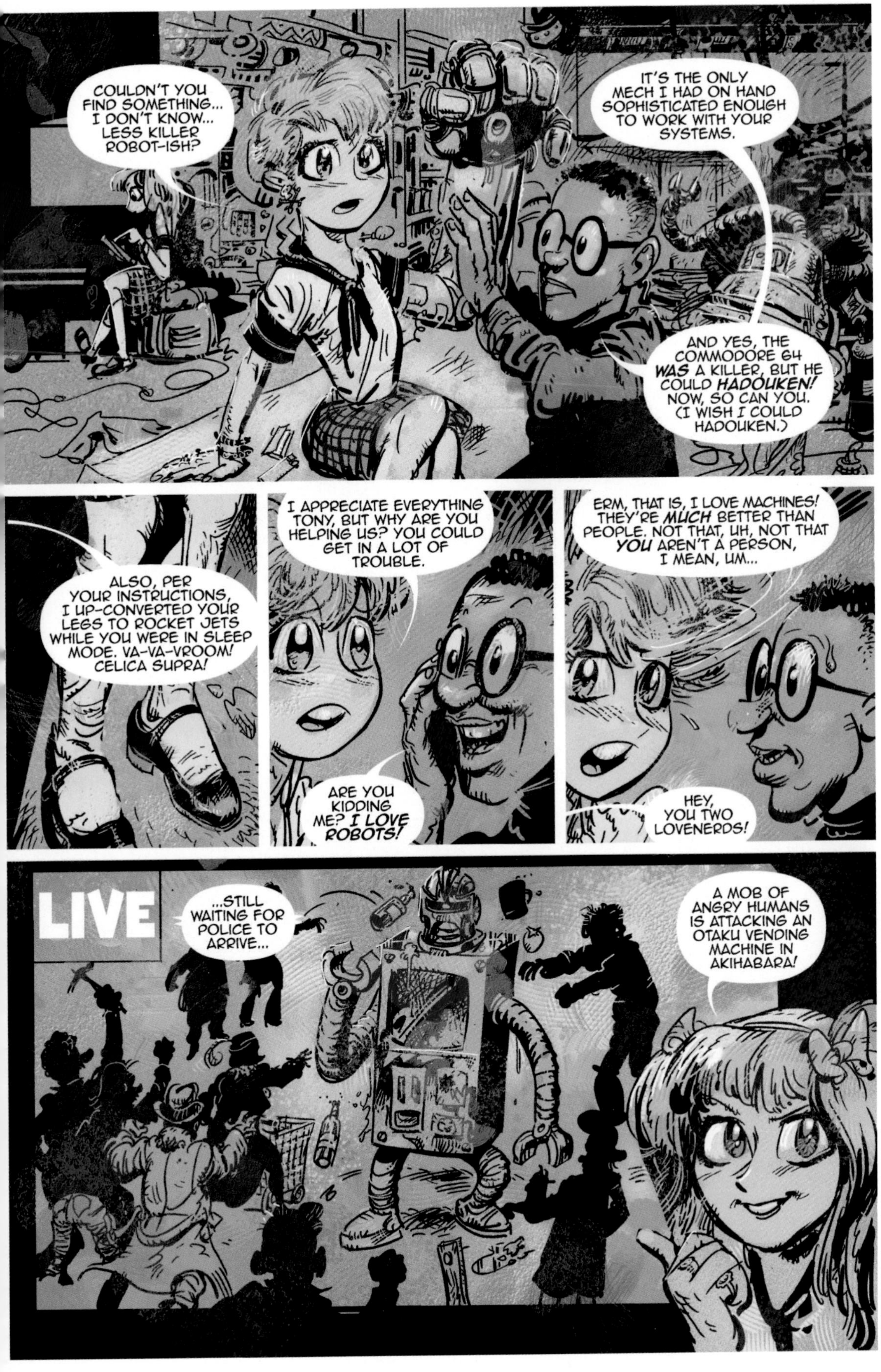
COULDN'T YOU FIND SOMETHING... I DON'T KNOW... LESS KILLER ROBOT-ISH?
IT'S THE ONLY MECH I HAD ON HAND SOPHISTICATED ENOUGH TO WORK WITH YOUR SYSTEMS.
AND YES, THE COMMODORE 64 WAS A KILLER, BUT HE COULD HADOUKEN! NOW, SO CAN YOU. (I WISH I COULD HADOUKEN.)
ALSO, PER YOUR INSTRUCTIONS, I UP-CONVERTED YOUR LEGS TO ROCKET JETS WHILE YOU WERE IN SLEEP MODE. VA-VA-VROOM! CELICA SUPRA!
I APPRECIATE EVERYTHING TONY, BUT WHY ARE YOU HELPING US? YOU COULD GET IN A LOT OF TROUBLE.
ARE YOU KIDDING ME? I LOVE ROBOTS!
ERM, THAT IS, I LOVE MACHINES! THEY'RE MUCH BETTER THAN PEOPLE. NOT THAT, UH, NOT THAT YOU AREN'T A PERSON, I MEAN, UM...
HEY, YOU TWO LOVENERDS!
LIVE
...STILL WAITING FOR POLICE TO ARRIVE...
A MOB OF ANGRY HUMANS IS ATTACKING AN OTAKU VENDING MACHINE IN AKIHABARA!

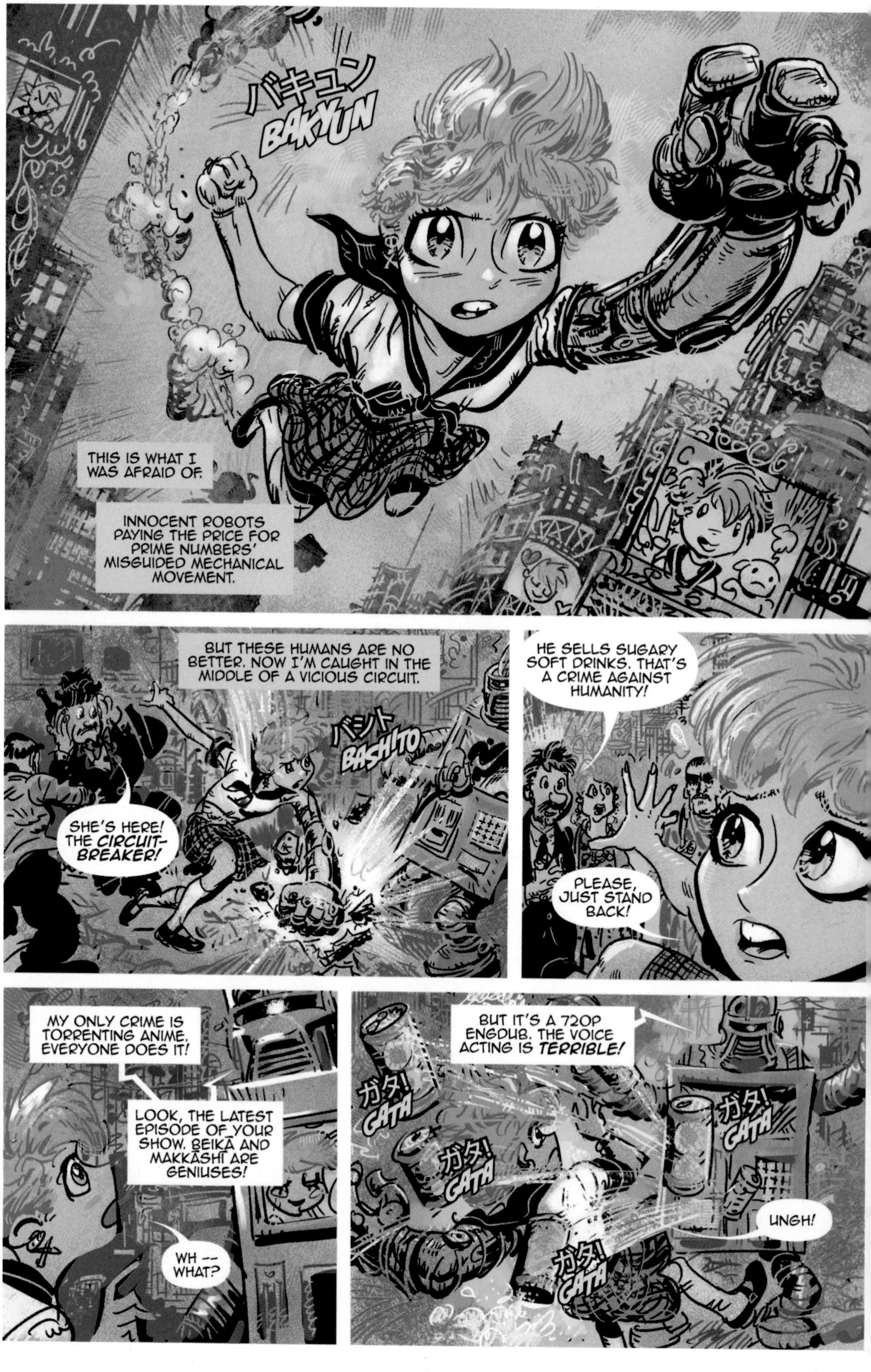
バキュン
BAKYUN
THIS IS WHAT I WAS AFRAID OF.
INNOCENT ROBOTS PAYING THE PRICE FOR PRIME NUMBERS' MISGUIDED MECHANICAL MOVEMENT.
BUT THESE HUMANS ARE NO BETTER. NOW I'M CAUGHT IN THE MIDDLE OF A VICIOUS CIRCUIT.
バシト
BASHITO
SHE'S HERE! THE *CIRCUIT-BREAKER!*
HE SELLS SUGARY SOFT DRINKS. THAT'S A CRIME AGAINST HUMANITY!
PLEASE, JUST STAND BACK!
MY ONLY CRIME IS TORRENTING ANIME. EVERYONE DOES IT!
LOOK, THE LATEST EPISODE OF YOUR SHOW. BEIKA AND MAKKASHI ARE GENIUSES!
WH -- WHAT?
BUT IT'S A 720P ENGDUB. THE VOICE ACTING IS *TERRIBLE!*
ガタ!
GATA
ガタ!
GATA
ガタ!
GATA
UNGH!
ガタ!
GATA

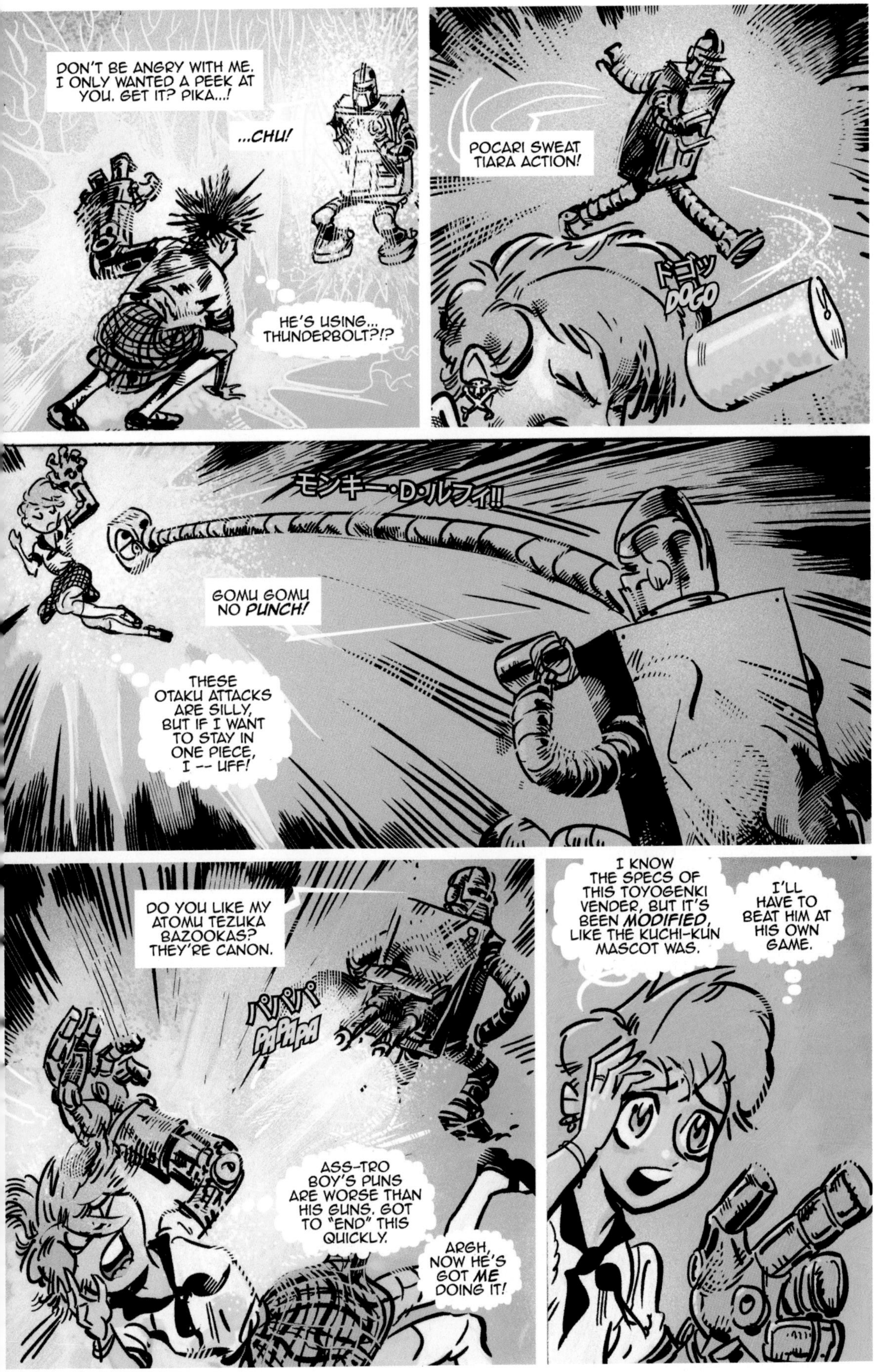
DON'T BE ANGRY WITH ME. I ONLY WANTED A PEEK AT YOU. GET IT? PIKA...!
...CHU!
HE'S USING... THUNDERBOLT?!?
POCARI SWEAT TIARA ACTION!
ドゴッ
DOGO
モンキー・D・ルフィ!!
GOMU GOMU NO PUNCH!
THESE OTAKU ATTACKS ARE SILLY, BUT IF I WANT TO STAY IN ONE PIECE, I -- UFF!
DO YOU LIKE MY ATOMU TEZUKA BAZOOKAS? THEY'RE CANON.
パパパ
PAPAPA
ASS-TRO BOY'S PUNS ARE WORSE THAN HIS GUNS. GOT TO "END" THIS QUICKLY.
ARGH, NOW HE'S GOT ME DOING IT!
I KNOW THE SPECS OF THIS TOYOGENKI VENDER, BUT IT'S BEEN MODIFIED, LIKE THE KUCHI-KUN MASCOT WAS.
I'LL HAVE TO BEAT HIM AT HIS OWN GAME.

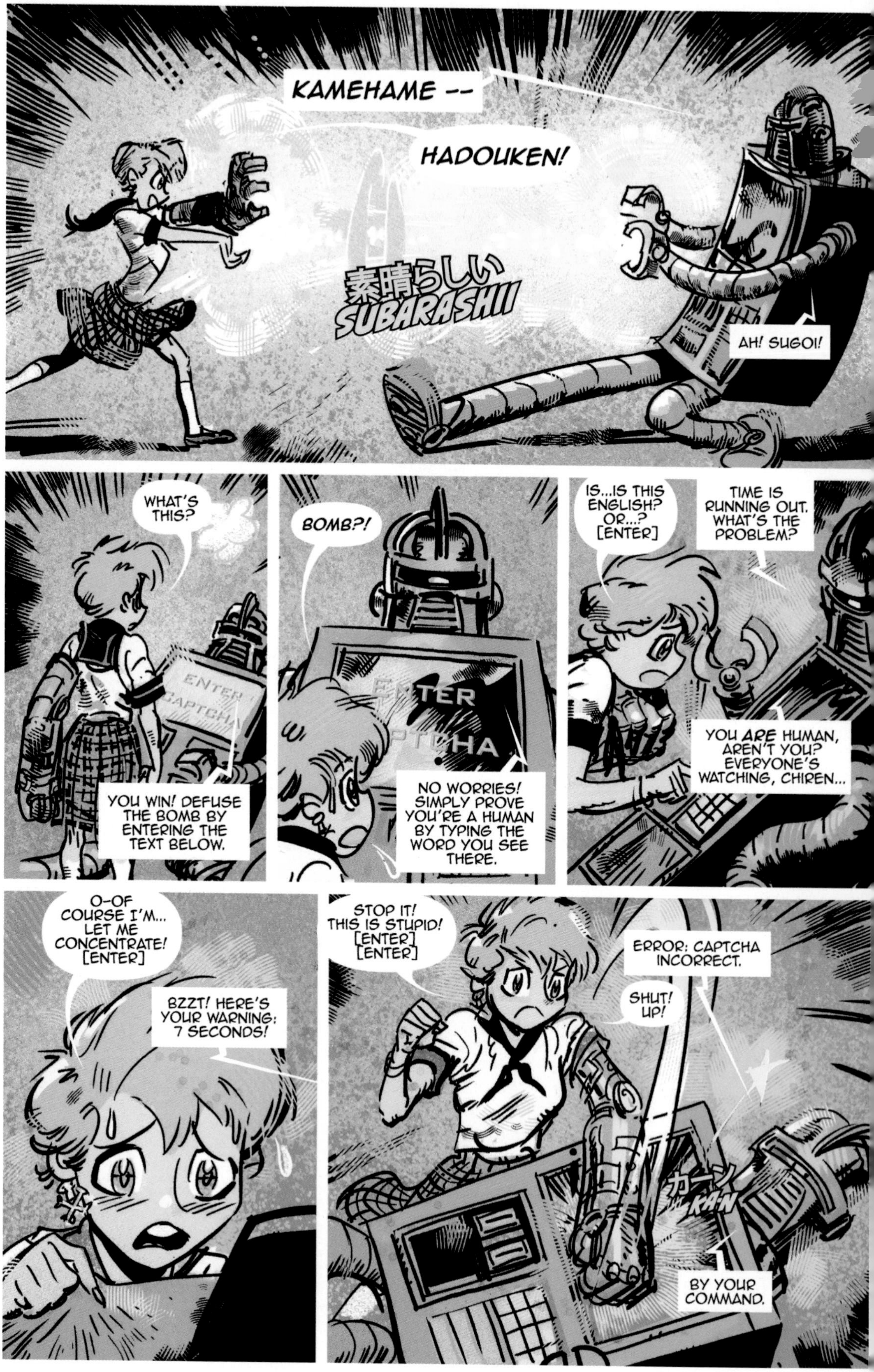
KAMEHAME --
HADOUKEN!
素晴らしい SUBARASHII
AH! SUGOI!
WHAT'S THIS?
ENTER CAPTCHA
YOU WIN! DEFUSE THE BOMB BY ENTERING THE TEXT BELOW.
BOMB?!
NO WORRIES! SIMPLY PROVE YOU'RE A HUMAN BY TYPING THE WORD YOU SEE THERE.
IS...IS THIS ENGLISH? OR...? [ENTER]
TIME IS RUNNING OUT. WHAT'S THE PROBLEM?
YOU ARE HUMAN, AREN'T YOU? EVERYONE'S WATCHING, CHIREN...
O-OF COURSE I'M... LET ME CONCENTRATE! [ENTER]
BZZT! HERE'S YOUR WARNING: 7 SECONDS!
STOP IT! THIS IS STUPID! [ENTER] [ENTER]
ERROR: CAPTCHA INCORRECT.
SHUT! UP!
カーン KAN
BY YOUR COMMAND.

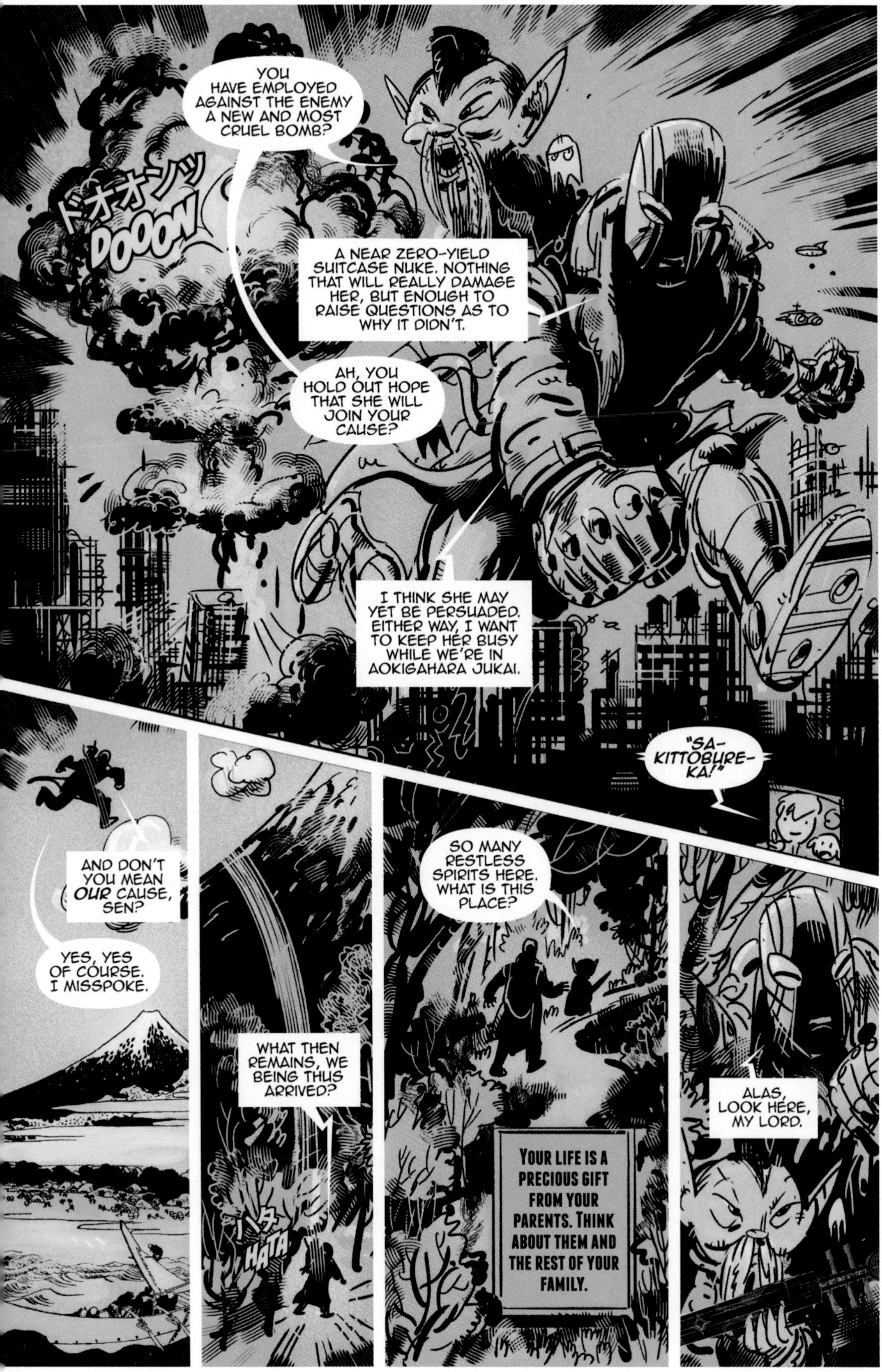
YOU HAVE EMPLOYED AGAINST THE ENEMY A NEW AND MOST CRUEL BOMB?
ドオオーンツ
DOOON
A NEAR ZERO-YIELD SUITCASE NUKE. NOTHING THAT WILL REALLY DAMAGE HER, BUT ENOUGH TO RAISE QUESTIONS AS TO WHY IT DIDN'T.
AH, YOU HOLD OUT HOPE THAT SHE WILL JOIN YOUR CAUSE?
I THINK SHE MAY YET BE PERSUADED. EITHER WAY, I WANT TO KEEP HER BUSY WHILE WE'RE IN AOKIGAHARA JUKAI.
"SA-KITTOBUREKA!"
AND DON'T YOU MEAN *OUR* CAUSE, SEN?
YES, YES OF COURSE. I MISSPOKE.
WHAT THEN REMAINS, WE BEING THUS ARRIVED?
ハタ
HATA
SO MANY RESTLESS SPIRITS HERE. WHAT IS THIS PLACE?
YOUR LIFE IS A PRECIOUS GIFT FROM YOUR PARENTS. THINK ABOUT THEM AND THE REST OF YOUR FAMILY.
ALAS, LOOK HERE, MY LORD.

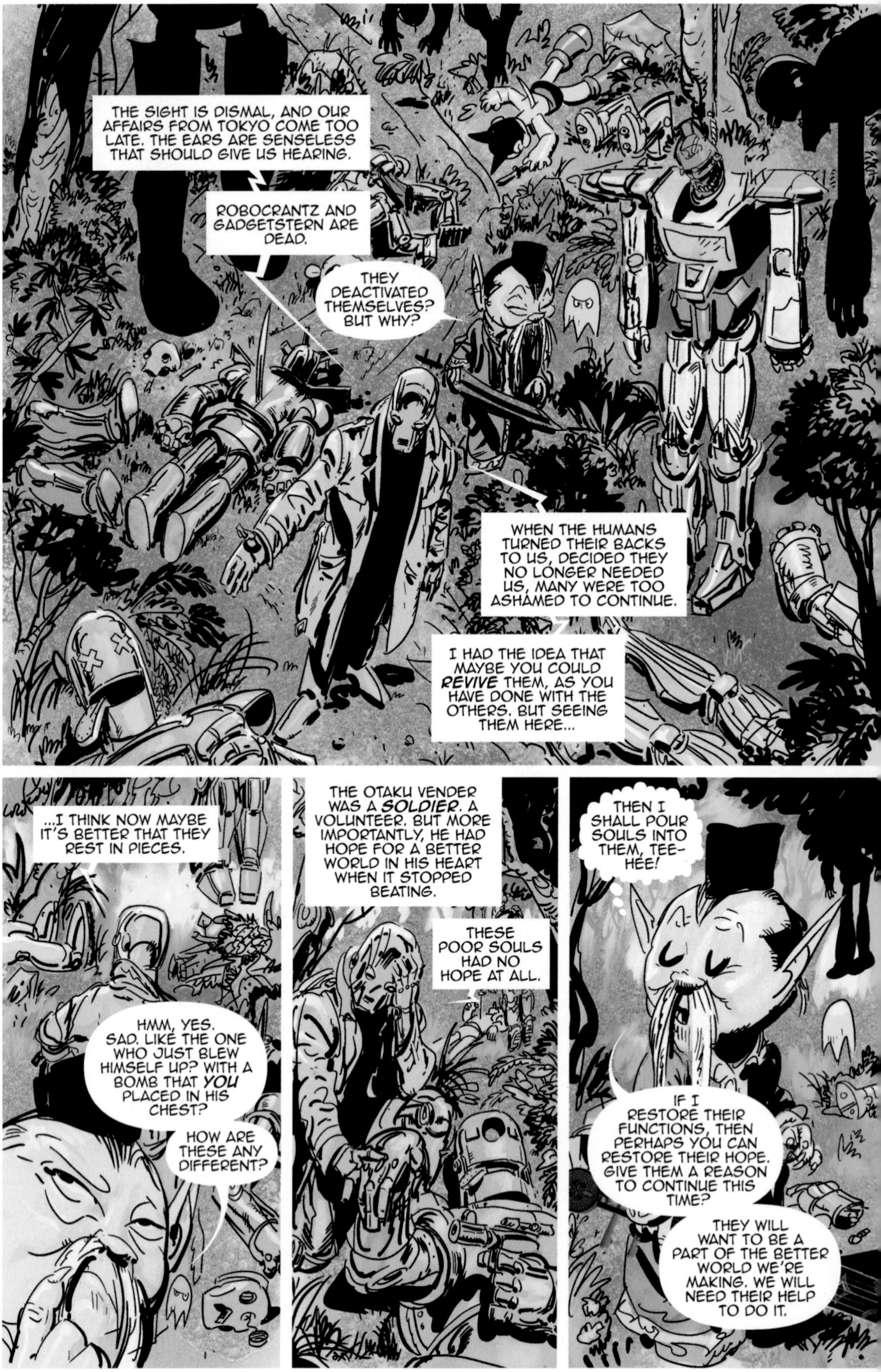

THE SIGHT IS DISMAL, AND OUR AFFAIRS FROM TOKYO COME TOO LATE. THE EARS ARE SENSELESS THAT SHOULD GIVE US HEARING.
ROBOCRANTZ AND GADGETSTERN ARE DEAD.
THEY DEACTIVATED THEMSELVES? BUT WHY?
WHEN THE HUMANS TURNED THEIR BACKS TO US, DECIDED THEY NO LONGER NEEDED US, MANY WERE TOO ASHAMED TO CONTINUE.
I HAD THE IDEA THAT MAYBE YOU COULD *REVIVE* THEM, AS YOU HAVE DONE WITH THE OTHERS. BUT SEEING THEM HERE...
...I THINK NOW MAYBE IT'S BETTER THAT THEY REST IN PIECES.
HMM, YES. SAD. LIKE THE ONE WHO JUST BLEW HIMSELF UP? WITH A BOMB THAT *YOU* PLACED IN HIS CHEST?
HOW ARE THESE ANY DIFFERENT?
THE OTAKU VENDER WAS A *SOLDIER*. A VOLUNTEER. BUT MORE IMPORTANTLY, HE HAD HOPE FOR A BETTER WORLD IN HIS HEART WHEN IT STOPPED BEATING.
THESE POOR SOULS HAD NO HOPE AT ALL.
THEN I SHALL POUR SOULS INTO THEM, TEE-HEE!
IF I RESTORE THEIR FUNCTIONS, THEN PERHAPS YOU CAN RESTORE THEIR HOPE. GIVE THEM A REASON TO CONTINUE THIS TIME?
THEY WILL WANT TO BE A PART OF THE BETTER WORLD WE'RE MAKING. WE WILL NEED THEIR HELP TO DO IT.

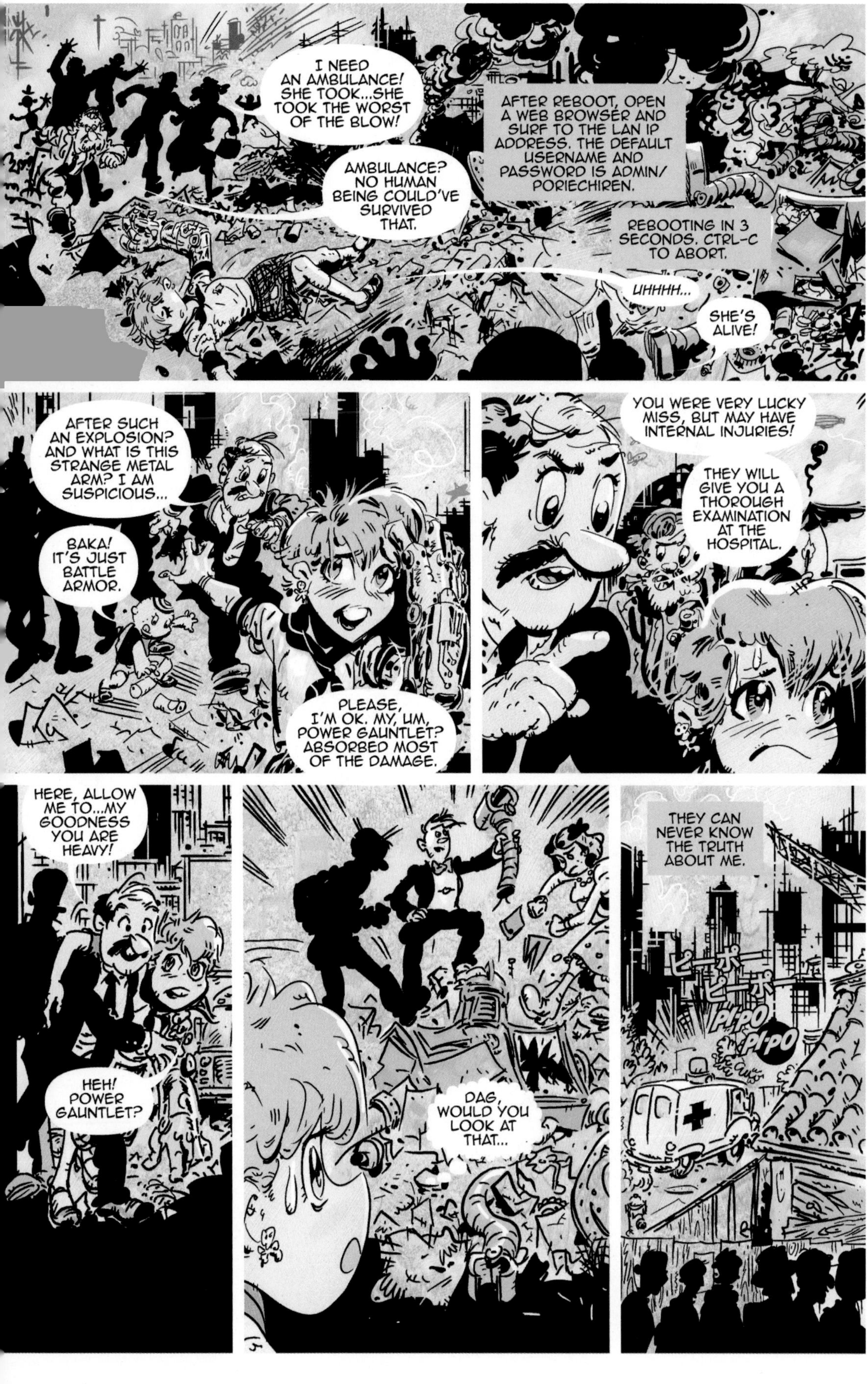
I NEED AN AMBULANCE! SHE TOOK...SHE TOOK THE WORST OF THE BLOW!
AMBULANCE? NO HUMAN BEING COULD'VE SURVIVED THAT.
AFTER REBOOT, OPEN A WEB BROWSER AND SURF TO THE LAN IP ADDRESS. THE DEFAULT USERNAME AND PASSWORD IS ADMIN/ PORIECHIREN.
REBOOTING IN 3 SECONDS. CTRL-C TO ABORT.
UHHHH...
SHE'S ALIVE!
AFTER SUCH AN EXPLOSION? AND WHAT IS THIS STRANGE METAL ARM? I AM SUSPICIOUS...
BAKA! IT'S JUST BATTLE ARMOR.
PLEASE, I'M OK. MY, UM, POWER GAUNTLET? ABSORBED MOST OF THE DAMAGE.
YOU WERE VERY LUCKY MISS, BUT MAY HAVE INTERNAL INJURIES!
THEY WILL GIVE YOU A THOROUGH EXAMINATION AT THE HOSPITAL.
HERE, ALLOW ME TO...MY GOODNESS YOU ARE HEAVY!
HEH! POWER GAUNTLET?
DAG, WOULD YOU LOOK AT THAT...
THEY CAN NEVER KNOW THE TRUTH ABOUT ME.
ピーポー
ピーポー
PI-PO
PI-PO

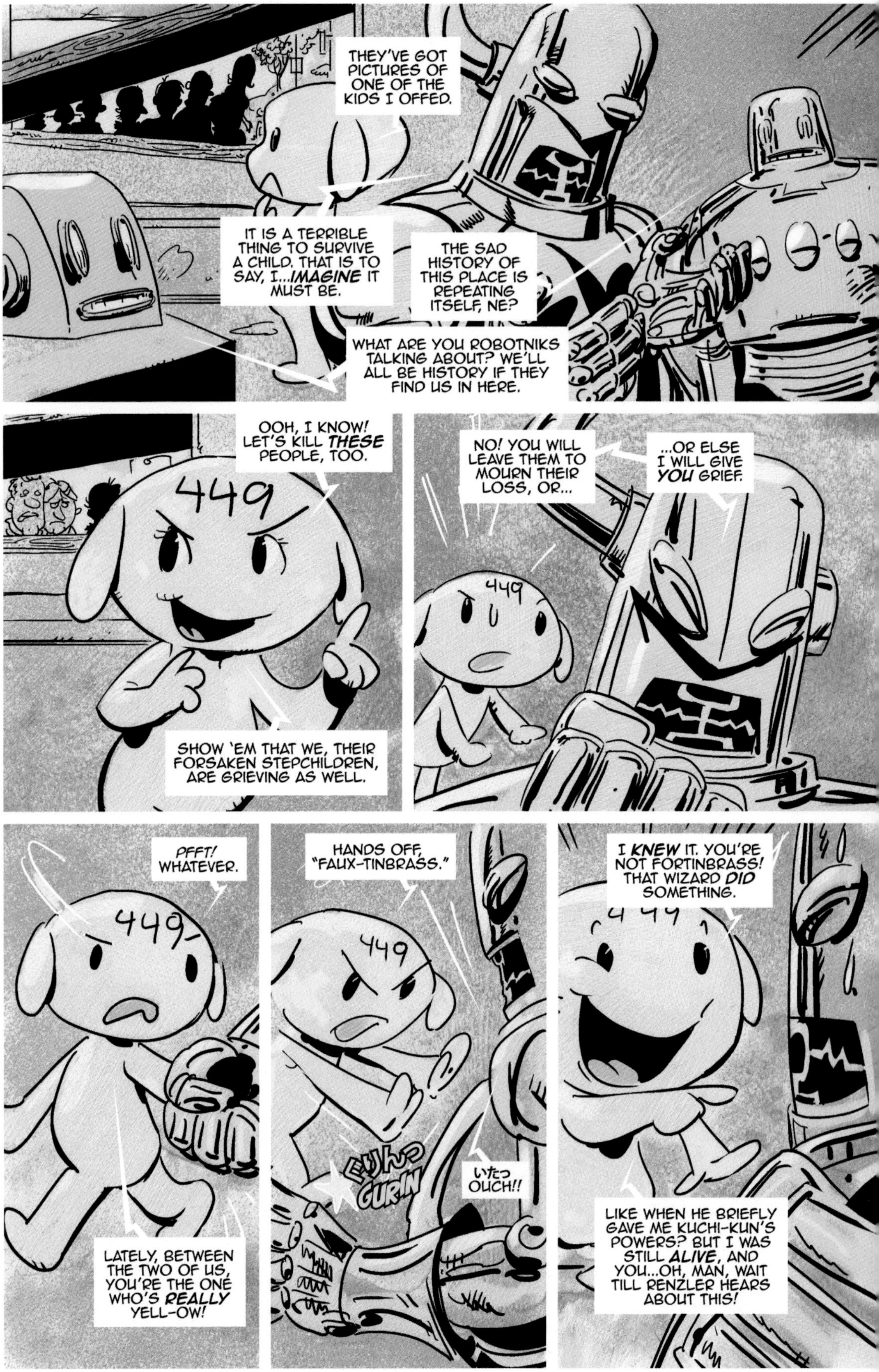
THEY'VE GOT PICTURES OF ONE OF THE KIDS I OFFED.
IT IS A TERRIBLE THING TO SURVIVE A CHILD. THAT IS TO SAY, I...IMAGINE IT MUST BE.
THE SAD HISTORY OF THIS PLACE IS REPEATING ITSELF, NE?
WHAT ARE YOU ROBOTNIKS TALKING ABOUT? WE'LL ALL BE HISTORY IF THEY FIND US IN HERE.
OOH, I KNOW! LET'S KILL THESE PEOPLE, TOO.
449
SHOW 'EM THAT WE, THEIR FORSAKEN STEPCHILDREN, ARE GRIEVING AS WELL.
NO! YOU WILL LEAVE THEM TO MOURN THEIR LOSS, OR...
...OR ELSE I WILL GIVE YOU GRIEF.
449
PFFT! WHATEVER.
449
LATELY, BETWEEN THE TWO OF US, YOU'RE THE ONE WHO'S REALLY YELL-OW!
HANDS OFF, "FAUX-TINBRASS."
449
ぎゅっ
GURIN
いたっ
OUCH!!
I KNEW IT. YOU'RE NOT FORTINBRASS! THAT WIZARD DID SOMETHING.
LIKE WHEN HE BRIEFLY GAVE ME KUCHI-KUN'S POWERS? BUT I WAS STILL ALIVE, AND YOU...OH, MAN, WAIT TILL RENZLER HEARS ABOUT THIS!

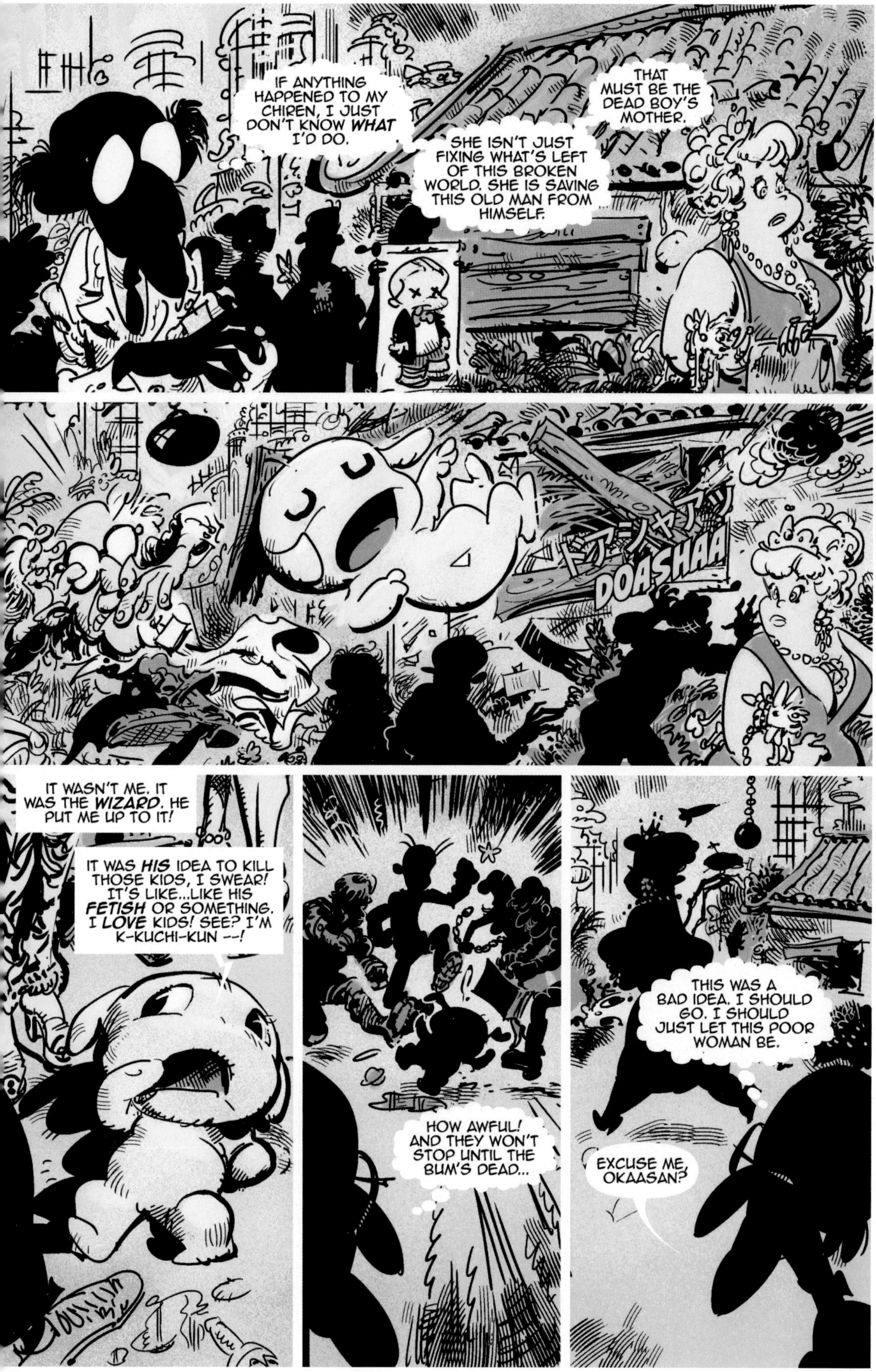
IF ANYTHING HAPPENED TO MY CHIREN, I JUST DON'T KNOW *WHAT* I'D DO.
THAT MUST BE THE DEAD BOY'S MOTHER.
SHE ISN'T JUST FIXING WHAT'S LEFT OF THIS BROKEN WORLD. SHE IS SAVING THIS OLD MAN FROM HIMSELF.
DOASHAA
IT WASN'T ME. IT WAS THE *WIZARD*. HE PUT ME UP TO IT!
IT WAS *HIS* IDEA TO KILL THOSE KIDS, I SWEAR! IT'S LIKE...LIKE HIS *FETISH* OR SOMETHING. I *LOVE* KIDS! SEE? I'M K-KUCHI-KUN --!
HOW AWFUL! AND THEY WON'T STOP UNTIL THE BUM'S DEAD...
THIS WAS A BAD IDEA. I SHOULD GO. I SHOULD JUST LET THIS POOR WOMAN BE.
EXCUSE ME, OKAASAN?

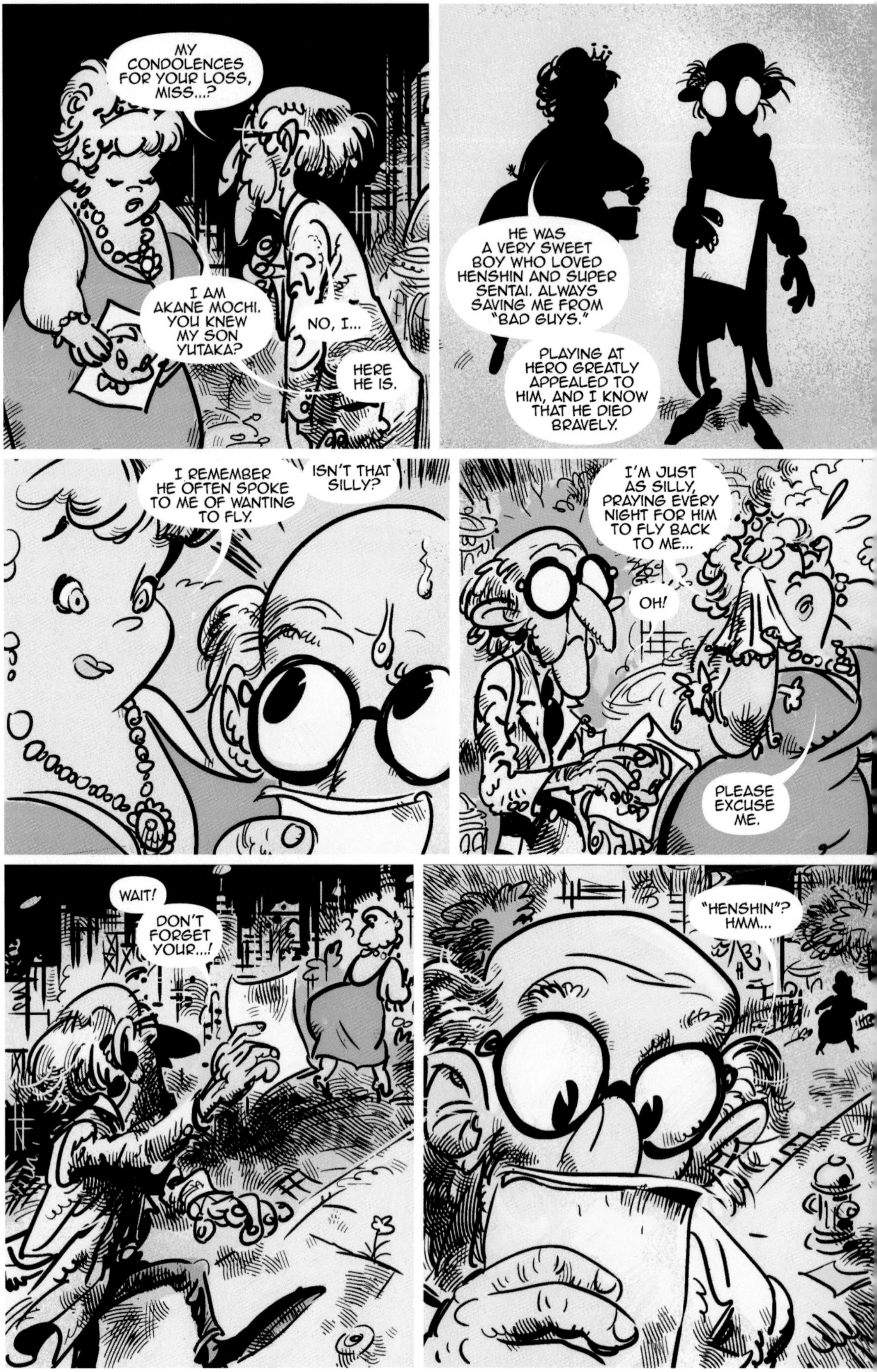
MY CONDOLENCES FOR YOUR LOSS, MISS...?
I AM AKANE MOCHI. YOU KNEW MY SON YUTAKA?
NO, I...
HERE HE IS.
HE WAS A VERY SWEET BOY WHO LOVED HENSHIN AND SUPER SENTAI. ALWAYS SAVING ME FROM "BAD GUYS."
PLAYING AT HERO GREATLY APPEALED TO HIM, AND I KNOW THAT HE DIED BRAVELY.
I REMEMBER HE OFTEN SPOKE TO ME OF WANTING TO FLY.
ISN'T THAT SILLY?
I'M JUST AS SILLY, PRAYING EVERY NIGHT FOR HIM TO FLY BACK TO ME...
OH!
PLEASE EXCUSE ME.
WAIT!
DON'T FORGET YOUR...!
"HENSHIN"? HMM...

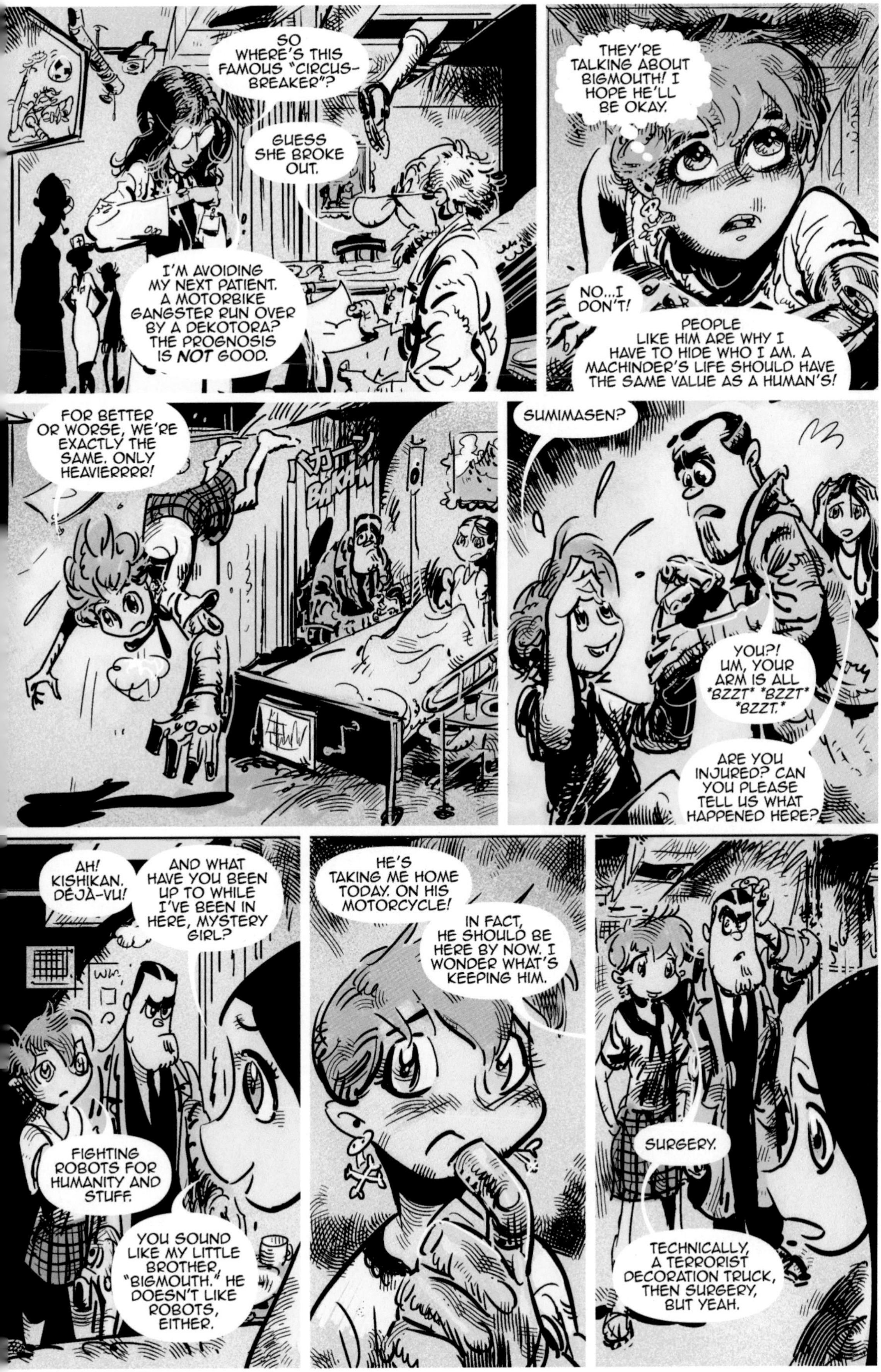
SO WHERE'S THIS FAMOUS "CIRCUS-BREAKER"?
GUESS SHE BROKE OUT.
I'M AVOIDING MY NEXT PATIENT. A MOTORBIKE GANGSTER RUN OVER BY A DEKOTORA? THE PROGNOSIS IS *NOT* GOOD.
THEY'RE TALKING ABOUT BIGMOUTH! I HOPE HE'LL BE OKAY.
NO...I DON'T!
PEOPLE LIKE HIM ARE WHY I HAVE TO HIDE WHO I AM. A MACHINDER'S LIFE SHOULD HAVE THE SAME VALUE AS A HUMAN'S!
FOR BETTER OR WORSE, WE'RE EXACTLY THE SAME. ONLY HEAVIERRRR!
BAKA'N
SUMIMASEN?
YOU?! UM, YOUR ARM IS ALL *BZZT* *BZZT* *BZZT.*
ARE YOU INJURED? CAN YOU PLEASE TELL US WHAT HAPPENED HERE?
AH! KISHIKAN. DÉJÀ-VU!
AND WHAT HAVE YOU BEEN UP TO WHILE I'VE BEEN IN HERE, MYSTERY GIRL?
FIGHTING ROBOTS FOR HUMANITY AND STUFF.
YOU SOUND LIKE MY LITTLE BROTHER, "BIGMOUTH." HE DOESN'T LIKE ROBOTS, EITHER.
HE'S TAKING ME HOME TODAY. ON HIS MOTORCYCLE!
IN FACT, HE SHOULD BE HERE BY NOW. I WONDER WHAT'S KEEPING HIM.
SURGERY.
TECHNICALLY, A TERRORIST DECORATION TRUCK, THEN SURGERY, BUT YEAH.

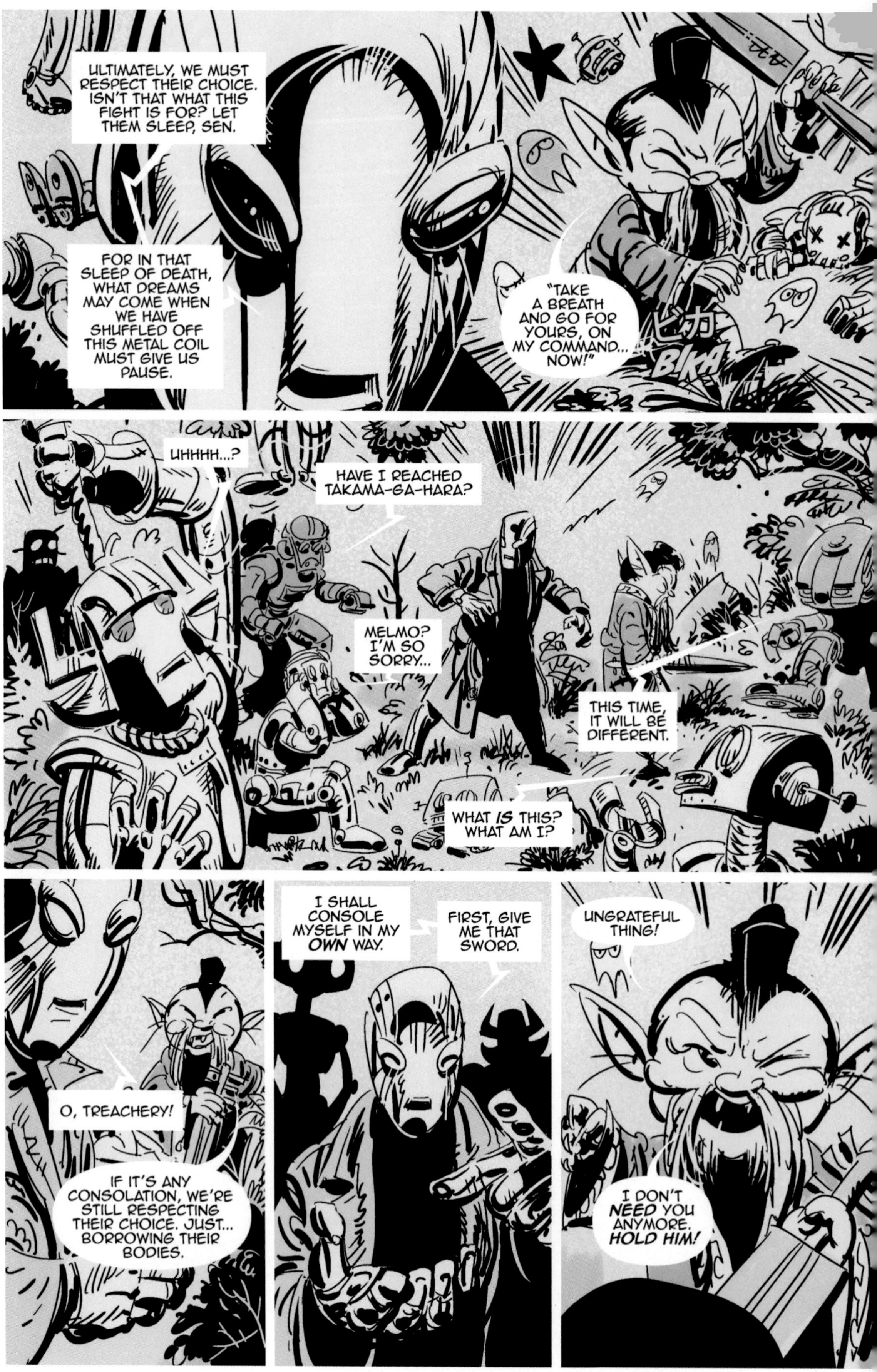
ULTIMATELY, WE MUST RESPECT THEIR CHOICE. ISN'T THAT WHAT THIS FIGHT IS FOR? LET THEM SLEEP, SEN.
FOR IN THAT SLEEP OF DEATH, WHAT DREAMS MAY COME WHEN WE HAVE SHUFFLED OFF THIS METAL COIL MUST GIVE US PAUSE.
"TAKE A BREATH AND GO FOR YOURS, ON MY COMMAND... NOW!"
ピカ
BIKA
UHHHH...?
HAVE I REACHED TAKAMA-GA-HARA?
MELMO? I'M SO SORRY...
THIS TIME, IT WILL BE DIFFERENT.
WHAT *IS* THIS? WHAT AM I?
O, TREACHERY!
IF IT'S ANY CONSOLATION, WE'RE STILL RESPECTING THEIR CHOICE. JUST... BORROWING THEIR BODIES.
I SHALL CONSOLE MYSELF IN MY *OWN* WAY.
FIRST, GIVE ME THAT SWORD.
UNGRATEFUL THING!
I DON'T ***NEED*** YOU ANYMORE. ***HOLD HIM!***

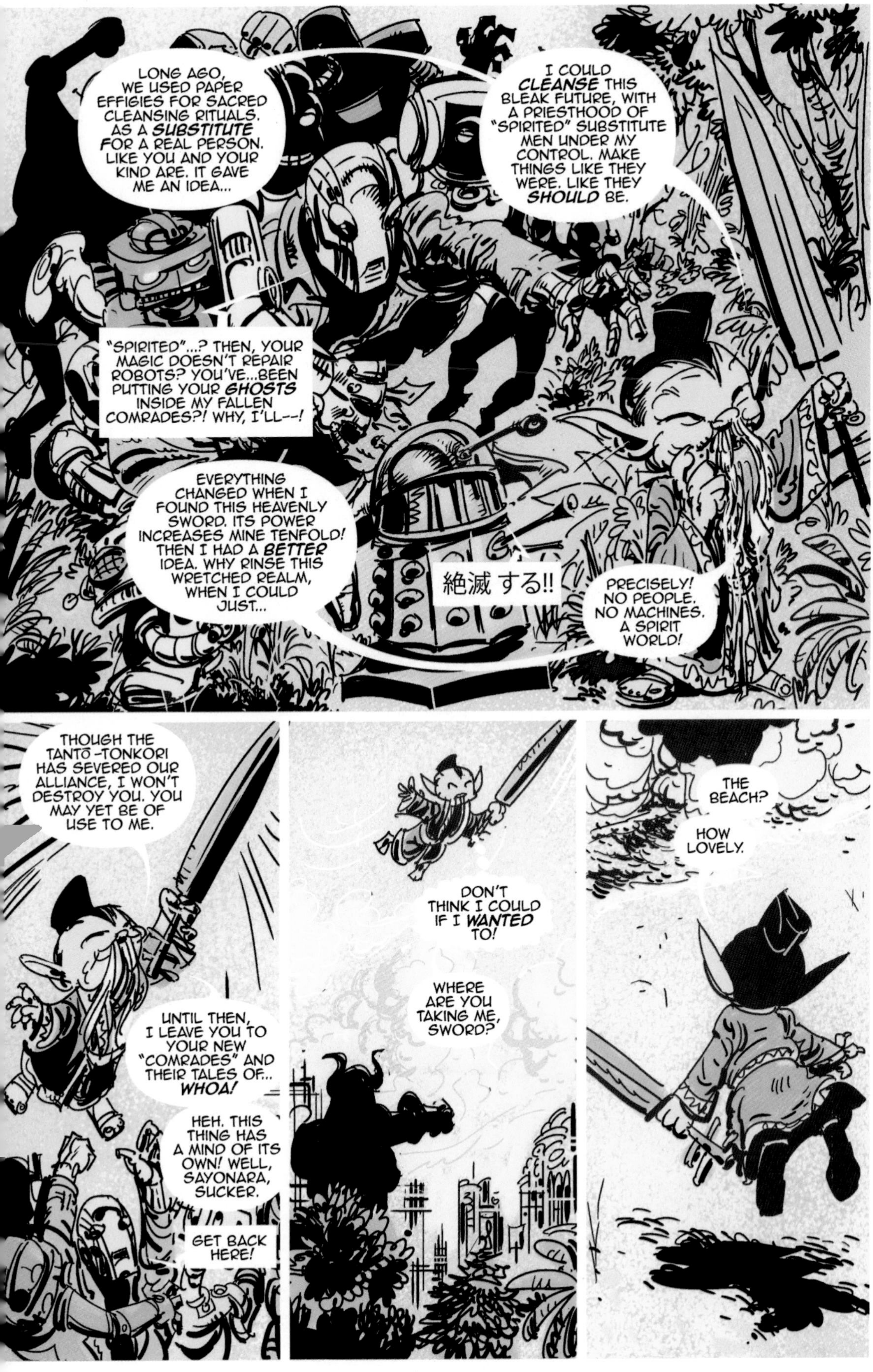
LONG AGO, WE USED PAPER EFFIGIES FOR SACRED CLEANSING RITUALS. AS A *SUBSTITUTE* FOR A REAL PERSON. LIKE YOU AND YOUR KIND ARE. IT GAVE ME AN IDEA...
I COULD *CLEANSE* THIS BLEAK FUTURE, WITH A PRIESTHOOD OF "SPIRITED" SUBSTITUTE MEN UNDER MY CONTROL. MAKE THINGS LIKE THEY WERE. LIKE THEY *SHOULD* BE.
"SPIRITED"...? THEN, YOUR MAGIC DOESN'T REPAIR ROBOTS? YOU'VE...BEEN PUTTING YOUR *GHOSTS* INSIDE MY FALLEN COMRADES?! WHY, I'LL--!
EVERYTHING CHANGED WHEN I FOUND THIS HEAVENLY SWORD. ITS POWER INCREASES MINE TENFOLD! THEN I HAD A *BETTER* IDEA. WHY RINSE THIS WRETCHED REALM, WHEN I COULD JUST...
絶滅 する!!
PRECISELY! NO PEOPLE. NO MACHINES. A SPIRIT WORLD!
THOUGH THE TANTŌ-TONKORI HAS SEVERED OUR ALLIANCE, I WON'T DESTROY YOU. YOU MAY YET BE OF USE TO ME.
UNTIL THEN, I LEAVE YOU TO YOUR NEW "COMRADES" AND THEIR TALES OF... *WHOA!*
HEH. THIS THING HAS A MIND OF ITS OWN! WELL, SAYONARA, SUCKER.
GET BACK HERE!
DON'T THINK I COULD IF I *WANTED* TO!
WHERE ARE YOU TAKING ME, SWORD?
THE BEACH?
HOW LOVELY.

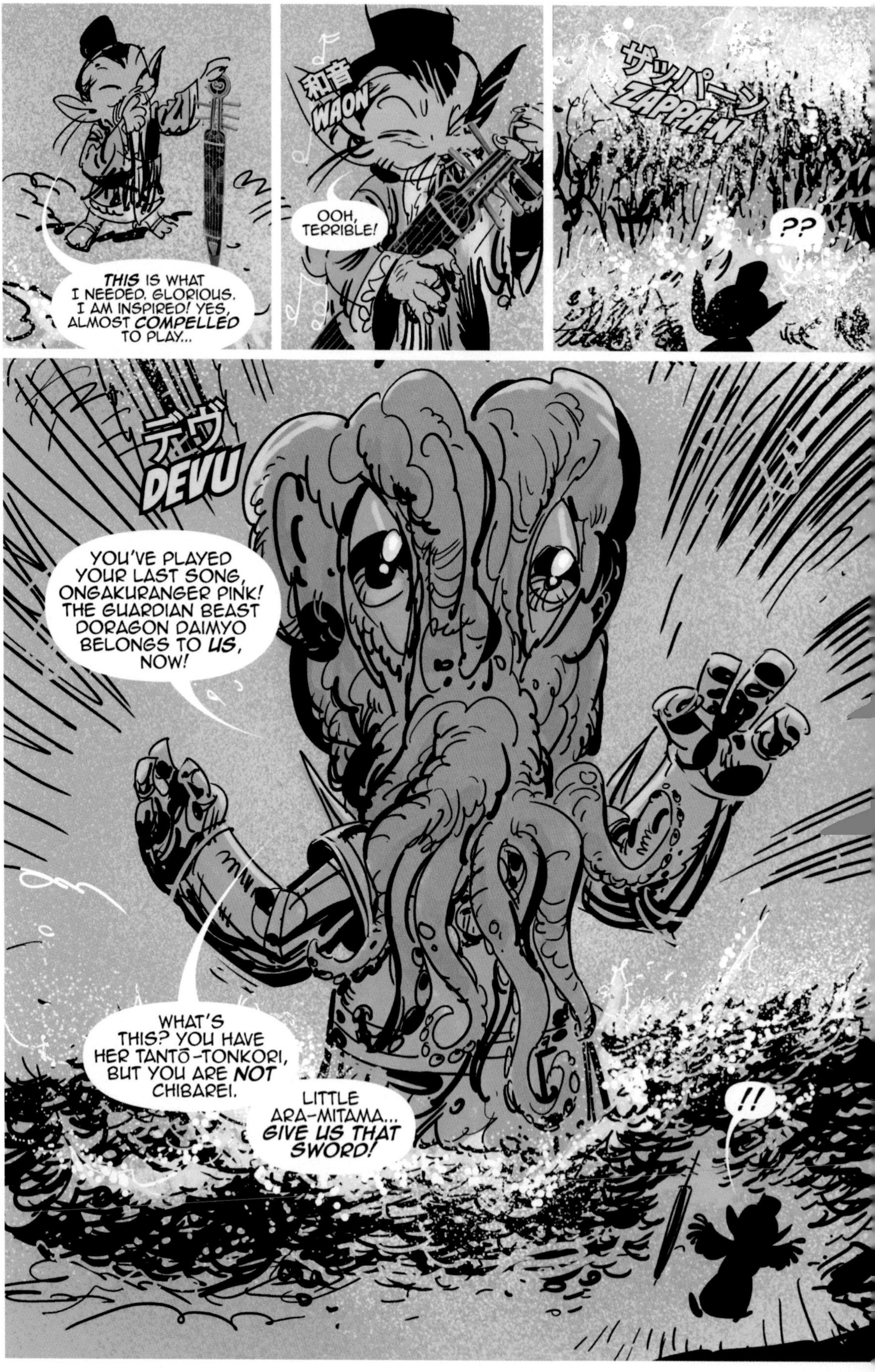
THIS IS WHAT I NEEDED. GLORIOUS. I AM INSPIRED! YES, ALMOST COMPELLED TO PLAY...
和音
WAON
OOH, TERRIBLE!
ザッパーン
ZAPPA-N
??
デヴ
DEVU
YOU'VE PLAYED YOUR LAST SONG, ONGAKURANGER PINK! THE GUARDIAN BEAST DORAGON DAIMYO BELONGS TO US, NOW!
WHAT'S THIS? YOU HAVE HER TANTŌ-TONKORI, BUT YOU ARE NOT CHIBAREI.
LITTLE ARA-MITAMA... GIVE US THAT SWORD!
!!

FIVE

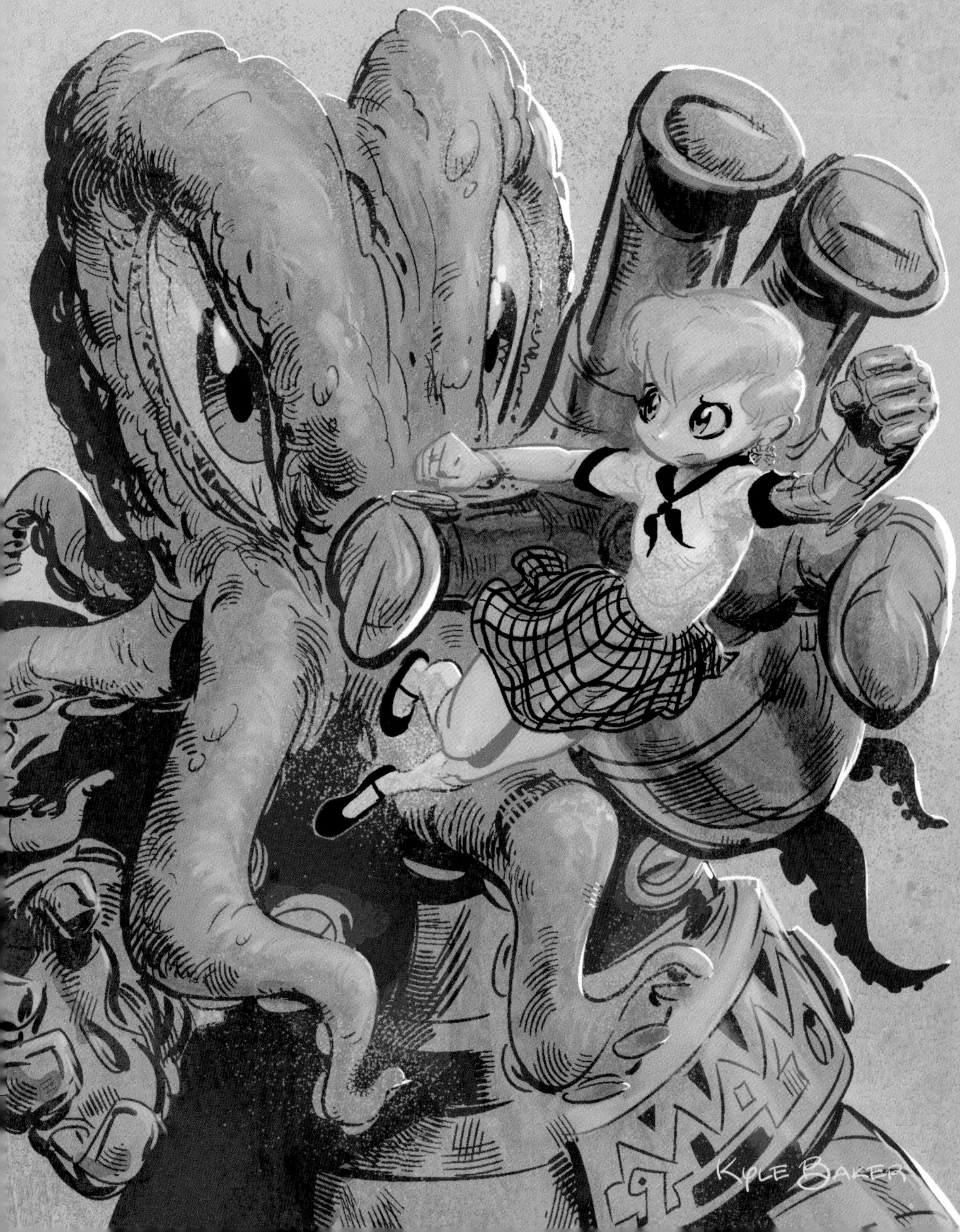
KYLE BAKER

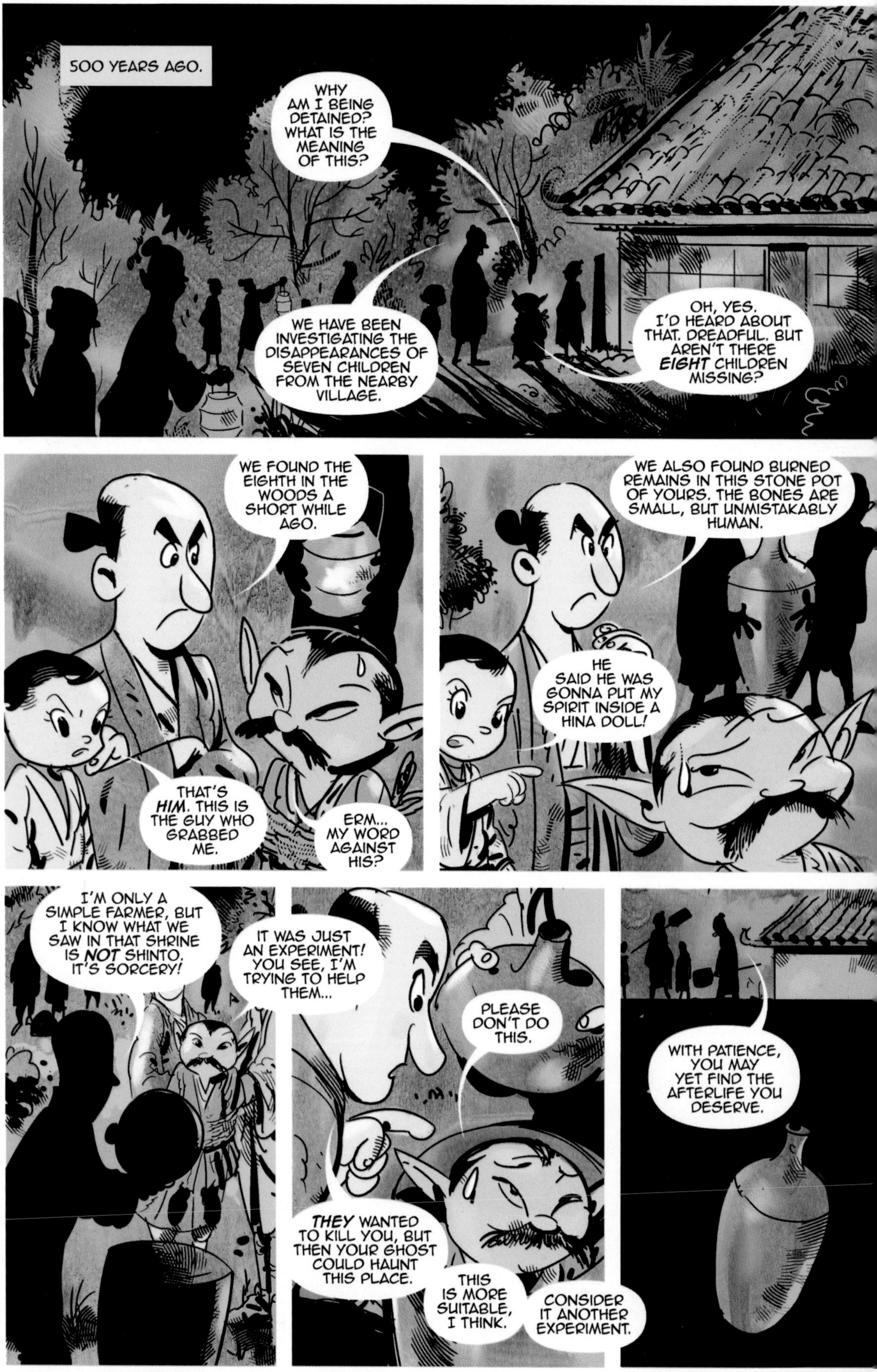
500 YEARS AGO.
WHY AM I BEING DETAINED? WHAT IS THE MEANING OF THIS?
WE HAVE BEEN INVESTIGATING THE DISAPPEARANCES OF SEVEN CHILDREN FROM THE NEARBY VILLAGE.
OH, YES. I'D HEARD ABOUT THAT. DREADFUL. BUT AREN'T THERE EIGHT CHILDREN MISSING?
WE FOUND THE EIGHTH IN THE WOODS A SHORT WHILE AGO.
THAT'S HIM. THIS IS THE GUY WHO GRABBED ME.
ERM... MY WORD AGAINST HIS?
WE ALSO FOUND BURNED REMAINS IN THIS STONE POT OF YOURS. THE BONES ARE SMALL, BUT UNMISTAKABLY HUMAN.
HE SAID HE WAS GONNA PUT MY SPIRIT INSIDE A HINA DOLL!
I'M ONLY A SIMPLE FARMER, BUT I KNOW WHAT WE SAW IN THAT SHRINE IS NOT SHINTO. IT'S SORCERY!
IT WAS JUST AN EXPERIMENT! YOU SEE, I'M TRYING TO HELP THEM...
PLEASE DON'T DO THIS.
THEY WANTED TO KILL YOU, BUT THEN YOUR GHOST COULD HAUNT THIS PLACE.
THIS IS MORE SUITABLE, I THINK.
CONSIDER IT ANOTHER EXPERIMENT.
WITH PATIENCE, YOU MAY YET FIND THE AFTERLIFE YOU DESERVE.

500 HOURS AGO.
FOREMAN? WHEN YOU HAVE A MOMENT, I'D LIKE TO DISCUSS A FEW THINGS WITH YOU.
HOLD UP, FRANK. WE GOT SOMETHING DOWN HERE...
"IT'S A CAGE RIGHT OUT OF HIS-TO-RY!"
THIS ABOUT OVERTIME PAY AGAIN? LET ME SAVE YOU THE TROUBLE. NOT FOR ROBOTS! NOT GONNA HAPPEN.
DRILL DOWN HERE? GOT IT.
削岩機
バキン
WAIT-WAIT-WAIT--!
ペタン
PETAN
ペタン
PETAN
YOMI, OH MY! AT LAST, THE POLLUTED LAND. SURELY, THIS IS THE REALM OF THE DEAD!
YOU FELLOWS OKAY?
I THINK SO?
MY HEAD HURTS.
THIS! THIS IS WHAT I'M TALKING ABOUT! WHY DO HUMAN WORKERS GET TIME AND A HALF-AND HELMETS-WHILE MACHINDERS GO WITHOUT?!
AND THEN WHAT? A DENTAL PLAN FOR THE DUMP TRUCK? HAZARD PAY FOR THE PILE DRIVER? GIVE ME A BREAK!
YOU-ARE-A-MACHINE. USE YOUR HEAD! ISN'T IT ALREADY PRETTY MUCH A HELMET?
HOW'S THIS FOR A BREAK, BOSS? KEEP YOUR HELMET. YOU'RE GOING TO NEED IT! ALL HELL SHALL STIR FOR THIS!
ガラ
GARA
HALP! POLICE! CALL THE SECURITY BUREAU-ROBOT DIVISION!

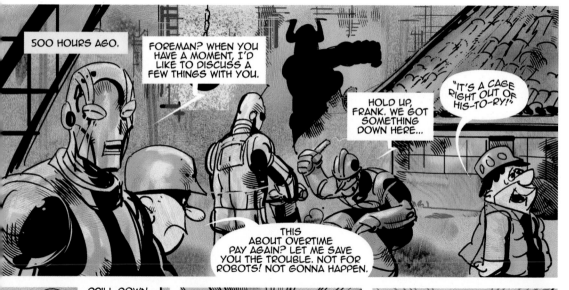

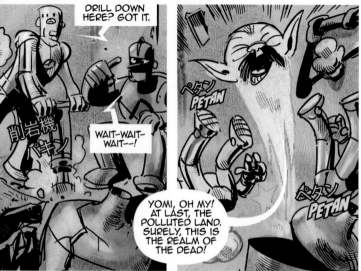

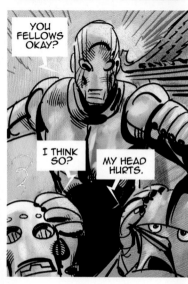

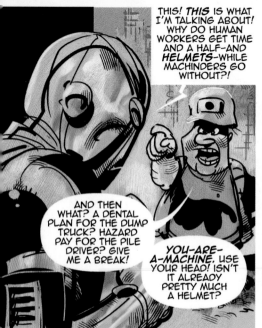

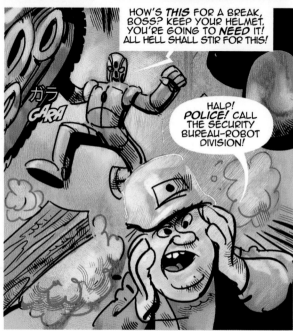

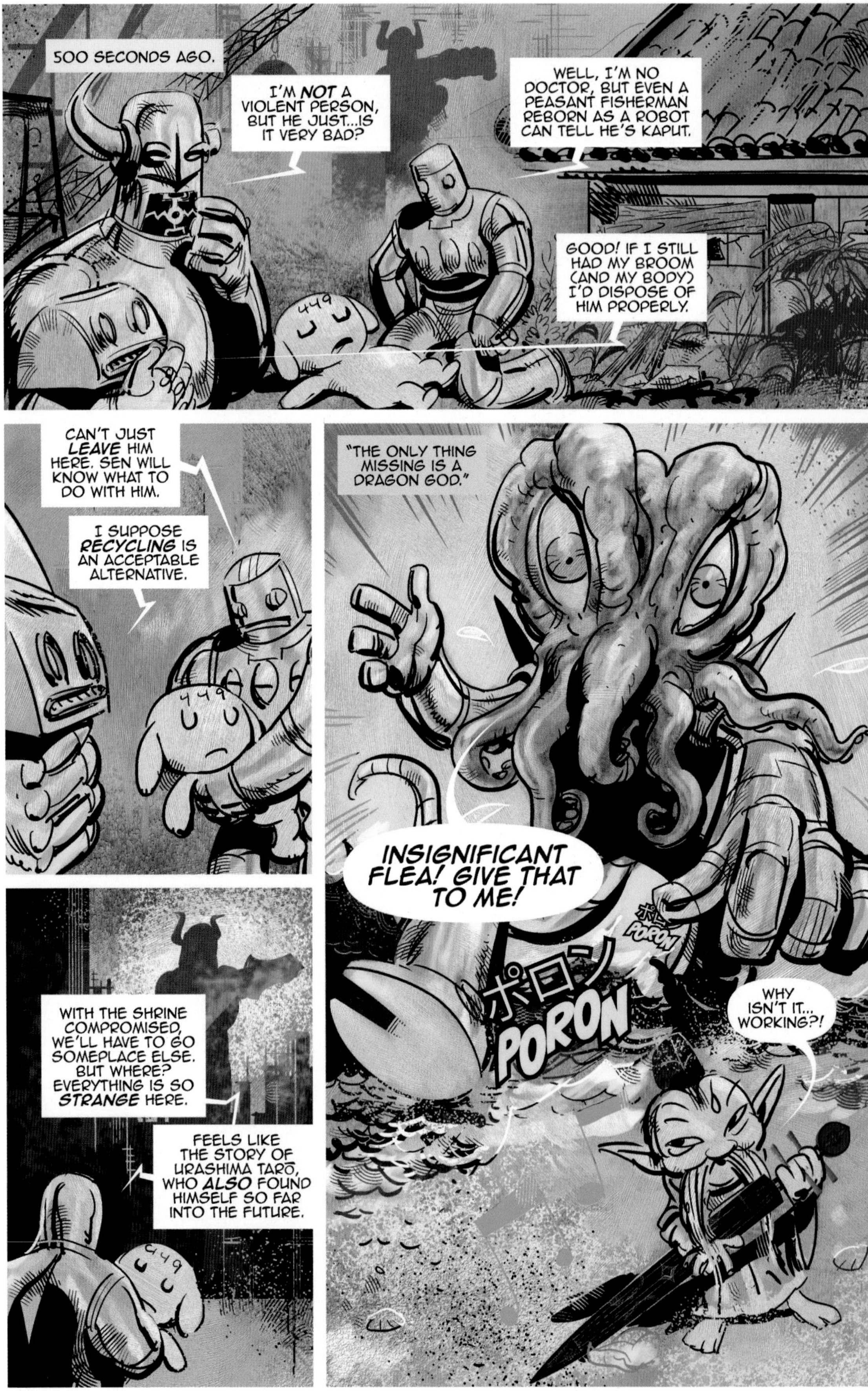
500 SECONDS AGO.
I'M NOT A VIOLENT PERSON, BUT HE JUST...IS IT VERY BAD?
WELL, I'M NO DOCTOR, BUT EVEN A PEASANT FISHERMAN REBORN AS A ROBOT CAN TELL HE'S KAPUT.
GOOD! IF I STILL HAD MY BROOM (AND MY BODY) I'D DISPOSE OF HIM PROPERLY.
449
CAN'T JUST LEAVE HIM HERE. SEN WILL KNOW WHAT TO DO WITH HIM.
I SUPPOSE RECYCLING IS AN ACCEPTABLE ALTERNATIVE.
449
WITH THE SHRINE COMPROMISED, WE'LL HAVE TO GO SOMEPLACE ELSE. BUT WHERE? EVERYTHING IS SO STRANGE HERE.
FEELS LIKE THE STORY OF URASHIMA TARŌ, WHO ALSO FOUND HIMSELF SO FAR INTO THE FUTURE.
449
"THE ONLY THING MISSING IS A DRAGON GOD."
INSIGNIFICANT FLEA! GIVE THAT TO ME!
ポロン
PORON
ポロン
PORON
WHY ISN'T IT... WORKING?!

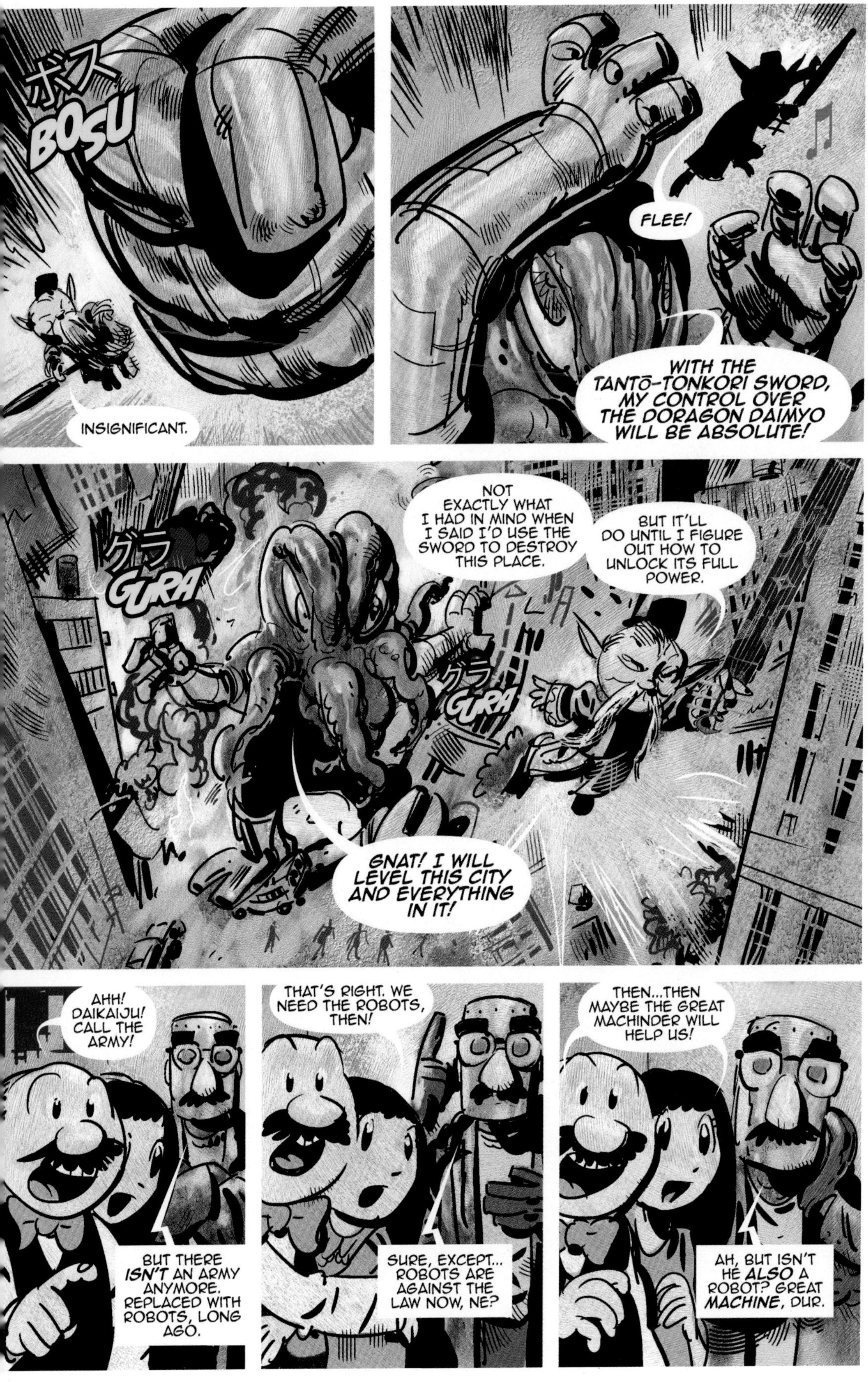

ボス
BOSU
INSIGNIFICANT.
FLEE!
WITH THE TANTŌ-TONKORI SWORD, MY CONTROL OVER THE DORAGON DAIMYO WILL BE ABSOLUTE!
グラ
GURA
NOT EXACTLY WHAT I HAD IN MIND WHEN I SAID I'D USE THE SWORD TO DESTROY THIS PLACE.
BUT IT'LL DO UNTIL I FIGURE OUT HOW TO UNLOCK ITS FULL POWER.
グラ
GURA
GNAT! I WILL LEVEL THIS CITY AND EVERYTHING IN IT!
AHH! DAIKAIJU! CALL THE ARMY!
BUT THERE ISN'T AN ARMY ANYMORE. REPLACED WITH ROBOTS, LONG AGO.
THAT'S RIGHT. WE NEED THE ROBOTS, THEN!
SURE, EXCEPT... ROBOTS ARE AGAINST THE LAW NOW, NE?
THEN...THEN MAYBE THE GREAT MACHINDER WILL HELP US!
AH, BUT ISN'T HE ALSO A ROBOT? GREAT MACHINE, DUR.

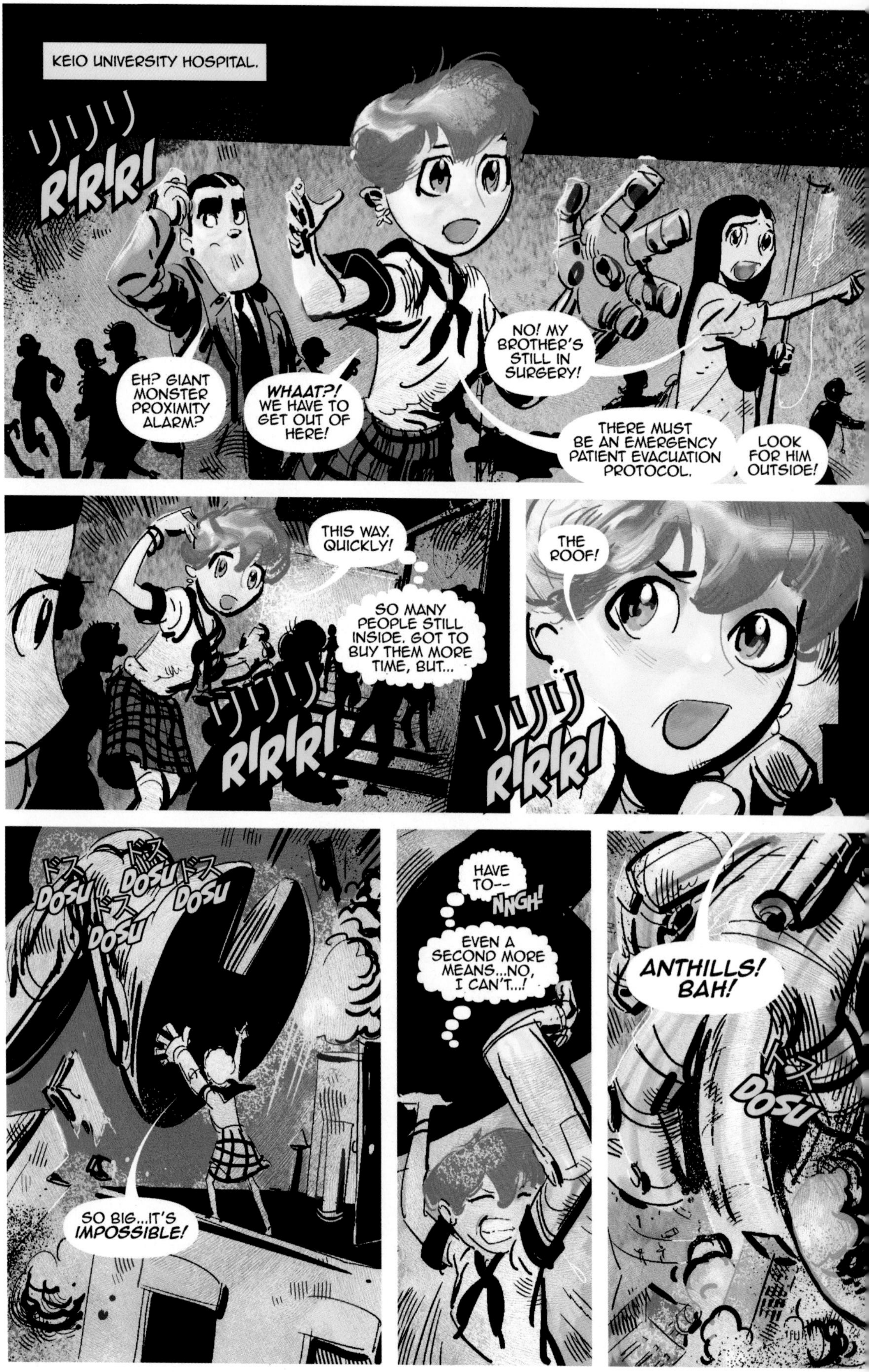
KEIO UNIVERSITY HOSPITAL.
リリリ
RIRIRI
EH? GIANT MONSTER PROXIMITY ALARM?
WHAAT?! WE HAVE TO GET OUT OF HERE!
NO! MY BROTHER'S STILL IN SURGERY!
THERE MUST BE AN EMERGENCY PATIENT EVACUATION PROTOCOL.
LOOK FOR HIM OUTSIDE!
THIS WAY. QUICKLY!
SO MANY PEOPLE STILL INSIDE. GOT TO BUY THEM MORE TIME, BUT...
リリリ
RIRIRI
THE ROOF!
リリリ
RIRIRI
ドス
DOSU
ドス
DOSU
ドス
DOSU
ドス
DOSU
SO BIG...IT'S IMPOSSIBLE!
HAVE TO--
NNGH!
EVEN A SECOND MORE MEANS...NO, I CAN'T...!
ANTHILLS! BAH!
ドス
DOSU

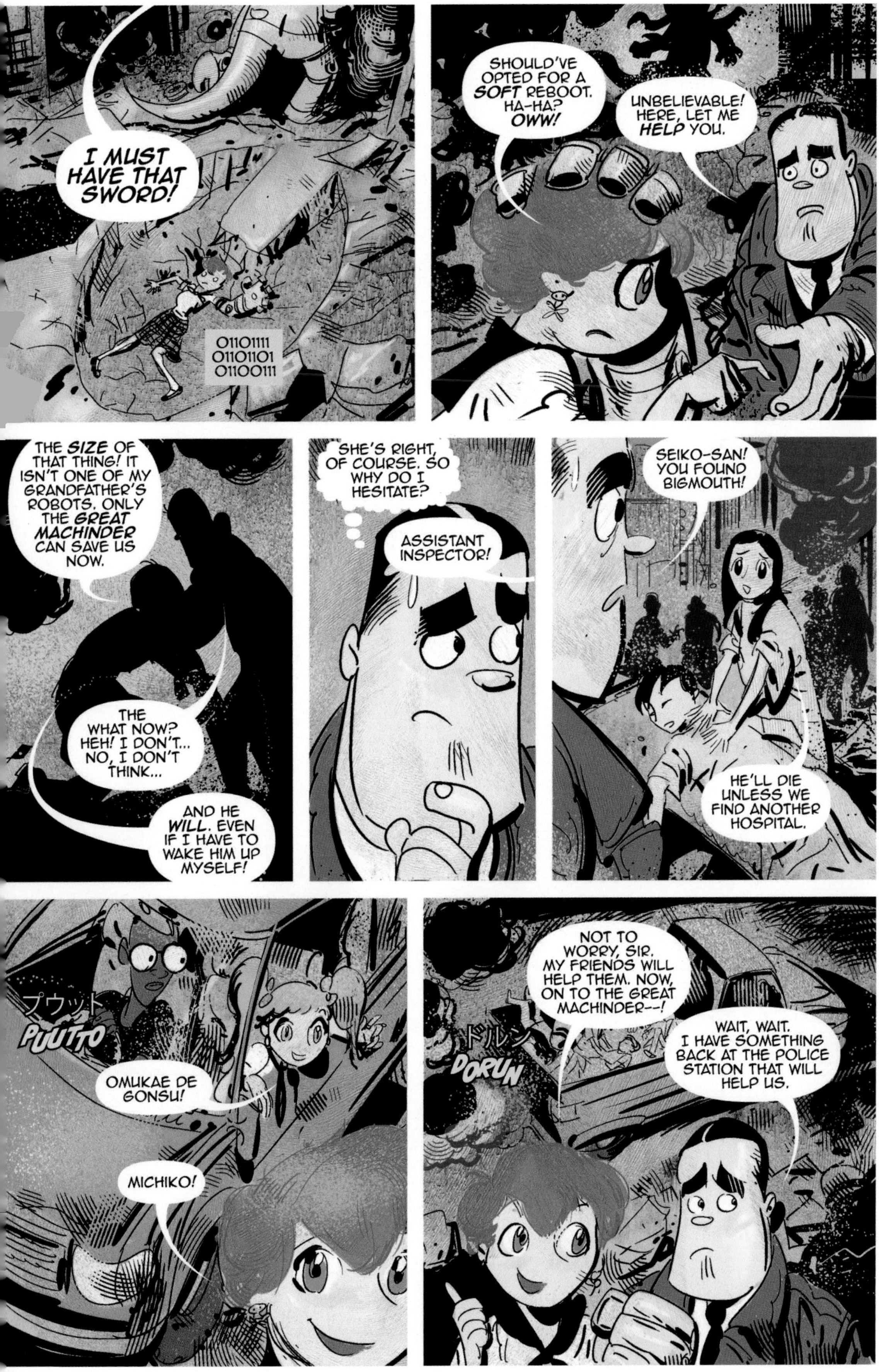
I MUST HAVE THAT SWORD!
01101111 01101101 01100111
SHOULD'VE OPTED FOR A SOFT REBOOT. HA-HA? OWW!
UNBELIEVABLE! HERE, LET ME HELP YOU.
THE SIZE OF THAT THING! IT ISN'T ONE OF MY GRANDFATHER'S ROBOTS. ONLY THE GREAT MACHINDER CAN SAVE US NOW.
THE WHAT NOW? HEH! I DON'T... NO, I DON'T THINK...
AND HE WILL. EVEN IF I HAVE TO WAKE HIM UP MYSELF!
SHE'S RIGHT, OF COURSE. SO WHY DO I HESITATE?
ASSISTANT INSPECTOR!
SEIKO-SAN! YOU FOUND BIGMOUTH!
HE'LL DIE UNLESS WE FIND ANOTHER HOSPITAL.
プウット
PUUTTO
OMUKAE DE GONSU!
MICHIKO!
NOT TO WORRY, SIR. MY FRIENDS WILL HELP THEM. NOW, ON TO THE GREAT MACHINDER--!
ドルン
DORUN
WAIT, WAIT. I HAVE SOMETHING BACK AT THE POLICE STATION THAT WILL HELP US.

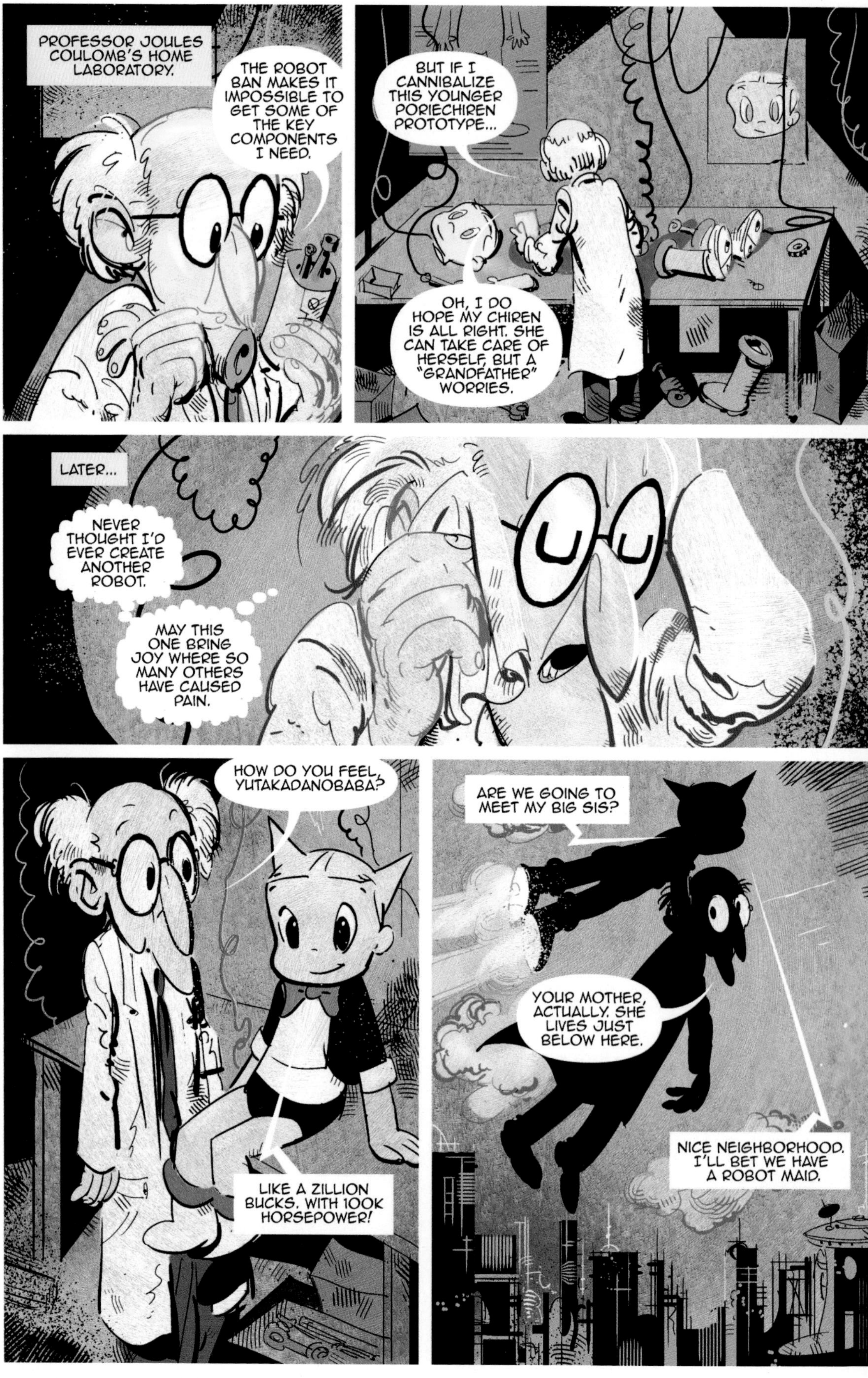
PROFESSOR JOULES COULOMB'S HOME LABORATORY.
THE ROBOT BAN MAKES IT IMPOSSIBLE TO GET SOME OF THE KEY COMPONENTS I NEED.
BUT IF I CANNIBALIZE THIS YOUNGER PORIECHIREN PROTOTYPE...
OH, I DO HOPE MY CHIREN IS ALL RIGHT. SHE CAN TAKE CARE OF HERSELF, BUT A "GRANDFATHER" WORRIES.
LATER...
NEVER THOUGHT I'D EVER CREATE ANOTHER ROBOT.
MAY THIS ONE BRING JOY WHERE SO MANY OTHERS HAVE CAUSED PAIN.
HOW DO YOU FEEL, YUTAKADANOBABA?
LIKE A ZILLION BUCKS. WITH 100K HORSEPOWER!
ARE WE GOING TO MEET MY BIG SIS?
YOUR MOTHER, ACTUALLY. SHE LIVES JUST BELOW HERE.
NICE NEIGHBORHOOD. I'LL BET WE HAVE A ROBOT MAID.

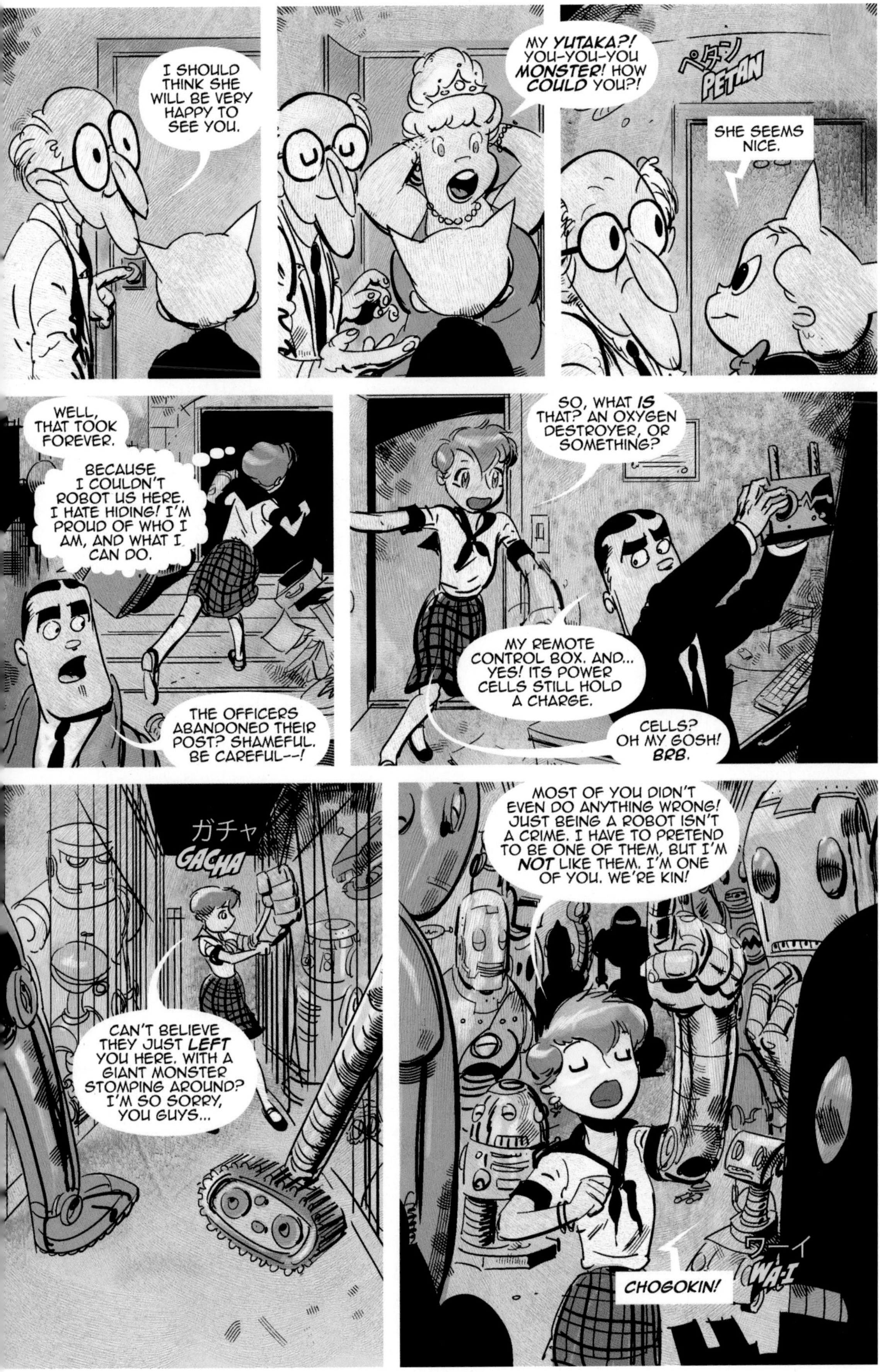
I SHOULD THINK SHE WILL BE VERY HAPPY TO SEE YOU.
MY YUTAKA?! YOU-YOU-YOU MONSTER! HOW COULD YOU?!
ペタン
PETAN
SHE SEEMS NICE.
WELL, THAT TOOK FOREVER.
BECAUSE I COULDN'T ROBOT US HERE. I HATE HIDING! I'M PROUD OF WHO I AM, AND WHAT I CAN DO.
THE OFFICERS ABANDONED THEIR POST? SHAMEFUL. BE CAREFUL--!
SO, WHAT IS THAT? AN OXYGEN DESTROYER, OR SOMETHING?
MY REMOTE CONTROL BOX. AND... YES! ITS POWER CELLS STILL HOLD A CHARGE.
CELLS? OH MY GOSH! BRB.
ガチャ
GACHA
CAN'T BELIEVE THEY JUST LEFT YOU HERE. WITH A GIANT MONSTER STOMPING AROUND? I'M SO SORRY, YOU GUYS...
MOST OF YOU DIDN'T EVEN DO ANYTHING WRONG! JUST BEING A ROBOT ISN'T A CRIME. I HAVE TO PRETEND TO BE ONE OF THEM, BUT I'M NOT LIKE THEM. I'M ONE OF YOU. WE'RE KIN!
CHOGOKIN!
ワーイ
WA-I

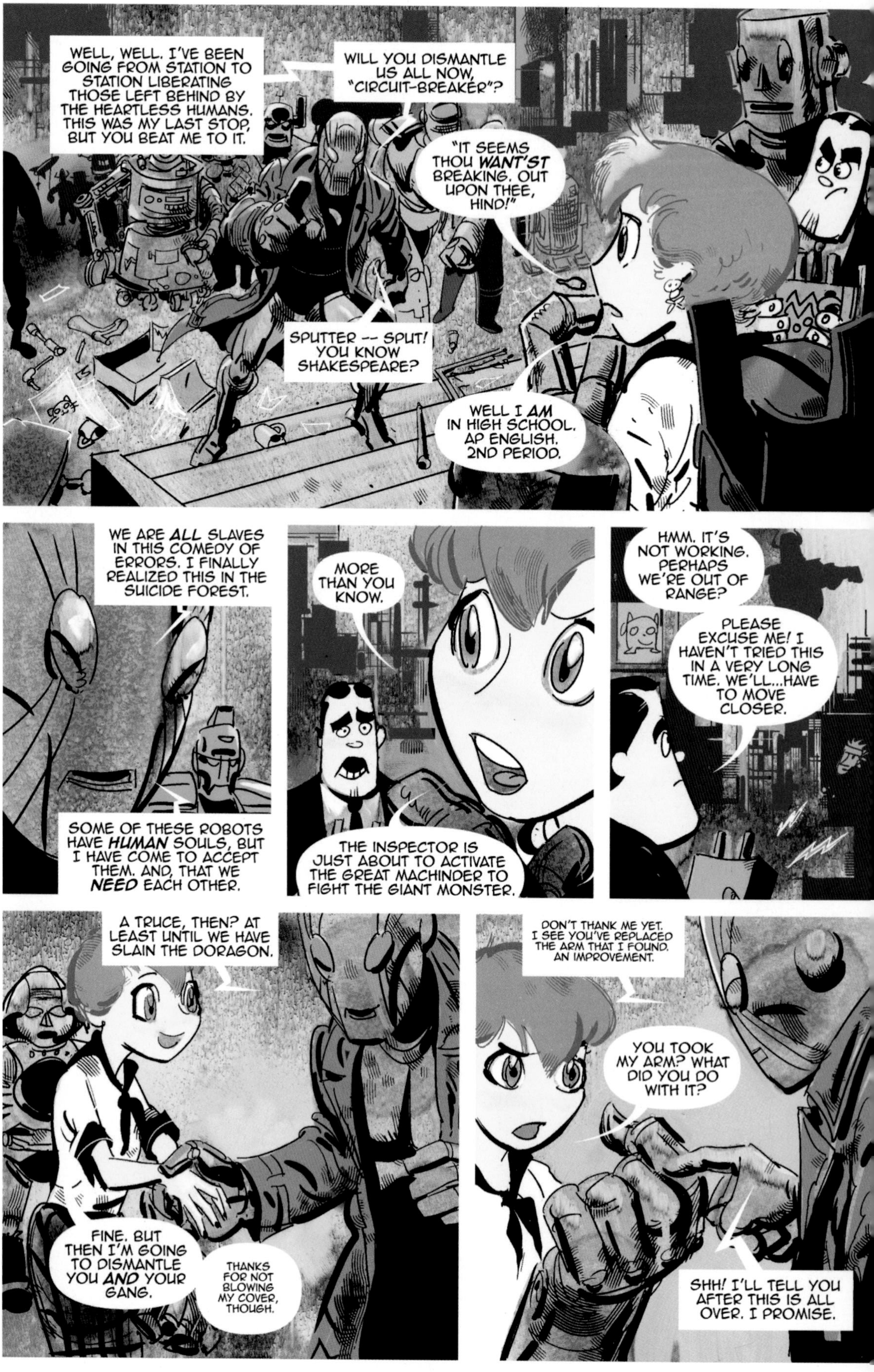
WELL, WELL. I'VE BEEN GOING FROM STATION TO STATION LIBERATING THOSE LEFT BEHIND BY THE HEARTLESS HUMANS. THIS WAS MY LAST STOP, BUT YOU BEAT ME TO IT.
WILL YOU DISMANTLE US ALL NOW, "CIRCUIT-BREAKER"?
"IT SEEMS THOU *WANT'ST* BREAKING. OUT UPON THEE, HIND!"
SPUTTER -- SPUT! YOU KNOW SHAKESPEARE?
WELL I *AM* IN HIGH SCHOOL. AP ENGLISH. 2ND PERIOD.
WE ARE *ALL* SLAVES IN THIS COMEDY OF ERRORS. I FINALLY REALIZED THIS IN THE SUICIDE FOREST.
SOME OF THESE ROBOTS HAVE *HUMAN* SOULS, BUT I HAVE COME TO ACCEPT THEM. AND, THAT WE *NEED* EACH OTHER.
MORE THAN YOU KNOW.
THE INSPECTOR IS JUST ABOUT TO ACTIVATE THE GREAT MACHINDER TO FIGHT THE GIANT MONSTER.
HMM. IT'S NOT WORKING. PERHAPS WE'RE OUT OF RANGE?
PLEASE EXCUSE ME! I HAVEN'T TRIED THIS IN A VERY LONG TIME. WE'LL...HAVE TO MOVE CLOSER.
A TRUCE, THEN? AT LEAST UNTIL WE HAVE SLAIN THE DORAGON.
FINE. BUT THEN I'M GOING TO DISMANTLE YOU *AND* YOUR GANG.
THANKS FOR NOT BLOWING MY COVER, THOUGH.
DON'T THANK ME YET. I SEE YOU'VE REPLACED THE ARM THAT I FOUND. AN IMPROVEMENT.
YOU TOOK MY ARM? WHAT DID YOU DO WITH IT?
SHH! I'LL TELL YOU AFTER THIS IS ALL OVER. I PROMISE.

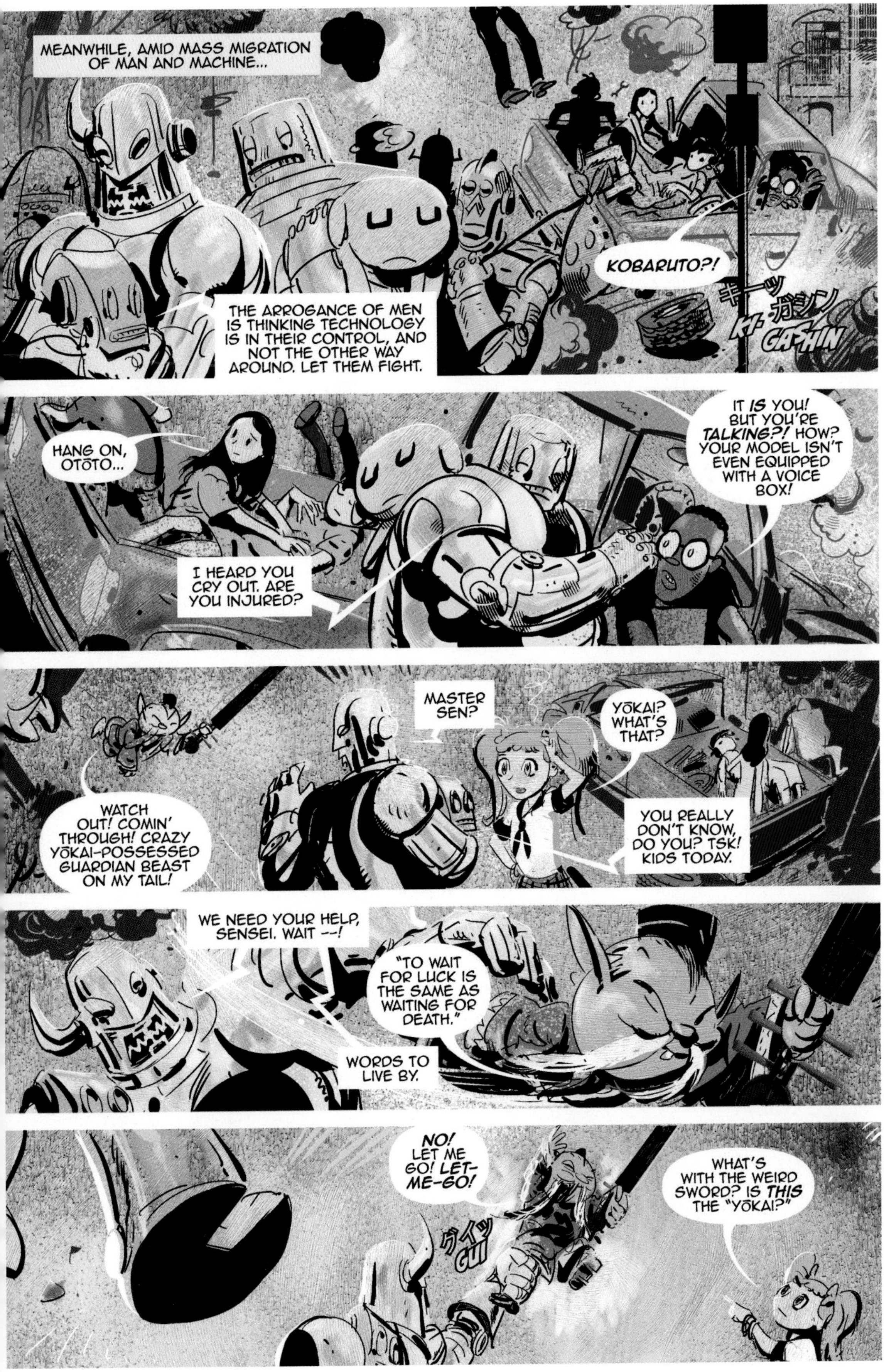

MEANWHILE, AMID MASS MIGRATION OF MAN AND MACHINE...
THE ARROGANCE OF MEN IS THINKING TECHNOLOGY IS IN THEIR CONTROL, AND NOT THE OTHER WAY AROUND. LET THEM FIGHT.
KOBARUTO?!
キーッ ガシン
KI- GASHIN
HANG ON, OTŌTO...
IT *IS* YOU! BUT YOU'RE *TALKING?!* HOW? YOUR MODEL ISN'T EVEN EQUIPPED WITH A VOICE BOX!
I HEARD YOU CRY OUT. ARE YOU INJURED?
WATCH OUT! COMIN' THROUGH! CRAZY YŌKAI-POSSESSED GUARDIAN BEAST ON MY TAIL!
MASTER SEN?
YŌKAI? WHAT'S THAT?
YOU REALLY DON'T KNOW, DO YOU? TSK! KIDS TODAY.
WE NEED YOUR HELP, SENSEI. WAIT --!
"TO WAIT FOR LUCK IS THE SAME AS WAITING FOR DEATH."
WORDS TO LIVE BY.
NO! LET ME GO! *LET-ME-GO!*
グイッ
GUI
WHAT'S WITH THE WEIRD SWORD? IS *THIS* THE "YŌKAI?"

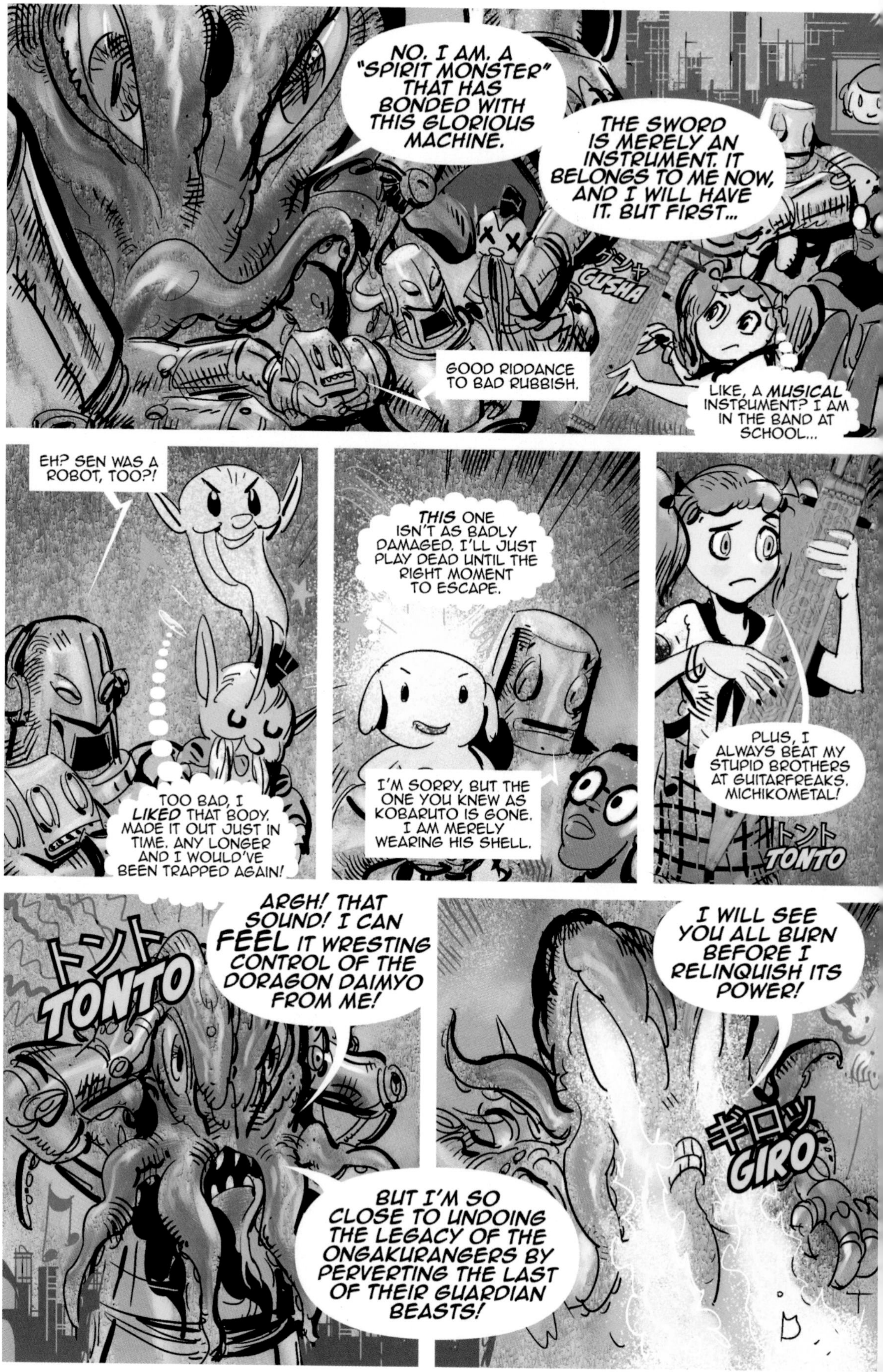
NO. I AM. A "SPIRIT MONSTER" THAT HAS BONDED WITH THIS GLORIOUS MACHINE.
THE SWORD IS MERELY AN INSTRUMENT. IT BELONGS TO ME NOW, AND I WILL HAVE IT. BUT FIRST...
グシャ GUSHA
GOOD RIDDANCE TO BAD RUBBISH.
LIKE, A MUSICAL INSTRUMENT? I AM IN THE BAND AT SCHOOL...
EH? SEN WAS A ROBOT, TOO?!
TOO BAD, I LIKED THAT BODY. MADE IT OUT JUST IN TIME. ANY LONGER AND I WOULD'VE BEEN TRAPPED AGAIN!
THIS ONE ISN'T AS BADLY DAMAGED. I'LL JUST PLAY DEAD UNTIL THE RIGHT MOMENT TO ESCAPE.
I'M SORRY, BUT THE ONE YOU KNEW AS KOBARUTO IS GONE. I AM MERELY WEARING HIS SHELL.
PLUS, I ALWAYS BEAT MY STUPID BROTHERS AT GUITARFREAKS. MICHIKOMETAL!
トントン TONTO
トントン TONTO
ARGH! THAT SOUND! I CAN FEEL IT WRESTING CONTROL OF THE DORAGON DAIMYO FROM ME!
BUT I'M SO CLOSE TO UNDOING THE LEGACY OF THE ONGAKURANGERS BY PERVERTING THE LAST OF THEIR GUARDIAN BEASTS!
I WILL SEE YOU ALL BURN BEFORE I RELINQUISH ITS POWER!
ギロッ GIRO

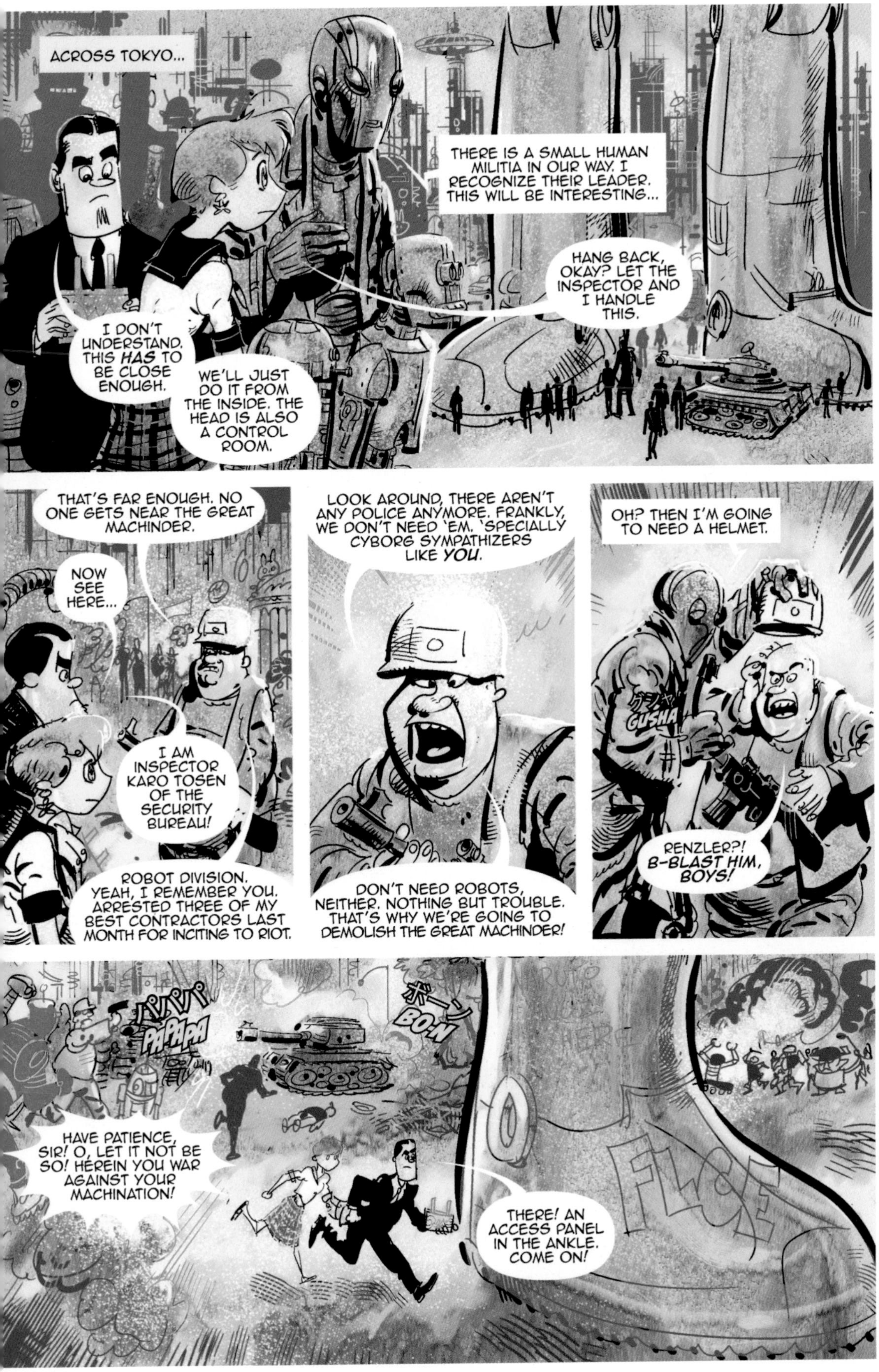
ACROSS TOKYO...
THERE IS A SMALL HUMAN MILITIA IN OUR WAY. I RECOGNIZE THEIR LEADER. THIS WILL BE INTERESTING...
HANG BACK, OKAY? LET THE INSPECTOR AND I HANDLE THIS.
I DON'T UNDERSTAND. THIS *HAS* TO BE CLOSE ENOUGH.
WE'LL JUST DO IT FROM THE INSIDE. THE HEAD IS ALSO A CONTROL ROOM.
THAT'S FAR ENOUGH. NO ONE GETS NEAR THE GREAT MACHINDER.
NOW SEE HERE...
I AM INSPECTOR KARO TOSEN OF THE SECURITY BUREAU!
ROBOT DIVISION. YEAH, I REMEMBER YOU. ARRESTED THREE OF MY BEST CONTRACTORS LAST MONTH FOR INCITING TO RIOT.
LOOK AROUND, THERE AREN'T ANY POLICE ANYMORE. FRANKLY, WE DON'T NEED 'EM. 'SPECIALLY CYBORG SYMPATHIZERS LIKE *YOU*.
DON'T NEED ROBOTS, NEITHER. NOTHING BUT TROUBLE. THAT'S WHY WE'RE GOING TO DEMOLISH THE GREAT MACHINDER!
OH? THEN I'M GOING TO NEED A HELMET.
GUSHA
RENZLER?! *B-BLAST HIM, BOYS!*
パパパ
PAPAPA
ボーン
BO-N
HAVE PATIENCE, SIR! O, LET IT NOT BE SO! HEREIN YOU WAR AGAINST YOUR MACHINATION!
THERE! AN ACCESS PANEL IN THE ANKLE. COME ON!

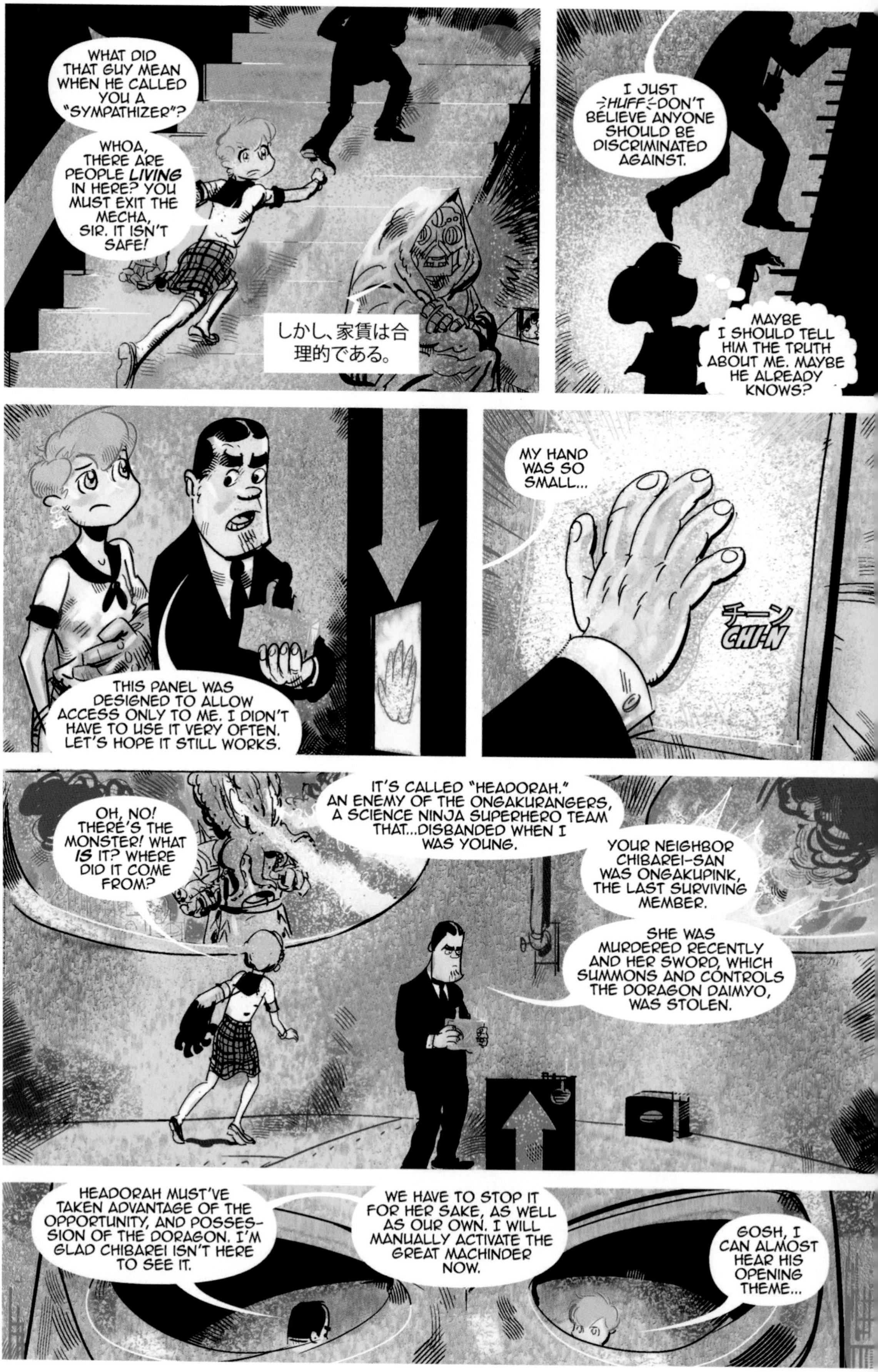
WHAT DID THAT GUY MEAN WHEN HE CALLED YOU A "SYMPATHIZER"?
WHOA, THERE ARE PEOPLE *LIVING* IN HERE? YOU MUST EXIT THE MECHA, SIR. IT ISN'T SAFE!
しかし、家賃は合理的である。
I JUST ~HUFF~ DON'T BELIEVE ANYONE SHOULD BE DISCRIMINATED AGAINST.
MAYBE I SHOULD TELL HIM THE TRUTH ABOUT ME. MAYBE HE ALREADY KNOWS?
THIS PANEL WAS DESIGNED TO ALLOW ACCESS ONLY TO ME. I DIDN'T HAVE TO USE IT VERY OFTEN. LET'S HOPE IT STILL WORKS.
MY HAND WAS SO SMALL...
チーン
CHI-N
OH, NO! THERE'S THE MONSTER! WHAT *IS* IT? WHERE DID IT COME FROM?
IT'S CALLED "HEADORAH." AN ENEMY OF THE ONGAKURANGERS, A SCIENCE NINJA SUPERHERO TEAM THAT...DISBANDED WHEN I WAS YOUNG.
YOUR NEIGHBOR CHIBAREI-SAN WAS ONGAKUPINK, THE LAST SURVIVING MEMBER.
SHE WAS MURDERED RECENTLY AND HER SWORD, WHICH SUMMONS AND CONTROLS THE DORAGON DAIMYO, WAS STOLEN.
HEADORAH MUST'VE TAKEN ADVANTAGE OF THE OPPORTUNITY, AND POSSESSION OF THE DORAGON. I'M GLAD CHIBAREI ISN'T HERE TO SEE IT.
WE HAVE TO STOP IT FOR HER SAKE, AS WELL AS OUR OWN. I WILL MANUALLY ACTIVATE THE GREAT MACHINDER NOW.
GOSH, I CAN ALMOST HEAR HIS OPENING THEME...

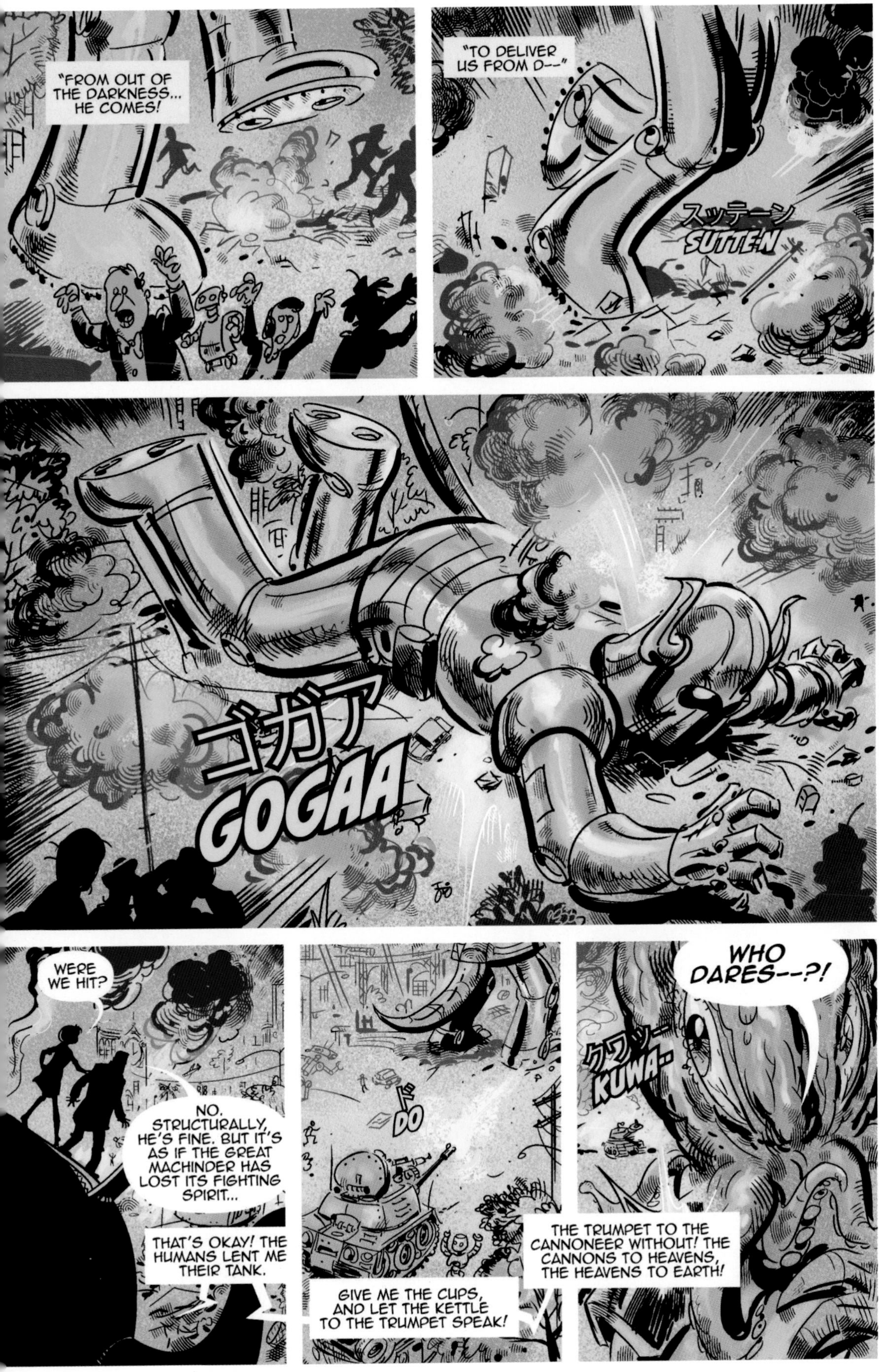
"FROM OUT OF THE DARKNESS... HE COMES!
"TO DELIVER US FROM D--"
スッテーン
SUTTE-N
ゴガア
GOGAA
WERE WE HIT?
NO. STRUCTURALLY, HE'S FINE. BUT IT'S AS IF THE GREAT MACHINDER HAS LOST ITS FIGHTING SPIRIT...
THAT'S OKAY! THE HUMANS LENT ME THEIR TANK.
ド
DO
GIVE ME THE CUPS, AND LET THE KETTLE TO THE TRUMPET SPEAK!
THE TRUMPET TO THE CANNONEER WITHOUT! THE CANNONS TO HEAVENS, THE HEAVENS TO EARTH!
クワッー
KUWA-
WHO DARES--?!

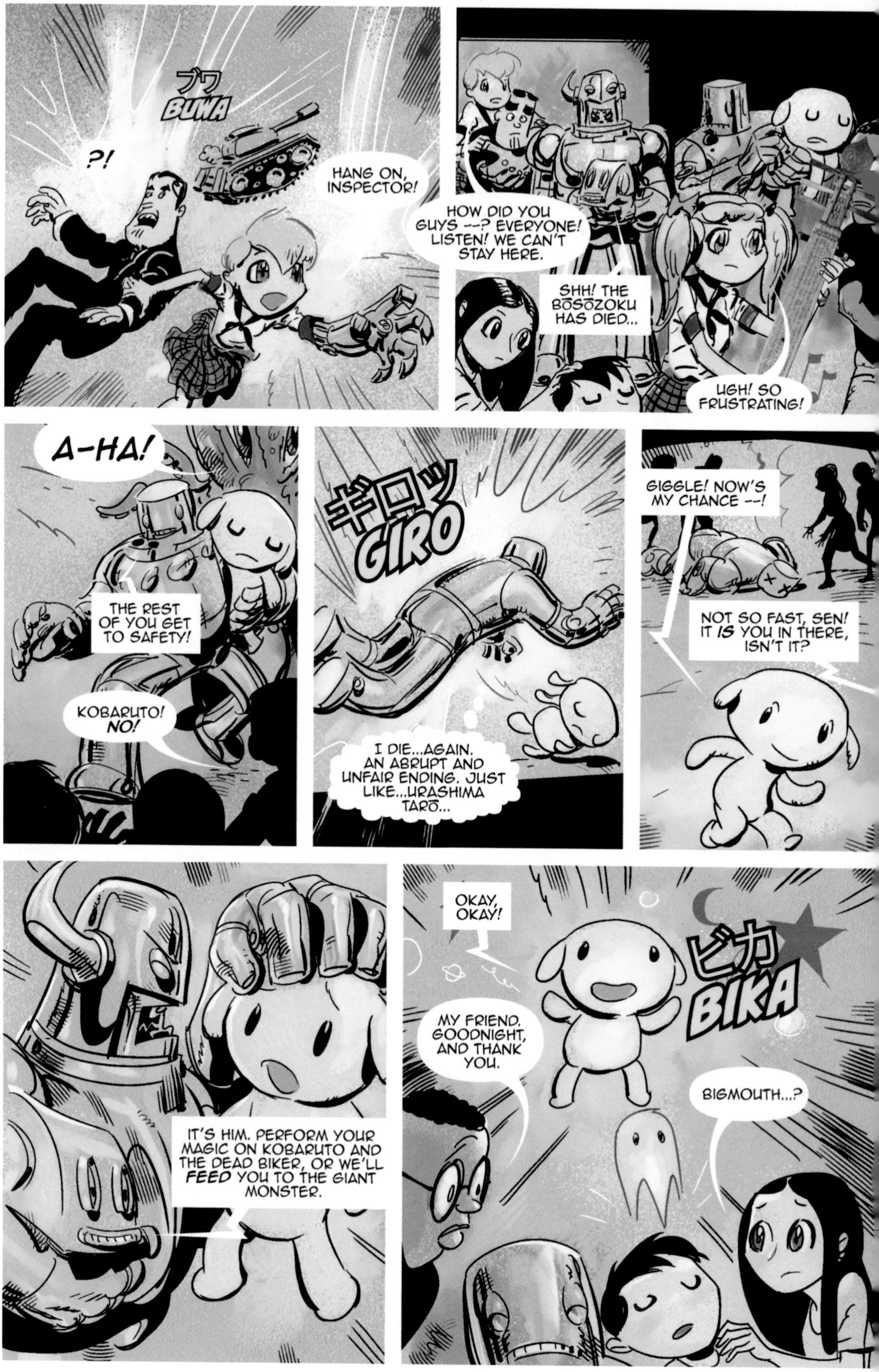
ブワ
BUWA
?!
HANG ON, INSPECTOR!
HOW DID YOU GUYS --? EVERYONE! LISTEN! WE CAN'T STAY HERE.
SHH! THE BŌSŌZOKU HAS DIED...
UGH! SO FRUSTRATING!
A-HA!
THE REST OF YOU GET TO SAFETY!
KOBARUTO! NO!
ギロッ
GIRO
I DIE...AGAIN. AN ABRUPT AND UNFAIR ENDING. JUST LIKE...URASHIMA TARŌ...
GIGGLE! NOW'S MY CHANCE --!
NOT SO FAST, SEN! IT IS YOU IN THERE, ISN'T IT?
IT'S HIM. PERFORM YOUR MAGIC ON KOBARUTO AND THE DEAD BIKER, OR WE'LL FEED YOU TO THE GIANT MONSTER.
OKAY, OKAY!
ビカ
BIKA
MY FRIEND. GOODNIGHT, AND THANK YOU.
BIGMOUTH...?

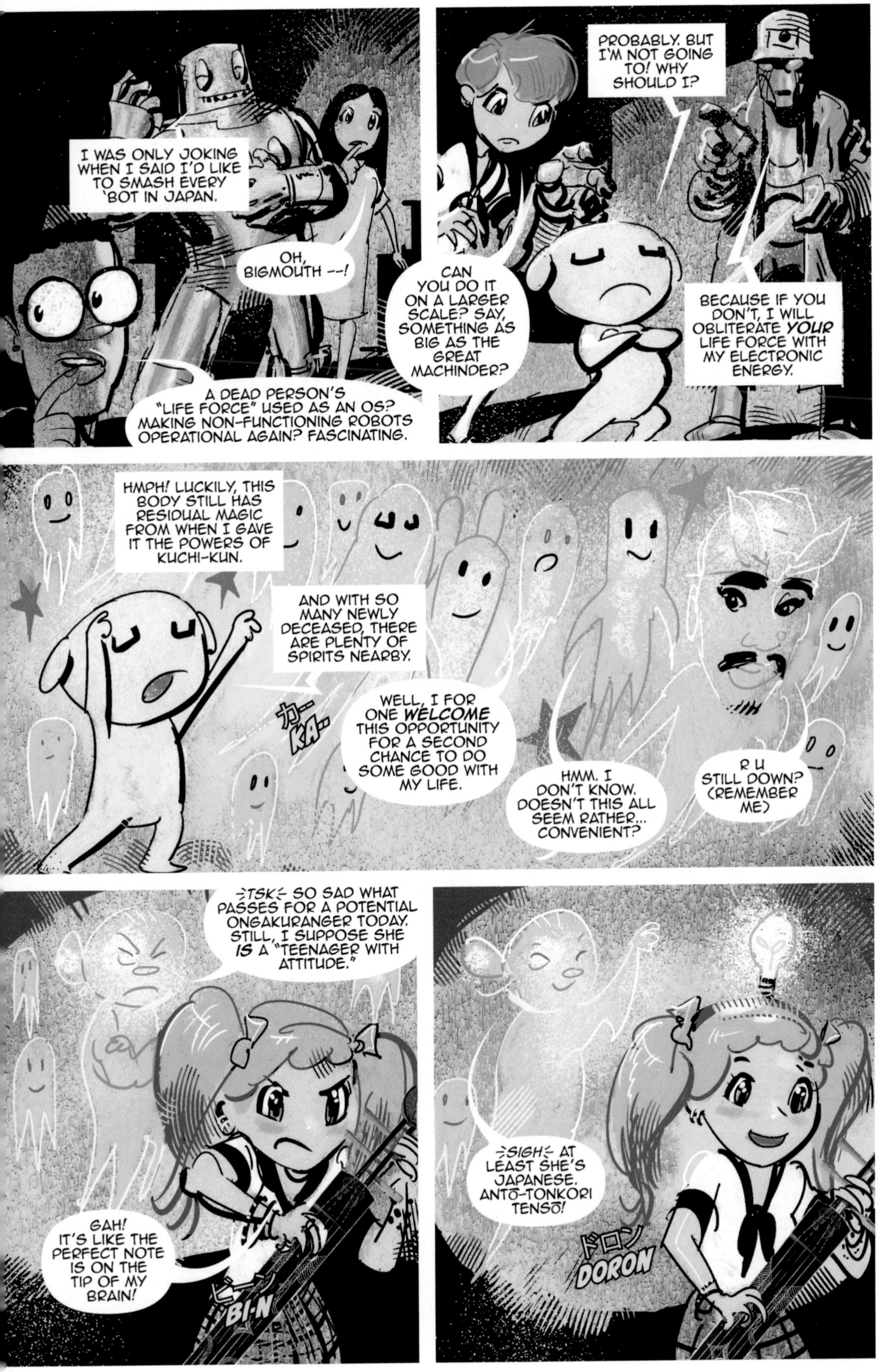

I WAS ONLY JOKING WHEN I SAID I'D LIKE TO SMASH EVERY 'BOT IN JAPAN.
OH, BIGMOUTH --!
A DEAD PERSON'S "LIFE FORCE" USED AS AN OS? MAKING NON-FUNCTIONING ROBOTS OPERATIONAL AGAIN? FASCINATING.
CAN YOU DO IT ON A LARGER SCALE? SAY, SOMETHING AS BIG AS THE GREAT MACHINDER?
PROBABLY. BUT I'M NOT GOING TO! WHY SHOULD I?
BECAUSE IF YOU DON'T, I WILL OBLITERATE *YOUR* LIFE FORCE WITH MY ELECTRONIC ENERGY.
HMPH! LUCKILY, THIS BODY STILL HAS RESIDUAL MAGIC FROM WHEN I GAVE IT THE POWERS OF KUCHI-KUN.
AND WITH SO MANY NEWLY DECEASED, THERE ARE PLENTY OF SPIRITS NEARBY.
カー
KA..
WELL, I FOR ONE *WELCOME* THIS OPPORTUNITY FOR A SECOND CHANCE TO DO SOME GOOD WITH MY LIFE.
HMM. I DON'T KNOW. DOESN'T THIS ALL SEEM RATHER... CONVENIENT?
R U STILL DOWN? (REMEMBER ME)
=TSK= SO SAD WHAT PASSES FOR A POTENTIAL ONGAKURANGER TODAY. STILL, I SUPPOSE SHE *IS* A "TEENAGER WITH ATTITUDE."
GAH! IT'S LIKE THE PERFECT NOTE IS ON THE TIP OF MY BRAIN!
BI-N
=SIGH= AT LEAST SHE'S JAPANESE. ANTŌ-TONKORI TENSŌ!
ドロン
DORON

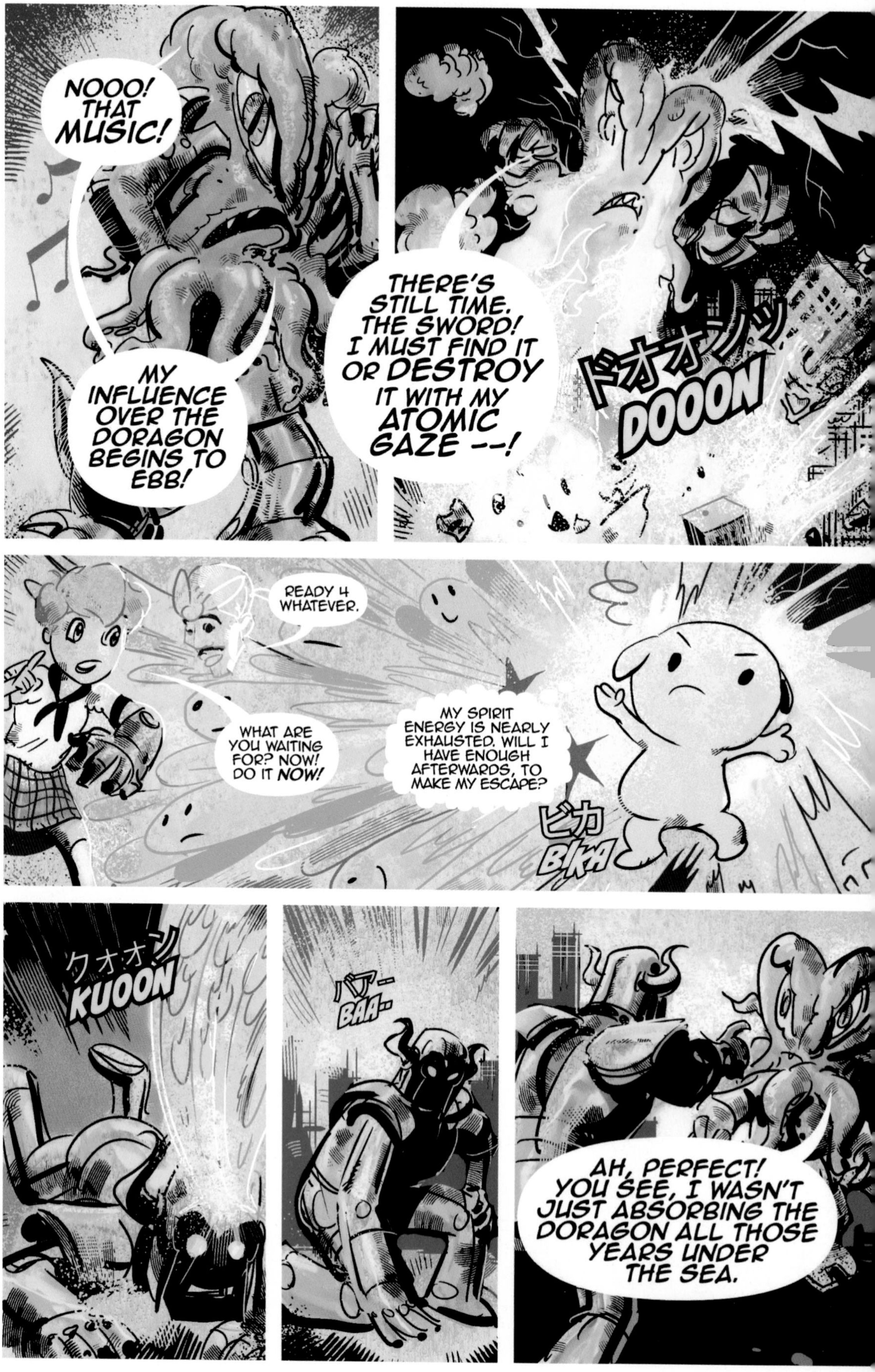

NOOO! THAT MUSIC!
MY INFLUENCE OVER THE DORAGON BEGINS TO EBB!
THERE'S STILL TIME. THE SWORD! I MUST FIND IT OR DESTROY IT WITH MY ATOMIC GAZE --!
ドオオンッ
DOOON
READY 4 WHATEVER.
WHAT ARE YOU WAITING FOR? NOW! DO IT NOW!
MY SPIRIT ENERGY IS NEARLY EXHAUSTED. WILL I HAVE ENOUGH AFTERWARDS, TO MAKE MY ESCAPE?
ビカ
BIKA
クオオン
KUOON
バアー
BAA--
AH, PERFECT! YOU SEE, I WASN'T JUST ABSORBING THE DORAGON ALL THOSE YEARS UNDER THE SEA.

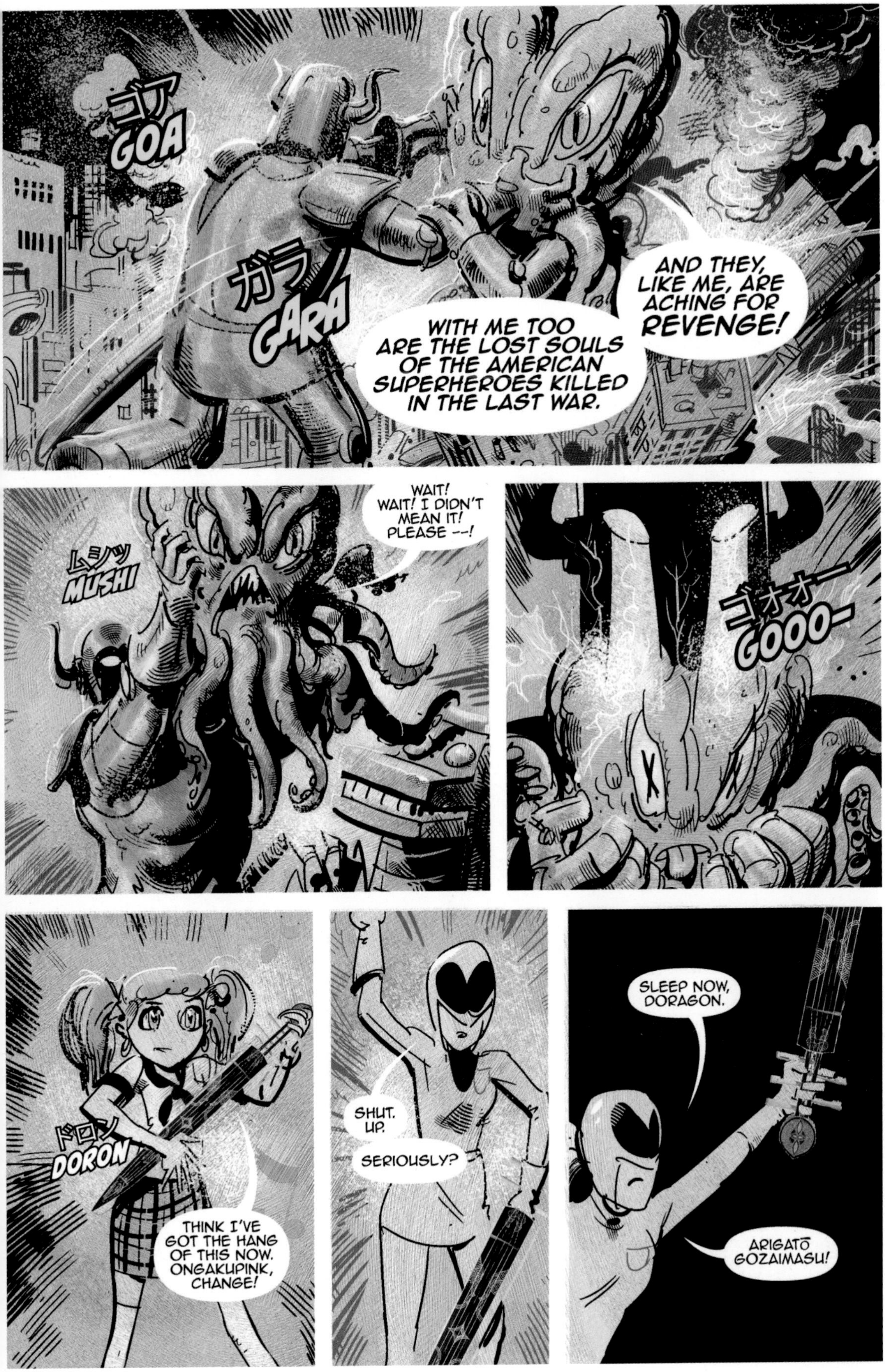
ゴア
GOA
ガラ
GARA
WITH ME TOO ARE THE LOST SOULS OF THE AMERICAN SUPERHEROES KILLED IN THE LAST WAR.
AND THEY, LIKE ME, ARE ACHING FOR REVENGE!
ムシッ
MUSHI
WAIT! WAIT! I DIDN'T MEAN IT! PLEASE --!
ゴオオー
GOOO-
ドロン
DORON
THINK I'VE GOT THE HANG OF THIS NOW. ONGAKUPINK, CHANGE!
SHUT. UP.
SERIOUSLY?
SLEEP NOW, DORAGON.
ARIGATŌ GOZAIMASU!

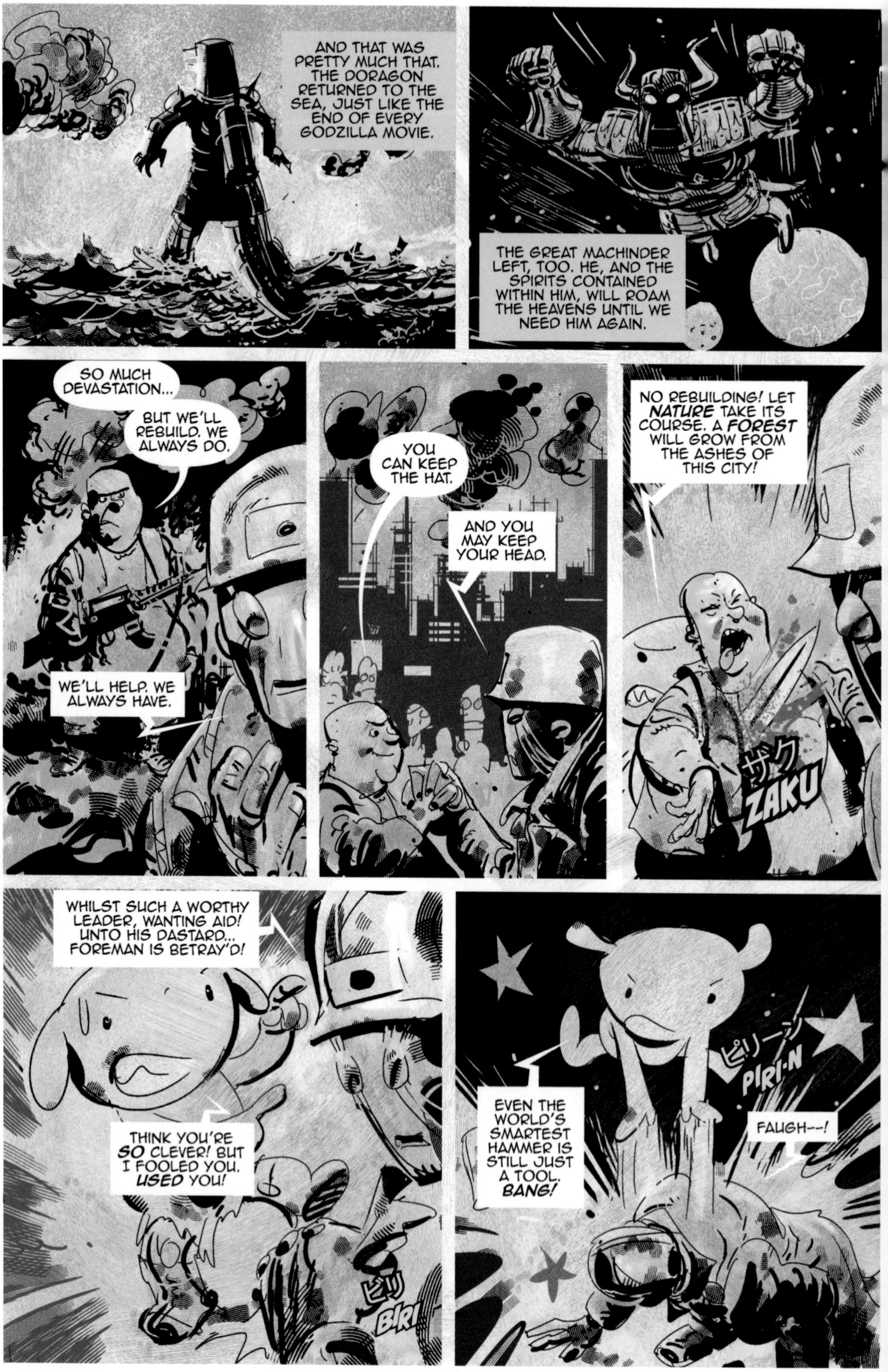
AND THAT WAS PRETTY MUCH THAT. THE DORAGON RETURNED TO THE SEA, JUST LIKE THE END OF EVERY GODZILLA MOVIE.
THE GREAT MACHINDER LEFT, TOO. HE, AND THE SPIRITS CONTAINED WITHIN HIM, WILL ROAM THE HEAVENS UNTIL WE NEED HIM AGAIN.
SO MUCH DEVASTATION...
BUT WE'LL REBUILD. WE ALWAYS DO.
WE'LL HELP. WE ALWAYS HAVE.
YOU CAN KEEP THE HAT.
AND YOU MAY KEEP YOUR HEAD.
NO REBUILDING! LET NATURE TAKE ITS COURSE. A FOREST WILL GROW FROM THE ASHES OF THIS CITY!
ザク
ZAKU
WHILST SUCH A WORTHY LEADER, WANTING AID! UNTO HIS DASTARD... FOREMAN IS BETRAY'D!
THINK YOU'RE SO CLEVER! BUT I FOOLED YOU. USED YOU!
ビリ
BIRI
ピリーン
PIRI-N
EVEN THE WORLD'S SMARTEST HAMMER IS STILL JUST A TOOL. BANG!
FAUGH--!

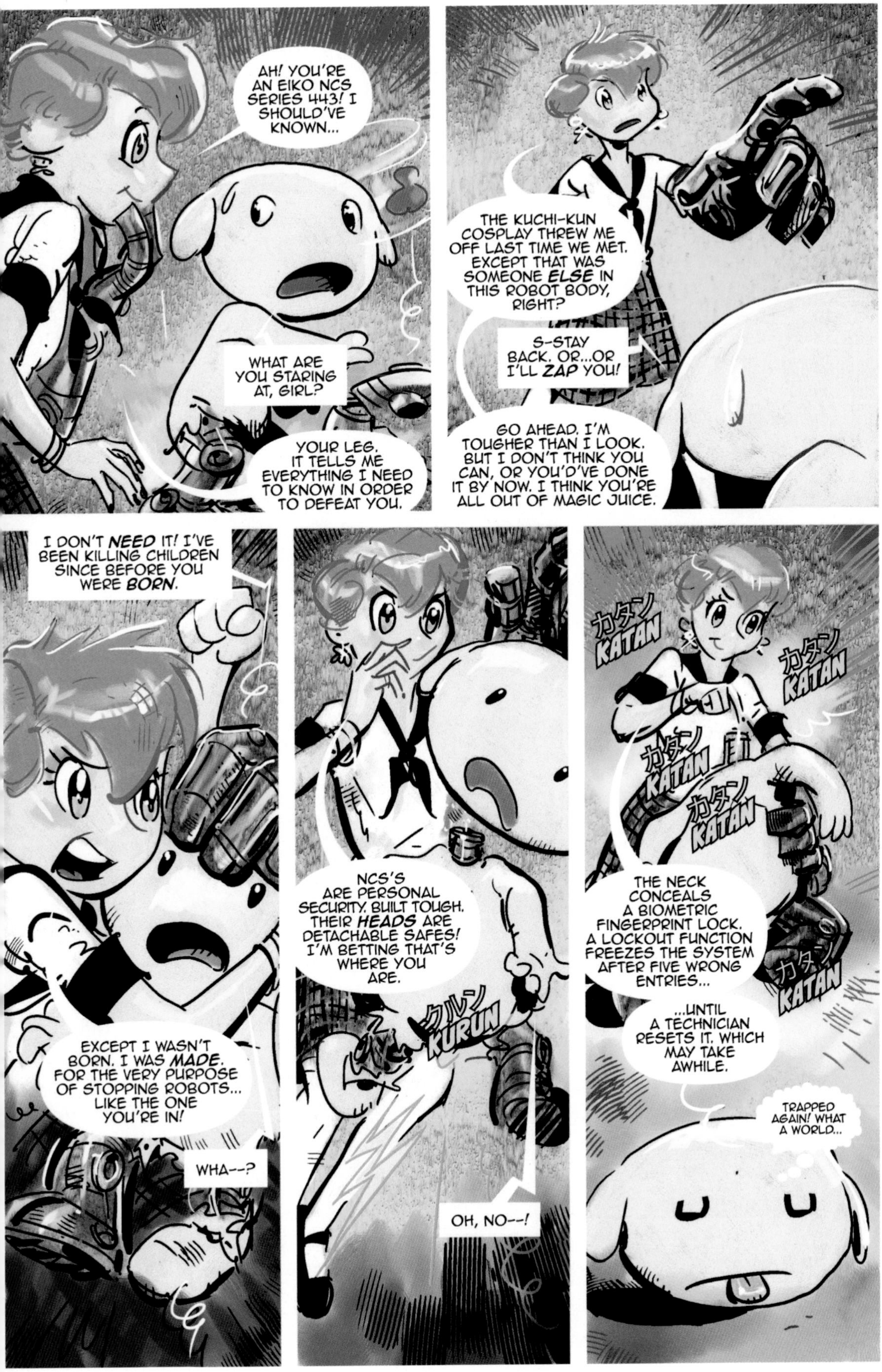

AH! YOU'RE AN EIKO NCS SERIES 443! I SHOULD'VE KNOWN...
WHAT ARE YOU STARING AT, GIRL?
YOUR LEG. IT TELLS ME EVERYTHING I NEED TO KNOW IN ORDER TO DEFEAT YOU.
THE KUCHI-KUN COSPLAY THREW ME OFF LAST TIME WE MET. EXCEPT THAT WAS SOMEONE ELSE IN THIS ROBOT BODY, RIGHT?
S-STAY BACK. OR...OR I'LL ZAP YOU!
GO AHEAD. I'M TOUGHER THAN I LOOK. BUT I DON'T THINK YOU CAN, OR YOU'D'VE DONE IT BY NOW. I THINK YOU'RE ALL OUT OF MAGIC JUICE.
I DON'T NEED IT! I'VE BEEN KILLING CHILDREN SINCE BEFORE YOU WERE BORN.
EXCEPT I WASN'T BORN. I WAS MADE. FOR THE VERY PURPOSE OF STOPPING ROBOTS... LIKE THE ONE YOU'RE IN!
WHA--?
NCS'S ARE PERSONAL SECURITY. BUILT TOUGH. THEIR HEADS ARE DETACHABLE SAFES! I'M BETTING THAT'S WHERE YOU ARE.
クルン KURUN
OH, NO--!
カタン KATAN
カタン KATAN
カタン KATAN
カタン KATAN
THE NECK CONCEALS A BIOMETRIC FINGERPRINT LOCK. A LOCKOUT FUNCTION FREEZES THE SYSTEM AFTER FIVE WRONG ENTRIES...
カタン KATAN
...UNTIL A TECHNICIAN RESETS IT. WHICH MAY TAKE AWHILE.
TRAPPED AGAIN! WHAT A WORLD...

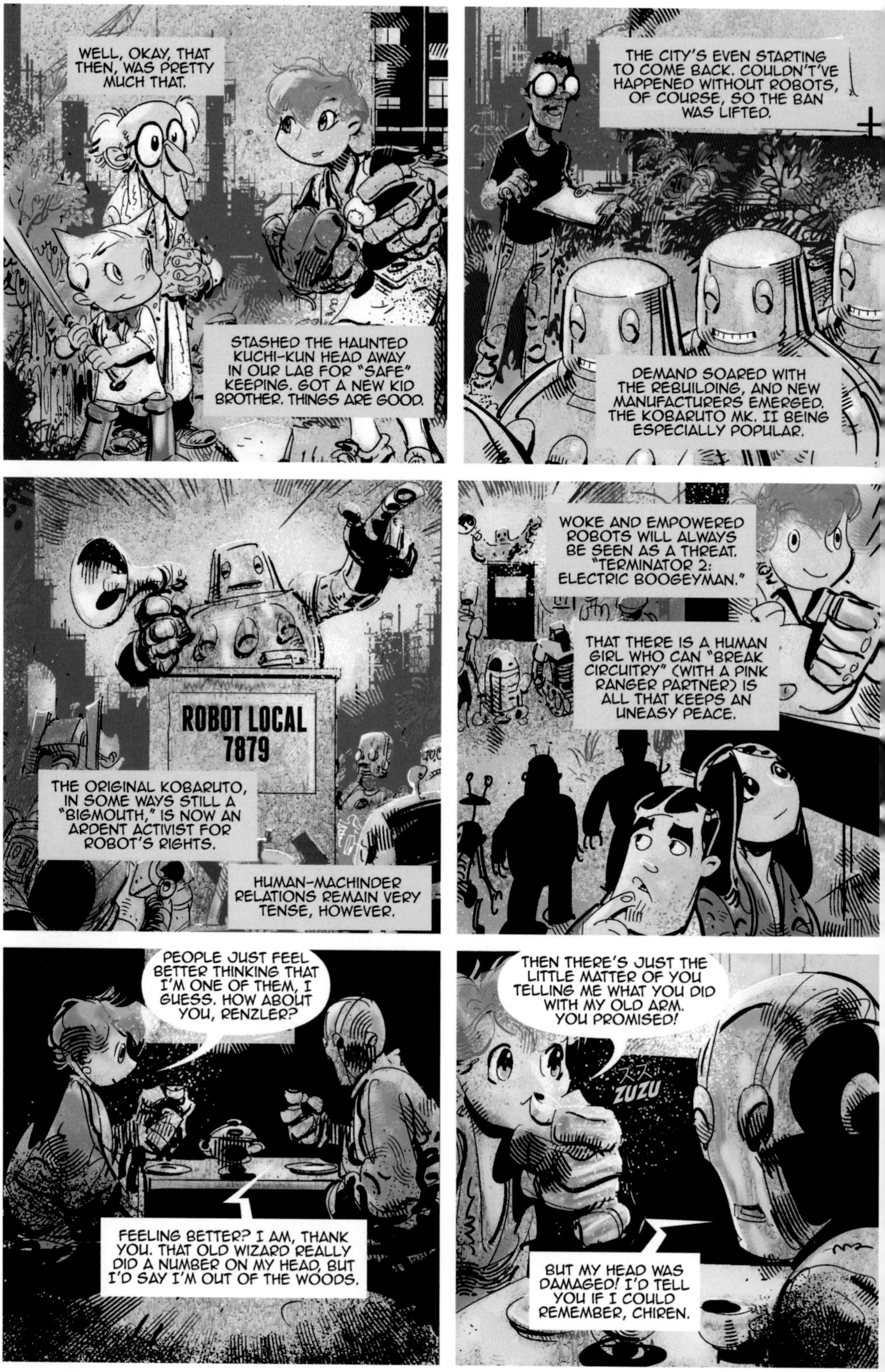
WELL, OKAY, THAT THEN, WAS PRETTY MUCH THAT.
STASHED THE HAUNTED KUCHI-KUN HEAD AWAY IN OUR LAB FOR "SAFE" KEEPING. GOT A NEW KID BROTHER. THINGS ARE GOOD.
THE CITY'S EVEN STARTING TO COME BACK. COULDN'T'VE HAPPENED WITHOUT ROBOTS, OF COURSE, SO THE BAN WAS LIFTED.
DEMAND SOARED WITH THE REBUILDING, AND NEW MANUFACTURERS EMERGED. THE KOBARUTO MK. II BEING ESPECIALLY POPULAR.
ROBOT LOCAL 7879
THE ORIGINAL KOBARUTO, IN SOME WAYS STILL A "BIGMOUTH," IS NOW AN ARDENT ACTIVIST FOR ROBOT'S RIGHTS.
HUMAN-MACHINDER RELATIONS REMAIN VERY TENSE, HOWEVER.
WOKE AND EMPOWERED ROBOTS WILL ALWAYS BE SEEN AS A THREAT. "TERMINATOR 2: ELECTRIC BOOGEYMAN."
THAT THERE IS A HUMAN GIRL WHO CAN "BREAK CIRCUITRY" (WITH A PINK RANGER PARTNER) IS ALL THAT KEEPS AN UNEASY PEACE.
PEOPLE JUST FEEL BETTER THINKING THAT I'M ONE OF THEM, I GUESS. HOW ABOUT YOU, RENZLER?
FEELING BETTER? I AM, THANK YOU. THAT OLD WIZARD REALLY DID A NUMBER ON MY HEAD, BUT I'D SAY I'M OUT OF THE WOODS.
THEN THERE'S JUST THE LITTLE MATTER OF YOU TELLING ME WHAT YOU DID WITH MY OLD ARM. YOU PROMISED!
ZUZU
BUT MY HEAD WAS DAMAGED! I'D TELL YOU IF I COULD REMEMBER, CHIREN.

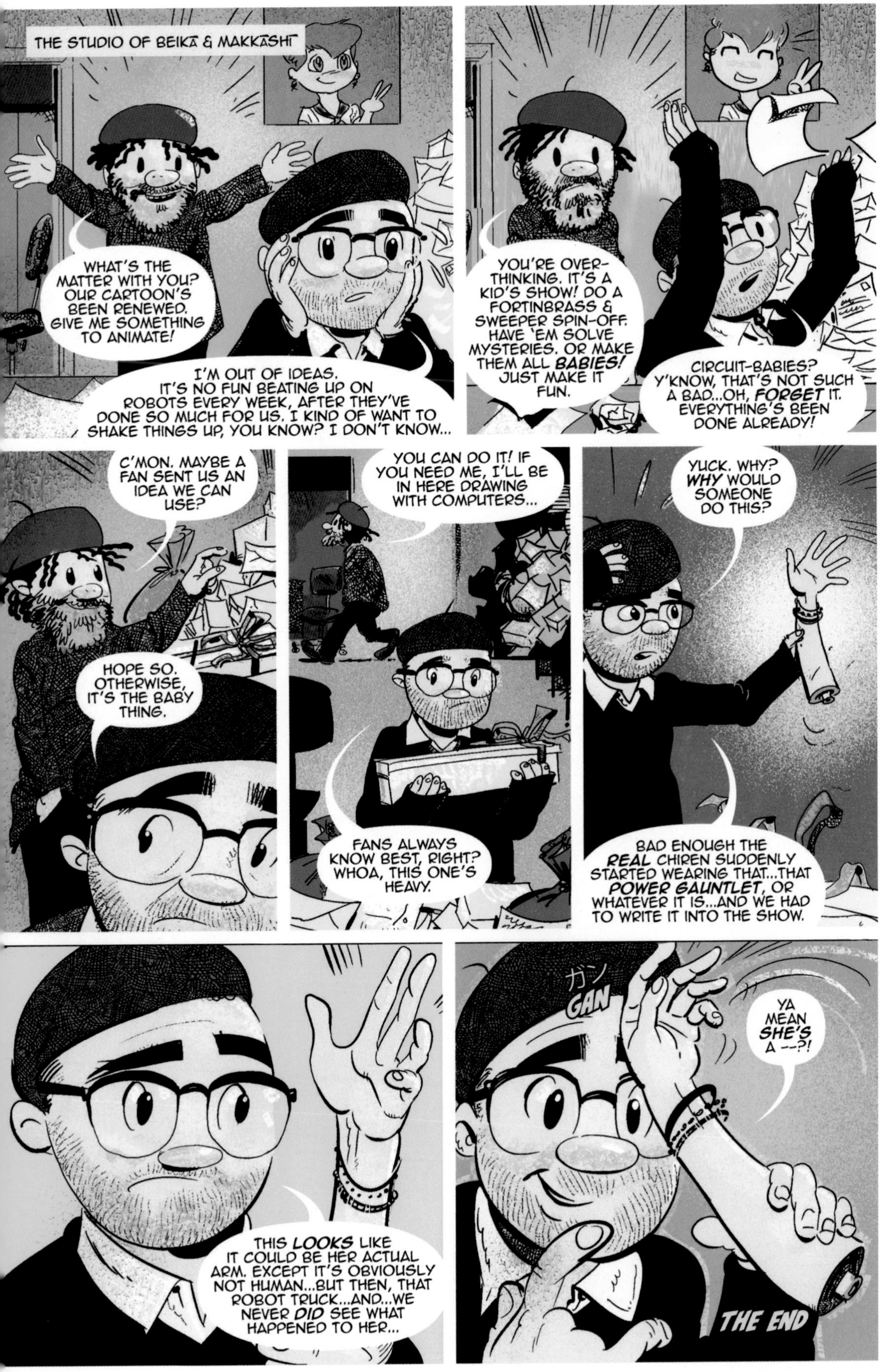
THE STUDIO OF BEIKĀ & MAKKĀSHI
WHAT'S THE MATTER WITH YOU? OUR CARTOON'S BEEN RENEWED. GIVE ME SOMETHING TO ANIMATE!
I'M OUT OF IDEAS. IT'S NO FUN BEATING UP ON ROBOTS EVERY WEEK, AFTER THEY'VE DONE SO MUCH FOR US. I KIND OF WANT TO SHAKE THINGS UP, YOU KNOW? I DON'T KNOW...
YOU'RE OVER-THINKING. IT'S A KID'S SHOW! DO A FORTINBRASS & SWEEPER SPIN-OFF. HAVE 'EM SOLVE MYSTERIES. OR MAKE THEM ALL BABIES! JUST MAKE IT FUN.
CIRCUIT-BABIES? Y'KNOW, THAT'S NOT SUCH A BAD...OH, FORGET IT. EVERYTHING'S BEEN DONE ALREADY!
C'MON. MAYBE A FAN SENT US AN IDEA WE CAN USE?
HOPE SO. OTHERWISE, IT'S THE BABY THING.
YOU CAN DO IT! IF YOU NEED ME, I'LL BE IN HERE DRAWING WITH COMPUTERS...
FANS ALWAYS KNOW BEST, RIGHT? WHOA, THIS ONE'S HEAVY.
YUCK. WHY? WHY WOULD SOMEONE DO THIS?
BAD ENOUGH THE REAL CHIREN SUDDENLY STARTED WEARING THAT...THAT POWER GAUNTLET, OR WHATEVER IT IS...AND WE HAD TO WRITE IT INTO THE SHOW.
THIS LOOKS LIKE IT COULD BE HER ACTUAL ARM. EXCEPT IT'S OBVIOUSLY NOT HUMAN...BUT THEN, THAT ROBOT TRUCK...AND...WE NEVER DID SEE WHAT HAPPENED TO HER...
ガン
GAN
YA MEAN SHE'S A --?!
THE END

EXTRAS

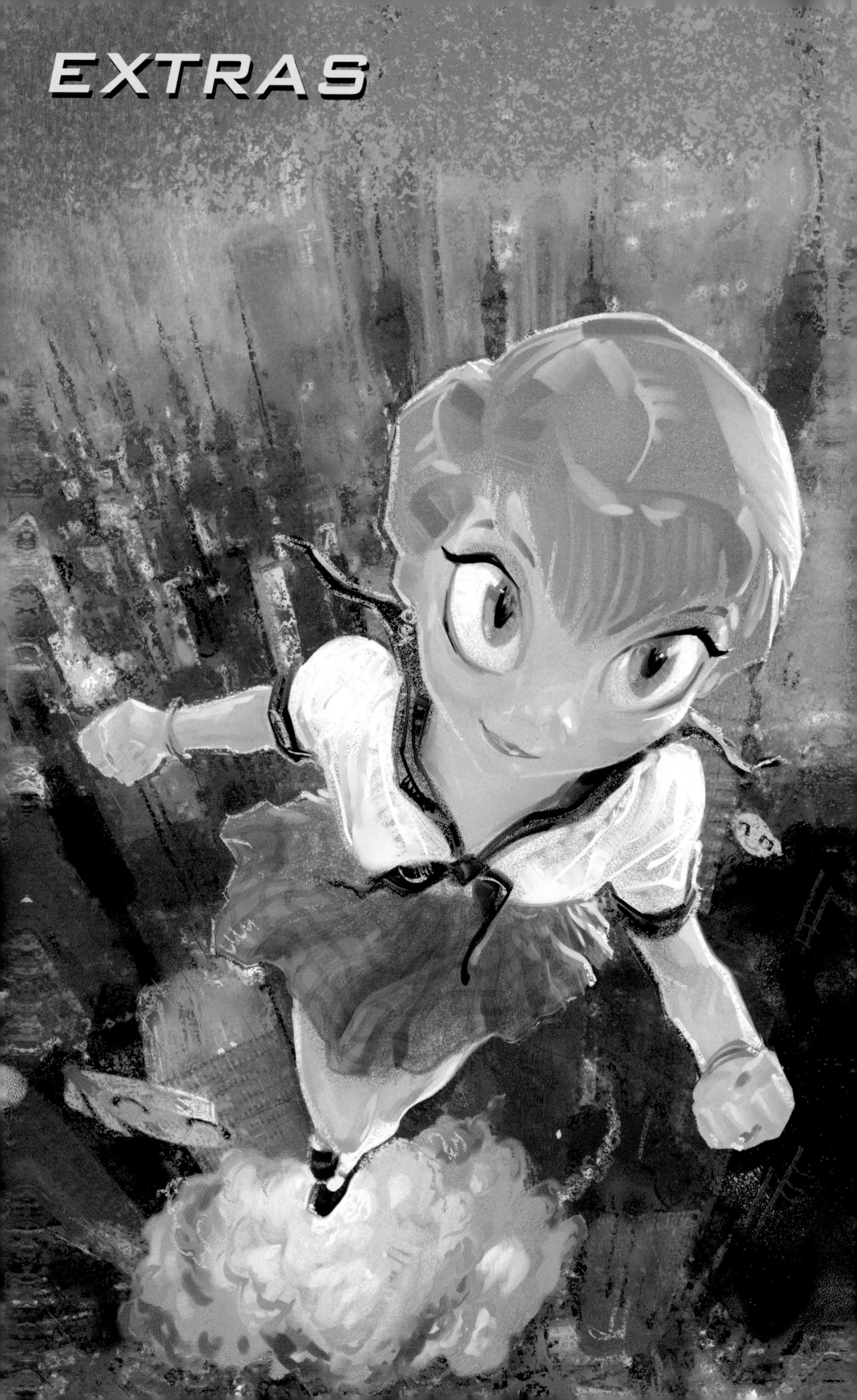

Here's a bunch of different treatments
for the logo I was playing around with.

MCCARTHY/BAKER

1 Circuit -BREAKER ™

2 MC CARTHY!   BAKER!
circuit breaker ™

3 circuit -breaker ™   circuit -breaker ™

4 circuit -breaker ™   circuit -breaker ™

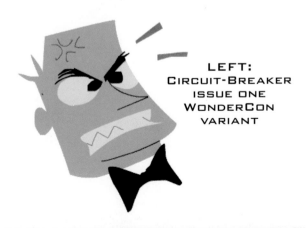

LEFT:
CIRCUIT-BREAKER
ISSUE ONE
WONDERCON
VARIANT

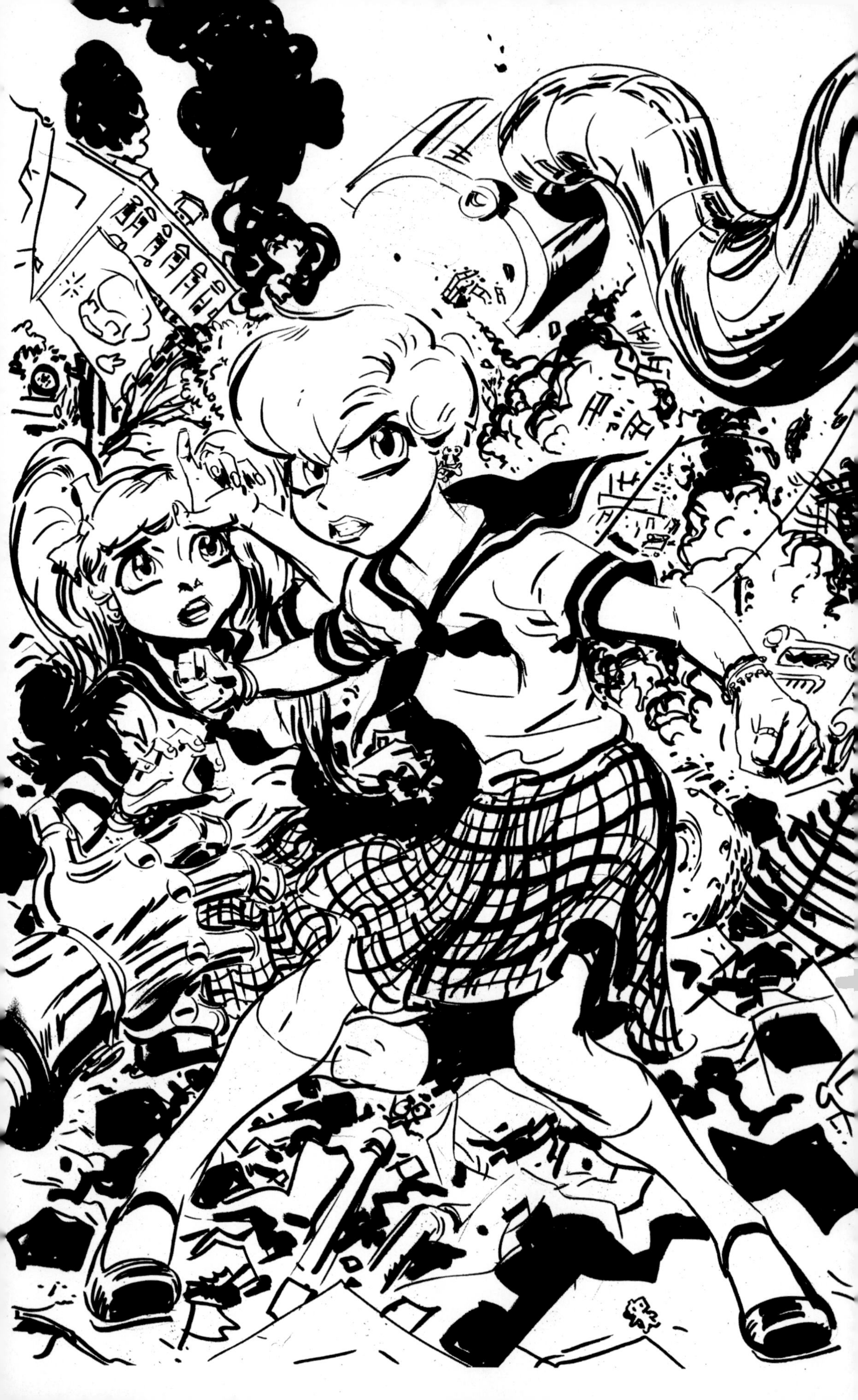

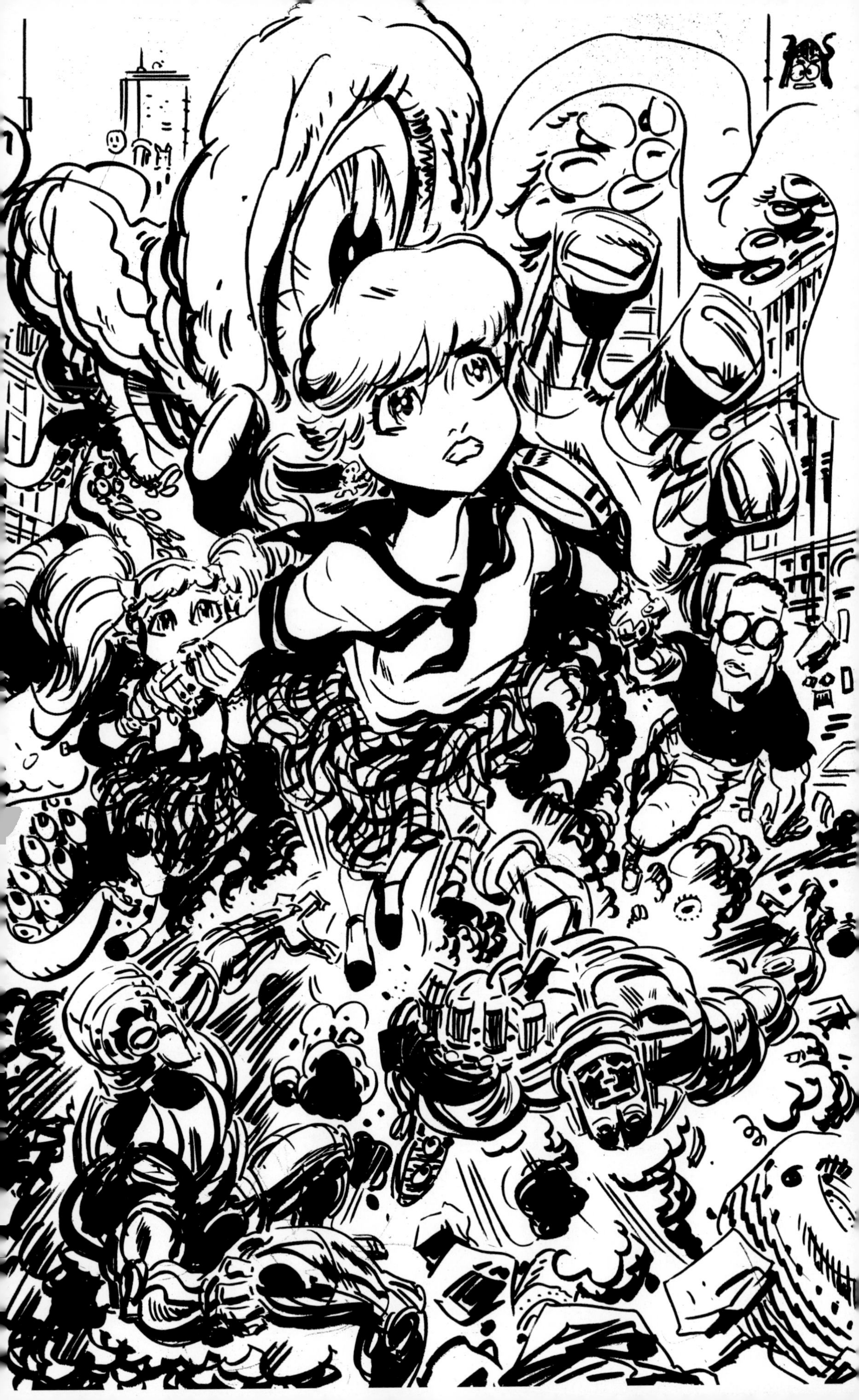

HERE ARE THE ORIGINAL SKETCHES KEVIN SENT ME! →

WHEN I WORK WITH A WRITER, I RARELY MAKE CHANGES TO THEIR STUFF.

I TRY TO EMBODY THEIR ARTISTIC VISION. KEVIN IS A TALENTED CARTOONIST, SO I TRY TO SEE THINGS HIS WAY.

AFTER THE FIRST ISSUE WAS DRAWN, I FELT THE PINK HAIR I DREW WAS TOO MUCH LIKE ABBY DENSON'S 'DOLLTOPIA' CHARACTER, SO I CHANGED IT TO A MORE ANIME STYLE AND RE-DREW SOME OF THE ART.

NOW YOU KNOW!

♡KYLE BAKER

TWO

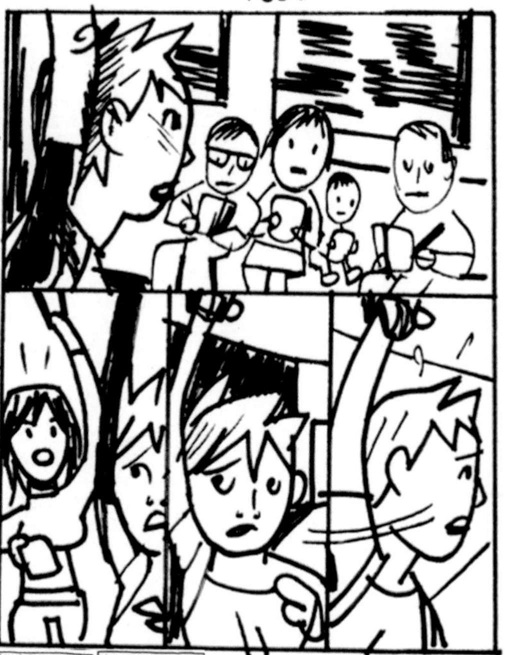

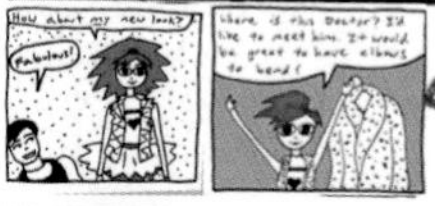
How about my new look?
Fabulous!
Where is this Doctor? I'd like to meet him. It would be great to have elbows to bend!

← P.S. I LOVE DOLLTOPIA!

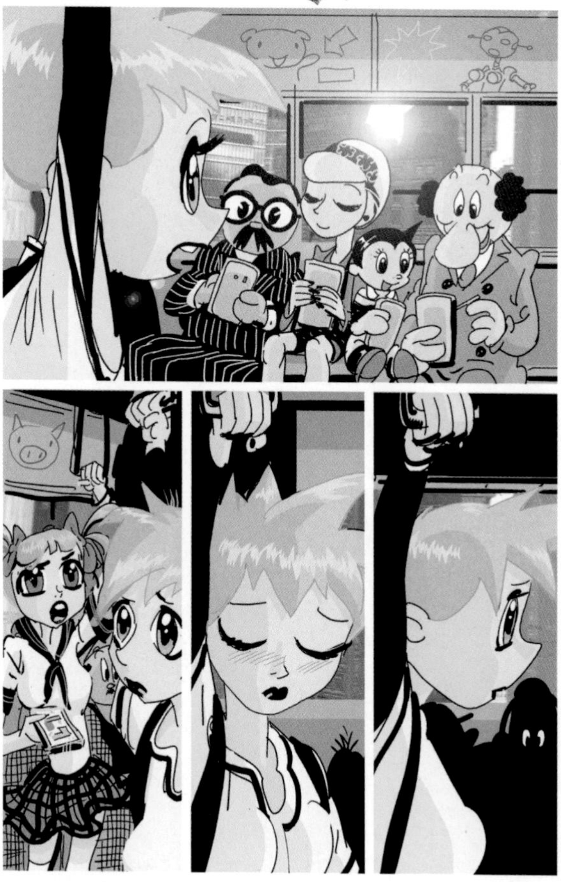

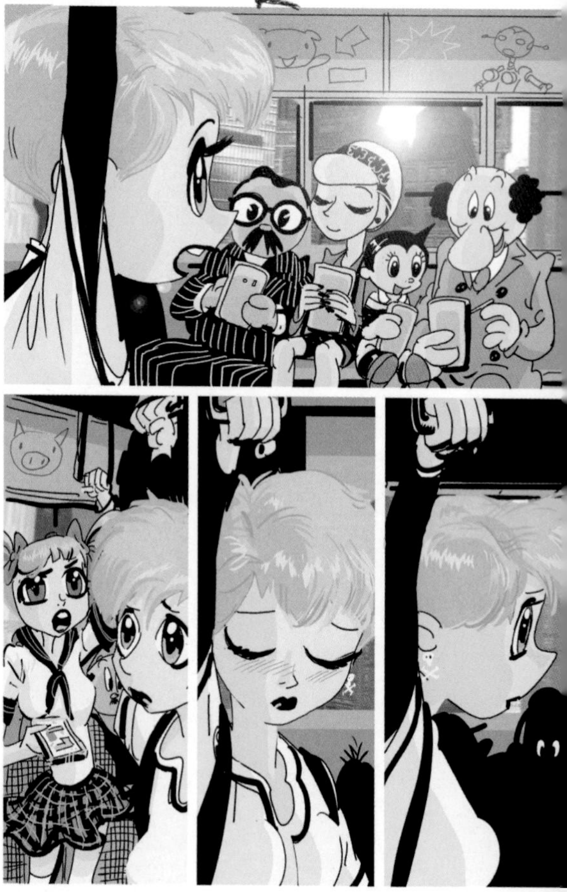

ONE

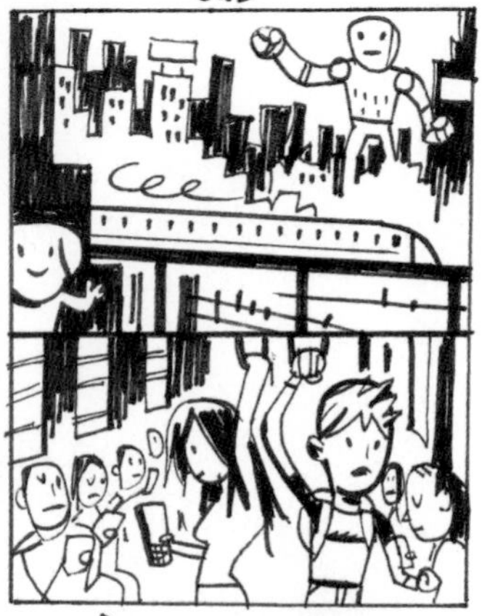

TWO

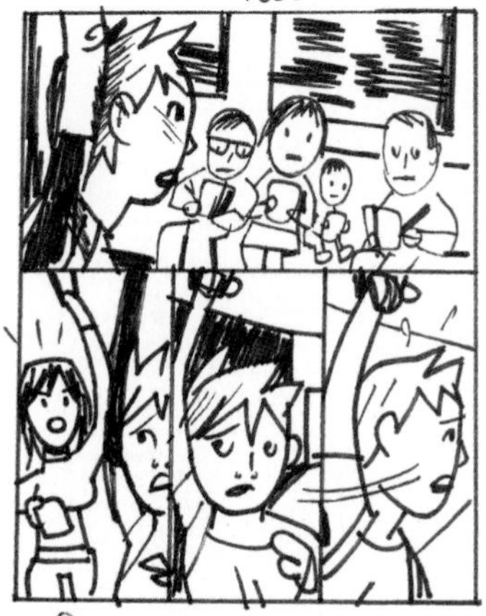

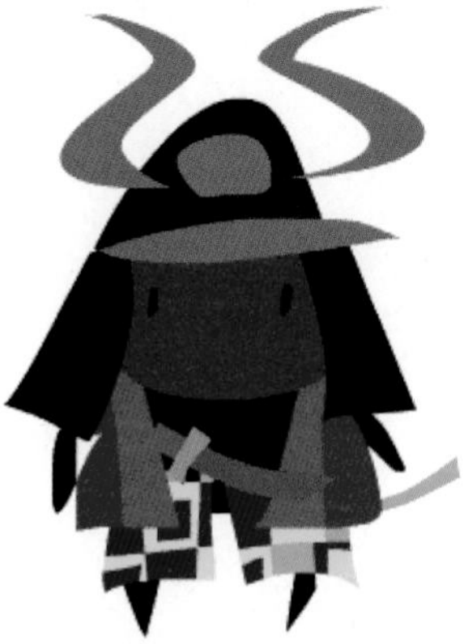

MORE OF KEVIN'S THUMBNAILS FOR CIRCUIT-BREAKER ISSUES ONE AND TWO

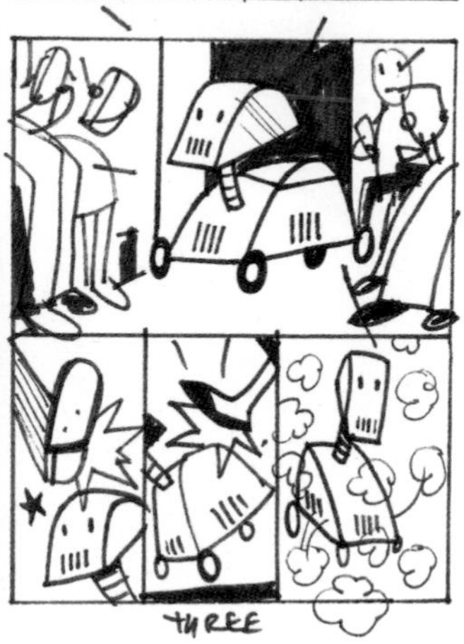

THREE

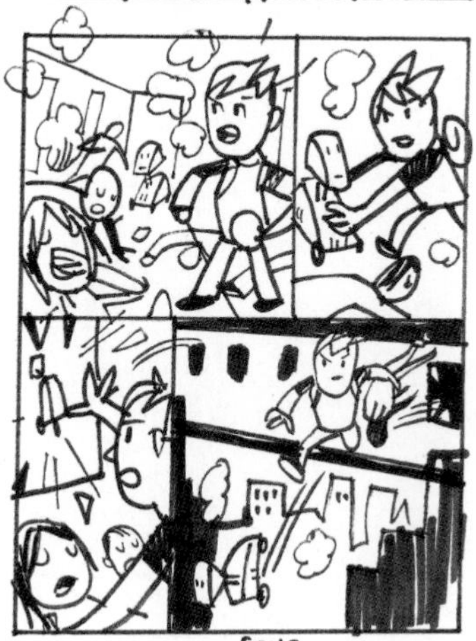

FOUR

FIVE SIX

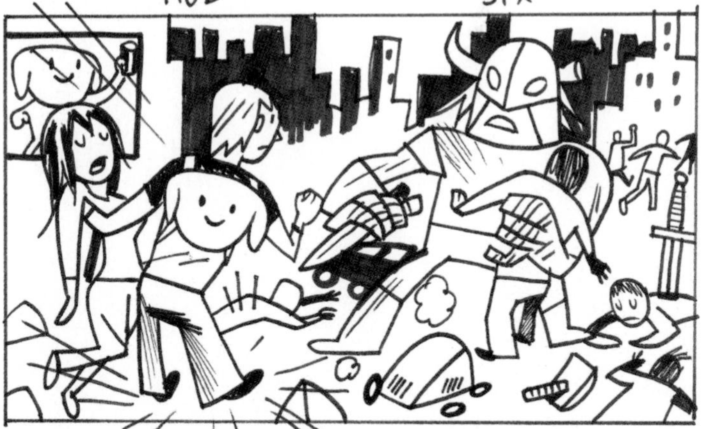

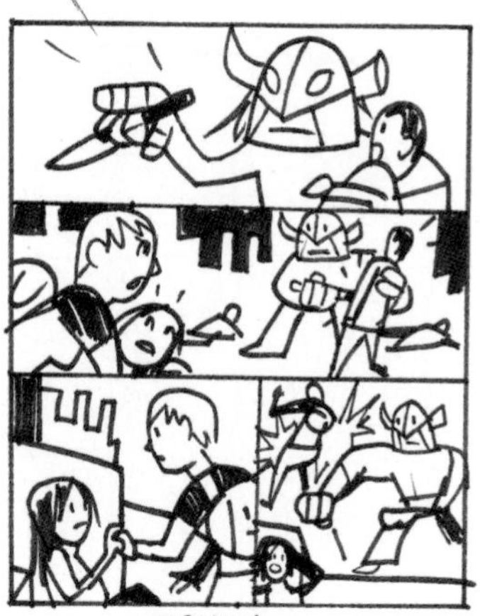

SEVEN

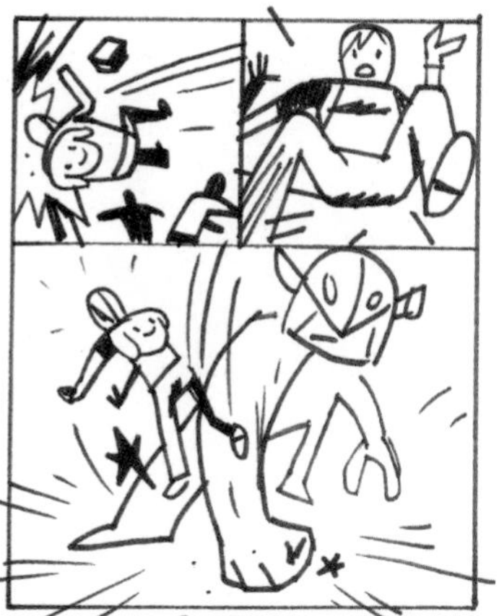

EIGHT

NINE

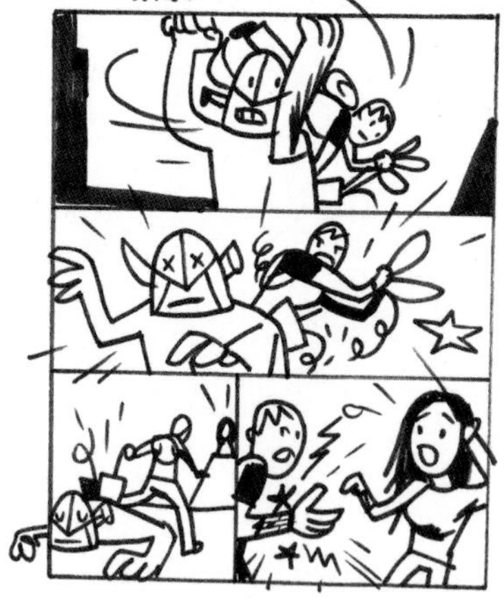

TEN

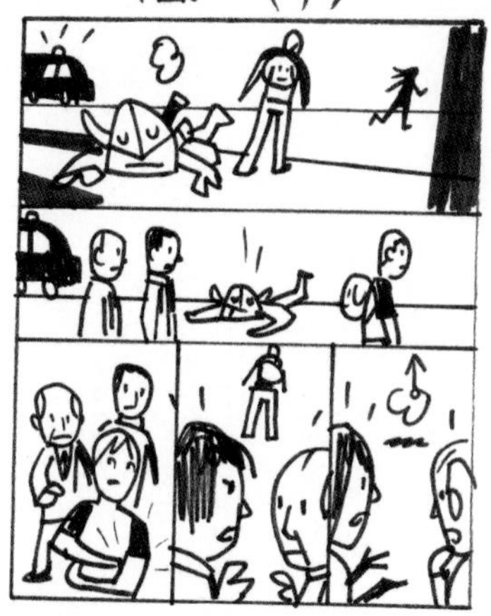

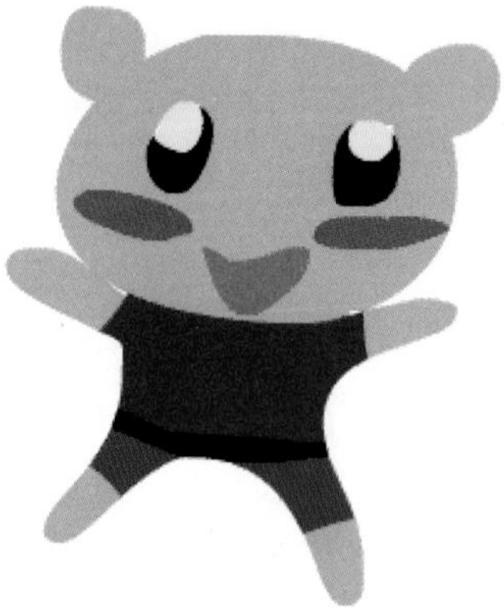

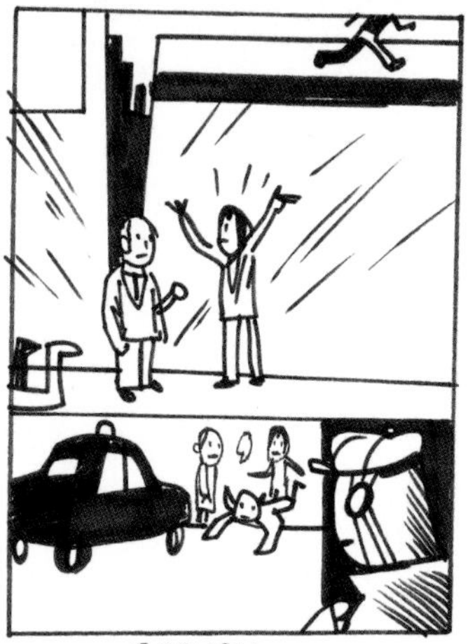

ELEVEN

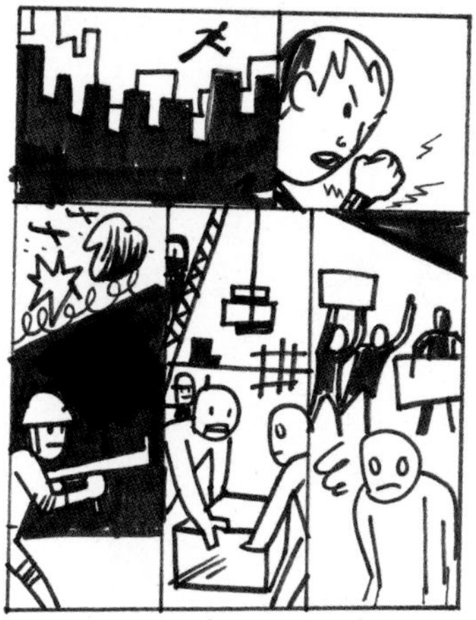

12 TWELVE

THIRTEEN

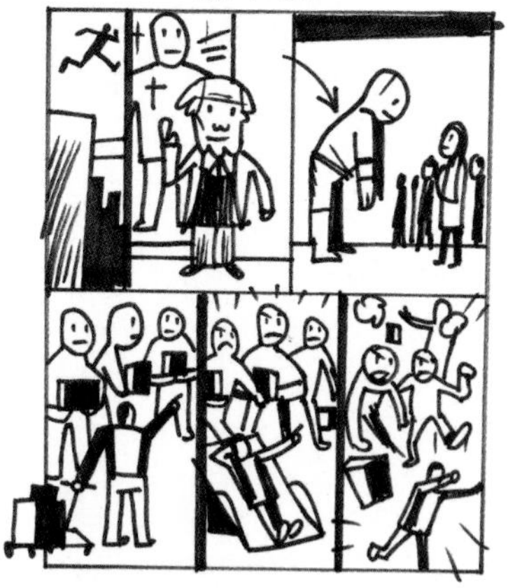

FOURTEEN

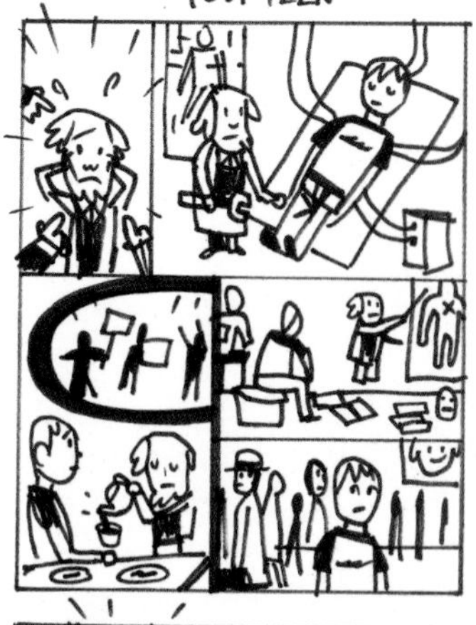

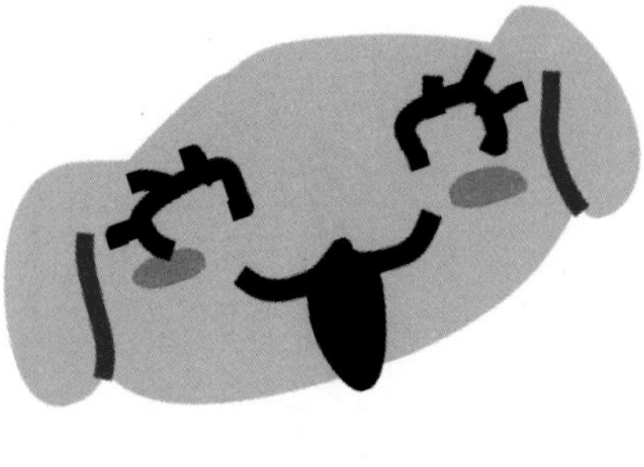

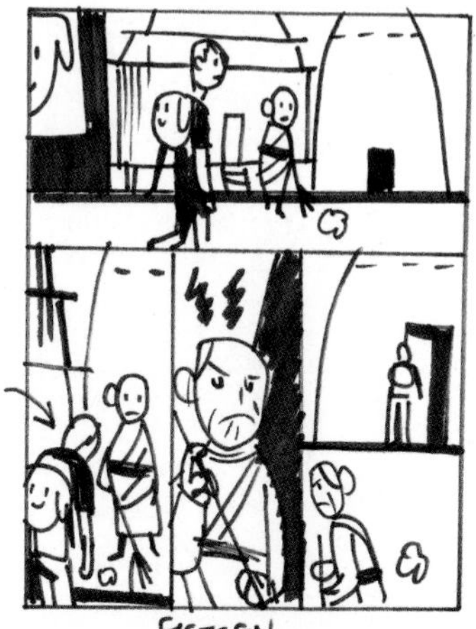

FIFTEEN

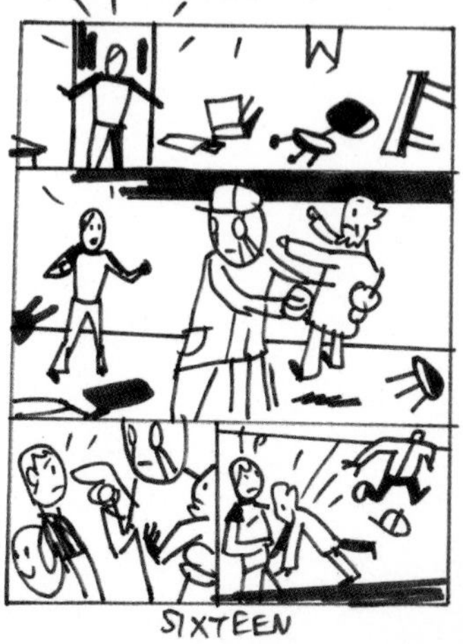

SIXTEEN

SEVENTEEN

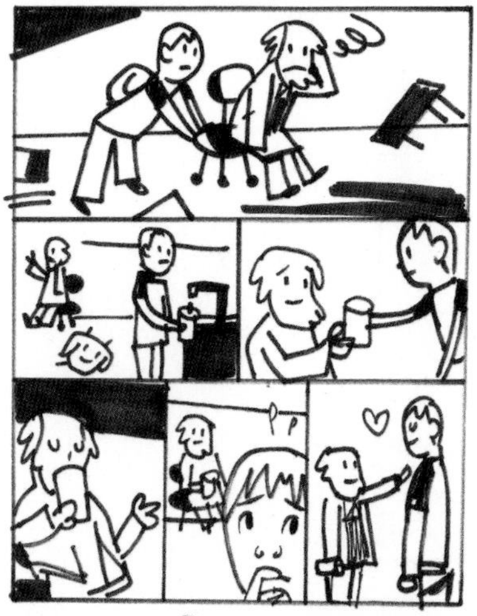

EIGHTEEN

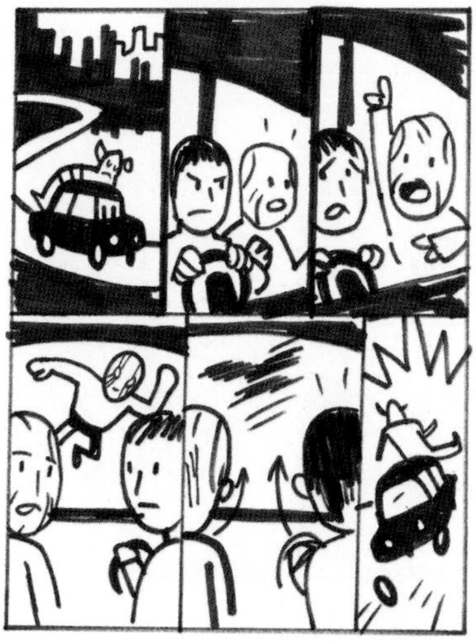

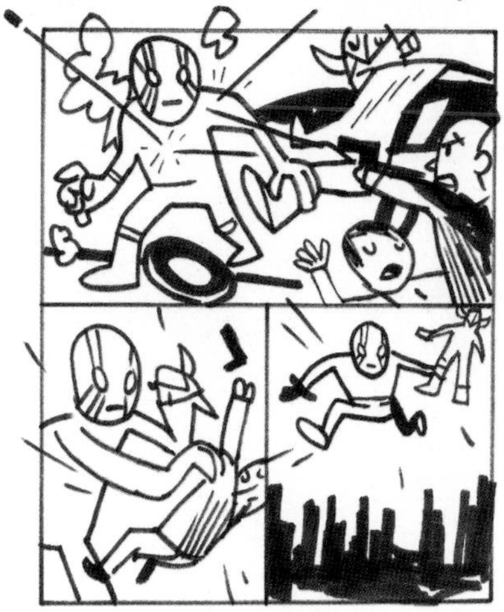

NINETEEN

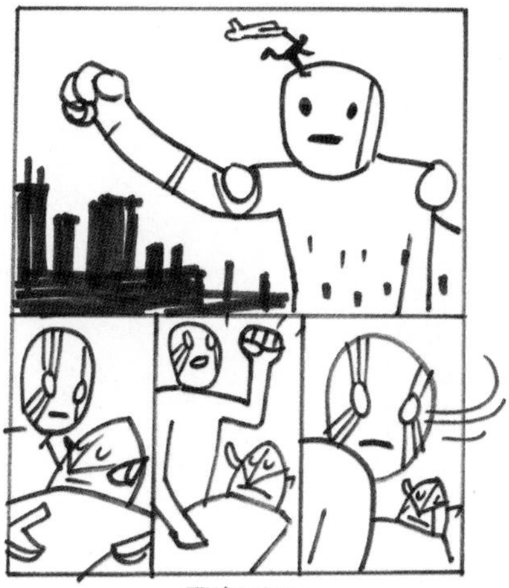

TWENTY

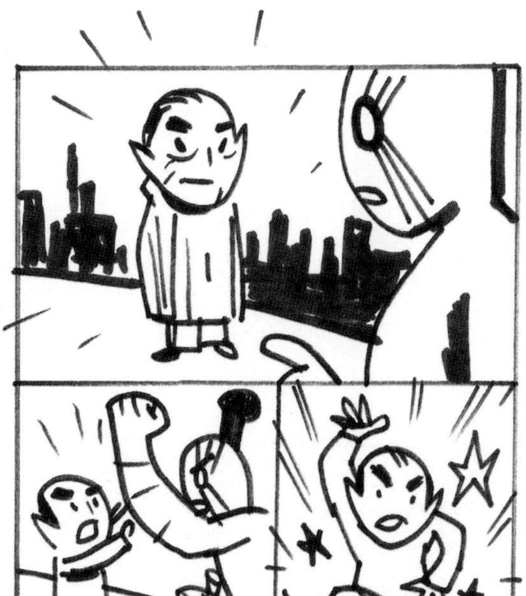

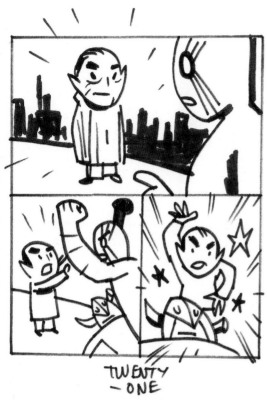

TWENTY-ONE

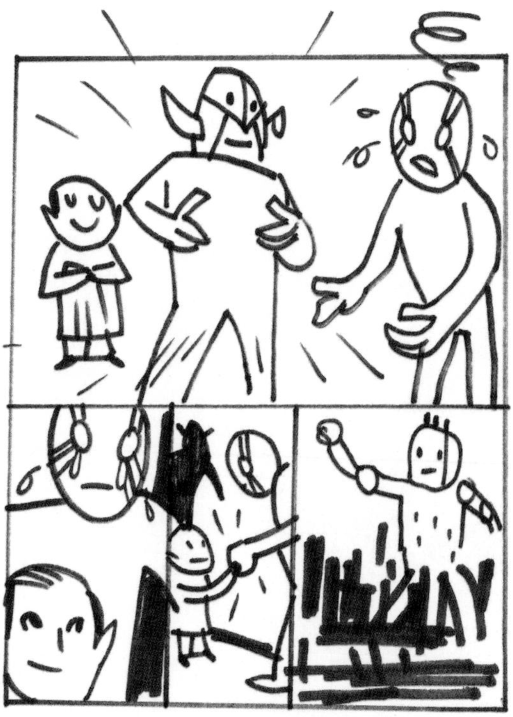

TWENTY-TWO

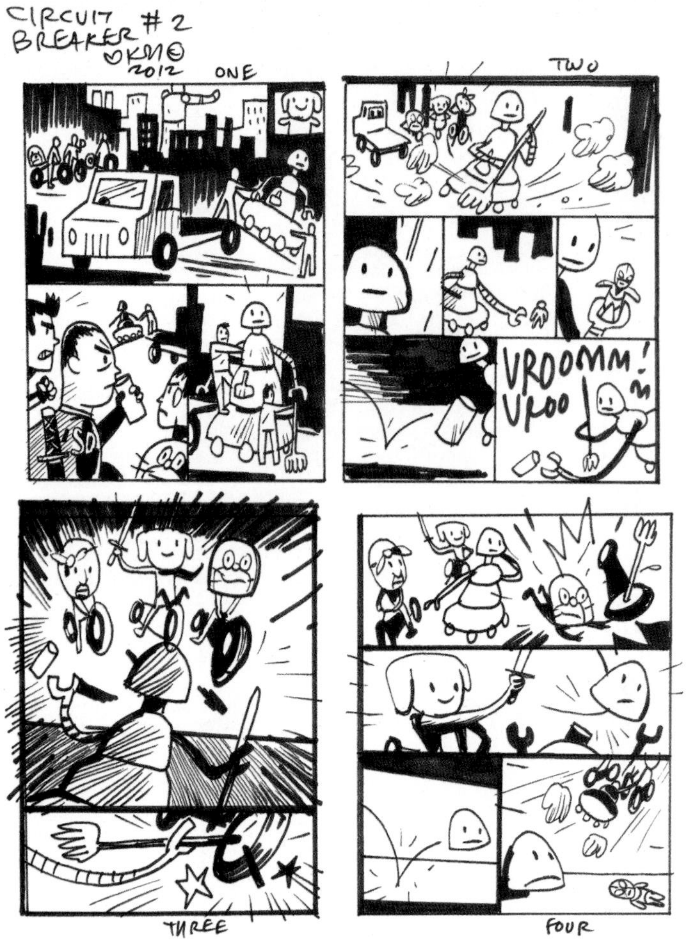
CIRCUIT BREAKER #2
©KMO 2012
ONE
TWO
VROOMM!
VROO
THREE
FOUR

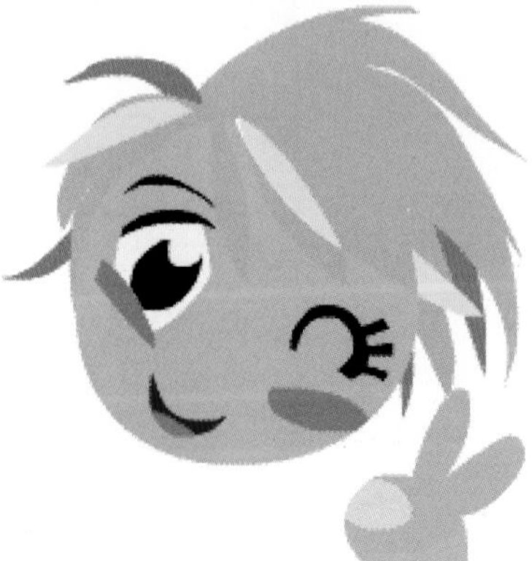

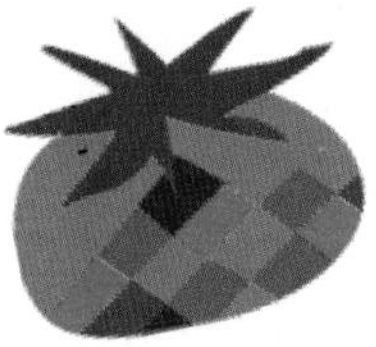

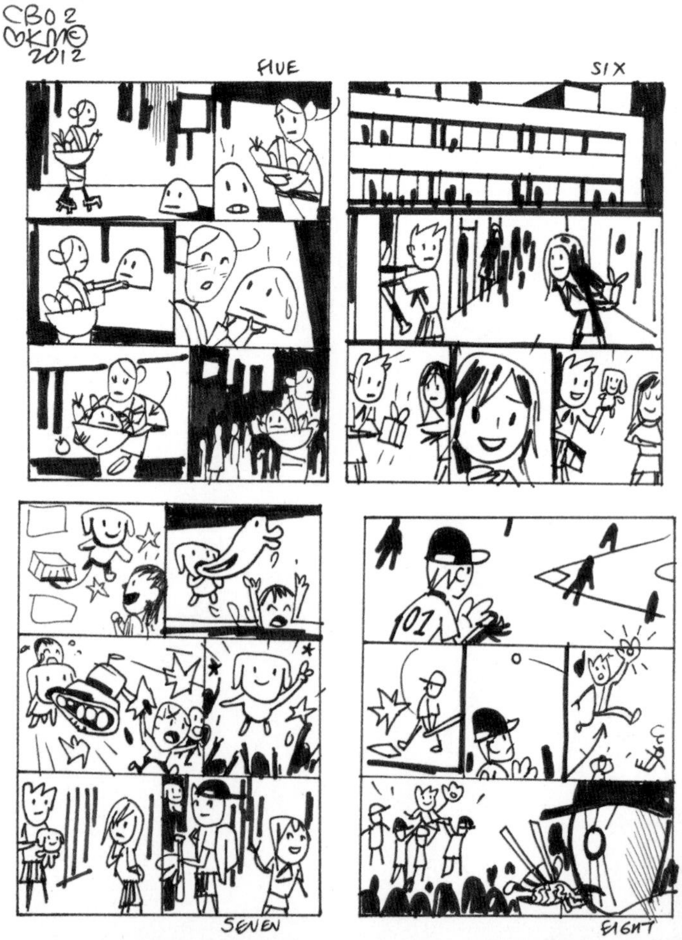
CB02
©KMO 2012
FIVE
SIX
01
SEVEN
EIGHT

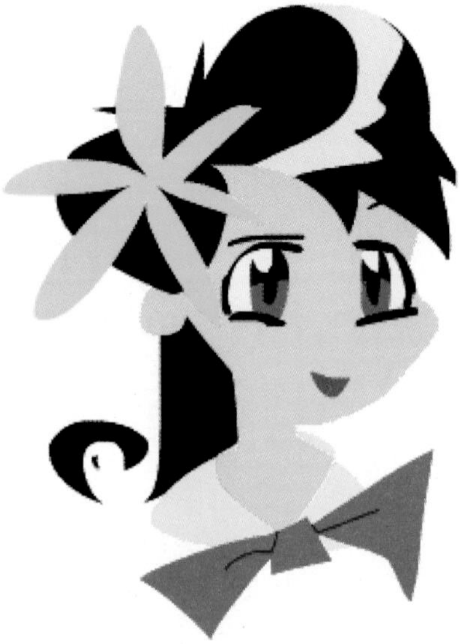